Sea of Secrets

For Liz - I hope you enjoy Oriel's story!

Amanda DeWees

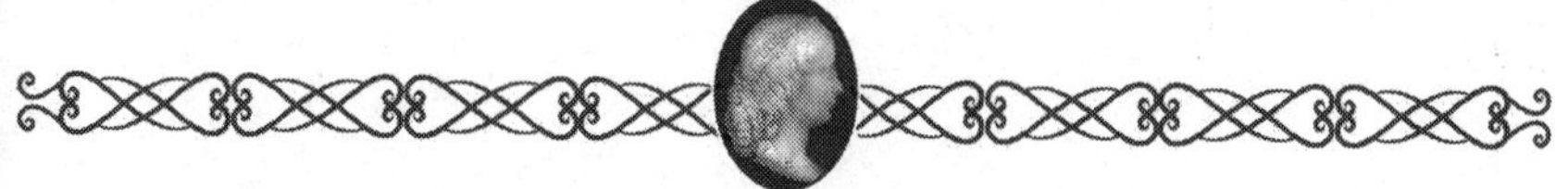

Sea of Secrets

This is a work of fiction. Names, characters, places, and incidents either are products of the author's imagination or are used fictitiously. Any resemblance to actual events or locales or persons, living or dead, is entirely coincidental.

ISBN-13: 978-1978476103
ISBN-10: 1978476108

Cover design by Victoria Cooper Art

Visit the author at www.amandadewees.com

Find me on Facebook:
Author Amanda DeWees

This book is dedicated with gratitude to Bo, Jim, and M— C—,
the three most important gentlemen in my writing life,
both past and present.

About the Author

Award-winning author Amanda DeWees is a native of Atlanta and received her PhD from the University of Georgia. Learn more about her and her books at AmandaDeWees.com.

Books by Amanda DeWees

Cursed Once More

The Last Serenade

Nocturne for a Widow

Sea of Secrets

With This Curse

The Ash Grove Chronicles:

The Shadow and the Rose

Casting Shadows

Among the Shadows

CHAPTER ONE

After the funeral we returned to the house. We sat in the parlor listening to the drumming of rain against the windows until Father strode to the drapes and jerked them closed as if slamming the door on an eavesdropper.

It had rained all through the funeral. Not the gentle trickle that a sentimental person could interpret as tears from a sympathetic Nature; this was a soaking, squelching rain, the kind that gets under collars and into boots and eyes. Nor was it some special manifestation for the funeral; it had been raining like this all month. My brother Lionel, who had never troubled to guard his speech around me, would have said that it was pissing down.

It was Lionel we had buried today.

Because of the filthy weather the minister had rushed through the service, and the few mourners willing to brave the downpour at the graveside shook our hands quickly and damply before slogging off to their waiting carriages. Their hasty words of consolation were as grey and comfortless as the weather.

"You may be proud that he died a hero's death," intoned Abel Crowley, one of my father's colleagues.

"Indeed; a bullet in the head at twenty-three is far more gratifying than pneumonia at seventy," returned Father, and Crowley, a man not highly attuned to sarcasm, nodded sagely and clapped my father on the back before ambling away. Mrs. Merridew, the pastor's wife, was the next to say the wrong thing.

"He is strolling the streets of heaven now, and is one with the angels above," she quavered, all three of her chins trembling with emotion. I smothered a hysterical giggle in my handkerchief. If Mrs. Merridew had set eyes on Lionel since the day of his baptism, she would have known that he would most likely not have been admitted into heaven at all. As much as I loved Lionel, I was well aware that he was more likely to be throwing dice in a warmer clime. If by some oversight he had been admitted into the Elysian Fields, he was probably wishing he were at a dog race instead.

My father, a partisan of evolutionary theory, attended church only for the sake of appearances, so that his law practice would not suffer from his views. He gave the good lady a level look of scorn, which she was fortunately too near-sighted to catch.

But it was left to Mrs. Armadale from down the street to make the most foolish attempt to console my father for his loss.

"At least you still have your daughter," she said.

Father stiffened. I kept my eyes lowered, but I could sense the withering glance he directed at me.

"Madam," said Father, in his deep, solemn voice, "you cannot imagine how that fact has cheered me."

* * *

Now I sat in a chair as near the fire as I dared, spreading out my rain-sodden skirts to try to dry them. Father stood on the hearth, feet planted wide, staring into the flames. It was one of his favorite positions: it both established his mastery and effectively blocked any of the fire's warmth from reaching me. He was a handsome man, and created an imposing picture in his mourning black, which contrasted with his silver hair and moustache. He wore no beard, perhaps because one would have hidden his strong jaw.

He rang for tea, and Molly, the housemaid, brought it in. My hands were still stiff with cold from our vigil in the graveyard, and when I poured, tea slopped into the saucer. My father watched me with a derisive twist to his mouth.

"Such is my consolation," he said drily. "My brave, handsome son is killed in battle, and my blundering, useless daughter remains to cheer me. How comforting it will be during the decades to come that you will always be here with me. Every day, every hour I will have the solace of seeing your face and being reminded that, while I have lost my son, I will never lose my daughter."

I cleaned up the spilled tea as best I could and handed him his cup without answering. I had learned years ago that it was safest to say as little to Father as possible. Consequently, he added dullness to the list of my shortcomings.

Not least of these was my plainness. A daughter with dimples and glossy gold ringlets might have won his approval, even a smattering of affection. Since, however, I was from my earliest days small, thin, and drab, with no natural vivacity to lend any semblance of beauty, my father dismissed me as a financial burden and an inconvenience; sometimes, in a temper, he would go further and call me far worse.

I learned very early in life just what he thought of me. I remember being six years old and practicing at the pianoforte when he abruptly appeared at the door.

"Cease that blasted noise, girl," he snapped. "I am attempting to get some work done."

My instructress fluttered to him with an anxious smile. "Miss Pembroke must practice, sir, if she is to be musical."

"Your optimism does you credit, Miss Dalby." He regarded me with the cool calculation I know so well. He is a tall man, and at that time he seemed to tower over me, his deep-set eyes glaring out from under the strong silver brows. "She has no talent to foster; your lessons these few months have made that fact amply plain. I had hoped that, since the girl is utterly lacking in looks or charm, she might at least be accomplished, but it seems I am to be denied even this feeble compensation. I am saddled for the rest of my life with an unmarriageable brat who cannot even provide an evening's entertainment in exchange for her room and board." He turned swiftly to Miss Dalby, whose eyes were as wide in shock as was her mouth. "Madam, I see no reason to retain your services. Good day."

The pianoforte was removed the next afternoon.

Now, not wishing to attract more rancor, I poured a cup of tea for myself and rose to take it to my room.

"Sit down," he said without looking at me. "You are perfectly aware that we must be at home to condoling callers for the rest of the day. For once it is in your power to do something helpful, and you will not leave me to receive them alone."

"Yes, Father." I sometimes thought of myself as being one of the students in a Socratic dialogue when I spoke with Father. To whatever he said, however caustic or cruel, I answered only Yes, Father; As you say, Father; To be sure, Father. I wondered if Socrates' students, like me, had entertained secret longings to reply, "What rubbish, Socrates"; "You're a hypocritical tyrant, Socrates."

Father glanced at me sharply. "And stop grinning, girl. You look completely witless."

I erased the smile from my face. "I beg your pardon, Father."

"What you can find to smile about on the day you bury your brother, I cannot fathom."

That smarted, as he knew it would. Lionel had been the dearest person on earth to me, and the only one to have shown me any affection.

Our closeness did not arise from any likeness to each other; indeed, we resembled each other scarcely at all. He possessed all the blond good looks and appealing manner that I did not, and seemed incapable of being unhappy for a more sustained period than a quarter of an hour, while I have always, due perhaps to the difference in our upbringing, been inclined to seriousness. Although I found his unflappable buoyancy endearing, it could also be exasperating. Our fondness for each other was mixed on both sides with a sense of condescension: he found my gravity endlessly amusing, while I shook my head at his genial lack of understanding and his sometimes disreputable escapades. Not through malice, but through a lack of forethought, he seemed constantly embroiled in some scrape, from getting a housemaid in trouble to losing his horse in a card game—which two events he considered to be about equally trivial.

It was in the same spirit of thoughtlessness that he went to the Crimea to fight. That was the only time I ever saw Father angry with Lionel. My brother's disastrous encounters with cards, drink, and women were met with an indulgent smile, but this was one exploit my father protested.

"I'll not have you going off and getting yourself killed," he boomed. "Leave that to the fools who won't be missed. I won't tolerate my son and heir getting his young head blown off, or rotting of malaria in some army hospital."

"Surely there are more alternatives than the two." I could hear the smile in my brother's voice from where I sat sewing in the room next to the study in which they wrangled. I could envision Lionel lounging in an armchair, stroking the luxuriant golden moustache he took such pride in. He fostered that moustache as tenderly as a mother would her firstborn.

"My boy, you are too important to risk your life in this offhand manner. You are young, handsome, brilliant"—only Father would have applied this adjective to Lionel—"and need only reach out your hand for the best the world can offer. Everything you want is yours for the taking—so why choose this?"

I could hear him shift uncomfortably in the armchair, his spurs jingling. "To tell the truth, Pater, I'm bored. There's not much to do 'round here, and I'd love the chance to be in some real fighting. You needn't worry so; you know I'm a crack shot. I shall return heaped with laurels."

"And if you do not return?"—grimly. "What is to become of the Pembroke line then? And of your father?"

"Dash it, it's not as if you'd be all alone. The Mouse will be here to look after you. Besides, she'll be married one of these days and you'll be looking forward to whole battalions of new heirs to bounce on your knee."

There was a pause, while my father probably entertained that possibility and assessed it.

"My boy," he said finally, "I consider myself to be an enlightened man, and I hesitate to stake my confidence in miracles."

In spite of Father's protests, Lionel had left within a fortnight, bidding us farewell with a jaunty grin and a demand for letters, which he agreed to consider replying to.

"And you, Mouse," he said to me, "must promise to be careful while I'm gone. Any day young bucks will be thronging around you, and they may just try to take advantage of my absence. Until I come back to defend your honor—"

"Lionel, really."

"—I want to know that you won't let yourself be won over by any smooth-tongued young blade."

I laughed; the prospect was so ridiculous that I could only marvel at his serious tone. It was typical of him to be oblivious to the fact that I had never been sought out by so much as one shy curate, let alone a succession of scheming seducers. "Lionel, I don't think you need worry about that."

"But I do worry," he said, sounding so earnest that I wanted to hug him. For all his two years' advantage, I frequently felt as if I were much older than my brother.

"I think I have enough sense to tell a cad from a gentleman," I said, to soothe him.

"The trouble is, so many gentlemen are cads," he said doubtfully. But he let himself be coaxed out of his worries, and it was only as he swung himself into the waiting hansom that I felt regret that I hadn't continued the argument and thus delayed his departure a few minutes more.

Father, too, was silent and morose as the coach drove away. It was the one time I can remember when we were so in accord. Our apprehensions were fulfilled; Lionel was killed in battle less than a month later.

* * *

We received a number of visitors that afternoon, but not many friends of my brother's: most were in the Crimea themselves, chasing after the dream of glory and excitement that had betrayed Lionel. The few who did call stood around awkwardly, holding a cup of tea with as much unease as if it had been a baby we had forced into their hands, and obviously wishing for stronger refreshment. Father's cool reception of their stammered expressions of sympathy robbed them of the power of speech altogether, and since, as I have said, I speak as little in my father's presence as is possible, we were not a lively group.

Nevertheless, I was sorry to see the last of the mourners leave, since that meant I was alone again with my father. More than ever I missed Lionel, who had acted as a buffer between us. In Lionel's presence Father had treated me less harshly, made less display of his contempt for me; it surprised and amused him that Lionel was fond of me, but he humored the quirk as he humored all Lionel's weaknesses. Since my brother had left for the war, the evenings had been tense; one night, when I dropped my thimble and startled Father out of a reverie, he stood, seized my mending, and flung it on the fire.

At dinner he was unusually silent. Even though he thinks little of my conversation, Father enjoys speaking—perhaps it is a characteristic of those in his profession—and would carry on a monologue in my presence, content for it to be punctuated by my murmurs of agreement. Tonight he watched me thoughtfully over the rim of his wine glass and spoke little. It made me nervous; but then, I am never relaxed in Father's company. I wondered what he had in store for me. Doubtless it would not be pleasant.

"I'll take port in my study, Molly," he announced at the end of dinner, dabbing at his moustache with his napkin.

To my surprise, the maid continued to hover. "If you please sir, there's a card for you," she blurted, her black eyes bright with excitement. "It was left this afternoon."

"This afternoon?" Pushing back his chair, he glanced at but did not reach for the square of pasteboard on the salver she extended. "You knew I was at home; why didn't you admit whoever it was?"

"It was left by a messenger, sir." Molly took a deep breath, and I wondered what sensational morsel she was about to unburden herself of. "Her Grace did not call in person."

Her words did indeed cause a gratifying reaction. Father flung away his napkin and darted his hand out for the calling card, a hawk snatching at prey. "Her Grace?" he demanded, and even as his eyes gave him the name, Molly announced it, in ringing tones of personal pride.

"Gwendolyn, Duchess of Ellsworth." She let the words die away solemnly, then added in an avid whisper, "her that's just gone and married her brother-in-law."

Now she had caught my attention as well. Gossip had made free with the duchess of late: a few weeks ago everyone had been gabbling about the scandal, so much so that even I, with my severely limited acquaintance, was familiar with the facts. Scant weeks after the death of her husband the duke, the duchess had married his younger brother. Many winks and nudges and knowing nods had registered awareness of her haste. There was more than a dash of spite in the gossip, as well, since the duchess had flown in the face of the law, which prohibited such marriages; there were grumblings about her having received special permission for the match.

Some even cast a critical eye on the social convention that decreed she would continue to be addressed as a duchess even though her new husband held no title in his own right. I could understand Molly's excitement at the knowledge that such a celebrated—or notorious—figure had sent her card to us. As for Father, I knew of old his reverence for the peerage. Little wonder now that he was exulting in this evidence that a lady of such rank had bestowed notice on his household.

The question was why she had. How would my father be acquainted with the duchess? And if she paid him enough notice to leave her card, why had she done so by proxy, instead of calling in person? It seemed as if she wanted to show her awareness of our bereavement without running the risk of seeing us face to face.

I was rapt in contemplation of the caprices of the peerage when Father's voice broke into my thoughts.

"Thank you, Molly. I am glad to know Her Grace's card was safe in your keeping all this time." He had evidently recovered from his exultation, and the acid tone of his voice made her wince. Bobbing a quick curtsey, she removed herself as rapidly as she could. To me he added, "Bring the sherry and come with me."

As usual, I said, "Yes, Father."

To my surprise, the sherry was for me. When we reached his study, Father told me to pour myself a glass. He strode to the buffet where the port decanter was kept, and when his own glass was filled he turned to face me where I stood, standing awkwardly since he had not told me to be seated. He lifted his glass for a toast and, wondering, I raised my own.

"To the memory of Lionel," he said.

"To Lionel," I said.

He emptied his glass in one brief swallow and flung it into the fireplace. I hesitated, but he watched me impatiently, waiting for me to follow his example. The unexpected sentiment of his toast had tightened my throat, making it difficult to swallow, but I forced the sherry down before sending my glass after his. The crash of the glasses was shocking in the stillness of the room.

"Now, to business," he said briskly. Opening his desk, he took out a paper and tossed it over to me. Startled, I did not quite catch it before it fell to the ground. Father shook his head in exasperation and turned his back to me, drawing a cigar from the humidor. "Read it," he ordered, striking a match.

"'I, Hugo Pembroke, being of sound mind and—'" I broke off in confusion. "Your will?" Had I misjudged him, or failed to see a softer side than I had known him to possess? My father had never seemed the sort of man to let the death of another wake in him any sentiment about his own mortality.

"What a brilliant conclusion." He frowned at me as I stared at him, expecting an explanation. "Keep reading, girl, and don't gape at me in that half-witted fashion."

I read to the end. It was very brief: it left the bulk of his estate to his college for the construction of a new wing to be named after him. A few modest bequests went to the servants, and some personal possessions to colleagues. "You must have made this very recently, since Lionel's death," I said, surprise—or the sherry—loosening my tongue.

He took his customary position at the fireplace and blew smoke toward the ceiling. "Correct. I wrote it the day the telegram came. Does anything else strike your lightning intellect—or your self-interest?"

I folded the will and placed it on his desk. "I am unprovided for, if that is what you mean."

My flash of impertinence, for once, he let pass. His expression remained calm as he puffed at his cigar. "Correct again," he said, in what was for him an almost genial tone. "Really, I am beginning to think I was mistaken in my assessment of your mental capacities. You are showing nearly average intelligence. You will be learning chess next."

I had often beaten Lionel at chess, in fact. "May I ask why you have shown me this, Father?" I settled into a chair and folded my hands in my lap.

"I hoped you would." He actually smiled. "After twenty-one years of supporting you, I consider my obligations as your father fulfilled. I'm disinheriting you, daughter."

I nodded, since he seemed to be expecting me to reply.

"What's more"—he tapped cigar ash into the grate—"I'm disowning you."

"What?" I exclaimed without thinking.

That brought a broad, satisfied smile from him: my shock evidently pleased him. "Yes, my girl, as of the first day of next month I will no longer claim you. I give you until then to make arrangements for your future. Three weeks should be ample time in which to find a position as a governess or companion or a similarly situated drudge. At the end of that time, should you still be in the house, I will have your belongings burnt and your person removed from my property by main force. Once you have left my house I will take no responsibility for you and make no recognition of you. You will cease to become my daughter. Should you find yourself in need of assistance, financial or otherwise, it will be useless to apply to me. I will return letters unread, telegrams unopened. You, my dear, will be a stranger to me."

And with that endearment—the first he had ever spoken to me—he ended our life as father and daughter.

If he expected tears, protestations, hysterics, he must have been disappointed. He had schooled me well: since any display of emotion on my part acted as a goad to him, I had trained myself to become a blank wall. Perhaps I had taught myself too well, since I did not even feel anything.

"I won't ask you why you are doing this," I said at last. "I know only too well that you have always hated me."

"How perceptive of you to have noticed." The smile was gone when I met his eyes, and the hatred was so intense that it startled me, even though I was accustomed to seeing it. "Your mother would be alive now, but for you."

"So you have always said." I had heard him tell the story so often I could have quoted it back to him, even parroting his phrases: bearing me was too taxing for my mother's frail nerves, and after my birth she never regained her old spirits, sinking into a profound melancholy that was only worsened by my fretfulness, for I was a fractious, demanding infant. At last her poor nerves gave way and, driven past endurance, she flung herself into the ocean.

I had no memories of my mother's death, having been less than a year old at the time, and my father's version was the only one I knew. In spite of what the tale suggested of my mother's feelings for me, I had never ceased to miss her. I had not even the consolation of memories of her; so many times I had tried to force a recollection of her—a fragrance, or a snatch of song, would have sufficed—to come away with nothing. My father had never spoken of her to me, beyond enforcing upon me my part in her destruction. I had marveled time and time again that he who had always been so hostile and cold to me could have loved my mother with such devotion that he could not conquer his anger at her death. It would have seemed strange that so powerful a love could be transmuted into an equally powerful hatred, but that I was so familiar with him.

"I wonder if you would have hated me less had I been the firstborn," I mused, half to myself. "If Lionel had been the child who drove Mother to drown herself, would you have treated him as you have me? But I would still be plain and unmarriageable, and Lionel… it would be impossible for anyone not to have loved Lionel."

"He would have been a great man," said Father, regret vibrating fiercely in his voice. "He would have made a name for the Pembrokes. But you—how could you ever distinguish yourself, or do anything to add luster to your family? You could never be anything but a dead weight."

I rose, not angry, but weary of hearing the same refrain.

"You forget," I said. "It is no longer my family. You are nothing to me now, as I am nothing to you. You have made it so yourself."

He flicked cigar ash into the fire. "If you're trying to play on my sympathies and evoke some gush of paternal sentiment, you may as well save yourself the trouble. You won't alter my decision."

"I would not dream of trying to do so," I said, and made my curtsey. "Good night."

"Go on, get out." He waved me away, even though I was already going. "I know you're longing to escape to your room and snivel over my heartless treatment of you."

Once in my room I did not cry. I had not cried since I was a child. Like any display of emotion, it was too dangerous an indulgence; my father treated tears as hysteria, smacking me smartly across the face until they ceased. Now, after long years of such training, I seemed to have lost the ability. I had not even been able to weep for Lionel.

I drew a chair up to the window, where I could watch the small patch of stars visible between the roofs of surrounding houses. I felt no fear, no sorrow, not even anger; it seemed strangely right that my life with my father should be severed in this way. We had never, after all, been father and daughter in any real sense, and now it seemed the best thing to put an end to the pretense. As soon as I had been able to think after the news of Lionel's death, I had known that I would not be able to continue living in my father's house. My presence there had only been bearable when Lionel had been there to smooth things. After he had left for the war conditions had become strained, to be sure, but I never seriously expected him to be gone for long; never did I consider that he might die. It seemed impossible for one so blazingly alive, whose energy fairly crackled around him, to be snuffed out. But I had been wrong.

But even the gnawing of my grief for Lionel could not utterly blot out the strange feeling of exhilaration, even of happiness, that was pouring over me, as invigorating and refreshing as cold water. I would no longer be subject to my father's vicious temper and cold contempt. I was free to find my own place, without having even to win it. Without knowing it, Father had done me a service. He had given me my freedom.

Now, I asked myself, what would I do with it? In that first hour, alone with the soft unwinking light of the stars, I felt only the excitement of liberty, the tantalizing array of choices spread richly before me. The world seemed a trove of glittering opportunities beckoning to me, welcoming me. Later I would realize the immensity of this naïveté; but in that first hour of freedom I never doubted that the world awaited only a word from me before pouring all it could offer into my lap.

What would my choice be? It was not the first time I had considered my future. Seven years ago I had seized upon the plan of joining an Anglican sisterhood. A life of contemplation and sacred hush attracted me; I would be freed from the stigma of spinsterhood (at fourteen already an inevitability) and be able to spend as much time as I wished in reading and translating. Having done all of Lionel's lessons for him from an early age, I was quite proficient in languages and indeed took a great satisfaction in such study. One of my favorite memories had been overhearing Lionel's unsuspecting tutor praising what he believed to be my brother's translation of Catullus. "You've caught all the earthy nuances of the jaded lover upbraiding his mistress," raved Mr. Peabody, and Lionel, who until now had had no idea of what his sister had been writing on his behalf, exclaimed blankly, "Good God, I have?"

However, after a few years of passionately devoting myself to this dream, I realized that even a benevolent God might not smile upon an acolyte who took such pleasure and pride in reading Catullus and Gautier. It was more than likely that one who had consecrated herself to a holy life should not be so receptive to the scandalous satire of Byron. Besides, who was to say that a spiritual Father would be any kinder, any less harsh, cold, or exacting than my earthly one? I was not ready to blindly submit myself to a new lord after my treatment at the hands of the present one. Fathers struck dread in me. The Holy Mother was a more attractive figure, but she seemed to be, at best, an intermediary. So at seventeen I abandoned this plan and cast about for another.

It was at this time that Father seemed to regain some hope that I might be salvaged. Perhaps I showed some signs of a hitherto unsuspected beauty; more likely, he did not wish to completely dismiss all hopes of me without strong proof that they were in vain. Father did not attain his prestigious career by abandoning unpromising avenues without exhausting all their possibilities first. With some such aim in mind, no doubt, he introduced into the household a relative of my mother's, a countess, whose purpose was to sniff out any dormant charm I might possess and chivy it into the light.

She went about her task with a formidable energy and persistence that were exhausting to me, if not to her. My comfortable, simple dresses and practical boots were rejected in favor of a cruelly fashionable new toilette, which included a corset, dozens of petticoats, and painfully tiny slippers; thus encumbered I had singing lessons (when I could not draw breath for my stays) and dancing lessons (when every step pinched unbearably). The countess and her maid spent hours every day in a grim struggle with my heavy, straight hair as they attempted to skewer it into beauty. In the end their efforts, zealous as they had been, came to nothing; after a disastrous presentation at a tea for a bevy of society ladies, I was relegated again to my semi-solitude in the upper regions of the house, and the countess was dismissed. She left immediately, taking with her my expensive new wardrobe. I was not sorry to see the end of either, although Lionel had been charmed by my new look; in fact, I recalled sending the poor woman's coach away with a shower of hairpins.

I had been leaning on my elbows on the windowsill, in my habitually unladylike position since no one was ever there to correct me, but now I sat up abruptly. The countess had been a relative of my mother's; that I remembered. Yet she had not appeared at the funeral. I had not thought anything about it at the time because I never saw any of my mother's family; I had never met any but the countess, in fact. For the first time it occurred to me to wonder if my mother's death had caused some breach between my father and his wife's relatives. Of course, this may have been excited imagination; more likely they had died out, or moved far away. Still, it was strange that Father never referred to them, especially since I knew he would be quick to advertise his connection to anyone with a title.

I sat thinking until I heard Father's steps on the floor below going to his room. When I was certain he had retired and would not emerge again, I crept noiselessly out of my room and down the stairs to his study. Skeptic he may have been, but my father still kept the old Bible in which, I hoped, the branches of the family would be recorded. I had never seen it opened, but it was displayed impressively on its own stand by his desk.

I had not been mistaken. When I lit the gas and unfastened the clasps on the great book, I found at once what I sought. All my relatives for generations back were recorded, the most recent entries in my father's angular, precise hand. There was Lionel's name, with the date of his death inked in beneath in strong black strokes. Next to his was my name, Oriel Pembroke, the only legacy my mother had left me.

But ours were not the only names on the line reserved for the present generation. The line, in fact, was almost full; four more names elbowed in next to Lionel's and mine.

I had cousins.

Astonished, I stared at the page. I was so unprepared for this that I could almost convince myself that my father had made a mistake, that the names had been carelessly placed and these relatives belonged to some long-dead branch of the family. But my father, whatever his imperfections, was a meticulous man; he would not have committed to paper anything but the scrupulous truth. I had cousins whose presence I had never suspected, whom I had never known. Where were they, that we had never met? Were these my mother's family?

The names of their parents should give me the answer. Almost dizzily I traced upward from the unfamiliar clutch of names—two male and two female—to find myself staring at one I knew instantly. Gwendolyn Reginald, third Duchess of Ellsworth. My mother's stepsister.

Chapter Two

My dear girl (the letter read),

What a delightful surprise your note was! I never dreamed of hearing from you. Indeed, I did not know you were living; it has been so many years since I have seen you, and you but a tiny baby then. You must be the image of your sweet mother by now, and quite grown up.

Yes, by all means do call while I am in town. I am longing for us to become acquainted, and I would welcome the opportunity to express my sympathy for the loss of your poor brother in person. I am at home on Tuesday and Thursday afternoons. Do call soon so that we may begin to make up for the years we have been lost to one another.

Affectionately, Gwendolyn Ellsworth

The room I was shown into was a haven of warmth, light, and color after the dreary rain-drenched day outside. The maid took my dripping cloak with the faintest curl of her lip to register the puddles it was leaving on the pale carpet. But she said civilly enough, "Her Grace and the other ladies will be returning soon, if you will wait in here."

I thanked her, wondering about the "other ladies," but I did not want to display my ignorance before her. I had not bargained for a gathering, and my courage, already halfhearted, threatened to turn tail and flee. I made myself sit down, when I really wished to follow the maid back out of the room and leave the way I had come.

The duchess's London house was in one of the fashionable cul-de-sacs I had never had cause to venture into before, and the noise of the traffic barely penetrated. There was a restful quiet here, underscored by the self-deprecating tick of the mantel clock and the crackling of the fire. My tired feet, which had carried me all the way from my own house since I had no pocket money for a hansom, sank gratefully into a thick carpet patterned with cherry blossoms. This sitting room was evidently the duchess's own domain, for everything about the room bespoke femininity: the rose-hued damask curtains and coverings, the touches of gilt, the delicate curving lines of the furniture. After the tasteful but austere surroundings I was accustomed to, this room was a revelation. In spite of myself I began to relax under its serene influence.

That serenity was swept aside an instant later when the double doors burst open to admit what seemed in that first moment to be a dozen young women. After the first commotion was past I was able to see that there were only four women, and not all young, but the room seemed full to brimming over with the cheerful clamor of voices, the rustling of their massive skirts, and the gay colors of their dresses. Holding out her hands to me, the prettiest of the women approached me, and I got to my feet to curtsey.

"My dear child! So you did come. I so hoped you would, but I wasn't certain—what with your being in mourning. Poor child, how dreadful for you, and your only brother. I am more sorry than I can say. But how glad I am that you came! It is all that was wanting to make my visit complete."

"Your Grace," I said feebly, feeling overwhelmed by this enthusiastic barrage of commiseration and delight. "It is such an honor to meet you—"

"Oh, come now, child, there's no need for such formality among family," she chided me, laughing. "For we are family.

How good it is to see you again! Your mother was very dear to me, for all that we saw each other so little.... Felicity, Aminta, this is the young lady I told you about—your step-cousin, after all these years! Oh, it's such a pleasure to see you, child!" And she flew to kiss my cheek and draw me down next to her on a divan, still chattering gaily on.

I was glad of the respite so that I could collect myself. This was the duchess? From the scandal that was still linked with her name, I had expected something like the tragic heroine of a classical drama; surely a woman who had defied convention to make such a sudden, shocking second marriage would reflect it in her appearance. I had pictured a handsome, darkly exotic woman with a fiery temperament and passionate, knowing eyes. It was difficult to reconcile my imaginings with this golden-haired, dimpled creature, who looked at first glance to be little older than myself.

Her eyes were blue and candid—not at all the sloe eyes of the temptress!—and bright earrings bobbed and chimed in response to her animation as she spoke. Her hands were small and dainty, her waist as slender as an eighteen-year-old's, and instead of the rich velvets I had expected her to wear she was dressed in a confection that brought a rush of pure longing to my heart: pale blue taffeta, with at least six flounces on the skirt, each scalloped and trimmed with white silk fringe. To my dazzled, inexperienced eyes, she looked like a fairy princess, where I had expected a Cleopatra.

"But I'm forgetting my manners," she said now. "I haven't introduced you properly. I mustn't selfishly keep you all to myself." Now that I dragged my eyes away from the fascinating duchess I could form more of an impression of the other three women. They were hanging back tactfully, trying not to look as if they were observing me—all except for the youngest, who was frankly staring. The duchess observed this at the same moment.

"The young lady who is so interested in you is Felicity, my niece—no, my daughter now!" she amended gaily. At her nod, Felicity made a neat curtsey. She could indeed have been the duchess's daughter from her appearance: her long ringlets were honey-blonde like her aunt's, and her dress, mint green with emerald trim, was almost a duplicate of the older woman's. I guessed that she was a devoted admirer of her aunt-turned-stepmother. She must not have been out yet, since she still wore short skirts and looked to be perhaps seventeen. The smile she offered me was friendly, but inquisitive.

"And I'm Lady Montrose, Felicity's older sister." A woman in her middle twenties, with a heavy chignon of titian hair, stepped forward to clasp my hand in welcome. She was dressed in a more matronly fashion, but still very richly, and when she had stripped off her gloves she revealed a wedding band on her left hand. "Do call me Aminta," she added. I was to find out later that her husband was a viscount, but she did not stand on ceremony with family.

Felicity was still regarding me with open curiosity. "How old are you?" she said abruptly.

"Miss Reginald, really!" exclaimed the last woman, and darted me a look that combined exasperation and apology. "I do beg your pardon, Miss Pembroke. You'd think she'd never learned manners."

Felicity blushed. "I'm sorry," she said. "I didn't mean to be rude. Poor Miss Yates despairs of me, I am so thoughtless. I believe that is why she forces me to recite poetry in company, so that I won't embarrass her with such blunders." She gave Miss Yates a teasing look, her own embarrassment forgotten.

"Miss Yates is Felicity's governess, and as such I believe she qualifies for sainthood," explained Aminta, settling herself in a chair and spreading her rust-colored skirts around her. She had a low, pleasant voice and a wide mouth that frequently quirked with amusement, especially when she regarded her sister.

Miss Yates, shaking her head amiably, took a seat near the fire. I had thought her a member of the family, from her self-assured bearing and her obvious place in the group of women. She had a face that must have been handsome twenty years before, and she dressed like no governess I had ever had, in a gown of poppy-colored wool and a rich paisley shawl. I envied Felicity; my own governesses had been of a very different stamp, tending toward moldy grey sateens, false hair, and moustaches.

"To be sure, Felicity is forever speaking before she thinks," the duchess conceded. "But she's a good girl at heart, and means nothing by it. I do hope you won't hold her impetuous behavior against her, my dear."

"Of course not," I said. It was obvious that there was not a particle of spite in Felicity, and equally obvious that the others were used to her ways and indulged them; even, for all her scolding, Miss Yates. "There's nothing in the question to offend. I'm twenty-one."

"But you can't be!" exclaimed Aminta, and I saw her eyes go to my hair. I wore it in a braid down my back—a schoolgirl style that, I was well aware, I should have abandoned years ago. But by the time I was old enough to put my hair up, Father had dismissed the last of my governesses—who never stayed long in any case—and I had never learned how to dress my hair in a fashion more appropriate to my age. Since I was never present when we had guests, and most certainly never visited others, I had never worried about my appearance. Now I thought about what an eccentric image I must present: my black gown was a necessity of mourning, but the severe, unadorned style and unfashionably narrow cut of the skirt and sleeves set me apart from the others as dramatically as if I wore a nun's habit. Even the maid had worn a dress more fashionable than mine. I was long used to such plain clothes, since I made my own dresses with fabric grudgingly provided by Father, but I realized now how I must look to outsiders, and I felt my cheeks grow warm.

The silence threatened to become awkward, and the duchess broke it. "But how remiss of me; I have not offered you anything. Aminta, dear, ring for Eliza and ask for tea. I am sure we would all be glad of something to warm us."

While we waited for the tea to arrive, she turned the subject to less personal matters. Grateful for her tact, I began to forget my self-consciousness, and the elegant array of cakes and savories brought by the maid provided a pleasant distraction. The duchess and her companions had been shopping that morning, and I listened hungrily to the details of the gowns they had ordered and the bonnets they had tried. Evidently the duchess had just come to London for a few days' shopping, and was soon to rejoin her new husband.

"We return to Ellsmere in a few days," she explained, helping me to more bread and butter. "I had planned to stay in town for another week, but I find I'm impatient to return to my real home."

"And to Papa," interjected Felicity, with a giggle that won a stern look from Miss Yates.

The duchess dimpled. She looked as roguish, and as young, as her new stepdaughter. "Yes, I confess it. And of course I am eager to be with Herron again."

"The duke," explained Aminta to me. "Our cousin, and yours. I don't suppose you'll ever have met him."

I shook my head.

"But you must meet him," exclaimed the duchess. "And your other cousin, Felicity and Aminta's brother. How terrible that you have been unknown to us for so long! You must promise to visit us at Ellsmere. We should try to make up for all these years of separation."

I smiled politely. It was kindly meant, but why should they wish to court the acquaintance of an obscure relation like myself? The invitation could be for form's sake only. "You're very kind, ma'am."

"For Christmas, perhaps." The duchess was undeterred by the coolness of my reply. "We shall be having a large party to stay with us, so it will be a very merry time. Do say you'll come and stay for a few weeks."

"And there'll be a ball," put in Felicity.

"And the house is always so lovely when it's decorated for the holidays. Imagine, reunited with your dear mother's family for Christmas! Do say you'll come."

She gazed at me with eager expectant eyes, as if she were a child pleading for a treat instead of one of the most powerful aristocrats in the country. Evidently she was sincere. I swallowed a bite of cake and smiled; a bit sadly, for the invitation was tempting. "I wish I could, ma'am," I said. "Unfortunately, I cannot make plans so far in advance. I have no idea where I shall be in December."

"Whyever not?" asked—of course—Felicity.

"I am looking for a position," I explained before the other ladies could rebuke her. Taking a deep breath for courage, I looked at the duchess. "In fact, ma'am, one reason I wished to meet you was to ask if you might know of a family who needs a governess. I have never worked as one before, but I am qualified to teach Latin and Greek as well as French, and my history and mathematics are fairly sound. I had hoped you might be able to suggest someone who would be willing to employ me. I have no one else to ask, and I"—there was no sense in disguising the urgency of it—"will need to find work at once."

I waited, searching for a hopeful sign in her face, but her expression was—deliberately?—neutral. She set her teacup down with a faint chinking sound, her eyes fixed on me. Then, abruptly, as if recalling herself, she turned to the others.

"Miss Yates, do forgive me," she said with a bright smile, "I forgot that I am keeping Felicity from her lessons. You have been very patient to let me detain her so long, and I'm sure her cousin will understand if she excuses herself. Oh, and Aminta, would you be an angel and speak to Cook? I have not yet settled tonight's menu with her; she must be in a taking by now. I'd be so grateful."

It was delicately handled, but no less definite a dismissal. The other ladies immediately rose and said their goodbyes to me before leaving us. Almost at once the double doors closed behind the last rustling skirt, and I was alone with the duchess.

"I hope I was not rude to send them away," she said, but she was perfectly composed, and poured us both more tea. "Perhaps it was unnecessary, but I thought you might find it less awkward to discuss the matter in private. You'll forgive me for being personal, child, but why are you in need of a position? I understood your father to be well situated financially. Has he suffered reverses of late?"

"Not financial ones." I hesitated, staring into my teacup as I tried to decide how much to tell. There was no way I could make her understand the strange gulf that had always existed between Father and me. How could she believe such coldness could exist between parent and child, she who had evidently lived all her life secure in the admiration of those around her? I decided to tell her a part of the truth, a part that she might be able to accept.

"Since my brother's death, I have been more of a burden to Father than a comfort," I said carefully. "He set great store by Lionel; we both did," and for a moment I had to stop and swallow hard before I could continue. The duchess patted my hand but did not interrupt. "It would be impossible for me to take Lionel's place, or to cease reminding Father of his loss. It would be better for both of us if I went away."

"And you must support yourself? You have no protector?"

"None."

She regarded me in silence for a few minutes, with no trace of the frivolity she had shown until now. For the first time her bearing seemed more that of a duchess than a belle. Her expression was pensive, with a kind of understanding that suggested decades more experience than I possessed; the butterfly of a moment before, who gave the impression of having known no greater sorrow than a torn petticoat, had given way to a woman of dignity and perception. The metamorphosis was disconcerting: which was the true duchess? And was I safe to trust so chameleon-like a creature?

She was watching me with a scrutiny so keen that I dropped my eyes to my hands, fearing she would guess my thoughts. At that moment I could have believed that she had the power to read my mind.

"I think I understand," she said finally, and again I was surprised at the gravity of her tone. "You find it impossible to remain under your father's guardianship, and you are unwilling or unable to benefit from his money or connections. You are prepared to work at the lowest occupation available to a gentlewoman, and are forced to seek a position from a distant relative who is essentially a stranger to you—as well as a figure of some notoriety." Light but implacable fingers tipped my chin up so that I was forced to meet her eyes. "I suspect you have told me something less than the truth," she said gently. "While loyalty is a commendable quality, if you ever wish to tell me the full story, you will not find me unsympathetic."

"Yes, ma'am," I whispered, guilt and hope mingling in me. Releasing my chin, she rose with something of her former energy and swept over to a tiny desk.

"Well, there is only one thing to be done. At the end of the week when we return to Ellsmere, you will accompany us." She wrote a few lines on one of her calling cards and held it out to me. Uncomprehending, I took it. "Show this at the railway station and one of the attendants will take you to my car. Our train leaves on Friday at eleven. I trust you can be ready to depart by then?"

Stunned as much by this unexpected efficiency as by its import, I stammered, "Yes, of course. But—excuse me, ma'am—have you thought of a position for me? Do you wish for me to tutor His Grace?"

She flung back her head and gave a peal of laughter. "Oh, gracious, my dear, I hardly think so. His Grace the duke is full twenty years old."

"I beg your pardon." I could feel myself blushing, and the duchess, immediately repentant, came gliding back to the sofa to catch my hands.

"My dear, I did not mean to laugh at you. But I cannot bear to think of you fretting about a position. You'll come to Ellsmere with us, and leave your future to me. I assure you, you shall not be forced to eke out an existence by drilling geography and history into a litter of spoiled children. We can do better for you than that!" Laughing, she drew me to my feet, and I found myself smiling. "There, that is better," she said approvingly. "Put yourself in my hands, and have no fear for the future."

"Thank you, ma'am." It was foolishly inadequate, but she did not seem to mind.

"Until Friday, then. Shall I send a carriage to your house?"

I stopped short. "Oh, please no—I'd much rather my father didn't know where I'll be." He probably had little interest in my whereabouts, in any case, but I felt obscurely safer knowing that I would be out of his reach. "In fact, ma'am, if you don't mind, I would be glad if we could keep what I've said between us."

To my astonishment, she put her arms around me and embraced me before I realized what she was about. Her eyes were very solemn when she drew back to look at me. "You poor child, of course," she exclaimed. "I shall tell Claude and the boys merely that I was lucky enough to encounter you in town and invited you to stay with us. That is all they need know."

Awkwardly, I attempted once more to express my gratitude, but before I had gotten half a dozen words out, Eliza the maid appeared with my wrap. I had not even noticed when the duchess had rung for her.

"Goodbye, my dear," she said. "Or, rather, farewell, as we shall meet soon again!"

In moments I was running through the drizzle to the hansom Eliza had called for me. Settling into the unaccustomed luxury of the cushions, I gazed out the window at the receding view of the duchess's house, with all the ride home in which to go over in my mind the events of that unusual morning.

* * *

As I had expected, Father showed no curiosity about my plans. He had formally ended our relationship; thus, whatever

I did with myself would be of no interest to him, since it could not possibly affect him. I was glad of his lack of interest. It convinced me, if I had needed convincing, that we would both be happier freed of our obligations to each other, and it allowed me to pack and prepare for my journey unencumbered by the necessity of inventing a story for his benefit.

"I have observed that you are already making preparations to leave," he commented one evening at supper. "I trust you will recall that the furnishings and decorations in your room are all my property, and I will treat any attempt to remove them from the house as theft."

Since the decorations in question were a mildewed sampler I had stitched at age eight and a dreary mezzotint entitled "Waifs of the Storm," I could assure Father with perfect truth that I had no intention of trying to abscond with them. I had little enough to pack: my few dresses, my sewing things, and my books. I would have liked to have had Lionel's Latin and Greek texts, which had always been more mine than his, but Father had disposed of them along with most of his possessions. The only mementos I had of my brother were a brooch with his hair, a miniature portrait of him at eighteen years old, and the copy of *Varney, the Vampyre; or, the Feast of Blood* he had pressed on me before he left (he had always enjoyed sensation fiction).

But, however scanty these souvenirs might be, they were more than I had with which to remember my mother. I had never asked my father for any of her possessions; I didn't even know if he had kept anything belonging to her. As I ate in my usual silence it began to seem unsupportable to leave my father's house forever without taking from it something of my mother. Even if it was only a tidbit of knowledge of her—the name of a song she had sung to me, her favorite author, the way she had dressed her hair—I could not go away empty-handed.

"Father," I said, and it was so unusual for me to address him that he put down his fork to narrow his eyes at me, "I have never asked you this before, but as I am leaving in two days' time and will trouble you no more, I must ask you now: what happened to Mother's belongings after she died?"

He regarded me for a moment, then resumed chewing. He swallowed, took a sip of claret, and said, "I burnt them."

The ruthlessness of it momentarily robbed me of breath.

"Why?"

"What a ridiculous question. Why does a man whose wife has just died do anything? I should scarcely be held accountable for my actions at such a time." Calmly he speared another bite of mutton.

"But there must have been things you would have kept. Her letters, her jewelry—"

"Ha, jewelry!" He smiled wryly. "The true nature of your interest emerges. You're greedy for whatever fine jewels and valuables she may have left."

I could not even find any anger in me to greet this accusation. "Very well, I can understand that it would be painful for you to be reminded of her. But surely you would not have destroyed a portrait."

"Who said there was a portrait?"

"There must have been one, if—" I had started to say, if she had been the stepsister of a duchess, surely she would have been painted, but I did not wish to reveal my new knowledge. Instead I said, "When you married, I would have expected you to want a portrait of your wife. Any bridegroom would."

He chuckled as he poured himself more claret. "And what would you know about bridegrooms, girl? That's a subject you'll never have any experience in."

"Yes, Father," I said, falling back on the established formula.

Perhaps it was the wine, or the knowledge that I would be leaving in two days, but for whatever reason he seemed to be in a fairly benign mood. Instead of letting the subject die, as I expected him to, he said after a moment, "Yes, there was a portrait."

"Was?" My heart lurched. "You didn't burn it, too?"

A slow smile spread across his face, and he gazed almost dreamily at his glass of claret, turning it so that the gaslight glinted off the faceted crystal and set the wine glowing like a drowned flame. "No. I did not burn it."

He was enjoying himself, drawing this out deliberately to keep me in suspense, but I had to ask the question he was waiting to hear. "Where is it, then? May I see it?"

Another long, deliberate pause, and he slowly tipped the last of his wine down his throat. Then, setting the glass on the table, he pushed back his chair and stood. Swiftly, I stood as well, and he rang for Molly to clear.

"Yes," he said. "I think you may see it. Since, as you say, you will be leaving soon, it is right that you should look on your mother's face before you go."

Scarcely daring to breathe for fear he would change his mind, so unexpected was his agreeable, accommodating mood, I followed him out of the dining room to the stairs. He paused to get an oil lamp, and then we began our ascent.

I followed him all the way to the top of the house, to a low narrow door I had never opened. The key Father used was rusty, the lock stiff, and when the door finally opened with a jerk we were greeted with a rising cloud of dust. When it settled, the lamp cast a warm glow on a jumble of disorder: broken chairs, crumbling sheaves of paper, boxes, trunks, crates. Everything was furred heavily with dust so that it blended into a dun-colored mass, and as we moved into the attic, squeaks and scrabbling sounds preceded us. Spiders had made free of the place; generations of webs draped the rafters, and Father, in front of me, had to brush them aside to move forward. The condition of the attic dispelled any notion I might have had that Father made sentimental pilgrimages to visit his dead wife's portrait, and I wondered why he had not stored it in a place where it would be safe from vermin and decay.

At least he—or a servant—had covered it, so that it was not naked to the dust that had grown moss-like over every other surface. The tall rectangle standing at the far end of the room was swathed completely in a cloth that may once have been white but was now the same grimy color as everything surrounding it. Father set the lamp on a nearby trunk so that it cast its light on the shrouded shape. Then, with thinned lips showing his distaste, he grasped a corner of the drape and pulled. Instantly he fell back as another choking cloud of dust arose, and I held my handkerchief to my nose as I stared at the painting, waiting for it to emerge from the haze.

I could feel my heart quickening. After so long, finally to know what she looked like, to see whether I even—oh, please—resembled her. To see in her face what her character was, whether she had been flirtatious, or gentle, or strong, to know what kind of person she had been who had ended her own life when she was no older than I. Through the settling dust came colors first, then shapes: a bright pink gown, a blue bonnet, hands folded over a fan. My heart was beating fast and joyful as my eyes sought her face.

They met blankness. Beneath the meticulously rendered plumes and frills of the bonnet there was no face, but a hole of vacant white canvas. Nausea touched me and I fell back a step, shaken by the terrible void where I had expected to find the features of a human face.

"The artist never even saw your mother."

I had forgotten Father's presence. Unable to speak, I looked at him where he stood next to me and saw unmistakable satisfaction in his eyes. "Tragic, isn't it? The only surviving portrait of your dear mother, and it lacks its subject." When I still said nothing, he went on, and he was actually smiling. "She was a very sickly little thing, your mother. If she wasn't taking the waters at a spa she was convalescing in Italy. The artist had to paint everything else first, and she was dead before he so much as met her."

"But... the hands?" I asked faintly, finding my voice.

He waved dismissively. "A model, no doubt."

A shiver went through me. Not even these held anything of my mother. All they spoke of was an anonymous shop girl or actress who had worn my mother's dress for the time it took to be set on canvas. I would never even have the slight knowledge they would have afforded: would she have had long fingers, clever with a needle or at the pianoforte? Or the plump, dimpled hands of a belle? Would she have had a smudge of Prussian blue paint on one finger, or ink from writing letters? Would her grasp on the fan have been languid, tentative, or firm?

I stared at the portrait with numb eyes, then moved to retrieve the discarded cloth and covered the painting up again. When I turned around my father was watching me with folded arms and the same satisfied expression.

"All this time," I said, "you let me believe that you loved her—so much that you had no love left for me. But if you'd had any love for her you would never have used her portrait to try to hurt me."

His smile split in half, into a wolfish grin of gleaming white. "Brava, my girl. Very good."

"Why, then? If she meant nothing to you, then why do you hold her death against me still? What have you lost?"

"You spoke of jewels, earlier. For years I have been waiting for you to ask to wear your mother's jewels. It would have been a natural request from anyone less timorous, not to say spineless. The fact is that your mother's jewels, and everything else she possessed of value, were merely lent her. She owned no property; she left no inheritance." His voice was losing its restraint and beginning to take on an edge of remembered fury and resentment. "Her family pulled the wool over my eyes beautifully. A modest dowry, and her allowance, were all I ever got. She would never inherit anything, nor I through her; her father was too cautious. If I had known when I married her that the family money would be tied up..."

The numbness was receding. A white tide of anger was rising in its place, and I even thought I could hear its roaring in my ears. "That is what you've mourned all these years?" I said, not caring if I was interrupting. "Money? How can you dare to blame me, when it was your gullibility and greed that led to your disappointment?"

The look he leveled at me would have made me quail at any other time. "You stupid girl, when she died, her allowance died with her. All that magnificent income, and a place in society, destroyed by a colicky brat. Do you think her family cared after that if I had enough money to live on? Do you think they continued to sponsor me in society, to give me entrée into the class I'd married into? In one blow I was robbed of wife, money, position." His voice had dropped to a vicious whisper. "Now do you understand why I hate you?"

I was shaking, but not with fear or grief. I had always assumed that, even in his contempt for me, he had never spoken less than the truth. Now I saw in one searing glimpse how he had manipulated me by fostering such an assumption. The one thing about him that had seemed to draw us together—his feeling for my mother—was perhaps the most irreconcilable gulf, and he had used my sympathy, had nurtured it as he seemed to reject it.

"I can well understand," I said, and my voice trembled. "If there is one thing you have taught me to understand, it is hate. I have always feared you—for all you think me a fool, I am too intelligent not to fear you—but I have never hated you until now. Now I know that I hate you."

I turned, fumbling away from him out of the reach of the lamplight, and as I felt my way to the door I heard him laugh. It was the sound of delight, of gratification, and of triumph.

"So I have succeeded in teaching you something," he said, his voice almost purring in its deep contentment. "You have inherited something from me after all—the capacity for hate. That will be your legacy."

I stumbled out of the attic, but his laughter followed, a soft delighted crooning that sickened me. I flung myself headlong down the stairs to escape it, to lock myself in my room and huddle on my bed until daybreak, to tell myself again and again that I had not become what he wanted to make of me, that my newborn hatred did not brand me his creature and his kin—his daughter.

CHAPTER THREE

Next morning I departed for Ellsmere.

Looking back much later, I would realize how little prepared I was when I embarked on my new life. I was armed with a strange combination of learning and inexperience: from my unorthodox reading (unorthodox, that is, for a young woman) I had culled an accumulation of worldly knowledge but, having led a sheltered and mostly solitary life for more than twenty years, I was nevertheless hugely naïve.

I knew that evil existed, and that the world was not always a just place; had I not just received shattering proof of this? I knew also a great deal more than I should have about matters considered improper for ladies' sensibilities—the earthier aspects of love, for example (here I was indebted to Catullus and Byron).

Of real human evil, though, I was ignorant. My father's tender mercies had taught me that parents could be unnatural, that where I should most expect caring I might find only calculation. But I thought him an isolated case, an extreme—certainly not one of a multitude. If only there had been some wiser soul to warn me that other families hid secrets just as malignant.

At the time, though, I would not have heeded any such warning. I was eager to trust, and to love. Only later would I learn the dangers of both.

When my necessaries had been loaded into the hansom cab I stood for a long moment before the door to my father's study. He was keeping his normal schedule; no need to interrupt it to bid farewell to someone who was no longer his daughter. He had easily made the transition from father to childless widower. Molly already had orders to move the furniture out of the room I had occupied so that it might be made into a library.

But I could not sever myself from him so easily. It did not matter that there was no love between us, that he had never shown the slightest interest in me other than as a reflection upon him; for all that, he was my father, and something like loneliness swelled painfully beneath my ribs as I stood ready to leave him.

If only I could have won his respect, if not his love; I had always hoped somehow that I could achieve something that would win a fraction of the approval and commendation he gave Lionel. My translations for Lionel, I had thought, might impress him; but when I made the mistake of telling him of them, he reviled me as a jealous liar, trying to steal the credit for my brother's accomplishments, and in the same breath derided me as a bluestocking. My skill in sewing he turned to good use, since if I made my own dresses he did not have to pay a seamstress, but he dismissed it as a brainless accomplishment, the only one elementary enough for a girl who could not play or draw. It had taken me time to learn the futility of running to him with every small accomplishment in hopes of winning his admiration.

Even so, in spite of the years since in which I had told myself that it was best and easiest to help him to forget my presence rather than to draw attention to it, there was still a part of me that longed for his approval. I wondered if he would be proud of me, even for a moment, if I told him of my acquaintance with the duchess and of her patronage of me. He would be impressed, that was certain; his dearest wish was to move among the aristocracy, and he might even spare a morsel of admiration for me, knowing that I was to achieve what he so prized.

I raised my hand to knock. I would tell him. But then the memory of the faceless painting of my mother came before my eyes, and a return of that flush of anger and revulsion. He might be proud of me—but it would be because he thought I was using the duchess to foster my own ambition, as he would have done. I would be no better than him if I tried to plume myself on the acquaintance. Heat rushed to my face as I realized how close I had come to lowering myself to that level, and I turned and almost ran out the door and to the waiting cab.

When I reached the railway station the duchess had named, I discovered that I had no need to ask anyone for directions to her car. The duchess literally had her own, identified by her coat of arms and teeming with liveried footmen. Newly awed, I made my way to it, followed by a porter who carried my boxes. As I neared it, I could read the motto on the family crest: *Esse quam videri.* I translated it automatically: "To be, rather than to seem." A sentiment I admired; I hoped it was an apt one.

While I was thinking this, Lady Montrose—Aminta—emerged at the top of the steps.

"Why, good morning!" she exclaimed warmly. "I did not know if we would meet. I was just seeing Aunt and Felicity off." She swept her voluminous skirts expertly down the steps and came to meet me. "I am glad I was able to see you before you left."

"You are not traveling with us?" I felt a dart of disappointment; even though we had only met once before, I had been impressed by Aminta's calm, pleasant manner and unobtrusive good sense. She made an attractive counterpoint to her more ebullient sister and stepmother, and I would miss her company.

She smiled and slipped a hand through my arm to give me a reassuring squeeze. "Oh, you needn't think you're rid of me for good. Now that we know we have a cousin, Felicity and I won't be so easily avoided. In any case, my family and I will be coming to Ellsmere for Christmas."

"How nice," I said, thinking how companionable that sounded. I had never known what it was like to have such a family gathering. "How many children do you have?"

"Two. Freddy is five, a perfect cherub, and India is my two-year-old tempest. But I must let you get settled," she added, walking me toward the railway carriage; "I'm certain

Aunt Gwendolyn is waiting for you, and Felicity will be impatient to ask you all the questions she has thought up in the last three days."

Smiling at the likelihood of this, I mounted the narrow steps to the door through which my porter had already disappeared, then stopped as I heard Aminta call out again. "I almost forgot. Do you mind?" She handed up a heavy square package wrapped in paper. "Charles asked me to find some books for him, and I did not remember to give these to Aunt Gwendolyn. If you could take them to him…? Thank you. And give him my love."

I promised to deliver both books and love, even as I wondered who Charles was. Perhaps her brother, and my fourth cousin? I would have to ask Felicity. Surely she would not mind if I posed a few questions after having run the gamut of hers. I felt every bit as inquisitive about my new family as Felicity had shown herself to be about me.

Preoccupied with these thoughts, I entered the car, and was abruptly startled out of my abstraction by its appearance. Could this really be a railway car? The interior looked astonishingly like the duchess's sitting room. The only thing lacking seemed to be a fireplace: otherwise the interior of the car had the same elegant complement of sofas, chairs, dainty side tables, and mirrors, and was coordinated in soft shades of Wedgwood blue and ivory. The duchess, Felicity, and Miss Yates were enjoying what seemed to be a late breakfast at one of the tables, and as I entered, a footman came briskly up to take my wrap.

"My dear, there you are!" exclaimed the duchess, waving me to a seat next to her. "I had begun to worry. You had no difficulty in finding us? Good. Do have something hot to drink. How glad I am to leave London behind! For all its lovely shops, no place on earth is so dismal in cold weather."

I sat down with them and accepted a cup of tea; the china pattern repeated the blue and ivory of the decor. "Will it take us long to reach Ellsmere?" I ventured.

"We should arrive in good time to dress for dinner," said the duchess comfortably. Unaware of the dismay this prospect struck into my heart, she went on, "Since I gather you have no maid at present, I will ask Jane to wait on you, if that is agreeable. She's a good girl, and knows how to keep quiet about one's waist measurement."

Felicity, perhaps guessing the nature of my silence, asked bluntly, "Have you a dinner dress?"

"...with you?" added the duchess smoothly.

"I am afraid I don't," I admitted, even as I appreciated her tact. "None of my dresses is truly suited for evening." But surely it would not matter if I had nothing to compare with her wardrobe; indeed, there could be few who could match her in the magnificence of her dress. Today she wore a less elaborate gown for travel, but it was of lilac shot silk, and the skirt and sleeves were edged with a design of flowers in cut velvet. She was even wearing one of the new crinolines, whose steel or whalebone hoops lent her skirts the coveted bell-shaped silhouette. I was wearing the dress in which we had first met, over my two meager petticoats.

"I knew it!" exclaimed Felicity. "You are a Quaker, aren't you?"

"Felicity!" The duchess was half shocked, half laughing. Even I could not keep from smiling, though the laughter was at my own expense.

"I am sorry to disappoint you, but no," I said. Felicity subsided, disappointed, and her aunt patted my hand.

"Of course we know you are in mourning, my dear. But that does not mean you must deny yourself pretty frocks," she said coaxingly, and I realized she too had misunderstood my unfashionable dress. Evidently the only reason she could imagine for the style of my dresses was that they had been made expressly for mourning clothes; the truth was that I had simply dyed my everyday dresses black. "I would dearly love to see you in a deep wine color, or violet. Nothing too elaborate for mourning, of course, but with a bit of décolletage... we shall see what we can do." She smiled with such sly delight that it would have been churlish of me to object to her designs. Clearly she did not see them as charity, but simply enjoyed indulging her generosity.

The dingy views of London gradually gave way to brighter shades of landscape as we traveled farther into the country. It was another grey, rainy day, but there had not yet been a hard frost to blanch the countryside, and through the windows of our traveling parlor, streaming with rain, I could see an enchantingly dimmed and rain-softened landscape, whose emerald greens glowed mysteriously through their veil of grey. The duchess wrote letters and gave instructions to the footmen, and when Miss Yates began to doze, Felicity came to perch next to me on the couch from which I watched the changing scenery.

"It isn't much of a view," she said. "There won't be anything interesting to look at for ages and ages yet."

Taking the hint, I turned away from the window. "Perhaps you wouldn't mind entertaining me, then? At least until the scenery improves."

"Oh, good; I was so hoping you'd feel like talking." She gave an eager bounce on the sofa and I tried not to smile; she might have been ten instead of seventeen. "I'm longing to know more about you."

"And I you," I said. "I would very much like to know more about the family. How many of you are there?"

"Let me see." She frowned prettily. "Aminta and her husband have their own place in Derbyshire, so they don't count. At Ellsmere there are Aunt and Miss Yates, of course, and me; Papa, and Charles—my brother; he's *much* older—and Herron. Not very many of us at all; we scarcely take up one wing unless we have visitors, and Miss Yates will be leaving this summer, when I come out. I shall miss her terribly, but I cannot wait to be done with lessons and to put my hair up and go to parties and balls like Aunt Gwendolyn." She greeted this prospect with a beatific smile, and I felt a twinge of sympathy for Miss Yates, who must find her work difficult with so distracted a student. "If Charles is well enough by the beginning of the season he will be my escort. He has only been home for less than two months. He was in the Crimea—like your brother—only Charles was invalided out."

"He was injured?" I asked, thoughts of Lionel instantly engaging my sympathy.

She shook her head, her green eyes wide with relief. "No, he was dreadfully ill with malaria. It's frightening to see him so pale and thin, when he used to be so strong and good-looking. He tries to hurry himself along, but he is still convalescing. But he hates to be treated as an invalid." She leaned forward and lowered her voice to a thrilling whisper. "He's terribly brave. Sometimes I know he must get awfully frustrated that he doesn't have his strength back, but he never complains. I think he is wonderful."

"He sounds a perfect paragon," I said, hoping I was concealing my skepticism. "Has he no faults at all?"

"Well, he can be very obstinate at times—for instance, refusing to take good care of himself. Aunt and Aminta and I have to simply *force* him to rest sometimes. Aminta says all men are like that. Was your brother? Stubborn, I mean."

I laughed, feeling a catch in my throat as memories thronged to mind. "He was. Thoroughly stubborn."

"Well, so is Charles. He's a dear, of course, but he refuses to listen to me just because I happen to be younger. I am very fond of him, but he can be quite maddening."

I smiled at the lofty condescension of her tone, and the familiarity of her feelings. How many times had I thought of Lionel in just such a fashion? "What does this brother look like?"

"Oh, he's awfully handsome. All the Reginalds are handsome," she said complacently, sure of her place among these fortunates. "He has very blue eyes, and a fine gold moustache, and the longest eyelashes I've ever seen. It makes me frantic with jealousy; they are *inches* longer than mine. It's so unfair they should be wasted on a man, don't you think? You should see the way the ladies gush over him when we have guests. It is really rather revolting; they have no dignity at all. Even though he has been ill, he is still the most popular bachelor in the county. You will adore him."

"I'm sure I will," I said, positive I would detest him. I could envision him all too well: a middle-aged, convalescent Prince Consort, all drooping blond moustache and melting-eyed attentiveness, languidly reclining on a sofa whenever he grew fatigued from kissing the hands of the local beauties. I would not be surprised to find that he also played the flute and collected botanical specimens. So much for my fourth cousin.

"And the duke?"

"The—? Oh, you mean Herron. I cannot think of him as the duke." Her forehead wrinkled in thought, and she sat back. "Herron is very different. He is quite dark, for a start, and all the rest of the Reginalds are fair. To say the truth, he rather frightens me; one never knows what he is thinking. He seems so contemptuous of everyone, and when he looks at you, it's as if his eyes burn right through and come out the other side." She shivered, wrinkling her nose in distaste.

"Has he always been so?"

"No-o-o," she said, drawing the word out doubtfully. "That is, he has always been the quiet one of the family, but he used to be rather jolly, and we always got on well. But lately…" She hesitated, looking beyond me toward the duchess, but was evidently satisfied that her attention was elsewhere. "He was devastated by his father's death," she whispered, leaning closer once again in a conspiratorial manner. "He broods dreadfully, and avoids any kind of company, even *me*" (indignantly). "I think it very tiresome of him, but Aunt Gwendolyn says we must be patient, that some people must mourn longer than others."

"I imagine so," I said and, trying to be delicate, added, "you may have had experience of that yourself."

"I? No, my mother died bearing me; I never knew her." Perhaps this explained her impatience with the duke's grief. I myself could well understand that a young man still reeling from his father's death would find the company of this lively cousin a bit trying. "Aminta and Miss Yates always took care of me. That is why I am so pleased to have a real mother at last."

"And your father?" This was no idle question. I was deeply curious about the duchess's new husband. Before meeting her I had imagined that she must have been the instigator of this scandalous marriage, but now that I had begun to know her, I was forced to wonder if Lord Claude's was the will behind the marriage. The thought increased my discomfiting awareness of my precarious position. If he were a powerful, ruthless man—the kind, indeed, who would not scruple to seize upon his brother's new widow—he might well be someone to fear. He might not wish to receive a relative from the rejected branch of the family; worse, he might try to effect a reconciliation between myself and my father. I knew Felicity's opinion would scarcely be unbiased, but it might be of help and prepare me, at least in part, for my host.

Whatever information I had hoped for from her, I was disappointed with the actuality. Felicity was evidently growing bored with discussing her family, and said offhandedly that her Papa was "a perfect darling, but you'll meet him soon enough."

"He is nothing at all like your father, from what I have been able to hear," she added with her usual candor. "Aunt Gwendolyn said that she could not fathom what your mother ever saw in him."

"She told you that?"

Felicity shrugged. "She didn't know I was listening. She and Aminta only talk about truly interesting things when they believe I cannot hear." She hesitated, and this was so unlike her that I knew some more than usually personal question must be fighting to emerge. She blurted, "Isn't it difficult for you, coming to the place where your own mother died so horribly?"

I should have expected it; I should have made the logical connection once I had discovered the identity of my mother's family. But I was still unprepared for the knowledge that my mother had drowned at Ellsmere.

"I had no idea of it," I said, in a voice I hoped was steady.

Her eyes widened, but with excitement rather than alarm. "You did not know?" she exclaimed, but softly, so as not to alert her stepmother. "Oh, I am sorry to tell you so plainly, but does it not seem like fate? Aminta says I'm foolish to believe in portents, but it does look as though your destiny led you to us, and to Ellsmere. I wonder what is in store for you next!"

"You do destiny too much credit," I said, trying to speak lightly. But after Felicity left me to take a nap on the duchess's orders (protesting volubly that she was not tired, then falling asleep within five minutes), I wondered if something out of my hands was shaping my future. I could not help but marvel at how, after spending all my life knowing nothing of my mother's family, in the space of a few days I had not only discovered them but had been practically adopted by them.

And I had always been possessed by a strange feeling—part curiosity, part attraction—toward the sea. It may seem strange that I did not fear it or hold a grudge against it for having stolen my mother away from me, but I did not feel that it had. Although I had no memory of ever having been near the ocean, I did not wish to avoid it; now that I knew Ellsmere was on the coast I had no desire to change my mind about accepting the duchess's hospitality. My peculiar attachment to the ocean may have resulted from loneliness. In my childhood Lionel was a dear but sporadic and frequently dismissive presence, and as I grew older I could imagine that my mother went into the waters feeling, not fear or desperation or even sorrow, but solace. I had always imagined that she would have seen the agent of her death as a comforting certainty, a friend who could not and would not reject her or turn away. She had thrown herself into its arms, and it had welcomed her. And now I would know for myself this being whose embrace my mother had sought. The prospect excited and cheered me—perhaps in this place of strangers I would find reassurance in the sea, the companionship my mother must have felt before me.

We dined there in the railway car, and despite the lack of normal kitchen facilities the five courses were as elegant as anything ever served me in a stationary dwelling. Afterward Miss Yates and Felicity played cribbage, and the duchess took me aside to show me the purchases she had made in London.

"This cane is for Charles; very elegant, don't you think, with the carved handle?" I agreed, admiring the hound's head, worked in silver, that served as the grip. "He is still recovering from malaria, as Felicity probably told you, and has not regained all his strength yet." She glanced over at her stepdaughter and smiled at me with just the conspiratorial expression Felicity had shown earlier. "I expect Felicity told you a great deal about Charles," she said, lowering her voice, which was touched with amusement. "He is so much older than she that she is inclined toward hero-worship."

I said that I had gathered as much. "But she does not seem to be as close to the duke."

To my surprise, the duchess laughed. "Felicity is still too young to appreciate someone as introspective as Herron. In a year or two I fancy her feelings will change, and she will be extolling him as the Byronic ideal. She is a bit hurt that her old playfellow has no time for her now." Her amusement faded from her face, and she shook her head. "How could she understand what it is like for him? Even I cannot truly comprehend what he must be feeling, and he confides in no one. He has withdrawn himself so."

She no longer seemed to be speaking to me at all; these confidences seemed unconscious, her thoughts speaking themselves.

"Perhaps I indulged him too much, protected him too much," she mused. "But he was such a beautiful child..." As if suddenly remembering my presence, she looked up from the cane, whose handle she had been stroking, and her reflective mood vanished like frost under sunlight as she dimpled. "Despite what Felicity says, I at least think my son the handsomest of all the Reginalds," she confided. "If I were a young lady her age I should be madly in love with him. But then, perhaps as his mother I am not completely impartial.

Now, I must show you the set of ruby buttons I found for Claude..."

I admired the jeweled buttons in their elegant gold settings, and after them the other purchases she showed me, including a handsomely bound edition of *Childe Harold* for the duke. As I was stroking the leather bindings and turning the yet-uncut pages, the duchess's voice came quietly to me, lowered so that the other two, chattering gaily over their game, would not hear.

"Your father called on me two days ago," she said, and my head jerked up, the book forgotten. At once I realized the display of purchases had been only a pretext for talking to me apart.

"You need not look so anxious," she added gently. "He knows nothing of your being with us, and he has said nothing to make me change my good opinion of you."

"Oh," I said. It was a great sigh of relief, as all the breath left my lungs, and I felt the tension ease out of my shoulders. "Why did he call, then, if not to ask about me?"

"I had a business matter to discuss with him; that is why I had left my card. Don't fear, child; your father is not all-seeing, and he does not know we have met."

I nodded, thankful but still far from easy in my mind. "Did he—did he say anything about me?"

She frowned and took the volume of Byron from me, wrapping it up again with the rest of the set. I thought she might be taking the time to choose her words, perhaps to avoid hurting me, but when she spoke she sounded so puzzled that I wondered if she was still trying to account to herself for their conversation.

"I asked after you, as if I had not seen you since your infancy," she said slowly, "and he looked straight at me and said, 'I must tell you that my daughter is dead to me. If Your Grace has no objection, I would prefer to speak of other subjects.' Snubbed in my own drawing room, if you please! When I pressed him, he simply refused to say anything further." She flung up her hands in exasperation, her jeweled rings twinkling. "I declare, the man has changed little in twenty years."

I dropped my eyes to the carpet. "You must wonder what I have done to make him speak of me in such a fashion."

"Oh, child, I believe I am a good enough judge of character to have no need of asking that," she said gently.

"Whatever rift there is between you cannot be rooted in anything you have done."

Encouraged by these words, I dared to meet her eyes again, and saw only sympathy. "I would rather tell you how it came about, ma'am, than risk having you doubt me later," I said.

"Of course, if you wish. I have told you I would be glad to listen."

Awkwardly, conscious of the proximity of Felicity and her avowed interest in eavesdropping, I described as briefly as I could the events that had led to my parting from Father. The duchess listened attentively, without interrupting, but the sound of my own words in my ears was unconvincing. All too aware of the implausibility of my story, I stumbled and faltered. Why would she believe such an outlandish tale? I must sound spiteful as well as mendacious.

"I hope you can understand now why I wanted my whereabouts to be secret from him," I said at last. "For the first time I feel free of him, of his disdain and disappointment. I know it seems unnatural in a daughter, unfilial—"

Miserably, I fell silent, biting my lips. I did not dare look at her again. In the silence the rumbling of the train pounded in my ears, and I waited in dread to hear what she would say.

Before she could speak, Felicity's voice came gaily from across the carriage. "Aunt Gwendolyn, you must not be so secret with my cousin! Miss Yates and I want to know what you are saying. Come now, tell us what has absorbed you so."

The duchess turned to them immediately, her usual warm smile supplanting whatever expression her face had worn an instant before. "Yes, we have been too exclusive, have we not? I cannot blame you for scolding. But if you will find the cards, dear, the four of us can have a game of speculation, and then we may all visit together."

She moved toward the others, shepherding me with one light hand on my shoulder. She said nothing to me, but her hand gave a reassuring squeeze, and when I looked up I saw that her eyes, regarding me so gently, were full of tears.

CHAPTER FOUR

Night had fallen when we reached Ellsmere, the early but consuming nightfall of autumn, so that my first view of the estate was no more than a clutch of fleeting impressions: a long stretch of woods giving way to parkland and a huge building of pale stone that almost glimmered in its own light, extending higher and broader than I could see, and studded with the warm sheets of light that were windows. Later, by day, I would see that the massive main wing was flanked by two others: the west, the oldest part of the house, which reared a crenellated tower, and the east, a newer addition, a mass of gables and balconies.

I was surprised and disappointed not to be able to hear the ocean, but I had little time in which to think about it. After the relative calm of our train journey, our arrival at Ellsmere was a pandemonium. As soon as our coach stopped we were met by a flood of servants, and the bustle of our arrival was evidently not the only urgent matter on their minds.

When the duchess had pieced together the cause for the general air of confusion and apprehension, she turned to me with a sigh. "My dear, I hope you will bear with us. The re-plastering of the guest rooms is not yet finished—why, I cannot fathom! I shall have to look into it later—and we must put you in Great-Aunt Agatha's room this evening. It is a nuisance, but it is only for one night."

"I have no objection, as long as Great-Aunt Agatha has none," I said, winning one of the duchess's trilling laughs.

"Great-Aunt Agatha has been dead these thirty years; I doubt she will be discommoded by your presence."

"I would sooner risk disturbing a living relative than a dead one," said Felicity, with a shiver of horror not unmixed with relish. "I hope for your sake she sleeps sound in the earth, cousin. She might choose to evict you."

The duchess gave her a gentle frown. "That is scarcely hospitable, Felicity, to greet our cousin with tales of bogles and haunts. I myself have never heard that Great-Aunt Agatha makes a habit of revisiting her old quarters. She led a very contented life, as far as I know, and left no unfinished business behind but her embroidered altar cloth. No, my main concern is that you will be alone on the third floor. I hope you will not feel terribly isolated, my dear; I would not put you there if there were any other room fit for you to occupy." She hesitated, a single worried crease appearing on her brow. "But we'll find something better for you tomorrow."

Even though it was on the top floor and had not been fitted with gas lighting, Great-aunt Agatha's room was a quaint and comfortable chamber full of enormous, heavy furniture that had a reassuringly solid appearance. The hangings were rich but faded and fraying, and altogether I felt much more comfortable in this old and frankly shabby room than I would have in a more fashionable apartment fitted out in the fragile, eggshell-hued furnishings the duchess seemed to favor.

The duchess assured herself that I had fresh linen and hot water before leaving to make her own toilet for dinner. After shutting the door behind her and making a brief tour of my new living quarters, I took off my gown and had begun gratefully to wash the travel grime from my arms and face when there was a knock at the door. I gathered my dress to me and, uncertainly, called out a welcome.

The door opened on the startling sight of a heap of clothes. After the first moment of bewilderment, I saw that the heap was surmounted by two brown eyes and a smart white cap. This, I reasoned belatedly, must be Jane, come to fit me out for dinner.

"Good evening, miss," said a voice from behind the mass of fabric. "The duchess has sent some things for you."

"Thank you." I felt awkward, never having had a personal maid before, and was unsure of what to say or how to behave. "Won't you come in?"

She did so, moving briskly to place her burden on the bed, and I was able to observe her more fully. She was even smaller than I, although sturdier of build, and looked no more than fourteen. I later discovered that she was every day of twenty and married to one of the footmen, but in that first glimpse she looked too young to be out of the schoolroom.

For her part, as soon as she had laid out the gown and petticoats she had brought in, she turned to give me a look of appraisal even more frank than mine. My surprise and discomfort at this scrutiny were short-lived, though, as she said thoughtfully, "The gown should fit very well with a bit of taking in. You and Her Grace are much of a height. Shall I lace you up?"

To her credit, she did not so much as blink when I told her I did not wear stays. Fortunately the gown fitted me without them, although Jane had to pin starched ruffles to my chemise to fill out the bosom. It was a finer gown than any I had ever worn, although the dark purple color and modest décolletage, cut just below the collarbone, made it appropriate for mourning. It was trimmed only with braid of the same color, but the wide pagoda sleeves and full skirts, swelled by the layers of petticoats, gave it an unmistakably fashionable shape. The duchess must have had it made on the death of her husband, although she wore no mourning now. She could not have worn the gown more than a few times, and I marveled at the extravagance of purchasing a mourning wardrobe that would only be used for a few weeks.

It was awkward being dressed by another person, when I had dressed myself since I was old enough to fasten a button; even though Jane did not subject me to any more measuring looks, I was fiercely self-conscious, and clumsy at getting my arms into the sleeves. When she had hooked me up I breathed an inward sigh of relief, but the ordeal was not over: she had orders to dress my hair as well. Sitting at the dressing table as her hands worked nimbly over my head, I wondered if I would be able to accustom myself to these strange ministrations and cease feeling like an invalid unable to fend for herself, or a spoiled princess who could not be permitted to raise a finger on her own behalf.

In the end I had to appreciate Jane's efforts, though. Instead of my usual braid, my hair had been coaxed into two shining wings that met in a graceful braided chignon at the back of my neck. The unexpected weight of it made me hold my head carefully, as if a governess had balanced a book on it, but the effect was undeniably attractive. The rich color of the borrowed dress suited me, as the duchess had predicted, and I felt my spirits rise. It was heartening that I would not have to meet the rest of my new family looking like a Quakeress.

I thanked Jane again, more warmly, and she accepted the thanks with a complacent curtsey, well aware of the feat she had wrought. I pinned on my mourning brooch, so bright with Lionel's gold hair that it seemed too ornamental for mourning. Then I rose to join the others. Despite my new confidence in my appearance, I was aware of my heart beating emphatically beneath the borrowed finery as I followed Jane down stairs and passages to the drawing room where she said the family assembled before dinner.

When I entered I thought at first that Jane had led me to the wrong room, for there was no sign of the duchess or of Felicity. The only sounds were the ticking of a massive grandfather clock and the occasional crack and spit of the fire. Rich, restful shades of russet and bronze warmed the carpet, furniture, and draperies, and two massive, welcoming armchairs flanked the Adam fireplace. As I hovered just inside the doorway, wondering if I should call Jane back, a small brown and white spaniel lifted its head and offered an inquisitive woofle. At the sound, a man's face appeared around the sheltering wing of one chair. Instantly it was followed by the rest of him.

"I beg your pardon; I didn't hear you come in." He used a cane to cross the room toward me, and this confirmed my conjecture as to his identity. "You were so quiet you might have been a ghost." His smile was friendly and guileless, his voice surprisingly deep.

"I used to be called Mouse, because I am so quiet," I said. It was probably not the best way to introduce myself, but without an intermediary to perform the introductions I felt uncertain and shy, and said the only words that came to me.

"Not a very flattering nickname," he said easily, not seeming to find my reply strange. "Or even very appropriate. But perhaps it suited you better when you were a child."

"Perhaps." I was already regretting having mentioned it; I had never liked Lionel's nickname for me, and now it was too painful a reminder of him. I stooped to pat the spaniel, who was investigating my skirts with a cold nose. "What is his name?"

"Zeus." He met my eye and we laughed. "That was Felicity's doing, not mine; I would have named him Candide, since he is such an optimist. He greets everyone as if they had a soup bone in their pocket." He was watching with an indulgent smile as Zeus and I got acquainted, his hands folded on his stick. "If you'll allow me to say so, you have improved greatly since our last meeting," he said presently.

I straightened in surprise. "We have met?"

"Yes, indeed. You were crying as if your heart was broken, and I remember asking if I could stuff a piece of sponge cake in your mouth to silence you." Seeing my confusion, he relented. "You were two weeks old," he explained, the deep voice solemn although his eyes shone with mischief. "I would be greatly surprised if you remembered."

"I am surprised you yourself remember," I commented. "You must have been very young."

"Oh, the incident is etched in my memory: my father scolded me so roundly for my lack of chivalry that my whole character was altered. Now I am a notorious pest for flinging my coat over puddles for ladies to walk on. May I offer you a seat? Father and Miss Yates should be down soon, but I am afraid we may have a long wait before Felicity and Aunt Gwendolyn join us."

"Oh? Why?"

His eyebrows quirked in exasperation and amusement. "I thought perhaps you could tell me. I have often wondered why it takes them a full hour to change gowns. Doubtless it is a mystery best not inquired into."

I took one of the armchairs by the hearth, and when I was seated he resumed his seat in the other. I noticed the way his knuckles whitened on the handle of his stick as he lowered himself into the chair, and scolded myself for having kept him standing; he must find it a strain to be on his feet for long, although he had said nothing.

Now that I met Felicity's paragon in the flesh, I found that the reality bore little resemblance to the creature I had envisioned. This was no dandy with drooping moustaches and macassar oil in his hair. Charles was indisputably moustached, to be sure, but this adornment was neatly clipped, and his straw-colored hair innocent of pomade. He was tall, but his height was balanced by the breadth of his shoulders, so that he was nothing like the languid weed I had envisioned. The loose fit of his suit suggested that he had grown thinner from his illness, but he seemed utterly unconscious of being an invalid.

He also seemed unaware of his own good looks, which Felicity, to my surprise, had not exaggerated. He had a narrow, fine-boned face, with expressive blond brows and eyes the wide and candid blue of the sky. Except for being so handsome, he seemed a fairly ordinary fellow, and one whose camaraderie was very welcoming. Already I felt more at ease; his manner was so like a brother's, although more courteous.

As if he had read my thoughts, he said, "I hear that you have lost your brother, and recently. I am very sorry."

"Thank you." I sounded abrupt, even to my ears, and added without intending to, "I still cannot quite believe it. He was away such a short time."

"He was in the Crimea, I believe." There was both understanding and concern in my cousin's voice.

"Yes. At Inkerman."

I could feel his eyes on my face, gauging whether to change the subject. "Would you prefer not to speak of him?" he asked quietly.

"Not at all; I wish I could speak of him more, in fact." All at once I wanted to confide in him. It would be a great relief to me, and I felt that Charles would understand. "But nobody will discuss it with me or tell me what I want to know; it isn't right for young ladies to know about war and killing. No one will let me bring up the subject. You would think it was something indecent."

"What is it you wish to know? I'll gladly help if I can."

"My brother was shot," I said in a rush. "We were told that he died almost instantly. And everyone tells us what a mercy it was, that he would have suffered so if he had survived to be taken to a hospital. What I need to know is if that is the truth, or if they are only trying to make his death easier to accept. Would he have suffered so? Were the hospitals so dreadful?"

He was silent for a moment, and dropped his eyes so that I could not read them. He reached down to scratch Zeus's ears, his long fingers moving absently in the spaniel's fur. "They were," he said, without looking at me. "The care of the wounded was criminally poor. The conditions of the hospitals... well, if I tell you that what I saw there convinced me to take up the study of medicine, perhaps that will give you an idea of the atrocity of it."

"You are a doctor?" I exclaimed. In a family as wealthy as the Reginalds, there could be no need for even the son of a younger son to work for a living. Charles must have been deeply affected by his experiences to take up a trade.

"I hope to become one. This summer I leave for Edinburgh to begin my studies in earnest. Now, while I am convalescing"—the wry lift of one eyebrow showed his opinion of that term—"I am trying to learn the fundamentals. I hope to find ways to reform the practices that lose so many lives needlessly."

"You must have suffered a great deal yourself," I ventured.

He brushed that away. "Believe me, your friends are not sugaring over the truth for your benefit," he said earnestly. "If your brother died quickly, he was surely spared a great deal of horror. And many more men died in hospital of illnesses they contracted there than of battle wounds. Your brother's death was probably the most merciful that could have happened under the circumstances."

I nodded, feeling a rush of gratitude toward him for having relieved some of my anxious uncertainty. "It is kind of you to be frank with me."

"Not at all. So many people don't wish to hear the truth about the war; it is a relief not to have to guard my tongue for once."

This was more kindness, I guessed; had he spoken with utter candor, I suspected, he could have described horrors I knew nothing of. I wondered if he had been able to talk of what he had experienced to anyone, or if he had been forced to offer only a partial and highly edited account for his family's hearing.

Although I had not heard anyone approach, Zeus's head popped up and he gave a pleased bark that announced another arrival. Charles and I rose and I found myself facing a man who must be Lord Claude. I stared to curtsey, but he caught my hands in his and drew me forward, beaming. Before I realized what he intended he had startled me by planting a kiss on my cheek.

"So this is Gwendolyn's long-lost niece," he said. "I see that you have already met Charles. I hope he has been making you feel at home. Did you have a pleasant journey?"

"Very pleasant, thank you, sir." Clearly I had no cause to worry about my reception.

"I am glad to hear it. I know Gwendolyn is delighted to have you here, as we all are." His eyes twinkled, and I saw the resemblance between him and his son. "I even believe she has given special instructions to Cook for something spectacular to welcome you with."

"She need not have troubled; I feel very welcome already," I said, dazzled by the lavish extent of this hospitality.

"It is no trouble, I assure you," he said with a chuckle, and Charles added, "My aunt would be sorely disappointed to lose the chance for a celebration."

Lord Claude was shorter and stockier than his son, but with the same good-humored expression, and the crinkles around his eyes suggested that he laughed often. He was a handsome man, the ruddy gold of his hair and beard unmixed with grey, and without any sign of paunchiness. Nevertheless, he was not a forceful presence: his voice and manner were quiet, calm, unobtrusive, never calling attention to himself. In a livelier company he might be forgotten altogether. Once more I was baffled by the difference between my expectations and the reality. Neither Lord Claude nor the duchess looked at all the sort of person I had naïvely expected to be involved in a scandal. For all their wealth and rank, they seemed to be pleasant but fairly normal people. Even their willingness to take in a virtually unknown distant relation bespoke an openheartedness I had not expected to find.

Lord Claude's voice broke in on my thoughts, although he was not speaking to me. "Have you any idea whether Herron will be joining us tonight?"

Charles shook his head. "I saw him earlier and told him that the ladies would be arriving today, but I couldn't say whether he will put in an appearance."

"Does His Grace have other plans?" I asked, and the two glanced at me, then each other, as if silently consulting about how much they should say.

"Not as such," said Charles—cautiously, I thought. "But he has been keeping to himself a great deal of late, and he does not always take his meals with the rest of the family."

"But I should hope that he'll behave himself this evening and put in an appearance, for his new cousin's sake if nothing else," put in his father, in what seemed weariness more than anger. "Ah, well, we shall see. Perhaps the boy will remember his manners."

But he did not sound optimistic, and I wondered for the first time if the duke and his new stepfather were on friendly terms. the sudden change in their relationship might have met with some resistance on one side—or both. I wondered if Lord Claude was being unjustly critical of the duke. My curiosity about this cousin was growing every moment, and I longed to see if he was anything like the idea I had formed of him in my mind. The accuracy of my predictions had certainly been poor thus far.

But I was disappointed in my hope of assessing him in person, since the duke failed to appear that evening. The duchess and Felicity eventually joined us, resplendent after their long toilet, but by the time the dinner gong went we were still only six, with Miss Yates. The duchess and her husband exchanged a long look, and I saw her lips press together as if to keep in her disappointment. But in a moment she gave a laugh, her face restored to its usual gaiety, and slipped her hand through her husband's arm.

"Well, there's nothing for it but to start without him. If he has any sense at all he will join us; Cook has outdone herself in your honor, my dear, and Herron will be the loser if he misses this meal. Charles, will you take your cousin in?"

Charles offered me his arm, and with Felicity and Miss Yates following after, we processed in to dinner.

"By the way," he said in an undertone as we crossed the great hall, a vast vaulted space with an echoing marble floor, "it might be best if you can learn to call Herron by his name. He hates being addressed by his title; in his mind, his father is still the duke." I said I would bear that in mind, and he added in a resigned tone, "Of course, if he persists in being so coy, you may never have occasion to speak to him at all."

This was discouraging, but as soon as we entered the dining room I was so distracted by the grandeur of my surroundings that I almost forgot my disappointment at the duke's absence. Although when they were not entertaining guests the family usually took dinner in the breakfast room, Charles told me, tonight they were using the banquet hall in my honor. The six of us were a ridiculously tiny group at the end of the long, gleaming table that would have seated thirty. Our voices echoes in the vast arched chamber, and despite the chandeliers, the light did not entirely dissipate the shadows. I felt awed, as if I were dining in a particularly opulent monastery. I wondered how long ago Ellsmere had been built: this room felt centuries old, as if the air was layered with the echoes of many lives.

The duchess evidently still held out hope that her son would join us, and when we had dawdled over the soup as long as was possible, she beckoned the butler over for a brief consultation. It ended in her sigh.

"Well, bring in the fish, Jenkins," she said in resignation. "I suppose my son is off wandering the cliffs again. We'll not see him tonight; there's no sense in waiting longer." She offered me a sad smile. "My dear, I do hope you will forgive this feeble showing on your first night with us."

I assured her that there was nothing to forgive, but I wondered at the cause of the duke's absence. Was it meant to show disdain or to hurt his mother? Surely, no matter how forgetful or grief-stricken, he would have made an appearance otherwise.

"Perhaps I should speak to the boy, remind him of his responsibilities." This from Lord Claude, who looked anything but eager to do so.

The duchess's shake of the head sent her ruby earrings dancing; I could not help but reflect that their flirtatious motion was ill suited to the gravity of her expression. "I doubt it would do any good, Claude. I cannot do a thing with him, myself, since his father—" She broke off, perhaps recalling the presence of others.

"I'm certain he'll return when he tires of being dashed with salt spray," said Charles, glancing at his stepmother's puckered brow. "Unless, of course, he's rehearsing for a tableau and wishes to portray Ariadne, pacing the shore of Naxos. Felicity could wrap herself in a counterpane to portray

Dionysus, and descend from the chandelier to whisk him away."

Felicity squealed indignantly, and the duchess looked up with what seemed to be a grateful smile, her shoulders visibly relaxing. She reached out to touch Charles's hand. "We mustn't put Felicity in such a precarious position, but tableaus are a wonderful idea. We must have a game one evening soon—as long as I may be sure of the safety of the chandeliers."

Charles went on to make other ridiculous suggestions for the tableaus, Felicity interrupted to scold him, and in the silliness the subject of the duke's absence seemed to be forgotten. The duchess's face lost its sad preoccupation, and when the ladies withdrew to leave the men to their port, she was so busy describing the new hangings for the blue salon to me that she did not even seem to remember the cause of her earlier distress.

As congenial as the company was, I felt tired after the day's events and found the prospect of an evening's conversation taxing. To my relief, the duchess rose to retire as soon as Charles and Lord Claude returned to join us in the drawing room.

"I'm certain we ladies are all a bit weary after our journey, and would like to retire." For some reason her cheeks were pink, although she had not been sitting by the fire, and she did not look at all tired as she took Lord Claude's arm. Then I remembered that they had only been a few weeks married, and felt an answering blush rise to my cheeks as belated understanding came to me.

"Have you everything you need, my dear?" the duchess paused to ask on her way out of the room with her husband. "If you find you lack anything, just ring for Jane. Good night, children, and sleep well."

And with that, they were gone. She seemed to have forgotten her concern over putting me in Great-Aunt Agatha's room, but that was little wonder. She was obviously too absorbed in her reunion with her husband to fret for long about guest accommodations.

Back in Great-Aunt Agatha's room I did not ring for Jane, but managed to wriggle out of my gown and petticoats by myself; the prospect of another awkward session with the maid was more than I had the fortitude to face. The unaccustomed weight of my chignon had made my head ache, and I was glad to be able to pull out the hairpins and brush my hair out. Evidently moving among the higher strata of society was going to involve the sacrifice of a certain amount of comfort to fashion.

I turned down the lamp and climbed into the high, canopied bed that had its own set of stairs. Had Great-Aunt Agatha's legs been as short as mine? I wondered.

I was warm and content under the faded velvet counterpane, and my room was perfectly silent. No sound, not even the noise of the sea, disturbed the stillness. Images of the preceding day drifted gently through my mind, and all of them assured me that I was welcome, that I would be able to be happy here. The first day of my new life had been a promising one. I had almost drifted off to sleep when a hollow noise gradually came to my ears. Although I waited for it to cease, it persisted, refusing to be ignored, until I was wakeful again with annoyance.

A steady, regular beat. Someone was pacing the floor of the room above. Evidently, I decided, a servant was having trouble sleeping, and was marching like a sentry back and forth… except (and the memory made my eyes snap open, and I sat up in bed), except there was no room over mine. I was on the top floor of the house, and why would any human being be walking the roof at night?

* * *

When I woke in the morning I did not spare more than a moment's thought for the footsteps. Doubtless there was some reasonable explanation for them, and the mystery had not kept me awake for long. In any case my mind was too full of anticipation to let me dwell long on anything else. As soon as I was awake I knew I would be able to think of nothing else until I had gone down to the shore. I needed to see the ocean.

Quickly, I donned one of my old dresses—sparing a moment to be glad that it buttoned up the front, so that I had no need of assistance—and twined my hair into a hasty braid. On the stairs I encountered a maid and asked directions of her. Once she had told me the way, I ran down the great stair and through the front door, opened for me by a footman too well trained to betray surprise.

The morning was cold but fair, the path up to the cliffs easily found: it was rough but wide and well trod (by Herron?)

and not steep enough to daunt someone accustomed to running up and down the stairs in a London row house. Not for the first time in my life I was glad that I wore no stays to hamper me; I was scarcely breathing hard when I crested the hill and stood looking down on the sea.

The cliffs stretched to my right in a bleak, jagged line, the uneven rocky faces sometimes falling sheer to the sea below, which seethed as if in anger around great boulders on the shore. To my left the cliffs gentled and smoothed, becoming a ribbon of soft green slopes. The morning sun was dazzling on the sea, which flung up sheets of froth as it ceaselessly beat itself against the shore far below. With a thrill of excitement I found that an opening between two crags led to a narrow footpath down to the strand. I began to pick my way down, going slowly because of the incline and the multitude of pebbles that might cause a more precipitous descent than I wished.

The breeze freshened as I descended, until my hair had fought loose from its clumsy braid and was slapping gaily around my face. As I came nearer to the surf, its noise also increased until the sound was overwhelming. The roar rose and ebbed, but was never allowed to quiet before another great wave hurled itself onto the rocky shore.

Uncertain, I stood where the footpath ended at the rock-strewn beach, not eager to climb over the crags that met me. The volume of sound and the fierce energy and motion of the surf were formidable, almost overpowering, and abruptly I felt small and feeble in the face of this element. This was far from the comforting, lulling ocean I had imagined, the place of solace and refuge I had sought. Instead it was a battering force, unruly and violent. I hesitated only a moment, then turned swiftly back to the path, almost colliding with someone who stood behind me.

"Watch where you're going," he said rudely. "You will have to pick your way with a great deal more care if you plan to stroll around the cliffs."

I looked up at a dark man. His eyes were in shadow, untouched by the still tentative light, but the rising sun picked out the angle of his face in a sharp gold sliver. Unaccountably, he was in shirt sleeves, even though I was shivering in my woolen dress. He must have followed me closely, unheard, all the way down the path.

Nettled at the intrusion, I pushed my vagrant hair out of my eyes and glared at him. "Perhaps I would fare better without meddlesome bystanders dogging my footsteps."

This received a thin, humorless smile. "Believe me, I had no intention of courting your company. Nothing would give me more pleasure at this moment than your absence."

"Are you always so gracious to the duchess's guests?"

"A guest of my mother?" He surveyed me, lifting an eyebrow at my windblown skirts—or their undistinguished cut. "I took you for a maid."

My shock at discovering his identity was almost conquered by indignation. "I am your cousin," I snapped. "I have come for a visit, Your Grace."

"In that case, I retract my advice, and encourage you to put yourself out of your misery as swiftly as you can. Tumbling off a cliff would be a pleasant alternative to living at Ellsmere." He seemed to look beyond me, but his eyes were still pools of darkness and I could not read them. "You may be sure that I've considered the idea myself, and have not yet discarded it." With that, he pushed roughly past me and vaulted the rocky barrier to the beach.

Startled, I stared after him. He seemed to know his way, for he strode down the shore with a sure foot, never glancing at his path. I watched him for several minutes as he moved farther and farther away, until a renewed gust reminded me that I, too, had come out without a cloak. It must be nearing time for breakfast, in any case, and I would need to make considerable repairs in my appearance before joining the others.

I turned and unceremoniously clambered back up to the cliff top, the roar of the tide pushing me all the way, and then I actually picked up my skirts and ran back to the warm, sheltering rooms of Ellsmere.

CHAPTER FIVE

This, then, was Herron.

The impression I had formed of him from that abrupt encounter was to serve me for several days, since it became clear that his preference for solitude extended not only to dinner but to all other hours of the day. He might as well have been invisible. Occasionally one of us would see him vanish around a doorway on entering a room, but he was as impossible to pin down as a ghost, and far more scanty of his presence than most haunts are purported to be. His mother despaired of him. It was painful to see her look around the table hopefully at every meal, as if believing he would surprise her with his presence, and to see her inevitable dismay at his absence. If his morbid tendencies were characteristic of his behavior lately, I could well understand her anxiety about him. Detaining her after breakfast that morning, I told her of my meeting with him and his startling explanation for his walks on the cliffs. I had feared to alarm her, but her response was calm: "Oh, my dear, I know it. He has spoken of such things ever since the death of his father."

"But can you be sure he won't do an injury to himself?" I ventured. "Should not someone stay with him?"

"No, he chafes so at company." Then, reading my expression, she patted my shoulder. "You are good to think of him, but truly, there is no danger. Those who talk of doing themselves harm never actually execute their threats. It is nothing but words, a way to win our notice. Probably he feels I have been neglecting him for Claude, and this is his revenge on me."

"I hope that is all it is, ma'am." I was far from convinced that the duke was safe from himself, but as I was unable to set eyes on him most of the time, let alone stand guard over his wanderings, there seemed to be little point in continuing to worry. After all, the duchess was his mother, I told myself; she should know her own son's heart.

"Now, that is enough of that," she said briskly, pulling on her gloves. "Such a glorious day is not meant for so serious a subject. We must find something diverting for you. Will you come riding with Claude and me? It is impossible to sit still on a morning like this, and there is the sweetest mare in the stables who would be just right for you. Do join us."

I declined, and she did not press me; I knew that, however sincerely meant was her offer, she would enjoy herself much more in the company of her husband, without an accompanying third. It had been clear since the first time I saw them together that the duchess and her new husband were deeply in love. Even in company they tended to lose themselves in gazing at each other, and it was touching to see the pleasure they took from each other's presence. In spite of the fact that they had grown children, they might have been eighteen again. When Lord Claude himself handed his wife into the saddle and she smiled her thanks down at him, I felt a flicker of something like envy, followed by the sort of tolerant superiority that I suppose lovers have always inspired in the rest of the world: their condition was endearing, but I could congratulate myself that I was not victim to it.

I could also admit to myself that I was making a virtue of necessity, but I chose to ignore that thought.

"They make a fine couple, don't you think?" came a voice, and I saw that Miss Yates was standing behind me on the steps. She crossed the terrace to join me at the balustrade, her checked taffeta skirts bobbing cheerfully.

"They seem well suited to each other, and very happy."

"Oh, indeed they are. I know Felicity and her brother could not be more pleased that they have found their way to marry."

I noticed that she did not include the duke. "And you?" She hesitated, and I remembered that it would be indiscreet of a governess to discuss the matter with a member of the family. "You may trust me not to repeat anything you say," I said quickly. "I would like to hear your opinion, as a valued friend of the family."

"It is not my place to comment, of course, but truly I think this marriage is the best thing that could have happened. Her Grace looks as if she has dropped ten years from her age, and Lord Claude—well, between us, he needs a strong wife to give him direction. He is a good man, but a trifle weak. The duchess has enough will for the both of them."

"The late duke did not allow her such freedom?"

She gave me a considering look, as if debating how much more to tell me, and said only "No."

"You must have been with the family a long time," I said.

"Since Felicity was five. I have grown very attached to the Reginalds in that time; they have come to feel like my own family." With a sudden twinkle she added, "And as you have gathered, I criticize them as freely as if they were my own flesh and blood."

"How is it that you have no family of your own—that you have not married?"

She chuckled comfortably, not in the least offended. Perhaps long exposure to Felicity had inured her to impertinent questions. "Oh, I am much too particular—or so Her Grace tells me." She glanced at me and smiled. "But I imagine that is what you answer when asked the same question."

I looked out across the drive and the level expanse of lawn. The two figures on horseback were growing smaller and farther away every moment. "Yes," I said. "I am too particular."

* * *

In spite of the duchess's dismissal of my fears, I could not rid myself of a nagging worry, as if I were carrying the anxiety that should have been hers. I was provided more cause for concern a few days later.

We had guests for dinner, and the duchess made some excuse to them for her son's absence. We started dinner without him, as had become usual, but halfway through the soup the duchess put down her spoon abruptly with an exclamation of pleasure.

"Why, my dear, how nice—"

Her words stopped as if they had been pinched off. Her face registered the strangest series of emotions: joyful surprise succeeded by shock, pain, and what might have been the beginnings of anger. Like everyone else, I turned to look.

Herron stood in the doorway, lounging against the jamb, making no move to come further into the room. Now that he no longer had a shadow over him I could get a true idea of his appearance, and I could not keep myself from staring. He was almost inhumanly beautiful.

His face tapered sharply from wide cheekbones, lending his features a faunlike appearance. The fierce angularity of his bones was balanced by his mouth, sweetly curved and generous. Black hair swept in unruly waves, slightly longer than fashion, from a high, clear brow, and eyes whose color shifted brown and gold like sunlight off the drowned leaves in a forest pool were fringed with long, soft lashes; his eyebrows were uncompromising slashes of black. He was surveying the company, those remarkable eyes moving restlessly. The combination of softness and strength in his face was arresting, and I knew I was not the only woman at the table to stare.

But although many were staring, not all felt my admiration. I heard the chiming clatter of a wine glass tipped, and Claude's words, hoarse with anger: "What do you think you're about, Herron? Don't you realize we have guests here?"

Herron arched his eyebrows and bowed with mocking obsequiousness. "My apologies. I had no idea my presence would be so repugnant to anyone but my own family."

"Herron, why?" It was the duchess, her voice almost a moan. Confused, I looked again at her son, seeking the cause of her disturbance.

I saw first that he was not in evening clothes. It had been easy to overlook this, since his suit was black, as were the other gentlemen's. Certainly that was inappropriate, even rude, but no cause for such pain and fury on the part of his mother and stepfather. Then, as Herron drew a chair from the wall and dropped into it, smiling tightly at his mother, I noticed what else he wore: a black cloth band, almost invisible against his black frock coat, on his right arm.

He was wearing mourning for his dead father.

"Go and change at once," ordered Lord Claude. His face was pale, and I saw that it was his wine that had spilled, a weak gold stain oozing over the snowy tablecloth. His hand shook as he righted the glass. "I will not have you appear in such a fashion before our friends."

Herron glanced at him and then deliberately, with a rudeness that made my eyes widen, plucked a black-bordered mourning handkerchief from his breast pocket and tossed it at his stepfather's place. "You've spilled your wine."

He might as well have thrown a gauntlet. Lord Claude rose so quickly that his chair tottered. I saw Charles reach out to right it. But it was the duchess who spoke.

"Herron, I know that you still miss your father. You aren't alone in that, believe me." Her voice was almost steady. "But you must realize this is neither the time nor the occasion for such a display."

"A display, you call it?" His voice was thin and sharp as a blade, and I shivered, glad it was not directed at me. "My dear lady mother, I will pay my father and myself the tribute of letting myself feel the pain of his loss. I refuse to disown that with a veneer of pretense." His mother's eyes flared at the emphasis, but he went on before she could speak. "If I felt less, I might be able to simper and profess pleasure at the inane conversation of society. But my grief, at least, is genuine, even if you find it objectionable."

She was truly angry now; her hands strangled the napkin in her lap, although her voice was controlled now when she said, "Herron, we will discuss this later. Alone."

"I see no reason to postpone what I, at least, consider an interesting discussion."

Everyone was still, embarrassed to be watching yet unable to look away. When Charles cleared his throat, it was a startling sound in the silence, and we all looked toward him.

"Herron, you may not feel any compunction at causing your mother pain, but may I remind you that she is not the only lady present? You are alarming your guests."

Once again Herron's brows arced mockingly. He darted a withering glance around the table, started to speak; then his eyes fell on me and after a moment he closed his lips again.

Encouraged by his silence, Lord Claude resumed his seat. "Have something to eat, my boy," he suggested, not unkindly. "You'll feel better. Jenkins, get His Grace a plate."

"Spoken like the master of the house," said Herron, but in such a low voice that I may have been the only one to have heard. Aloud he said, "Does my mother take part in the invitation?"

She smiled, not altogether successfully. "Of course, dear."

"Well, then. I accept."

The rest of the meal was, not surprisingly, carried out in an atmosphere of strain. The company made a valiant effort to restore a sense of normalcy: Lord Claude with heartily unfunny jokes, the duchess with blithe talk of trifles, and Charles with attempts to draw out the others, which were not unsuccessful but failed to erase the tension from our hostess's face. As for the duke, I glanced at him once to find his eyes on me, steady and, I thought, speculative, but he did not say another word all evening.

As soon as the duchess rose to signal the departure of the ladies, Herron rose as well and was the first to leave the room. His mother looked as if she longed to follow him, but she was ever conscious of her guests, and she led us all to the drawing room and settled herself with a bit of dainty embroidery as if she had no other concern.

As the hours passed and the gentlemen rejoined us after their port, I admired her more than ever: she maintained the same gentle, gracious smile, and always listened in rapt attention to the badinage, ready to join in with a question or observation to keep the conversation afloat. Perhaps Herron was right, I thought, as I listened to an elderly earl and Miss Yates debating the relative merits of the schottische and the polka ("but the one is so much more becoming to ladies!"); perhaps the genteel conversation of society was inane. But the duchess's demeanor never suggested she found it so. She might have been any society bride with no graver matter on her mind than the cut of her gown. Marveling at this skilled display of breeding, I contented myself with being an observer merely.

Lord Claude was almost as talented a dissembler, and joined in the chatter with alacrity. But then, he seemed willing to let the matter of Herron's dramatic behavior drop, and much happier among the company of guests and family. I wondered if he felt quite at ease with his new stepson: certainly, Herron's speech and actions indicated that he was not content with his new parent.

Charles, unlike his father, was restless; his eyes kept going to the window, and I wondered if he hoped to glimpse Herron in the grounds. When Felicity went to the pianoforte and asked him to turn pages for her, he did so, but with such an abstracted air that twice the player had to nudge him to remind him of his duty.

If he hoped to confront his stepbrother, he was denied the opportunity; by the time the company dispersed for the night Herron had not reappeared, and Jenkins replied to the duchess's inquiry with the statement that he had not seen Herron since dinner. We retired to our rooms without speaking of him. Lord Claude seemed relieved at the postponement, the duchess disappointed; the two emotions were mingled in me.

Later, after I had undressed and gone to bed, I lay for a long time trying to sleep. Anyone will testify that this is a vain enterprise: the very effort of trying to compel oneself to sleep makes one increasingly alert. The noise of the wind, which was sometimes so lulling, only communicated a feeling of violent energy and unrest as it whistled at the windows. I sighed and leaned over to grope for matches, when a moment's drop in the gusting of the wind allowed me to hear clearly another sound: a slow, steady beat overhead.

It was the footsteps I had heard on my first night at Ellsmere.

Their pace was unnervingly regular, like a metronome, and they wandered from directly over my chamber to a space more distant, so that at times they almost died out. The sound was muffled but carried a strange gravity with it, as if an unknown sentry walked the roof over the rooms of sleepers.

I succeeded in lighting my candle, which flickered in the draft from the windows, and slipped out of bed. My boots lay on the carpet where I had cast them off, and I stepped into them hastily; in a moment more I had wrapped myself in my old black cape and shut the door of my room behind me. The candle flame burned steadily in the relative stillness of the corridor, and by its light I looked around to see that no one else was there. The hall beyond was a wall of darkness, and the only sound came from above, the regular drumbeat of the walker's footsteps. I remembered the duchess's concern for me, alone on the topmost floor; had she known of the footsteps and feared for me to hear them? Or was I the only one to hear them because of the isolation of my room?

Whatever the reason, no one else had emerged to join me in seeking their source. Shielding the candle with my hand, I made my way quickly to the end of the corridor and the unassuming door that gave on the tower stairs: at the next landing was the door to the roof, and I supposed that if one continued to climb one would emerge atop the tower, but I had never ventured that far. I opened the door and stepped into the stairwell, and the sudden guttering of my candle flame told me that the door to the roof was already open. Whatever—whoever—walked above must have taken this way before me. For some reason, this was more unnerving than the sound of the footsteps itself, the knowledge that the unknown had crept unheard past my door.

Carefully, holding up my hem so that I would not trip on the narrow stair, I ascended to the roof. When I emerged into the night air the wind immediately snuffed my candle, but at once I saw another light: someone had placed a lamp near the parapet, and it cast a warm circle that reached almost to where I stood. Still I waited, looking for the source of the sound I had heard. I could hear the footsteps, sounding distant now, and I moved forward slowly, trying to peer around the chimneys that blocked my view.

The cloaked figure emerged so suddenly that I fell back a step. He was at the other end of the roof but approaching with that steady gait whose sound I had come to know so well. He—for he had the height, and his shoulders the breadth, of a man—came steadily closer, and in anticipation of seeing his face I moved toward him, until the lamplight lapped the hem of my cloak.

Immediately he drew up short. For a moment we both stood motionless. Then, so swiftly I had no time to move, he closed the space between us in four long strides and seized me by the arm. His grip was so strong that I cried out, but he paid me no heed, his other hand fumbling for my hood, which he flung back from my face. The light was behind him, so I could see nothing of his face, and he must have seen but little of mine, for he pulled me roughly toward the place where the lamp stood. In a moment we could see each other, and he let my arm drop.

"Oh," said the duke, "it's you," and three words have never been steeped with such bitter disappointment.

Rubbing my arm where he had grasped me, I reflected that his company that evening had hardly been pleasant enough that he could afford to criticize mine, but I said only, "What are you doing up here?"

"That is no concern of yours."

"It is my concern when your pacing keeps me awake," I said—unjustly, but I was past caring about fairness.

He ignored this. Now that he had seen who I was, he evidently had no use for me: he had turned his back and stood staring out over the darkened landscape toward the sea. When the wind died I could just hear the waves, and it was strange to be unable to see them.

Since he seemed disinclined to conversation, I took a few minutes to better look at our surroundings. The multitude of chimneys, some as wide as four men standing shoulder to shoulder, scattered seemingly at random, gave the roof the feel of a sparsely wooded forest; anything could be hiding a few feet away, unknown. Perhaps that was why Herron paced instead of keeping his vigil by the parapet: he wanted to be sure that nothing was concealed from him? But what would he be seeking? I wondered who he had expected to see when he uncovered my face.

A mistress, came the cynical thought; if he had been Lionel, that would have been likely. But the duke had not behaved as if greeting a beloved when he seized me.

He was pacing again, his hands thrust in his pockets, the wind ruffling his hair. I moved to relight my candle at his lamp and heard his steps pause. There was no sound as I coaxed my candle into life again, and an uneasy feeling crawled up my neck at the knowledge that he stood somewhere behind me, silent and watching.

"Do you believe that the dead return?"

The suddenness of the words was no less startling than their sense. I turned slowly, taking time to collect myself.

He was standing very near and staring at me intently, as if my answer was of great importance. Unnerved though I was, I could not help but notice the unearthly beauty of his face in the lamp's soft illumination. Covered in the cloak, he might have been a figure from another time, a visitant himself, doomed to walk on nights like this.

"Do you mean ghosts?" I asked, uncertain.

He shrugged impatiently. "Ghosts, revenants, haunts—whatever you wish to call them. Do you think the soul can return after the death of the body to move among the living?"

I had never given the subject any serious thought, and I felt a doubt lest he was baiting me. "Well, one of my governesses once told me that Anne Boleyn still walks in the Tower..."

At once I knew I had said the wrong thing. Pushing past me, he snatched up the lamp. "Is that all you know about? Servants' gossip and All Hallows' spooks? You're as useless as the rest." He was striding to the door, and I hurried after him and the receding circle of light, which suddenly seemed like a refuge.

"Wait, please. I haven't ever seen one, but that does not mean—" The meaning of his words struck me. "Have you? Is that what you're looking for?"

His step faltered, but only for an instant. He plunged down the stair, and by the time I had fastened the door behind me he was gone; only the penumbra of the lamp retreating down the hall gave any sign of his existence.

I fumbled my way back to my room and crept into bed. Burrowing into the welcome warmth, I played the strange encounter over again in my mind. I could not forget the sight of his face, staring out of the darkness, his eyes intent and seeming to see far beyond the present. Somehow he put me in mind of the old ballad of Tam Lin, the human whose beauty so captivated the Queen of Faery that she claimed him for her own. Generations might come and go, but when unwary mortals summoned him from the other world, he was still young, still fair, but with a terrible knowledge in his eyes. Herron had looked as I had always imagined Tam Lin to look: like a man who had seen worlds beyond this one, and knew they could endanger a man's very soul.

Had he seen something? Or did he only hope to?

* * *

After this incident, my life at Ellsmere fell into a fairly unexciting routine. It was not what I had expected when I had made plans with the duchess in the city: I had somehow imagined that I would be instantly assimilated into a new family, that my days would be crammed with company and conversation. I had eagerly anticipated discussing poetry with Herron, politics with Charles, and everything else with the duchess and Felicity. Since Lionel's departure I had been starved for someone to talk to, and I had not realized just to what extent until I found that, after all, I would spend much of the time in my new life as I had in the old—alone.

The duchess could hardly be blamed; with the enormous household to run, she was very busy, and I counted myself fortunate that she took time every day, even if it was only a few minutes before the dinner gong went, to ask after my activities and make certain that I had everything I desired. She was always in the midst of a hum of activity: paying a visit to the tenants or nearby neighbors; planning menus and arranging flowers; sending invitations and answering them; supervising the redecoration of the guest rooms in preparation for the house party that would be arriving the next month. She seemed amazed that I would wish to stay in Great-Aunt Agatha's room, with its unfashionable furnishings and dark, faded hangings, but I loved the rich forest-green velvet and damask; age had muted their splendor to mysterious, subtle hues, so that to my eyes the room had the tints and shadows of a wood at dusk.

Of Felicity I saw little, as well: Miss Yates had not relaxed her vigilance regarding lessons in spite of the short time remaining until Felicity would dispose of her services, and when Felicity was not closeted with the governess she was following the duchess around with the devotion of an acolyte. When forced to part from her idol she could generally be found practicing on the pianoforte, for which she had a great talent. She was pleasant, but on those occasions when she was disposed for my company, we found it difficult to find a subject on which to converse, since our interests and characters were so dissimilar. After we had assuaged our initial curiosity about each other, we were forced to fall back on discussion of the weather and the prospects of trifle for tea.

Her brother, while easier to talk to, spent much of the time in diligent study to prepare himself to take up his medical training in earnest when he left for Edinburgh.

During the mornings he was usually closeted in his study, but we occasionally encountered each other in the afternoon. To my surprise, he turned out to be widely read, and one day when I came upon him walking on the terrace we had a friendly argument about the new novel *John Halifax, Gentleman*, which I had just finished reading. I had found it rather saccharine, but Charles said he enjoyed melodrama.

However, as agreeable as Charles was in his fashion, it was Herron I wished to see more of. As abrasive as his company was, it was curiously stimulating, in a way that the rest of the family, for all their kindness, were not: I wanted to know more about the young duke who bore his title so reluctantly. His obvious unhappiness drew me to him; I felt as if, like me, he knew he was out of place here, even though he was among his own people and I was a stranger. The alien quality of his grief and the anger with which he armed himself separated him from his own flesh and blood as visibly as his dark coloring contrasted with their blondness. He might have been a changeling, this dark son of a golden family, placed among them by a mischievous goblin. In those early days, when I was still insecure in my new life, uncertain of my future and—perhaps in consequence—bitterly lonely for Lionel, I would have given much to speak to a fellow creature who knew something of the isolation I felt. But Herron continued to avoid all company, and, after my blundering intrusion on the roof, I was not surprised that he did not seek me out. I tried to put myself in his path again, but without success.

Although my hosts did not fully guess the extent to which I felt out of place, Lord Claude at least showed that he had considered my strange position in the household. One afternoon he invited me into his study to talk. I sat on the edge of a chair, facing him over the massive desk at which he sat. When he saw my nervousness he smiled at me kindly.

"There's no need to look so solemn, my dear, as if you were going to be scolded like one of the maids; I'm not going to accuse you of failing to dust under the bureau. I thought, though, that it might be best to discuss the terms of your stay here."

In spite of his reassurance, this sounded very business-like, and I waited apprehensively.

"I take it that my charming wife, who, between us, has been known to be slightly impulsive"—I could not help smiling at that—"invited you here without giving you a very clear idea of just what the nature of your visit would be. In which case I would imagine that you are in a somewhat uncomfortable position, with no certainty as to how long or under what conditions your stay will be."

"That is true," I said. "But, sir, if I am to be her new lady's maid, I must confess that I have no aptitude for that sort of work."

It was a feeble joke at best, but he leaned back in his chair and laughed, a relaxed, unconstrained sound. "My dear child, I have no intention of putting you to work. Indeed, I simply wanted to let you know that you should consider yourself truly one of our family. You are welcome here for as long as you choose to stay. Permanently, if you wish."

"But, sir, I couldn't possibly impose—"

"My dear, please do not think of such a thing. You are one of our family, and indeed I do believe Gwendolyn feels she has acquired a new daughter. Ellsmere is your home now, if you wish to claim it." He reached across the desk for my hand. I placed it in his, shyly, for I was still not used to gestures of affection. "It's settled, then?" he asked. "You'll be content to acquire an eccentric, slightly scandalous, but nonetheless loving family?"

The mischievous light in his eyes encouraged me even more than his words. "Indeed, sir, I find a bit of eccentricity invigorating. In any case, I've already grown very fond of this family. It's—very different from the one I knew before."

Lord Claude glanced at me when I said that, but did not take me up on it. Instead he told me of his arrangements for a dress allowance for me—an amount that made me blink—and for the renovation of the room next to mine as a study for me. "Gwen said that you're fond of languages," he said as I rose to go. "The library here is rather a good one. You must feel free to avail yourself of it."

When I found the library I realized how modest he had been in his praise of it. Two stories high, it was completely lined with books—even the doors had shelves built on to them—and I had to tip my head back to see the highest shelves. A gallery ran around the second level, and rolling ladders on both levels offered the means to reach the less accessible volumes. It would take a week simply to read all the titles. At random I chose a shelf and immediately found extensive sets of Virgil, Homer, and Cicero, as well as more recent works in different languages, some of which I had heard of but had not been allowed to read. I stood with a copy of *Mademoiselle de Maupin* in one hand and Apuleius's *Metamorphoses* in the other, almost dizzy as I surveyed the riches surrounding me.

Soon my daily routine—what there had been of it—was enhanced by long stays in the library. From time to time Lord Claude or Charles would wander in, but for the most part the library was my domain. For the first time in my life I was able to freely indulge in my favorite pursuit, for as long as I wanted; if I missed lunch, it was brought in to me, and I was never chastised. Indeed, the others seemed impressed with my literary tendencies, and when Lord Claude persuaded me to read to them from my translation of Ovid, they all declared themselves in awe of my talent. It was a heady feeling to be admired for what I had once had to do in secret, as a vice.

There was another factor that kept me from boredom and loneliness in my new life. One brilliantly sunny day, when even an endless array of books could not keep me inside, I ventured down the cliff path again. I had been troubled by my craven reaction to my first sight of the sea, and today, when it felt physically impossible to stay indoors, I decided to make another trial.

As before, the sound met me before the sight itself, and the breeze immediately seized upon me to rumple my hair and skirts, but this time I was not overwhelmed: under the bright blue sky the sea was dazzling, winking with coins of sunlight all over its bobbing surface. Something in me seemed to rise up to meet its energy and buoyancy, and I lifted my face up to the sunlight, delighted by the wild sense of restless, excited activity. Exhilarated, I stood there for a moment, my chin to the breeze, letting the spray settle tingling on my skin. The wavelets flung themselves up as if trying to pat my feet and I darted back, laughing, and picked up my skirts to chase them back as they receded, in a game of tag more ancient than I then knew. It was much later when, disheveled, flushed, and well content, I decided to explore further and set off down the shore.

After perhaps a mile I climbed over a line of rough, enormous rocks to find myself at the edge of a small bay. In contrast with the rough energy of the shore I had left, this place held peace as in the palm of a hand. There was scarcely any beach here, since the massive rocks that bound it came almost to the water's edge, and the water's surface was more placid. This great cool cup of green might have been a completely different entity from the boisterous scene I had come from. The stillness of it was entrancing. I found a rock that reached out over the water's surface and clambered up onto it. If I lay on my stomach and leaned over, I could trail my fingers in my reflection. Even the noise had receded, blocked by the high border of rocks that sealed this place off as with an enchantment.

These places became a refuge and a companion to me. Whenever I felt restless I would make my way down to the beach and let myself be buffeted by its roaring energy; when I wished for calm and quiet, however, I would climb over the rocks to the tiny bay and sit or lie on the lookout rock, letting myself be soothed by the tranquil, gently moving waters of that pocket of ocean.

CHAPTER SIX

One evening, almost a fortnight after I had arrived at Ellsmere, the duchess sent for me to come to her boudoir "for a surprise." I told Mary, her maid, that I would be along as soon as I finished my page of Homer, and went to her room a few minutes later with a feeling of combined anticipation and dread. I knew enough to expect another manifestation of my hostess's vast generosity, and while I could not help but be touched by her gifts to me, I was nonetheless a bit overwhelmed by them.

My hand was raised to knock when I heard Lord Claude's voice. I kept still so that I would not intrude on them in a private moment, but then the subject of their conversation dawned on me and I stayed to listen.

"—scarcely bear my presence, and you've seen the way he looks at me: as if he was passing judgment." His voice sounded far from that of the carefree bridegroom: I could hear weariness, and sadness as well.

I heard a sigh. "He behaves just the same toward me," said the duchess in tones as tired and defeated as her husband's. "It's as though my very existence offends him."

"And all this business of going off by himself. On my way to breakfast I saw him coming out of the door to the stable. Riding, and before dawn! Walking the cliffs at all hours! What can be the matter with him, Gwen?" His voice grew hushed. "Do you think there's something—er—wrong with him?"

The slight pause before her answer robbed her words of their certainty. "No, my dear, I'm sure of it. I doubt it's anything more than grief for his father's death—and anger at us for marrying before the 'proper' interval had passed."

A maid was coming down the hall toward me, and I knocked quickly, lest she realize I was eavesdropping. Without her presence to shame me into announcing myself, I own that I would gladly have stood listening as long as they spoke of Herron. Now the duchess's voice, as bright and careless as it had been downcast a moment ago, bade me enter.

Lord Claude rose from her side on the pink-sprigged divan as I joined them. He, too, was making an effort to appear carefree, but his face was less schooled than the duchess's, and there were signs of strain around his eyes. I felt a pang of sympathy for him: he seemed to want his stepson's friendship so sincerely and to be so dismayed at the denial of it. As I made my curtsey I wondered if Herron realized how good a stepfather he was rejecting. He had his reasons, of course, but I wondered if there was a way I could help to reconcile the two.

Of course, considering that I was not even on speaking terms with the duke, it was probably unlikely.

"Ah, good evening, my dear," he said with one of his kind, comfortable smiles. "My wife tells me that she is going to set about enlarging your wardrobe. I trust you will soon be needing to move to more capacious rooms."

"Claude, really!" she laughed, shaking her head at him so that her ringlets bounced. Even at this hour, when she retired to her room to rest before dinner, she was still as exquisitely groomed as if she were expecting callers: not one of her curls was awry, and her dressing gown (a peignoir, she called it) was trimmed with lace and rosettes of pink satin ribbon. "You're heartless. And now you've given away my surprise. I wanted to dazzle her with a brilliant display of treasures, like a storybook djinn, and now you reduce my role to that of a haberdasher!"

"From djinn to duchess—such a falling off!" he teased, giving a tug to one of the bobbing curls. They smiled at each other with an expression that made me all at once feel excluded. As far as they were concerned, I might not have been in the room. I should have been tactful and turned the other way, assuming a sudden interest in the fire screen or mantel ornaments, but I could not take my eyes away. I felt a stab of sheer envy at the adoration that blazed so nakedly in their faces. How fortunate they were—and how forlorn I suddenly felt, barred from the joy they knew.

As if my thoughts had spoken, the duchess's first words after her husband left us were, "we must get you a husband, child."

I laughed, instantly disgusted with my own foolishness. "Oh, never. I am one of nature's old maids. When I am fifty you will come visit me with your seventeen grandchildren and I shall teach them all to conjugate Latin verbs. That is my true place in life."

"Conjugation, rather than the conjugal?" She looked so pleased at her own witticism that I laughed again. "My dear, there is no reason you cannot have both."

"I doubt very much than any man of sense will have me—and I will not have any man who isn't sensible."

"Well, you certainly have fixed on a persuasive rationalization for rejecting suitors. Your determination is quite formidable."

"So far there have been none to test it."

"You exaggerate, my dear. In any case, we shall soon change all that." She was sweeping me toward the door to her dressing room, and when I started to reply she slapped me lightly on the wrist. "None of that! You are to enter the djinn's treasure house in appropriately awed silence. Jane, Mary, if you please."

As the door swung open, the maids each ran up with overflowing burdens of dress stuff: damasks, silks, muslin, mull, fabrics whose names I only learned later. More brilliant lengths spilled over chairs and from the shelves of the clothes press: pools of liquid topaz, dusky claret, shimmering silver. And on the bed, heaped like jewels in a casket, were finished gowns: one of a rose-colored wool, with belled sleeves and trim of grey velveteen; another of hyacinth blue, whose wide collar and cuffs were edged with snowy lace scalloping; and the third, unmistakably an evening dress, and the one that drew an involuntary "oh" of adoration from me: a heavy, gleaming satin that iridesced from blue to green like the sea, with the briefest of bodices but yards of billowing skirt. A wide, fringed hanging sash was its only trimming.

"I thought you'd like them," said the duchess complacently, holding the sea-green gown up to me to assess the effect. "I had ordered them for myself, but I knew as soon as we met that they would look much better on you. Mrs. Prescott will fit them to you today and we shall have them altered at once."

"But—" I stopped fondling the gleaming satin and looked anxiously up. "I can't take your gowns. You'll miss them."

"Miss them! Hardly. I ordered more than a dozen, and three out of all those will scarcely be an insupportable loss. Besides, they truly do not suit me. Look." She held the ball gown I coveted up to herself, and I saw that the bold hue eclipsed her fairness and made her look faded. "I do better in my 'flower frocks' as Claude calls them."

It was true. The delicate shades of pink, blue, and yellow she favored suited her, while I would have felt foolish and juvenile in them. The gowns she had set aside for me were also markedly plainer in cut than those she wore, which were always flounced, ruffled, beribboned, and generally fashioned a great deal like many-petaled flowers. I was relieved that she had offered me only the simplest gowns: the furbelows that looked dainty on her would only heighten my plainness by contrast, I was certain. Better by far not to appear as if I wished to hide my shortcomings by dressing like a belle; at least I could look neat and trim, if not pretty.

Once again she seemed to sense my thoughts. "If these are too plain, we can have them trimmed," she said, beckoning for Jane to unhook my dress. "But I had a feeling you wouldn't wish to go about in such heavily weighted things. These uncluttered styles are so much more elegant, really."

But this was tact; I saw the caressing glance she bestowed on her own new ball dress as she was hooked into it. Countless layers of frothy pink tulle, lavished with frills, it made no attempt to be "uncluttered."

"These are perfect," I sighed; then, my heart sinking as Mary approached with a corset, "must I be laced to wear them?"

She and Mary exchanged amused glances at the consternation in my voice. "But of course you must! We should get you into stays as soon as we can."

"But why?" I gasped for breath as the whalebone stays tightened under Mary's lacing. "I thought you said I was slender already."

"And so you are, dear; but the stays will give you a waist that will be the envy of every girl, and a tidier silhouette as well." With an approving nod at the maid's handiwork, she reached for a measuring tape. "I believe that dress is made with an eighteen-inch waist." Seeing the look on my face, she relented. "The day dresses are somewhat more generous."

Thank heaven for that. "Perhaps I will get used to it," I said, without much hope.

"Of course you will," she said comfortably. "I have not gone without stays since I was fifteen, and I would feel undressed without them. Soon you will feel the same." Correctly reading my silence as skepticism, she added, "And, you know, whenever you retire to your room you may change into a dressing gown. I find it very refreshing to spend a few hours out of my corset in the afternoon. Would you like to choose fabric for a few peignoirs?"

"I would feel very extravagant," I said, but it was only a halfhearted protest at most; it would be lovely to have a few loose things to wear in my own room. Despite her assurances, the idea of spending all day corseted was a daunting one. To my relief, she waved away my feeble objection.

"Nonsense, my dear. I assure you, you will be glad of them. What would you like? This pretty lavender crepe?"

Tantalized, I wandered over to the heaps of fabrics, touching the different textures. While the duchess's dressing gowns were all of light, delicate stuff, like the crepe she had suggested, I found myself drawn to the richest, deepest colors, the most luxurious weaves: a velour of cobalt blue as deep as a moonless midnight, and a cut velvet of wine-red shot with silver. When I held them up, shyly, the duchess's eyebrows rose. I knew they were more suited to ball gowns, and for a lady of her age, not an unmarried girl, but all she said was, "How beautiful. You'll look like a medieval princess. Mrs. Prescott, have those two made up in Mademoiselle's measurements."

"Very good, Your Grace," said the thin-lipped seamstress, whose plainness was a strange contrast to the gorgeous materials she worked with. She began fitting the hyacinth dress to me, and I had to stand very still to avoid being stuck with pins. When Mrs. Prescott had the dress fitted to her satisfaction, the duchess came to inspect me.

At once her face broke into dimples. "It's perfect for you—as I knew it would be. Here, child, have a look at yourself."

Walking carefully, my arms held out stiffly from my body lest I stab myself, I approached the duchess's cheval glass.

It was astonishing, the difference a dress could make. In the new dress, even with excess fabric pinned in pleats around me, I looked prettier than I could ever recall. My cheeks were flushed, perhaps with excitement, and I gave the duchess a dazzling smile in the mirror. I felt as though I had acquired, not a djinn perhaps, but a fairy godmother. Such beautiful new dresses, in such colors—

I dropped my eyes suddenly and turned away from the mirror, fumbling for the dress fastenings. Jane saw my struggles and hurried to unhook me, handling the dress carefully so as not to dislodge the pins. The duchess, sensing a change in my mood, rustled over.

"My dear child, what is the matter? Does it not please you?"

"It does," I said in a rush. "And it's so kind of you, ma'am. But I can't help feeling that I shouldn't put off my mourning yet. It's been such a short time—" I stopped, with a gulp.

"Oh. I see." Her face had instantly assumed the gravity of mine, and she said nothing more while I put my own dress on again. Then she gestured for the others to leave us. When the door had shut behind the stiffly disapproving back of Mrs. Prescott, who was evidently offended at my reception of her handiwork, she led me to the divan.

Taking my hands, she sat me down to face her. She still wore the pink ball gown, its frilled skirts spreading wide over the hooped crinoline, so that she seemed to sit in a mass of pink flowers.

"I realize it has not been long since your brother's death," she said gently. "Perhaps I should not influence you to leave off your mourning so soon. If you would rather not wear colors for a time—"

"But I would rather wear them," I blurted miserably. "That is what distresses me. I hate wearing everlasting black and grey and purple. I have always longed to wear lovely things. But I feel ashamed to wear them now, when it would wrong Lionel's memory."

The strangest expression was tugging at her face. If she had not been so grave, I would have thought she was trying to keep from smiling.

"I see," she said, one fine crease appearing on her brow. "That is a difficulty. If you intend to be guided by convention, then of course you are quite right to remain in mourning—however primitive a custom it is. The deities of propriety and decorum would have it that there is no other course."

Somehow the way she described the matter, the phrases she used, stirred a kind of dissatisfaction in me. Convention and propriety were such smug, stingy entities. I knew what my father would have said: that even to consider wearing colors within a year would destroy his reputation, that he would be pointed at as the man who had raised a cold, selfish, vain little brat. He would have had me cast my eyes on the ground every waking hour in ostentatious respect for the dead rather than risk a glimpse of something that would make me appreciate that I still lived. If Lionel could not enjoy it, nor should I. All that my brother had not lived to see should be forbidden me, the unworthy, living child.

I realized that I was hunched tensely on the edge of the divan, clenching my fists, and the duchess was watching me in concern. Embarrassed, I uncurled my fingers, feeling now the pain from embedding my fingernails so deeply into my palms. I clasped my hands to hide the angry red crescents and straightened.

She must have observed my resentment, but she took no direct notice of it. "Tradition is a helpful guide, but it fails to take circumstances into account," she said mildly. "Perhaps it is better to decide what is best for you, in your particular situation. What do you think Lionel would do, were he in your position?"

"Get intoxicated."

This time I was certain she smiled. "After that."

"He would probably have worn black for a week or two," I said, thinking it over; "but then I'm sure he would have been unable to resist his saffron tailcoat. Lionel loved nice clothes; he could not have borne covering himself in black for long." The idea was curiously heartening.

"And would you think any the less of him for ceasing to wear black for you?"

"No," I said, truthfully, although I knew where she was leading with her questions, and I could not help but be aware that it suited her purposes to get me out of mourning. While I was certain that her own generosity prompted her, I could not ignore the wry inner voice that told me it would be far pleasanter for her not to have so visible a reminder of her own abbreviated mourning period. I wondered if she had admitted to herself the reason for her eagerness to furnish me with a new wardrobe.

She sat back, beaming at me as if I had said something exceedingly clever. "Well then!" she exclaimed. "Why should you force yourself into clothes he would have detested as much as you? Will you not be acting more in accordance with his wishes to wear pretty dresses such as he would have liked to see you in? I do not mean to sound callous, my dear, but after all, you did not die with him. In any case, wearing colors does not mean you loved your brother any the less. It is what is in your heart, not on your back, that shows sincerest feeling."

This speech sounded more than a little glib, and I wondered if she had recited it frequently as a defense for dispensing with her own mourning. Nevertheless, I was willing to be persuaded; however uncomfortably her reasoning sat with me, I agreed with it in its general import, and soon we returned to the happy task of debating the relative merits of cherry-red satin and peacock-green taffeta.

At her insistence, I chose fabric for two more day dresses, a riding habit (I had never been on horseback), and three dinner gowns. Although she encouraged me to choose what I wished, the duchess gently led me toward more appropriate choices for my remaining costumes than I had made for my dressing gowns. This suited me; I did not wish to appear eccentric, and would gladly dress demurely in public as long as I could wear the rich things I loved for myself. She summoned back Mrs. Prescott, who softened sufficiently to agree to have the hyacinth dress ready for me to wear the next day, and after having deluged me with delicate new stockings, lingerie, and nightgowns of the softest silk, she let me go.

As I wandered back to my room to dress for dinner, my head spinning with visions of dazzling colors, I realized suddenly that my predilection for rich fabrics and colors was something I had in common with Lionel. I had never before had the opportunity to discover such a preference, and I found it comforting to feel this kinship with a brother who, although much loved, never seemed much like me. It made him seem nearer to me, as if some tiny flicker of his character lived still.

I hoped, however, that this newfound sympathy did not mean I would also discover a penchant for Madeira and cards.

At dinner I was able, for once, to converse on a subject dear to Felicity's heart, as she clamored to hear about my new gowns and told me in return all the details of the dresses she would be ordering once she was allowed to wear long skirts. Felicity was in a sort of no-man's-land at seventeen: although she still had a governess and wore short skirts she was allowed to take part in conversation with guests and even to flirt mildly with the bachelors, unusual liberties for a girl who had not yet come out. I wondered if this was due to the duchess's indulgence and blithe disregard for conventions—at least, for those that inconvenienced her. I was certain that Felicity and I both benefited from the duchess's protection; anyone of less stature than she would not be able to flout society's strictures so blatantly without enduring widespread censure, even rejection.

I wondered, though, if even her rank exempted the duchess completely; had she had to face down strong opposition when she discarded her mourning crepe and made her scandalous remarriage? Had she had to endure the humiliation of being cut by former friends? I remembered her compressed lips yesterday when she opened her mail, and the voice in which she had told Jenkins that the Willow Room and Clock Room would not be needed. Clearly some of her invitations were being rejected. No wonder she had made so wry an appraisal of convention that evening.

Now I recalled also Miss Yates's estimation of the duchess as a woman of strength, a quality I had not formerly associated with her. Perhaps the duchess was not the ingenuous creatures she appeared to be, but something like the gowns she wore: to all appearances insubstantial and frivolous, but with a foundation of steel and whalebone under all the ruffles. This new and intriguing line of thought occupied me through the end of the meal.

It was a miserable night, with rain pounding down and a rising wind whipping it against the windows with a sound like flung pebbles, and the drawing room after dinner was all the cozier by contrast. Charles and his father played at chess in front of the fire while Felicity tried out a new piece on the pianoforte.

"Come, Aunt Gwendolyn, sing for us," she urged, and with very little persuasion the duchess did so. Her sweetly clear soprano lured her husband's attention from the game, and at his suggestion I took his place at the board so that he could join the group at the piano. Charles caught my eye over the chess pieces and smiled as Lord Claude's pleasant baritone joined in the song.

"They complement each other very well, don't they?" he said in an undertone, and I had to agree. Lord Claude never returned to the chess board.

Herron had not appeared, and I wondered if he was keeping his rooftop vigil. Surely, though, on such a night even he would remain indoors.

By the time we retired, the wind had risen: it whined shrilly around the casements of my room, and sheets of rain battered the windows as I climbed into bed. It was so loud I could not have heard Herron's footsteps overhead if he had been there. I wriggled down under the covers and drew the eiderdown up around my shoulders, devoutly glad to be sheltered and warm.

The storm made me restless, though, and I did not feel like sleep. After an hour of wakefulness I sighed and left my bed long enough to fetch *Varney the Vampyre*, the book Lionel had urged on me before leaving for battle. It was not what I would have chosen, but a belated feeling of guilt at discarding my mourning suggested that reading it would be a sisterly gesture. And if any night was an appropriate setting for vampire attacks and disappearing corpses, it was this one. I burrowed under the bedclothes again and started to read, not without another sigh at the length of the book. Nine hundred pages seemed rather a large atonement for a new gown. Composing myself to patience, I lit a candle and embarked on the sanguine adventures of Sir Francis Varney.

Clear and distinct through the gusting of the storm came another sound. I looked up. The handle of my door was moving. Without taking my eyes from the door or stopping to think I reached a hand out and snuffed my candle, perhaps out of some obscure notion of hiding myself. The fire still cast its autumnal glow on the hearthrug, but I now sat in dimness.

Silent now, the door opened, and a figure moved into the room. I sat upright in amazement as Herron closed the door behind him with a faint click and stood there, his eyes searching the darkened room.

In the first moment I felt only shock, and never considered that I might be in a perilous position. Certainly nothing in his appearance or manner suggested that he had come here out of amorous motives, or even conscious choice. He streamed with rainwater; he wore no coat or cloak, and his shirt was sticking transparently to his body, so that he shivered, dripping, where he stood. Probably he had been driven from the roof to the first warm room by the elements. Surely he must realize by now that it was tenanted? Embarrassed, I cleared my throat to speak.

At the sound he turned such a devastated face to me that I was startled into pushing the bedclothes back and stepping to the floor with the half-formed intent of going to him.

"What is it?" I whispered, awed by the terrible anguish in his face. He raised an unsteady hand to push the hair out of his eyes. His whole body was trembling, in short hard spasms; it could not be only the cold. He looked at the end of his strength, and I wondered how long he would be able to stand.

"I'll ring for someone and—" I began.

"Father."

It was all he said before his knees buckled and, with a piercing stab of pity, I ran to him, thinking to help him to his feet. But kneeling he clutched at me, wrapping his arms around me so tightly that I had to catch at his shoulders to keep from falling. His face pressed into my waist, he began to cry, with great racking sobs like a child's. Through the thin silk of my nightdress they burned against my skin, and I shivered. Hesitantly I touched his hair, smoothed it.

"There, now. It's all right." What comfort could I offer in the face of such pain? Chafing at my helplessness, I put my arms around his shoulders, stroked his head.

"...wasn't there." His voice was muffled against my body.

"Hush now, dearest." He must be upbraiding himself for not having been there at the end. Had he been carrying that guilt all these weeks?

Still shaken with sobs, he said no more. When his arms loosened for a moment I slipped through them so that I knelt to face him. His face was damp with tears now as well as rain, and it seemed the most natural thing in the world to kiss the tear-streaked face. To keep on kissing it. Once or twice I even thought the kisses returned, but when I drew back to look at him his eyes were drifting closed, his breath quieting; he leaned against me more heavily.

I should, I suppose, have awakened one of the servants and had him taken to his own room. Instead I draped one of his arms around my shoulders and helped him to his feet. Half pulling, half supporting him I got him to the bed and into it. With a little trouble I peeled his wet shirt off him and hung it before the fire; I was able to remove his boots more swiftly. I crept around to the other side of the bed and leaned across to pull the covers over him; I could sleep on the sofa before the fire and need only a blanket. But I may have lingered longer than I needed to arranging the coverlet, and, as I started to draw back, his eyelids quivered and one hand fastened around my wrist.

"Don't go. Please."

The words were sleep-slurred, barely a murmur. Gazing at the flushed face, the long eyelashes spiky with tears where they lay against his cheeks, I did not even think of protesting. I lay down beside him and, with my hand clasped in his, he sighed once and slept.

I could not. Like Psyche with Eros, I could not resist the pleasure of observing him. I had never been in the presence of so beautiful a man, never seen such a lean, finely muscled body except in a sculpture. The arm that rested outside the counterpane swelled with a strength my own did not possess, and I marveled at the contrast. His skin was golden where the firelight touched, except where the beginnings of beard darkened his jaw. Carefully, for fear of waking him, I reached out with one finger to trace the strong line of his shoulder.

At the touch he stirred, turning on his side, so that his face rested very near mine on the pillow. His breath feathered against my cheek, and for a second my heart seemed to forget to beat at the pleasure of that touch. At last my eyes, lingering on his face, began to close, and breathing each other's breath we slept.

CHAPTER SEVEN

I woke before dawn, remembering his presence even before my eyes opened, knowing I must wake him and send him away before he was discovered with me. But he was already gone. His shirt and boots had vanished as well, and the only sign he had been there at all was the hollow in the pillow next to mine, still damp from his rain-wet hair. I stared for a moment at the empty place, then moved over to fill it, resting my head in the place where his had lain.

It was a gloomy day when it dawned. The rain had given way to implacable cold and a snow-colored sky, in whose sullen light the world looked stale and dreary. I lingered in bed, turning over the events of the night before. I was surprised at myself for having behaved with so little regard for propriety. I was even more surprised that I could not feel ashamed for it. I had acted partly out of an instinctive desire to comfort him, as if he'd been a child and I his mother. But only partly. Even in the chill austerity of morning I could call up the picture of him sleeping next to me and feel my heart thud against my ribs at the memory.

What would he say to me?

This thought struck me as I was getting out of bed, and I sat down again under the weight of it. Perhaps, I thought in a rush of humiliation that sent the blood to my cheeks, I had been too welcoming, too forward. Certainly any so-called lady who allowed a man into her room, let alone her bed, could expect to be branded a loose woman. But he had seemed so vulnerable. Surely he would not reward compassion, however unsuitable, with contempt—or, worse, with an attempt to take advantage of it.

Not for the first time since arriving at Ellsmere I wished I had had a more conventional upbringing. If I had been brought up properly, I would have simply shrieked and fainted when Herron appeared in my room, thereby avoiding the consequences of an ill-considered decision.

But I'm glad I didn't, I thought, remembering his face so near mine, his hair under my fingers. Oh, I'm glad I didn't faint.

Perhaps he would be dismissive, or even insulting. I knew so little about him, after all; maybe I had been unwise to greet him with such trust. But I could not forget that in his grief he had come to me, and no one else. That must mean something. With a rush of renewed optimism I bounded off the bed and snatched up my hairbrush.

"My, you're looking pleased with yourself, miss," commented Jane, as she brought in hot water to wash in. "You look like the cat with cream on her whiskers, if you don't mind my saying so."

"Not at all, Jane," I said, smiling as I plied the hairbrush. "Is my new dress ready? I'd like to wear it."

"Yes, of course, miss. I'll fetch it myself and send Mary in to lace you. She has stronger wrists than I."

That sent a qualm through me, but even the prospect of being strong-armed into a corset could not dampen me for long. If the events of last night had meant anything, it was that there was some special bond between Herron and me. Now I could be sure that it was not just my own feeling, but his as well. Surely it had not been a random search for shelter that had brought him to me, as I had thought at first: he must have sought me out deliberately.

When I reached the breakfast room I was not surprised to find only Charles and Lord Claude there. The duchess rose late, and Felicity and Miss Yates often took their breakfast apart from the family when they had morning lessons. Father and son were on their feet at once with their usual perfect manners. They wished me good morning, and Charles's eyebrows went up at the sight of me. The admiration in his eyes buoyed my high spirits even further.

"This must be one of the famous new gowns." He drew out a chair for me and stood back for a moment to survey me further. "My stepmother has talked of little else for days; now I understand why she was so pleased with herself. It suits you beautifully."

"It does?" I said, so hopefully that Charles smiled as he moved to the sideboard to serve me a plate.

"You look radiant. Don't you agree, father?"

"Yes, indeed. You look lovely, my dear. Although," he added, taking up his newspaper, "a bit flushed. You aren't feeling feverish, I hope?"

"Why, no; I've never felt better." I took a sip of tea to try to calm myself. My excitement must be very visible.

Lord Claude frowned nevertheless. "We can't have you getting ill, now. Charles, what do you think? Isn't her color high?"

He glanced at me over his shoulder as he spooned eggs onto my plate with abandon. "A bit, yes. But that may be the effect of the corset. I am correct in thinking my stepmother has forced one of those awful appurtenances onto you?"

"Charles, behave yourself," said his father mildly. "You'll embarrass her."

Charles put my plate down before me. It was heaped high with food, and I regarded it doubtfully. Even if I had not been too happy to eat, the grip of my new stays made swallowing more than two bites seem an impossibility.

"I'm sorry if I'm too frank," he said, seating himself next to me. "As a student of medicine I feel I have the right to speak openly about anything that can damage your health, and squeezing yourself into a steel-ribbed sausage casing..."

"Charles."

"Yes, yes. You're right, Father. I'll confine myself to observations about the weather; much safer. My dear Miss Pembroke, do you believe we shall have snow soon?"

I laughed and picked up my fork. "It does seem to threaten, Mr. Reginald."

"It does indeed. I wonder if snow will put a stop to Herron's Wertheresque wanderings." Charles offered me the strawberry preserves and, when I shook my head, applied them vigorously to a scone. "It would be a pity for him to contract pneumonia in the name of Romanticism."

"Perhaps something more than an excessive love for the works of Goethe is behind his wish to be alone," I said, feeling less cordial toward him. "Her—the duke does not strike me as someone who would put himself to such an effort merely for the sake of conforming to the Romantic standard."

"Do you think so?" He glanced at his father, who lowered his newspaper as if sensing the gaze.

"I believe I'll go see if I can raise Gwendolyn," he said, standing. "You'll excuse me, my dear." With a courteous bow he left the table, and Charles continued his remarks as soon as his father was out of earshot.

"I'll allow that Herron has reason to feel alone and unhappy. I'll never forget what I went through when my mother died. It's not that I think he shouldn't mourn. But it's surely not necessary—or kind, for that matter—for him to flaunt his unhappiness to such an extent."

"Flaunt!" I exclaimed before I could stop myself.

He shrugged. "That's the way it seems to me."

My former feelings of amiability toward Charles had waned considerably. I jabbed at my breakfast with the beginnings of ill temper. "Must you be so critical of him?"

Charles grinned good-naturedly. "It is the primary benefit of being a stepbrother."

"Of course," I murmured. "As a mere cousin, you must have been sadly restricted in your remarks."

He was silent for a moment, watching me pick at my rapidly cooling kippers. "I'm actually more than a little worried about him," he said in a different voice, "but he won't listen to me when I tell him to take more care of himself. He really will catch pneumonia one of these days, out roaming at all hours, never eating—"

"Forever the student of medicine." I reached for the teapot, having abandoned any attempt to eat. "Can a man not enjoy a stroll without risking his life, and your censure?"

He looked startled at my vehemence, but smiled. "Forgive me; you're quite right. At times I can become a monomaniac. If I say anything more about pneumonia, you may empty the teapot over my head." His face sobered. "Nevertheless, I cannot help but be concerned about him. Perhaps not his physical condition as much as—"

He broke off suddenly and I looked up to find the duchess rustling into the room on her husband's arm. She wore a morning dress of pale gold silk that looked like a trapped sunbeam. I could not restrain a slight sigh. Even in my beautiful new gown, I could never hope to hold anyone's eye if she was in the room. Her husband's adoration was printed plain in his face as he seated her across from me.

Charles rose at once to bid her good morning—and perhaps to distract her from what she might have heard.

"How lovely you look, my dear!" she exclaimed, beaming at me. She fairly bubbled with happiness, and with diamonds glinting at her ears and throat, she looked more than ever like an earthbound sunbeam. ("Ladies never wear diamonds in the morning," I remembered one of my governesses proclaiming; another convention reduced to shambles by the duchess.) "I knew that color would be perfect on you. Claude, love, would you ring for Jenkins? Herron wants a tray brought up to him."

Charles froze, and I stared. I had scolded Charles for his concerns, but it was true that Herron never seemed to remember to take any food. Sending for breakfast was something of a landmark event.

Lord Claude, whose thoughts were evidently similar to mine, said in a moment, "Herron has asked for breakfast?"

Fully aware of the sensation she had caused, the duchess bobbed her head. "Why, yes, is it not heartening? When I stopped by his room he was still in bed—I'm sure he hasn't slept so late in months! I was so glad not to find him out wandering like a lost sheep, and to say he would eat something as well. I cannot say how much he has relieved my mind."

Lord Claude reached over to pat her hand, meeting her bright gaze with a sympathetic smile. His face did not quite light up like his wife's, but his tone was brighter when he said, "I'm heartily glad of it if the boy's improving. I'll stop in and see if he'd like to ride around to see the tenants with me today."

"Oh, do, darling. I'd love for the two of you to spend some time together."

Jenkins moved to her side and she embarked on elaborate instructions regarding kippers and toast. Under cover of this, Charles murmured, "I'll be surprised if he accepts."

His father's face settled into resigned, weary lines. "So will I," he said.

* * *

The morning passed without any sign of Herron. Lord Claude was unsuccessful in his efforts to run him to earth and finally set out with Charles to visit the tenants. I knew I should not expect Herron to seek me out, but the suspense was making me fidgety. Even though I believed in my sudden new happiness, I needed to speak to him. After a struggle with myself I set out for the shore. It was, after all, where I had first seen him; but whether he was there or not, I felt the need to escape the placid confines of the house.

The sea was the color of metal under the blank sky. There was no color, no brightness in this world; only sound, and I stood for a long time there, letting myself be buffeted by the roar. It did not overwhelm me as it had once done; I found its energy and motion a mirror of what I was feeling. Its vastness and sheer power still reduced me to the status of a molecule, but I felt as if my small frame encompassed emotions as turbulent and powerful as the ocean itself, too big to be contained. In a strange way we were in sympathy. I waited for what may have been a long time in that peculiar communion, but Herron did not appear.

After tea I set out again, but this time with a new destination in mind. When Felicity started for the drawing room to practice on the pianoforte, I followed, waiting until we were well away from the others before asking my question.

She looked at me blankly. "Why, in the churchyard. Didn't you see the monument on Sunday?"

"I must not have been paying attention." Another question struck me. "You say the duke is buried in the churchyard? Why is he not in the church, in a vault?"

"The duchess wished him to have his own monument, apart from the rest of the family." Her expression indicated that she found my curiosity morbid at the very least; at most—perhaps I was, after all, a member of some eccentric religious sect, and wished to perform obscure rites over this stranger's grave. I forced down a grin at the thoughts that flitted across her face.

"Thank you," I said, and was unable to resist adding, "I believe I'll just walk over and pay my respects."

She was still staring after me as I went to fetch my cloak. I imagine Chopin had a difficult time holding her attention that afternoon.

The church was less than two miles distant, and I covered the distance quickly on foot; the grey chill of the day had not diminished, and frost crunched under my boots, but as yet there was no snow. My breath preceded me in misty puffs, but the cold was pleasantly invigorating. My guess as to Herron's whereabouts did not play me false. As I emerged from the woods at the edge of the churchyard, I saw him.

Why I had not before guessed that he would keep vigil at his father's grave I cannot tell; perhaps it was because the idea had not even occurred to those who knew him better. He stood at the foot of the grave, gloved hands clasped behind him, his dark clothes and hair blending into one black silhouette, as if he were not a presence but an absence, a hole cut out of the landscape. He was as motionless as the gravestones that stood ranked around him, but when I neared him, even though my steps were silent on the carpet of fir needles, he turned his head.

I hesitated in sudden uncertainty, wondering what my reception would be, but he turned back again to resume his study of the headstone. I came to his side and looked too.

The duke's monument was as great a tribute as a woman of his wife's devotion and fortune could make it. Marble of so pure a white that it hurt the eyes rose in an obelisk as tall as the trees. At the base two lightly draped women, evidently goddesses and hence impervious to the weather, crouched in attitudes of distress, and the Reginald coat of arms was set into the front surface. There was no name, no date, no verses. None were needed.

Herron's face was expressionless as he regarded the monument to his father. I wondered how many hours he had spent in this fashion, and what he was thinking. Whether he was remembering the night before, or if that brief visitation that had transformed everything I knew, casting a bright glow over all that would come after like light through colored glass, had already dwindled into his forgotten past. I wanted badly to ask him. But it was he who spoke first.

"Yesterday was his birthday. I thought he might come then. So I waited, as I have so many times, thinking that perhaps this night... but nothing. Nothing at all." He fell silent again, and I waited, wondering.

Finally, "His birthday?" I ventured.

He nodded. "Of course, such earthly anniversaries may cease to have any meaning after we leave this life. But I thought he might remember. I thought he might want to see me again, to leave me with—something."

At last I realized. I gazed at him as growing understanding, not unmixed with horror, sank into me. The rooftop vigil I had interrupted leapt into sudden clarity. "You've been waiting for your father, these nights," I said. "For his spirit."

He did not bother to answer. We stood together in silence, and after a brief struggle the horror faded in me, conquered by the yearning, stronger than ever, to offer some comfort to this man who suffered so much more deeply than even he appeared to. Who missed his father so desperately that he clung to the hope of being haunted by him. My eyes misted at the thought of him, even younger than myself—barely a man—having to endure so crippling a loneliness, and I turned my face away before he could see. I dared not let him see pity. Was not his ruthless arrogance a way to fight off pity, to keep others from penetrating his solitude and recognizing the terrible extent of his grief?

I realized I was crying. I had not been able to shed tears for the parting from my father, or even for Lionel, but now some constraint in me had broken. One more shackle of my father's forging was falling away, and even in the midst of my feeling for Herron I felt a kind of wonder at it. The frozen winter of my soul was at an end; the thaw had come.

I raised a hand to brush away my tears, and it was met by his. His fingers tipped my face up so that we regarded each other.

"I watched you, asleep," he said. His hand lingered on my cheek, but his voice was detached, incurious; he seemed to still be gazing somewhere beyond me. "You looked so peaceful. I felt that I'd sell my soul to be possessed of such peace."

He had watched me as I slept. The intimacy of it brought heat creeping into my face, and I dropped my eyes in something like shame. But I had done the same—had devoured the sight of him as he lay unconscious, vulnerable, open to my gaze.

"Not so peaceful as you may think," I said, unsure of how to reply. "I, too, have lost someone inexpressibly dear. I think that is why I believe I know something of what you suffer."

His fingers moved over my face, softly, touching my chin, my mouth. He seemed not to have heard me speak. "And I wondered if you had it in your gift, this serenity." His eyes at last met mine, and their darkness was startling, like a physical jolt: in them I saw sorrow ages older than he. "The only moments of Lethe I've known since he died, I found last night."

I reached up to take his face in my hands. "If I can give you that much, I am glad."

His lips were cold at first. But at their touch warmth flooded through me, beating in waves in my throat, my fingertips. If he sought comfort from my arms and mouth, then I took something from him too; perhaps not what I wished for, but close enough for now.

We stood for a long time together, not speaking. I wondered how his arms around my waist could fill me with a joy that made me want to shout even as I hurt for his grief. I could not tell if the painful constriction in my chest was sorrow or happiness, but I rested my head against his shoulder and did not try to decide.

As the white sky dimmed to lavender in the twilight, a soft cold touch on my face startled me into looking up. It was snowing. Within moments we stood in the midst of a silent, swift, insubstantial storm. The snow muffled the stillness further, and the landscape vanished gently into eerie white shadows that shone with the glow of dusk.

Herron, too, tipped his head back, letting snowflakes settle on his hair and eyelashes, starring their darkness. His face had relaxed and he looked young, peaceful. I felt a swell of triumph that I had brought this to him.

"Herron," I said, taking a childish pleasure in saying his name, "why did you come to me last night?"

He closed his eyes to the snow. There was time for me to hope a dozen things, or the same thing a dozen times.

"Because I knew I could trust you," he said at last.

"Trust me? How do you mean?" For a brief, terrible moment I doubted him.

"I knew I could trust your silence, confide in you. You won't tell anyone what I know—that Claude killed my father."

I stared at him, but he still stood with his face tipped up to the falling snow as if receiving benediction. His words hung frozen in the air, like smoke.

"No," I said quietly. "I won't tell."

My mind emptied itself of all hopes, all feelings or questions. This was too great, too much. There was no sound at all.

As if he felt my gaze he opened his eyes and drew me closer. Under the light, insistent fingertips of the snow we took warmth from each other's lips, and at our feet the mortal shell of his father slept on.

* * *

There were guests for dinner, so we were a large party when we adjourned to the drawing room after the men had finished their port. The duchess, of course, had a group gathered around her near the fire, and Felicity, at the pianoforte, had not one but two young men to turn pages for her. The duchess beckoned to Herron when she saw him come in. He still wore his mourning band, but his mother had evidently decided to overlook it since he was wearing the conventional evening dress.

"Herron, dear, come and sit by me." She patted the place beside her on the divan and smiled welcomingly.

He stopped short, then half bowed. "Thank you, but I believe I see a place more inviting." He dropped onto the rug beside the chair I had chosen, half in shadow, and I saw a look of surprise and disappointment on the duchess's face, quickly suppressed. Lord Claude took the empty place she had offered, however, and soon the flaxen head and the tawny one were bent close together, shining silver and gold in the firelight. I could not see Herron's face, but his fingers drummed silently on the carpet.

"He takes that place very quickly," he muttered.

Even I could not help but think this unreasonable. "He is her husband," I ventured.

"He took that place very quickly as well," was the reply.

I fell silent. Herron stretched out at my feet, lounging on his elbows, and I watched his face as he watched the others. Felicity was playing a duet now with one of the young men, and the lively music and the warm light of the gas lamps seemed to create a cheerful sphere we two were excluded from. I had deliberately wished to separate myself, uncomfortable at the thought of abandoning my customary position of obscure observer to put myself in the middle of company, but having a companion in isolation was new to me. It was pleasant to feel that, although apart from the noisy revelry, I was no longer alone. Herron's desire to remain apart seemed to draw him closer to me.

The duchess, as always, was a gay, vivacious hostess. Her earrings bobbing in sympathy with her laughter, she drew the guests into a friendly circle of company. Her husband, no less engaging but less energetic, sometimes fell silent to watch her with a smile. It was almost impossible for me to believe of him what Herron had said. How could this composed, courteous, gentle man have deliberately murdered his own brother? I could not imagine that kindly, humorous face ever contorted in a murderous rage, could not see the hands that offered cigars to his friends gripping a knife or measuring poison into a glass. At this thought I bent toward Herron.

"I am afraid I know nothing of the circumstances of your father's death," I said. "Can you tell me what happened?"

"Of course, you wouldn't know; it was all too suspicious. My mother hushed it up so that the newspapers wouldn't raise a scandal." He was watching his stepfather with a level intensity. "The two of them went hunting. There was no one else, no hunting party—there had been a great deal of rain. Just my father and *him*."

"Charles was not back from the Crimea, then?"

"He had just returned. He was still practically an invalid, and kept to the house."

"And you do not hunt?"

"Not a great deal, no. I was riding in a different part of the grounds. I could hear the guns sometimes."

I began to have an idea of what he was going to tell me, but I let him continue without interrupting again.

"It was nearly midday when I started back and heard the shouts. I rode toward them, and it was Claude"—he gave the name a vicious emphasis—"who met me. 'Go back to the house, Herron,' he said. As if I needed him to shield me. I could see past him to where my father lay. He was in a clearing, stretched out on the ground as if he were resting. I knew he was dead even then. There was blood everywhere; his eyes were…"

He sat up abruptly, folding his legs up. With his hands clasped around his knees he stared at his mother and stepfather, but I do not believe he saw them.

"He said my father's gun must have misfired, that he was some yards behind him and didn't see what happened. When he got to him it was too late. He found no heartbeat." His voice was matter-of-fact now, as if he were reciting racing odds. "My uncle went back to tell Mother, and sent two of the servants to help me with the—the body." That cost him some effort.

"And the gun?"

"I never saw it again. My uncle said he had it destroyed. I don't doubt it"—bitterly.

I reached out to touch his hand, so tightly gripping the other. "I'm sorry."

He nodded. Then, knowing I had to ask, "Why do you believe your uncle killed him? Could it not have been an accident, as he said?"

"An accident!" Several heads turned at this, and he lowered his voice. "Has ever an accident been so fortuitous, so beneficial as this has been to my uncle? Was he not the only one with my father in the woods, and wasn't he with him when I arrived? Did he not marry my mother before the flowers in the funeral wreaths had wilted? But there is another reason," he added, as I opened my mouth to speak. "It isn't mere suspicion on my part, or childish resentment of him for taking my father's place. No, I have another reason."

"What is it?"

At first I thought he was not going to reply. When he did at last speak, his voice was so low I had to bend to catch the words.

"The day of the funeral we were coming back from the church. It was foggy, difficult to see, but as we approached the house I could see a figure standing on the roof. It was as if he was waiting for me. In the fog I could just see him before he was gone, but—it was him. I'm certain of it."

All I could say was, "Did anyone else see him?"

He shook his head. "I don't think so. I was ahead of the others; I wanted to be apart from them. You understand?"

I nodded.

"I knew then that he had appeared to me for a reason, and that it could only be because he had died unnaturally. It can only have been my uncle. He killed my father." His voice trembled with intensity.

Troubled, I looked again at the group by the fire. I tried to visualize Lord Claude approaching his own brother with a gun. Aiming it coolly, pulling the trigger, taking a moment to ascertain that the bullet had done its work; then shouting out in pretended shock and alarm. Now, as he sat so relaxed at his wife's side, smiling at some witticism, was he playing a part? Was every expression calculated to disguise what he really felt? The thought made me hunch my shoulders in sudden chill. I could not bear to think that this man who, on such short acquaintance, had already won my respect and affection, could be so cruelly deceptive.

But still less could I bear to consider the alternative. If Lord Claude was innocent, then Herron...

"Have you seen the figure since then?" I asked.

"No, not once. I still believe he wants to contact me, to tell me what really happened, but I've not seen one sign of him during all those nights I've spent waiting." He rubbed at his temples, and a painful stab of sympathy pierced me. "Sometimes I just stand there where he stood the day I saw him and think how easy it would be to let myself fall. All I would have to do is lean forward a little—just a little—as if I were walking into a wind. Then it would all be over."

I searched his face, hoping he was exaggerating, but could find no trace of levity in his expression. I wanted to protest, but somehow I knew that to try to badger him out of the idea would only make him reluctant to confide in me again. I had to content myself with asking, "What would be the good of that?"

He turned to face me, and I was shocked anew at the simple, blank misery in his eyes. His resentment against his uncle seemed to have been forgotten for the moment, and he looked at me with the uncomprehending pain of a child. "All the good in the world," he said quietly. "Can you think of any better way to end all the mad unholy wretchedness of it all? To hover for a moment, pillowed on sheer air like a falcon, then to just—not be? You can't imagine how many times I've thought of it. To just slip gently off to sleep..."

"To sleep," I echoed, beguiled in spite of myself. I could imagine it, could feel what it would be like, arced briefly in the air, then gently overtaken by oblivion. Had my mother felt that curious comfort as she lay buoyed by the sea, letting the waters lap at her fingertips? Did she feel soothed as the waves closed over her face, as softly as a nursemaid pulling a coverlet over her?

"...instead of being forced to watch that Cain slither his way into my father's place." Herron's voice startled me; it had turned bitter again, with the note I disliked. But his resentment was less frightening than his strange fascination with following his father.

"Why do you stay, then?" I asked, although the thought of his leaving opened a gulf of emptiness in me. "You could go back to Oxford, couldn't you?"

He shrugged, and the gesture was a surrender. He looked as weary as a man three times his age, as if his spirit were broken. "I can't leave. I can't let myself lose a chance to see him again, no matter how small. I know I'm probably a fool to continue to hope, but I can't stop looking for him, waiting for him to come back. One of these nights he'll return, and I must be here when he does."

I thought of him keeping that dark vigil on all the nights since his father was buried, and I no longer wondered that he longed for the oblivion of sleep, even eternal sleep. Weariness was probably coloring his emotions; Charles had been right when he expressed concern over his stepbrother's health.

"You must be very tired," I said.

"I haven't slept much since he died," he said simply, and I reached out to touch his cheek, unable to speak. For a moment he held my hand against his face, pressing his lips to my palm. Involuntarily I glanced up to see if anyone had noticed. No one was watching us, but Charles was just looking away.

"I must go," said Herron, getting swiftly to his feet. "It's getting late. You understand."

I nodded, and he left without so much as a glance at the others. His parents looked up as the door closed behind him, and I hid my hand in my skirt, feeling his kiss still imprinted on my skin.

That night I lay awake for a long while, listening to Herron's footsteps drumming over my head. In a strange way it was comforting to know he was so near. But I could not relax; whenever the steps slowed, my body tensed, waiting for them to resume. I was seized with the fear that he might succumb to the desire he had spoken of. When at last I heard him descend the stair at the end of the hall, I sighed and slept.

CHAPTER EIGHT

"You spend so much time by the shore," Felicity said one day at tea. "Anyone would think you were waiting for a ship to come into harbor. What can you find that's so fascinating there?"

"It's very refreshing to walk on the beach. It clears my mind."

Felicity made a face. "I would much rather clear my mind with a cup of cocoa next to a warm fire. Wouldn't you, Zeus?" and she leaned down to feed a morsel of toast to the spaniel, who thumped his tail agreeably.

I could see her point of view. Indeed, sometimes the raw December wind, flinging the salt spray into my eyes, would drive me back indoors to toast my feet by the fire. But on most days when the weather was at all bearable I would make time for a walk by the sea. I had much to think about.

Herron's confidences, not unnaturally, had disturbed me profoundly, and I needed time to think through all that he had told me. I also needed time alone; although I was more strongly drawn to him than ever before, I found that when I was with him it was more difficult to think clearly. Those long walks along the shore, which to Felicity represented soaked hems and windblown hair, afforded vital time for contemplation, for adjusting my mind to all the astonishing and unpleasant ideas Herron had introduced into it.

That his uncle was a murderer I could not believe, but the thought was a grain of sand lodged in my mind: a tiny enough presence, but a constant irritant. Equally disturbing was the idea that Herron's ideas were rooted in some distemper of his mind. He did not seem to be mad—the very word was repellent, nauseating—but if he was not, if there was truth to his suspicions, then I was living in the presence of something more awful than anything in my former life had prepared me for.

Despite this, I could not deny my attraction to the man himself. Even though he carried darkness with him, with his anger and pain and distrust, there was yet a brightness banked within him that flashed out in rare moments. I may have been the only one to see it. His family, for all their love for him, could only see the way he had fallen off and become someone apart, a morose reminder of events they would choose to leave behind. But I saw something golden, and for its sake I could not choose but ally myself with him.

Sometimes when I went to the shore I found him there, and we would walk together in silence or sit on the rocks girdling the bay. "I believe I'll start calling you Ondine," he said one day when he came upon me. "You look so much at home here, stationed on your rock, as if you'll slip back down into the sea when I turn my eyes the other way. You seem to belong to the sea."

For some reason the fancy pleased me. No one had ever likened me to as ethereal a creature as a water nymph. At all events, Ondine was much more to my taste as a nickname than Mouse.

He still spent much of his time alone, on long solitary rides or walks. He did begin taking dinner regularly with the rest of us, though, and I know it reassured his anxious parents, even though he spoke little and pointedly sat beside me instead of at his mother's right hand. If he did not disappear altogether afterward he would find me, where I sat apart from the company, and lounge at my feet, staring into the fire. He watched his uncle sometimes, and always with the same level stare of hatred. It was unnerving to see and must have been even worse for Lord Claude. But the duchess, oblivious to subtleties of atmosphere, found his relatively gregarious behavior encouraging.

"I believe you're good for Herron, child," she told me. "He isn't as aloof and shy of company as he was before you came. He must find your company soothing."

"I'm glad," I said; it was all I could say. She looked at me keenly, and I wondered with some uneasiness if she was going to reprove me for being too free of my company. We had scarcely been discreet.

"Does he confide in you?"

I hesitated. "He speaks a great deal of his father, of course."

"Of course... and nothing else?" When I looked at her without speaking, she had the grace to blush. She gave a little laugh, embarrassed and rueful. "I know I'm prying, my dear. But when my own son will hardly bid me good day, I must rely on others to tell me of him. I have worried a great deal about him, and I would so like to know what is in his mind—unless you feel you should keep his counsel."

"He is still very distraught," I said carefully. As much as I could understand the duchess's hunger for news of her son, I felt uncomfortable divulging what he had told me privately. "But I believe it helps him to speak of his grief. He has said as much."

She let out a long breath. "Good. If he cannot confide in me—and, like any mother, I am selfish enough to wish he could—then I am glad he has found someone he can trust in you." She reached out to squeeze my hand and gave me a painful little smile. "I am glad to know that you will look after him, since he will not let me do so. I need not be so anxious about him."

I was anxious, though.

His vigils continued. Some nights he would come to my room when he gave up pacing the leads; I might wake to feel his body beside me, one arm thrown negligently over my waist as he slept. On other nights he would shake me out of sleep to huddle by the fire and talk, long into the night. If either of us thought of the dangerous impropriety of this, we quashed the idea. For me and, I believe, for him, our time together was as much a necessity as food and water.

He would lie on the hearth rug with his head in my lap and talk of his father as he remembered him, so that I came to have an image of a mighty, splendid man, majestic in his dignity and strength and wisdom; a massive, bearded Jove who watched over his wife with silent adoration and guided his son with calm sagacity. If sometimes this figure seemed too splendid to be an accurate depiction, I did not wonder at it: I had seen grief work this way on my father, removing all the imperfections of the dead. It seemed to be enough for Herron that I listened, so listen I did, running my fingers through his dark hair and gazing down at his face with its endlessly captivating contradiction of fierce brows and tender mouth.

Sometimes I spoke of Lionel. When I did it was with a stumbling and awkward tongue, since I found it difficult to put into words the way I missed that maddening, reckless, big-hearted boy. It was easier to sit in silence with Herron, whose dark velvet eyes seemed already to know all the sorrow I could not put into words.

At times his grief was quiet, and he could speak of his father calmly, subdued in his pain; at others it seemed to strike him anew like a lash, and under the scourge of it he would rage in futile protest against his father's death. In those moods he would press me to him with a kind of desperation and kiss me as deeply as if he were trying to drink in my soul. Even though I felt I was helping him, the dread never left me that one night he would cease to resist whatever was compelling him toward oblivion, and when he broached the subject I always felt a wrench of fear.

"It would be a sin to kill yourself," I pleaded one evening, a handful of days after he had told me of his suspicions of his uncle.

"Would it? Why should it be a sin to end a useless existence?" His back was toward me as he stood at my study window, staring out into the darkness. He had been waiting there for me when I returned from the drawing room after dinner. He must have only just lit the fire, since it had not taken the chill out of the room; I wrapped myself in a shawl and held my hands out to the flames. The snow had turned to rain, which fell hissing into the fire.

"It isn't useless; it only seems so because of your grief. I know what it feels like—"

"How could you know? You've never lost a father."

This silenced me. I had indeed lost my father, but not the kind of father Herron had known, or in any way he could understand. "Perhaps you are right," I said after a moment. "I only meant to say that I know how the loss of someone you love can make you feel as if your own life is futile and empty, as if there isn't any purpose in continuing to exist. It's only an illusion, but it feels like truth."

He turned swiftly to come to my side. "My sweet Ondine, forgive me. I was forgetting about your brother. Yes, of course you've known pain too." For a moment he held me and stroked my hair, and I hoped the subject I dreaded was lost for a time. But then he put me away from him so that he could look into my face. "Can you not then understand why I feel as I do? Why I can't imagine any point to dragging myself through the days, unless it is to kill him?"

A cold torrent seemed to flow over me. "You wouldn't do that."

"I think of it all the time."

"Herron, that isn't at all the same thing. Do you honestly feel yourself capable of killing another person? Much less your own uncle?"

He dropped his head into his hands and rubbed at his temples. "I don't know," he groaned. "I truly don't. Sometimes I'm afraid I'm a coward after all, and that I will never nerve myself to do it. I might as well destroy myself if I can't even summon the courage to execute my father's murderer."

"But if you kill your uncle you will be no better than what you think him to be. A murderer." I flung the word at him, hoping its ugliness would wake him to the enormity of his intentions.

"I would have justice on my side. It would be a fair requital—a life for a life."

"You don't even know that he really did what you believe of him."

He set his jaw. "I'm certain in my own heart."

"That's not proof."

"It is proof enough for me."

I seized him by the shoulders and actually shook him, trying to dislodge that faraway gaze that, together with his words, so unnerved me. "You can't convict a man on your heart's prompting. And even if you had proof of his guilt, don't you realize it isn't your obligation, or even your place, to try to exact justice from him? Can't you leave that to—to a higher court?"

I did not know whether I meant legal or spiritual justice, but Herron did not even seem to consider the former worth thought. He met my eyes with a bitter directness unlike his former abstraction.

"What justice can I believe in?" he said fiercely. "Would you have me put my faith and trust in a God who didn't intervene when my father was killed? Why should I believe there is any benevolent will behind such an act?"

My philosophers failed me; I had no answer for that. Feebly I said, "Perhaps there wasn't."

"Then why should it be a sin to turn my back on a world that's been left to chaos?" he demanded in triumph. "There can be no sin where there is no deity to sin against. And if there is a God, He can only be my enemy now. Why should I then hesitate to enact the justice that He fails to administer, or to end my own life if I feel it has no further purpose?"

I was out of my depth. I had not the means to sustain an argument on these grounds, when Herron had evidently thought deeply and intensely on the matter. I cast about for some weapon to use against his determination. "If you don't fear being damned for destroying yourself, then do you not have the least fear of death itself? Doesn't that give you pause?"

He gestured to the books that lay open on my desk. "Socrates tells us that it is foolish to fear death when we don't even know what it is."

I choked back the urge to damn and blast Socrates. "It would seem equally foolish to rush into the unknown. You can't be certain that the next world would be any better than this one." He was silent, and I pressed my advantage. "You talk of oblivion, and sleep—but in that sleep there is no waking, and what sort of dreams might haunt you? Imagine, Herron—you could be trapped with your nightmares for eternity." I knew he suffered from violent nightmares; he had wakened me with them more than once. "Instead of escaping from your afflictions, you might be rushing to meet new ones."

Still he said nothing, and he seemed to consider. I realized I was holding my breath as I waited for him to answer. The very calm with which he could weigh his own life came near to breaking me, and I put out my hands to him, pleading now, all policy forgotten. In that moment I lost sight of his suffering and even his salvation and remembered only my own fear.

"Don't leave me," I said.

Born of selfishness though it was, it was a plea more effective than all the reason and persuasion I had mustered up to that moment. In an instant he had drawn me to him and held me as tightly as if he were clinging to a precipice. Words tumbled from him, assurances, protestations, promises, and I drank them in greedily. There was something desperate in the way we clung to one another, but that may have been part of its sweetness. For now at least I was sure of him and was comforted.

* * *

But the comfort did not remain long. All too soon the fear of losing him—to his obsession, if not to the grave—returned to haunt me anew. I had to speak to someone; someone who would take my worries more seriously than had the duchess. I remembered when Charles had compared Herron to Werther. Had he really feared that Herron, like Goethe's melancholic, would kill himself? The next morning I seized on Charles as he made his way to the room that had been fitted up as his laboratory.

"I have not yet had a tour of the house, and you are going to remedy that," I informed him. "That is, unless you find your pet skeleton a more attractive companion." This new study aid had arrived that week, and Charles had assembled it in the drawing room to the accompaniment of much squealing from Felicity.

"No, indeed," he said, with an emphasis that surprised me, and I think, even himself, since he looked a bit embarrassed. Or perhaps he was startled by my directness; I rarely spoke so assertively. "I'll be happy to serve as cicerone, but my father would be far more informative."

"Oh, I don't know," I said vaguely. "He is so busy."

"Not too busy to join us for a quarter of an hour; he would be glad of such a diversion, I'm sure. I'll fetch him."

This was not at all what I wanted. "I wouldn't dream of troubling him," I said firmly, and took his arm. "His work is too important. Is there a portrait gallery? Shall we start there?"

"You may want a shawl," he said, capitulating. "The fire won't be lit."

The long gallery where the family portraits were displayed was also, Charles told me, where balls were held; now it was an immense emptiness that echoed as I entered. A gleaming expanse of floor, interrupted by carpets in soft shades of moss green and gold, reflected the drab light that entered through the long windows ranging down the length of the room. It was a grey, lowering day, and the sun that filtered through the lace curtains was cool and pale. The unlit chandeliers gleamed dimly, their crystals trembling at our footsteps like rain, and I was struck with the notion that this must be what the ocean floor was like: a vast shadowed place of stillness, with cloudy half-light swimming through the dimness in fitful gleams. Then Charles lit the gas wall brackets, and their bright matter-of-fact glow dispelled the mystery.

"It's quite a spectacle when the carpets are rolled up and the chandeliers lit," he said. "My aunt will be giving a ball soon, and then you'll be able to see for yourself. Ah, here's a portrait of the family from several years ago. Guess who the dashing young fellow in spats is?"

"You look very young," I said, assessing the painting. "Not more than eight or nine years older than Herron."

He grimaced. "Six, in fact."

Oh. "I'm sorry."

"There's no need to apologize. I don't recommend Sevastopol as a health cure."

Belatedly I remembered his record in the Crimea. I had thought him over thirty, but he must be no more than twenty-seven. It was certainly no wonder he looked older than his age after all he had been through. Yet his experiences had not hardened him; he looked mature, but not haggard, as were some men I had seen returned from the battlefields.

In the portrait he looked several years younger and a decade less experienced; he had not yet grown his moustache, and he lounged next to his sisters, who wore matching white dresses. On Aminta's other side stood Viscount Montrose, her husband, and a nursemaid with a small child who must have been Freddy. Viscount Montrose inclined toward gangliness, and was already losing his hair although he could have been no more than thirty-five; but, although he was no beauty, I decided I liked his face. Lord Claude stood a little apart from his offspring, halfway between them and the group on the sofa: the duke, the duchess, and Herron. His position was strangely solitary, as if he belonged with neither group.

The duke was very much as I had envisioned him from Herron's description: a barrel-chested man with a Roman nose and a great beard flowing over his chest. He sat stiffly, formally, one hand holding his wife's, his face half turned toward her as if even for the portrait he could not take his eyes from her. They seemed to be kind eyes, but there was a sternness to them that, together with the rigid austerity of his posture, made me wonder if during his life the duchess had been quite the carefree lady I knew now. In the portrait she smiled graciously, but without the merriment I associated with her. She actually appeared slightly older than she did in reality, although this may have been due in part to her gown, which was a severe, albeit elegant, evening dress of dark brocade. Instead of aging her, her husband's death seemed to have renewed her youth, as Miss Yates had suggested.

Herron, who must have been no more than seventeen, perched on the arm of the sofa, at the far end of the group. The portraitist had not flattered him: his intent dark gaze had a fixed appearance, and his mouth wore a sulky droop. Perhaps he had been chafing over having to sit still for long hours in his best suit.

Charles, too, was gazing at the portrait intently. "What do you think?" he asked at length.

"It's a handsome family. Was the duke as majestic as he looks?"

"Oh, yes. He had a magnificent deep voice and seemed to tower over everybody else in the room. When I was a boy I imagined that God must look exactly like him."

"He sounds like a man it would be easy to respect," I said, and left the last part of the thought unspoken. Charles seemed to sense it, however.

"And not so easy to love, you mean? Perhaps. I certainly went in fear of him until I was almost twenty. One look from those eyes could reduce me to the condition of a gibbering schoolboy caught stealing from the jam cupboard. But he was a deeply fair man, and very wise, and he loved his family a great deal even if he wasn't as much of a—well, a companion as my father."

"Did the duchess feel the same?"

He turned to me, arching one eyebrow with half a smile. "I had no idea gossip was so much to your taste."

"In general it isn't," I said, and at his skeptical look I laughed guiltily. "Very well, believe me or not as you please. But since it seems I'm to consider this family my own, I would like to know more about it. It seems to have had an eventful history—recently, at least."

"That's certain. Very well, I shall tell you what I know. But only because you badgered me without mercy."

He led me to another portrait, an older one, in which the former duke and duchess stood together in what I recognized to be the drawing room. It must have been their wedding portrait: the duchess, slightly plumper and smiling all over her cherubic face, was wearing an extraordinary gown of white silk whose train was painted with a design of flowers and ribbons. One gloved hand was tucked in the duke's arm, and she turned her face up to his. In the magnificent gown and heavy jeweled coronet she looked like a child dressing up in her mother's finery. The duke likewise wore the full regalia of his rank, but on him it seemed appropriate, and it lent him an almost military appearance that accorded with the formality of his posture. He looked very much as he had in the other portrait. I wondered how old he had been at the time of the wedding, and asked Charles.

"He was forty-three. My aunt was only seventeen—the same age Felicity is now, and, so I understand, much the same in temperament. She loved to dance and sing and attend parties and was always happiest in the midst of a group of young people. I believe there was some surprise when she married the duke: certainly it was an excellent match, and she became a gracious duchess, but I think she must have given up a great deal." I was surprised at this burst of confidence, and Charles seemed to feel he had been disloyal, for he explained quickly: "There was the difference in age, of course, and being a duchess carries a tremendous responsibility with it, as I'm sure you've noticed: she would have had to leave her girlish concerns behind very abruptly and learn how to manage the duke's affairs and comport herself in an entirely new way."

This was a new line of thought; I had imagined that she had always been as gay and lively as now. "She must have found it a strain."

"I'm sure so, even though she loved him devotedly. Now that she and my father are married, she seems a great deal more at ease, and does not work so hard to be formal and grave."

"Your father is much closer to her in age, isn't he?"

"Yes; there is less than ten years between them. He married my mother when he was very young."

My mind went back to the family portrait, where Lord Claude seemed to be set apart from the rest of his relatives. I asked Charles about this, and he hesitated.

"I think," he said slowly, "that he may have been falling in love with Aunt Gwendolyn at that time." He gave me a sheepish look. "That's pure speculation, and I probably shouldn't say it."

I hastened to assure him of my secrecy, and urged him to continue.

"You do draw a man out, cousin! I have the feeling that few can keep their secrets around you." Then he sobered. "But I do remember a change in the atmosphere dating from around that year—a difference in the way my father got along with the two of them."

"He and the duke quarreled?"

"Oh no, nothing so definite; at any rate, they were always close. That wasn't what changed." He seemed to be choosing his words with care, or trying to cast his mind back to that time. "Rather, it was a kind of diffidence on Father's part, a drawing back. I suppose he must have been trying to conquer his feelings, or to conceal them from Aunt Gwendolyn."

Or from the duke, I thought. But no doubt it was the instinct of a gentleman to try to remove himself from such a situation; no wonder he looked so uncomfortable, in such close proximity to the woman forbidden him. "It must have been difficult for him," I said with genuine sympathy. "I'm glad he found his happiness, even though he had to wait for it."

"Yes, he's happier than I've seen him in years—my aunt too, I must say. They are well matched in temperament; he is nearly as fond of fetes and entertainments as she." He grinned. "I expect this house party will be a very lively one indeed."

"No doubt," I said, although I did not care either way; I did not plan on taking part in the activities, so they held no interest for me. Nevertheless, the subject provided an opportunity for me to bring up the matter pressing upon me. "Do you suppose it will improve Herron's spirits?"

After a moment's silence, during which I kept my eyes on the portrait in affected nonchalance, Charles said, "I doubt it. I expect it will take more than whist and tableaus to bring him back to us."

It was no use pretending to be unconcerned; I turned my back on the portrait and faced Charles. He met my eyes gravely. "I feel the same way," I said. "Charles, you said once that he—you mentioned him in connection with Werther. Do you really think...?" I hoped he would cut me off, but he waited for me to finish the thought. To say the worst. "Do you think he might destroy himself?"

He did not answer at once. Looking past me at the painting, he raked his fingers through his hair. It was a habit of his when he was thinking deeply; I had seen him do this when he played chess with his father. "I certainly hope not," he said at last. "Why do you ask? Has he spoken of it?"

"Yes—more than once. Often."

He did not ask me when, and for that I was glad. "Does the duchess know of it?"

"I told her some time ago, but she seemed to think it was empty talk, a demand for attention."

"But you believe it to be more serious." It was not a question, but I nodded. "Well, you're probably right to fear for him," he said, looking at me with uncharacteristic solemnity. "He is certainly very troubled, however much his mother may wish to deny it."

For some reason I found it comforting that, instead of trying to dismiss or explain away my fears, he took them seriously. I felt I had an ally, someone to help me try to hold Herron back from the abyss. "What can we do?" I asked. "We cannot allow him to—to harm himself."

"If he is truly determined, there is little we can do." Then, seeing by my face that he may have been too blunt, he added, "But I'm probably being pessimistic. If he had wanted to end his life, he has had plenty of opportunity before now."

"That is true," I said, and in spite of myself my spirits rose. Charles must have heard hope in my voice, for he half smiled. "Perhaps the threat isn't so great as I feared. It may be that his fascination with death is after all an abstract interest, not a personal one, and he'll leave it behind in time. I've heard of such things. I was too quick to take alarm; he may only be speaking hypothetically."

"Perhaps," he said, but there was doubt in the word, and he was frowning again. "If we knew what the cause of his despondency was, we would have a better idea of how to help him. I only wish I knew what was in his mind." He shook his head, hard, as if to dislodge unpleasant thoughts. "We aren't as close now as we once were, and I regret that; I would have liked to think he could talk to me about what's troubling him. I can't help suspecting it's more than his father's death. But you may have some idea of the cause," he added suddenly, taking me by surprise: "He seems to find it easier to speak freely to you than to the rest of us."

His forthright blue gaze made me drop my eyes; I could not tell him that his own father was a murderer in Herron's mind.

Might that be the key to his rescue, though? If I could prove to him that his suspicions were unfounded, he might be freed from his misery. The thought restored me somewhat. It might be an impossible plan, but it was better to have something to do, some way to feel I was helping him, than to be forced to stand by and watch him wrestle with his demon alone. And surely there would be some way to convince him of his error, and then—then he would come back to us.

"He does seem to find that he can speak of his thoughts to me," I said, evading his question. "It may be that he will wear out his fascination by talking about it, and he will not feel the need to act on it."

"Let us hope so. In any case, having a confidante can only help him." He paused, and his voice was gentle when he said, in unconscious echo of the duchess, "You are very good for him."

I didn't know what to say to this any more now than I had then. "I hope so. I try to be."

Charles was the first to look away. His fingers tightened on his cane as he shifted his weight, and belatedly I realized that so long a period of standing must be exhausting for him in his condition. But he did not speak of his discomfort. "I hope Herron realizes how much he would be throwing away, should he act on his threat," he said instead. "He has one thing at least that's well worth living for."

"Oh? What is that?"

"Your love."

It was the first time a name had been put to my feeling for Herron, but I accepted it. Charles had recognized it before I had.

There seemed to be no reason to reply, and after a moment he offered me his arm. I took it, and we resumed our tour of the house.

CHAPTER NINE

The next day was unusually fine, and I was glad of this since I was to go with the duchess, Felicity and Miss Yates to take Christmas gifts around to the tenants. By mid-morning, under a pale winter sun, the carriage was drawn up to the door for us.

With our voluminous skirts and the crinolines worn by the duchess and Miss Yates, it was a surprise to me that we were all able to fit inside; indeed, the seat cushions were quickly submerged in a sea of tartan, since all of us wore dresses in that fashionable fabric, popularized by Her Majesty herself. When the hampers of food and the other bundles we were taking with us had been loaded, the carriage groaned on its springs. Lord Claude, seeing us off, laughed at us and said we looked like a gypsy caravan.

This was the first time I had visited any of the tenants' cottages, and I was favorably impressed by them: clean, well-ventilated, and spacious, they offered more comfortable conditions than much of the housing I had seen in London. Several had new roofs. "That's Lord Reginald's doing, miss," explained one woman. “In the last few weeks we’ve seen a lot of changes for the good.”

“Oh? The late duke did not maintain the cottages as well?”

We were gathered in the kitchen of the cottage, the hub of all household activity now that winter had come. Across the room, Felicity had warmed the soup we had brought and was feeding it to the youngest child, who lay coughing on a cot. The duchess and Miss Yates had discreetly tucked some new blankets around her and now helped to cajole the little girl into taking more soup.

“His Grace the duke was good to us, miss, don’t go mistaking me; but ’e didn’t take what you’d call an interest, like. If the ’ouse was in one piece, you’d not see him from one end of the month t’other. Lord Reginald, now”—my hostess beamed—“’e’s a lovely gentleman, miss. ’E’ll ask after me husband’s rheumatism and me vegetable garden. And ’e says we’re to have a new room built come spring.”

“How nice.” Such extensive refurbishing must be expensive. But it was obvious that the tenants were well pleased with their new landlord. I wanted to ask her more about her impressions of Lord Claude, but Felicity joined us then.

“Mrs. Downing, has the doctor been by to see Tilda? That’s a nasty cough she has.”

Mrs. Downing assured her that Lord Reginald had sent the doctor around just the day before, and he had declared her to be in no danger. I was impressed by this further evidence of Lord Claude’s attentiveness to his tenants. Whatever had been the cause of the old duke’s death, a great many people seemed to have benefited from it. Everywhere we went we saw and heard testimony to Lord Claude’s generosity. The gifts of food, wool, leather and candles we brought were almost incidental. Nevertheless, it was a new experience for me to take part in such gift-giving, and I enjoyed the chance to spend a morning as Lady Bountiful—or as one of her handmaidens.

“There!” exclaimed the duchess some hours later, relaxing against the coach’s cushions with a sigh. “I believe that’s everyone. I won’t be able to eat anything for the rest of the day, after having had so much bread and cheese and cider.” Most of the cottagers we had visited had pressed us to stay and eat a bite before continuing on our way, and the duchess had not wanted to disappoint any of them by refusing. Consequently we were all feeling a bit breathless, and I saw Miss Yates tug discreetly at her stays.

"I think a walk would do me good after eating so much," said Felicity. "I had intended to stop in the village in any case. Would you like to join me, cousin? I only need to make a few purchases, and then we can walk back to Ellsmere. It isn't far."

I acceded readily, and the coach pulled to a stop to let us off at the top of the village's main street. Felicity and I spent a contented half hour sorting through ribbons and other trifles in the shop; she laughed at my delight in the assortment of pretty things. "You must not have done much shopping before, cousin, if our little village store dazzles you so," she commented.

"Not much," I agreed.

She chattered blithely as we walked back to the house, telling me more about the families we had visited, exclaiming over the charm and comeliness of the children. Her knowledge of their lives impressed me: she knew just whose son had broken his wrist falling out of a tree, whose daughter had gone into service. I was beginning to realize that Felicity was not as flighty as she sometimes seemed.

"You seem to know them as well as your own family," I commented after one anecdote.

"Well, they practically are family, after all. A very extended family."

I unfastened my pelisse as the exercise warmed me. She was setting a brisk pace, careless of scuffing her boots or getting grass stains on her pantalettes, and in this too I was surprised. "Felicity, while we are on the subject of family, I was wondering..."

"Yes?"

"How did your father and Herron get along before the duke died?"

She didn't even have to reflect. "Famously."

"Truly?" I said, taken aback. "I was under the impression that Herron's father—?"

"Oh, Herron always worshipped his father, but I think he was a little awed by him too." Nimbly, she sidestepped a puddle. "Now, nobody could be afraid of Papa."

I turned this over. "So Herron was actually closer to his uncle than to his father?"

For the first time she hesitated. "I don't know that I'd say that, exactly. But with the duke Herron was always on his best behavior. We all were! I think Herron found it much less of a strain around Papa. They used to go to the theater together and 'take off' the performances later for me and Aminta and Aunt Gwendolyn. But he couldn't be silly like that with his own father." She darted a sideways glance at me. "It's only since the duke's death that Herron's taken such a dislike to Papa, if that is what you were wondering."

"It was," I admitted.

She gave a brisk nod. "If you ask me, Herron is feeling guilty. I expect he mourns his father so elaborately because, for all that he admired him so much in life, he had more in common with Papa—and he can't forgive himself for it."

This was so perceptive, and from so unexpected a source, that it halted me in my tracks. "However did you come to think of that?"

She laughed, unimpressed. "Oh, one gets to know one's own family. Hurry up, or we'll be late for lunch."

"Just one more question," I said, catching her arm. "Did the duke resent his son's closeness to Lord Claude?"

"Was he jealous, do you mean? Heavens, no. How could the sun be jealous?"

* * *

That evening I decided it was time to confront Lord Claude.

I knew that he liked to retreat to his study before retiring; from the library, which adjoined his study, I could sometimes hear him in conversation with Charles or chuckling over something he was reading. The connecting door usually remained closed, as it was now—he chose to enter his study by one of the other doors rather than risk disturbing me—and I stood before it for a long moment before I could bring myself to knock.

I was not even certain he was there, and even less certain that I should be approaching him. What I had in mind was uncomfortably like a betrayal of Herron's trust. But if I was to save him from his own suspicion I had to be able to offer some proof of his uncle's innocence, and the only way I knew how to do that was to test him—by using Herron's own evidence.

True, Herron had put his trust in me, had spoken freely with the understanding that his words would go no further. I could only pray that I would not destroy his faith in me by what I was about to do. But this was no war, I told myself; allying myself with Herron did not mean that I was in enmity with the rest of his family. Regardless of what he felt toward them, I could keep their interests in mind as well as Herron's. And perhaps by speaking now I could do something toward helping both parties.

This was no time to argue the whole matter over again to myself, though. Before my resolve could weaken further I knocked. For a moment there was no answer, and I had time to wonder if all my rationalizing had gone for naught, but then Lord Claude's voice bade me come in.

He was standing by the French doors, smoking; the sweet, fragrant smoke was heavy in the room. When he saw who I was he reached for an ash tray and made as if to knock the tobacco out of his pipe.

"Please, don't trouble yourself," I hastened to say. "I do not mind if you smoke. If I'm not disturbing you, I would like to speak with you about something."

"Of course, my dear. You're not disturbing me at all. Will you have a seat?" He indicated one of the leather-covered wing chairs by the fire. I was glad he did not want to hold our conversation across his desk, as he had once before; the formality would have made my undertaking all the more difficult.

He settled into the chair across from mine and regarded me benevolently. He wore a smoking jacked of mustard-colored velvet faced in red and consequently looked a great deal more dapper than in his usual drab suits. But his face showed signs of strain: I thought there were lines of anxiety now as well as laughter. When he spoke, though, the impression vanished, and I wondered if I had imagined it.

"Now, what can I do for you?" he inquired with a smile. "Do you need an increase in your dress allowance to see you through Christmas?"

"No, indeed; I have more than enough, thank you, sir. You've been most generous."

He waved his pipe deprecatingly. "Nonsense, my dear. What can I do for you, then, if it isn't money you need? Have you found a new edition of Virgil you'd like me to order for the library?"

"It isn't a matter of something I need, sir, but of something that's been troubling me. Someone, to be precise." This time he did not make a guess, and I continued. "I have come to be greatly concerned about His Grace." The title sounded foolish. "Herron," I amended.

His expression had sobered. "I see," he said slowly, tapping his pipe stem against his teeth without seeming to be aware of it. "I see. Anything particular that is concerning you?"

Now that it came to the point I found myself torn. It was not a betrayal, I reminded myself sternly; it was for Herron's own good—for the good of all of us. "You know, I am sure, that he still finds it difficult to accept his father's death." A single nod confirmed this. "And a part of his unhappiness is that of any son who has lost a parent. But there is more than that. Something particular is eating away at him."

At that, he leaned toward me, hands braced on his knees. "My dear, this is exactly what all of us have sensed—have feared," he exclaimed. "Do you know what it is?"

"Yes." I took a deep breath, hating myself. "He has told me that on the day of the funeral, upon returning to Ellsmere, he saw his father's ghost. He took the visitation to mean that his father died unhappily—that his spirit is not at peace."

This was my gamble, my sole reason for breaking Herron's confidence: if his uncle showed fear at this news, I would know that Herron had been right. I watched him intently from under my lashes, alert for any word or gesture that would betray his guilt.

But none came. With a long sigh, Lord Claude sat back in his chair, his eyes reflecting not dread of discovery or fear of retribution, but sorrow. Wonder was there as well, a tired unhappy amazement at the extent of his stepson's distress.

"How very tragic," he said at last. Not, I noted, "Did the ghost accuse anyone?" He was not thinking of himself. "And he truly believes in this spirit he thinks he saw?"

"Completely. He lives in hope of seeing it again and confronting it. He's certain his father was murdered, and believes the ghost will name the murderer." Again I watched him.

And again he passed the test. He shook his head gently, his brow furrowed. "Good God," he said softly. "I had not realized.... I have read of such cases, when the bereaved are so unwilling to accept a death that they convince themselves they are visited by their dead. The poor lad. Is there anything we can do to help him?"

"I wish I knew." This time I spoke without calculation, from my heart. "He seems beyond reason on that point. He has been keeping a vigil on the roof at night, where he believes he saw the spirit, and nothing I can say will sway him. Not a night passes but he is there, waiting." My voice cracked, and he reached out to cover my hands, which were plucking restlessly at my skirt, with his own.

"There, now. We'll find a way to bring the boy back to himself." The gentleness of his voice was comforting, and when I looked up our eyes met in shared grief. He squeezed my hand in sympathy. "It pains you to see him this way when you care about him, I know. It's the same for me, and for his mother. But if we love him enough, and are patient enough, we'll find a way to save him."

"I hope you're right, sir." He was watching me with concern, and I summoned up a smile to reassure him. Satisfied, he let go my hands and I groped for my handkerchief. "But he is not the only one I fear for."

His brows contracted. "He has not threatened to harm you?"

"Oh, no, nothing of the kind. Rather, he shows so much animosity towards you."

To my surprise he laughed at this. Rising, he went to his desk and retrieved his tobacco pouch. "I have observed it," he said calmly, cleaning out his pipe and proceeding to refill it, with as little concern as if we were speaking of the weather. "I find it perfectly understandable that he should be angry at me. To him, I have tried to replace his father, and I have had the further effrontery to take his mother's attention away just when he most wants company in his grief. I am sorry he resents me so—indeed, I greatly miss our former friendship—but I'm sure he'll recover from it in time."

"You are very fond of him, aren't you?"

His head was bent as he worked over his pipe, and I could not be sure of his expression. "He's like one of my own children."

There was silence as he finished refilling his pipe and lighting it, a lengthy process that seemed to involve a great deal of concentration. At last he had accomplished it to his satisfaction and returned to his chair, relaxing as he puffed at the pipe. We sat for a few minutes in a silence that was oddly companionable. As the smoke wreathed around his face, he regarded me through it with something like contentment, and I too was content to sit there in his company. Without speaking we seemed to be in sympathy, drawn closer together by our mutual concern, and the closeness itself as a comfort.

He may have felt it too, that sympathy, for when he spoke his voice held a kind of camaraderie or intimacy, as if there was some new understanding between us.

"It was kind of you to speak to me, my dear," he said. "I'm grateful, and moved, that you felt you could confide in me. You will, I hope, come to me in the future if you discover anything else about the boy—anything that I should know?"

I shifted uncomfortably. Again I felt overpoweringly torn in different directions: I wanted to believe in this sense of allegiance with Lord Claude, but my conscience was so uneasy.... Another confrontation like this might undo me. I wondered if I would ever feel free to come to him again about Herron.

My silence may have revealed something of my dilemma, for Lord Claude set his pipe aside and leaned forward again to look into my face. "You're a loyal little thing, aren't you?" he mused. "You've no wish to tattle on Herron, and you're already wondering if you've said too much. No, no, don't try to explain, my dear; I admire your fidelity to him. The last thing I want to do is to cause you any qualms of conscience." His voice was tender, and I felt myself being soothed out my agitation; almost, even, out of thought.

"You're the lad's true friend, and if you feel you'll help him more by keeping silent for him, I'll not try to dissuade you. But don't forget"—he gazed searchingly at me, his dark eyes earnest—"I'm the boy's friend, too. And I want to help him. You'll remember that, my dear?"

My mind spinning, I stood. I needed to get away from the spell of that quiet, lulling voice and think. "Thank you, sir. It was good of you to make time for me."

"Not at all." He rose to see me out, and at the door he took my hand again, this time in farewell. "Please don't hesitate to come to me whenever you need to talk. I assure you I will be glad to listen. And I thank you for your touching concern for me; it speaks of a womanly heart."

"You will be careful then, sir?"

The fine lines around his eyes crinkled in a smile. "I'll take the spirit, if not the letter, of your warning to heart. Have no fear for me; I shall take care not to goad the boy further if I can help it." He half bowed over my hand in a courtly way, then raised it to his lips. The kiss was the most delicate of touches. "Good night, child."

"Good night."

I had crossed the library before I looked back. He was not watching me, as I had half expected; he had vanished into his study, and the door had shut soundlessly. I stopped and took a few deep breaths before starting for my room. My thoughts were in more confusion than ever.

What a strange interview!

I had never before encountered such disturbing charm in a man. It was something I had never expected to find in Lord Claude, who was usually so self-effacing. It was as if he felt the division in this family, and had been wooing me over to his side.

At that, I shook my head angrily, trying to find different words to fit my impression. I was not being required to take sides in a battle or aid in a conspiracy, and I should be ashamed to ascribe his kindness to me to an ulterior motive. It was only natural for Lord Claude to want me to share my knowledge with him, in view of his affection and concern for his stepson, and there could be no harm in doing so.

Why, then, did I feel like a traitress?

At any rate, qualms of conscience aside, I could now dismiss the idea of Lord Claude as a murderer. Never in our conversation had he given any sign of guilt, of uneasy conscience. Certainly had he been guilty of murder he would have shown some anxiety over the mention of the ghost: whether or not he believed in such things, the rumor of an uneasy spirit would raise questions that would endanger the safety—at the very least, the peace of mind—of the duke's murderer. My mission had not been in vain. Now, if only I could convince Herron of my feelings... if possible, without revealing how much I had told.

Still mulling this over, I was so preoccupied as I entered my study that I did not at first notice the new addition to the effects on my desk. When I did notice I pulled up short in an instant of irrational fright.

From atop a stack of books a human skull was staring at me.

After a moment, when my heart had slowed to something like its normal pace, I approached and picked the thing up. It was cool and smooth to the touch, and when I tried the jawbone it dropped open obligingly. It was undoubtedly genuine.

Now that my brief panic was over and I could think sensibly again I knew where it must have come from. Charles, after all, was the only one in the house in possession of a skeleton. But how the skull had found its way to my desk was a more difficult mystery to solve. In that first glimpse it had struck me as an evil omen, even a warning perhaps, but from whom? "Why would anyone wish to frighten me?" I puzzled, but the silent gaping jaw offered no answer.

I sat down in front of the fire and held the skull in my lap, turning its face—what had once been a face—toward the light. It had ceased to be a thing of horror and now seemed only faintly ridiculous. What a sad and pathetic pass it was that a person could be reduced to this mindlessly grinning piece of bone. The thing was utterly anonymous; there was nothing to tell whether it had belonged to a man or woman, octogenarian or debutante. Perhaps the skull I was handling so casually had been a distinguished professor, a man of learning who would resent his present undignified position.

"I beg your pardon, sir," I apologized. "I realize I am taking great liberties with a gentleman to whom I haven't been properly introduced. But then, of course, you mightn't be offended at all. You may have been a young roué, and quite accustomed to having young ladies fondling your cheekbones. For shame, sir! I hope you are repenting for your behavior now, wherever you are." I smothered a giggle at my own fancy, and a voice behind me demanded, "Who are you speaking to?"

I started; Herron had entered without knocking and stood behind me. "Just a friend of Charles's," I said, and held it up in explanation.

"It seems unfair to make fun of him when he can't defend himself," he commented, sitting down on the hassock and holding out his hands for the skull.

"It can scarcely harm him now."

One of his rare smiles came and went, bright but quick, like a flash of lightning. "True; even if he had ears to hear with, which he doesn't. We can abuse him to our heart's content."

I watched as he turned the skull this way and that as I had done. "If it was a man, which we don't know," I pointed out. "I wonder if Charles has any idea, if he was told the identity. That would be gruesome."

"Why? You said yourself it's no longer a person. It's just the empty shell; the essence of the man—or woman—cast it off long ago." Dismissively he tossed it back at me, and I snatched at it in haste lest it fall; I did not want to hear the sound it would make if it struck the floor. "One carcass is much like another."

"Well, I suppose so; but think what it was before the essence abandoned it. This common bit of bone was what allowed that person to talk, and feel, and eat, and kiss—at least, I hope so. Perhaps it belonged to some lonely spinster who never got much use out of it."

"Don't waste your pity on it," said Herron idly, stretching his legs out before the fire. "Whatever its owner did during life, it's too late to change anything now."

"I wouldn't have expected you to be so cool about it," I said. "That skull may have had a father he loved... or a son."

For a moment he said nothing, and I wondered if I had gone too far. Then he said evenly, "I don't deny that. I simply find it difficult to feel any great emotion for a hunk of bone. I can't think of it as a person. The only reason to feel sorry for the thing is if the owner was robbed of its use before he was ready to relinquish it."

"Do you think that's what happened?"

He shrugged, but his face had hardened. "No holes from bullets or cracks from bludgeons, but there are other ways. Ones that wouldn't show on bone."

I rose at that, somewhat hastily, and replaced the skull on the desk—behind the stack of books, where its blank stare wouldn't be visible. "That's a horrible idea."

"Murder generally is, Ondine."

Taking a guess, I ventured, "Is that why you took it? To see if it showed signs of violence?"

He hesitated. "No, not exactly. I was... curious." So he had been the one to bring the thing here; not a warning, then, after all. "I wanted to see what we all look like in the end—if there's anything to distinguish a good dead man from an evil one. And there's not a bit of difference. It's strange that there should be no remnant of personality left. The machine is always the same; the only difference is the use to which it's put, and that dies with the man."

"Greatness doesn't die with the body, you know; things a man does in life can have powerful effects on those who come after."

"Yes, of course. But the man himself, be he martyr or murderer, will look like all his fellows in a century's time. Nothing he can do will change that; in the end we are all the same, a bare assemblage of bone. It makes all one's efforts or enterprises seem quite futile."

"Not quite that, surely. After all, the machine must be given to us for some purpose." I sat on the carpet beside the hassock, where I could rest my head against his knee. After a moment I felt his hand alight on my hair, abstractedly. "Herron," I said, "I've been thinking about all that you've told me, and I want to ask you something."

"Hmm?" His thoughts had already moved far away from me. It might be difficult to make him contemplate the subject I had in mind, but I would rather fight distraction than broach the topic when he was in one of his moods of bitterness. I nerved myself and plunged in.

"Have you considered that your uncle may be innocent? I know, you are convinced of his guilt. But think, Herron—did he and your father ever have any harsh words? From what everyone says they seem to have been on perfectly amiable terms. Why would your uncle suddenly take it into his head to kill a loved brother? And what's more," I went on quickly, as he started to speak, "your uncle doesn't show any signs of a guilty conscience. Surely if he were guilty of so monumental a crime his behavior would betray him. But speak of the duke before him and he'll not show fear, only sorrow. That can't be the way a murderer would react." I paused for breath, half fearful of his reply.

He sprang off the ottoman and strode across the room, his face turned away from me. "And what of my father's ghost?" he demanded. "Do you suggest that *he* was mistaken?"

"No," I said more slowly. "Not that. I know you believe that your father's spirit appeared in order to accuse him, but are you certain that was its object?" If indeed he had really appeared, but I could not suggest that I doubted the visitation he so clung to. "Could he not have appeared because"—I grasped after the logic of haunts, wishing I had more knowledge of these matters—"there is some other reason he cannot rest quietly? Perhaps his death was not murder after all; maybe he was troubled, or received word of some disaster that he could not face."

He pulled up short in his pacing and stared at me as if I had gone mad. "You suggest he killed himself?" he exclaimed, with such incredulous scorn that I winced. "My father? That's the most absurd thing I've ever heard."

"You've toyed with the idea often enough," I retorted. "Perhaps it's hereditary. No, no, I don't mean that, Herron. I'm sorry. All I meant to suggest was that your father may have had sorrows we know nothing about, and they may have driven him to do something extreme—even if it seems like an act that would not be in his character. Such things have happened."

"But not to my father." His face was still pinched with anger. "My father was not a weak man; he would have faced his troubles. He—" Herron broke off, realizing he was indicting himself, and for a few minutes neither of us spoke. Strain hung in the air like a fume. I had bungled badly, and done no good at all; worse than none. All I had accomplished was to anger and alienate him.

Suddenly he turned to me. "There is something to what you say, though. I can't believe that my uncle was not involved, but what if he had an accomplice? Perhaps my uncle is not the only guilty party."

I sagged against the ottoman under the weight of this awful idea. "But who could it be, Herron? Who would have any reason?"

He gave a bark of triumphant laughter. "My dearest mother, for one. She was quick enough to seize on her new husband; who's to say she did not hasten the first on his way to oblivion?"

"Herron, stop it." But unbidden came echoes of the refrain I had been hearing—the common feeling that the duchess's first marriage had not been a joyful one, that the duke had been too old and austere for her. Her own refusal to follow mourning customs, her undeniably hasty second marriage. But—"your own mother? How can you think it? She may have faults, but I cannot believe her capable of such coldblooded disloyalty, far less murder."

"Ah, but she would not have had to do the killing herself; she could have simply thought of the plan and made my uncle put it into execution. Heaven knows she has him twisted round her finger; he'd crawl on his belly over broken glass if she asked him to." His face was flushed, his eyes bright with a ferocious excitement. Alarmed, I stood and took his arm.

"Herron, I don't think you are quite yourself. Sit down; you're overexcited."

"Or perhaps it wasn't mother, but Charles." Shaking off my hand, he paced before the fire. I might not have spoken for all the good I was doing. "Yes, of course—we have only his word for it that he was too weak and frail to be abroad that day."

"You can't mean he was only pretending to be ill! Charles would never—and he was invalided home, he would have had to deceive surgeons, officers—"

"He could have made his way unseen into the woods, fired the shot, and crept back to the house so that his papa could 'discover' the body. What a perfect way to keep my uncle's hands clean." At my shocked exclamation he turned toward me. "Don't you see? He's killed before, in battle—ask him yourself. He'd have had no moral scruples about dispatching an unwanted uncle. Such a gentleman, our Charles: perfectly polite and considerate, but quite capable of putting a bullet through a man's head."

"How can you say such things? You're speaking of your own cousin, Herron—of Charles, whom you've known all your life!" Nevertheless there was an alarming logic behind the suspicions, however farfetched; Charles would indeed have had practice at killing, and he was fond enough of his father to make such an alliance a possibility. And his interest in medicine could have taught him how to feign illness...

Then I came to my senses. Even on short acquaintance I knew him better than to harbor such an idea. "And he'd have nothing to gain from killing your father, Herron."

This gave him pause.

"He could have done it out of loyalty to my uncle," he suggested, but without conviction.

"Murder out of loyalty?" I shook my head. "Even filial devotion would not stretch to that, unless there were some other reason. He wouldn't further any ends of his own by killing his uncle. And as for your mother, do you truly envision her plotting her own husband's death? After more than twenty years of marriage? If she hated him enough to kill him, she would have done so years ago. And we know she did not hate him."

He stood stock-still, his head bowed. "No," he said at last. "Perhaps not. But if my uncle managed to persuade her, to seduce her into acquiescence..." His voice trailed off. Then he raised his head to look at me. "You've given me much to think about," he said grimly. "Perhaps you're right, and it isn't as simple as I'd thought. I may have been wrong to think only of my uncle: there may be more than one murderer."

Appalled, I watched as he strode to the desk and picked up the skull. He stared into the empty eye sockets as if they communicated something to him. "I'd better return this to Charles. He'll be missing his friend."

"You won't say anything to him, will you? You'll not make any rash accusations?"

His smile was as ghoulish as the skull's. "Of course not, Ondine. You underestimate me. I shall simply observe."

That night sleep was a long time coming. Of late I had found it more and more difficult to sleep: I would lie awake for hours, my body stiff and tense, my mind whirling. The only way I could make myself drowsy was to imagine that I was floating on the sea, feeling the gentle motion of the waves as they buoyed me up, rocking me like a child in a cradle until at last sleep crept over me.

CHAPTER TEN

Christmas arrived with a clamor. All at once the placid tenor of the days gave way to a commotion of preparations, arrivals, and socializing.

Aminta and her husband, together with the children, their *bonne*, the valet, and the lady's maid, arrived the day before. The real onslaught of guests would not arrive until after Christmas, but the rooms were already filling, and on Christmas Eve there were twenty of us at dinner. So that the family might have its own celebration apart from the general festivities, the duchess told us all to gather in her boudoir on Christmas morning to exchange gifts.

Any notion of a quiet, intimate celebration of the holiday was quickly routed by Freddy and India. Aminta's children welcomed the advent of Father Christmas with shouts of glee, and even the normally placid Freddy grew mettlesome from sweetmeats, charging around the room and trying out his new toy drum. India tottered after on her short legs, waving wrapping paper like a banner.

"And I'll have a few things to say to you for giving him *that*, of all things," Aminta said under her breath to her father, the giver, but her shake of the head was tolerant under the fusillade of drumming. "Frederick, can you quiet him?"

"Here, old chap, that's enough," called Lord Montrose. "Time to call a halt. The troops can start up their march again after breakfast." Aminta's husband was a friendly, unpretentious man, with whom it was impossible to feel intimidated. He seemed cheerfully resigned to being neither handsome nor brilliant, and took undisguised delight in the exploits of his children. When we had first met, he had been crawling on the drawing room rug, with little India on his back. "Her Highness the Sultana of Arabia desired a camel ride," he had explained.

The impromptu parade was quelled and its participants soothed with scones and jam while the adults finished their breakfast and began exchanging gifts. Soon the duchess's boudoir was awash in wrapping paper and ribbons, and everyone was laughing and exclaiming over their prizes.

This was my first experience of a real Christmas celebration, and I was a bit dazed by the conviviality, the happy uproar in which I was a welcome part; as well, I was dazzled by the generosity of the gifts. Christmas at my father's house had been observed by a dinner to which Father invited his colleagues, my part in which was restricted to hearing the conversation that filtered up to me in my room. At Ellsmere, I was quickly included in the celebration, and the gifts heaped on me were touching testimony to my place among my new family.

Lord Claude in especial had been lavish in his gifts to us all. He had presented all the ladies with flat velvet boxes, which had disclosed pearl necklaces for Felicity and me, a garnet one for Aminta; the duchess, with much exclaiming, had opened her box to find a diamond-and-pearl parure: necklace, bracelets, earrings, brooch, even combs for her hair. Charles whistled appreciatively, and the rest of us murmured admiration as she held up the glittering pieces.

"Claude, you must have spent a fortune," she chided, but her eyes were shining as she turned the necklace in her hands. "Dearest, you really mustn't spoil me so."

"Who else deserves it so richly?" he countered, and chuckled as she flung her arms around him.

"None of that, now," Aminta admonished them. "Come, Aunt Gwendolyn, try them on and let's see how they suit you."

Flushed and wreathed in smiles, the duchess released her husband and let him fasten the necklace around her throat. With his assistance she had soon decked herself in all her new jewelry. She was wearing a morning dress of her favorite shade of pink, and the gems sparkled and glowed against their rosy background.

"Aunt Gwendolyn, you look like a princess in a fairy tale!" Felicity cried.

"Beauty and the Beast, perhaps," muttered Herron, and we all turned to look at him.

My euphoria waned. The only thing that had kept me from completely enjoying myself that morning was my awareness of Herron, sitting apart where he could watch us all with aloof detachment. His wry asides had begun to fret my nerves, and I was both saddened and irritated by his tendency to scrutinize his relatives as if they were suspects. Judging from our conversation of a few nights ago, he was considering that very possibility, and it nettled me. Why could I not be left to enjoy the warmth and fellowship of this first holiday with my family without this constant shadow of condemnation?

"Herron, you haven't opened your present," said Lord Claude easily. "I'd like to see what you think; I confess I'm rather proud of it."

"Yes, Herron, open it," urged Felicity. "I for one am about to *expire* to see what's in that enormous box."

Charles laughed at her italics, but said, "She's right, Herron. Put us out of our misery."

"Gladly." He bit the word out with venom, and I saw the other men exchange looks. With uncaring speed he stripped off the ribbon and bright paper, opened the box and hoisted out the present inside. It was a saddle. I knew nothing about such things, but it must have been a fine one: Lord Montrose and the duchess were warm in their approval, and even Herron's hard expression seemed to soften.

"It's beautiful," he said, and if the tone was grudging, his uncle was generous enough to overlook it.

"I'm glad it pleases you, my boy. It looked just the thing for you. You've been riding so much lately, and... well, I only hope you like the rest of your present as well."

"The rest of his present?" exclaimed the duchess, before Herron could. "Claude, you really are too extravagant. What on earth have you done?"

Lord Claude's face split in a grin. "Have a look in the stables, and you'll see soon enough." He turned to Herron, who sat perfectly still. "I know how fond you are of old Zephyr, but he's getting on in years, and when I found Caesar I couldn't resist. He's a spirited gelding, full of fire, and I know you like a mount with some dash to him. He's all yours, Herron."

Herron swallowed hard before he spoke. His parents' eyes were on him expectantly as he seemed to search for words. Finally he looked up at his uncle, with something like uncertainty, or even shyness.

"Thank you," he said at last. "It was good of you to think of me." He stood, still holding the saddle. "If you don't mind, I'd like to go down to the stables and see him."

"Of course, darling," said his mother, going to kiss him. "You go right along and do that. We understand." Her words were mild enough, but as soon as the door shut behind her son she whirled around, hugging herself with joy. "Claude, I think he's coming back to us at last. How brilliant of you!"

Her husband smiled in sympathy at her delight, but he did not seem inclined to share it. "Let us hope so, Gwendolyn; but it will take more than a new horse to win him over completely."

He's right, I thought: Herron won't be brought back to the fold that easily. But I too had felt a lightening of my heart to see that instant of self-doubt and hesitant liking. Perhaps I had given up hope too quickly. Maybe yet Herron would come to see, as I did, what a kind and compassionate man his uncle was.

When all the gifts had been unwrapped and the breakfast spread reduced to crumbs and dregs, the family began to disperse: with much kissing and thanks the different members began to depart to go about their day. I had expected the duchess to have a great many things waiting to claim her attention, as hostess to an increasingly large house party, but when I started to leave she detained me. "Do stay a moment, dear. I would like your advice on a matter concerning the library."

I agreed at once and hung back as she saw the others out. When she closed the door behind them and turned to me, she was smiling in a conspiratorial way.

"I must confess to a little deception," she said, twinkling as if well pleased with herself. "There is no pressing matter I need to consult you about, but I had one more Christmas gift for you that I did not want you to open in front of the others."

"But, ma'am, you've given me so much..."

Shushing me, she disappeared momentarily into her bedroom. When she reappeared she bore a large flat box covered in silver wrappings. "Now, sit down," she ordered. "And open it."

Unhappily, I took a seat on the divan, and she placed the package in my lap with a ceremonious air. When I had opened the box and brushed aside the covering tissue paper, I gasped. Inside the box was lace—yards of it, I saw, as the duchess held it up and draped it across my hands: heavy, hand-embroidered lace of exquisite workmanship, so fine that it could only be meant for one purpose.

"For your wedding veil," she said, as I gazed at it dumbly. "I had it made in Belgium just for you. Isn't it beautiful? Your dark hair will set it off perfectly." She drew a fold of the lace over my head to gauge the effect, and gave a satisfied nod at what she saw. "Just as I thought—you look a vision! Oh, my dear girl, what a lovely bride you'll make."

"But I am not getting married," I said, finding my tongue.

A peal of laughter greeted this. "Child, there's no need to be secretive around me. Were you afraid I would disapprove? Why, I could not be happier that you will be my daughter-in-law! You are just the girl I would have chosen for him."

"For whom?"

"For Herron, of course. You cannot deceive me; I know two people in love when I see them."

I had the precarious feeling that matters were slipping out of my control. "Herron has not proposed to me," I said, but she just patted my hand and went blithely on.

"Now, I have already told you, there's no need to keep it from me. Sooner or later I'll have to be told. The sooner the better, of course; there will be such an enormous amount of planning. Perhaps a June wedding? Or do you think a longer engagement? If you wish to marry soon, we can have the wedding at Ellsmere instead of in London..."

At last she saw something in my face that stopped her in the midst of her ecstasy of planning. “What is it, dear?” she inquired in concern. “You don’t look happy. Are you shy about a large wedding? Or is the lace not to your taste? We can change it for something else, you know.”

“The lace is beautiful,” I said desperately. “And much too fine for me. But, ma’am, I’m far from certain Herron wants to marry me.” I did not add that I myself had not thought of marriage. It was such an enormous step, when our love was still so new and there was so much we had not yet learned about each other. My mind reeled at the suddenness of the idea.

The duchess cocked her head on one side and regarded me with something approaching seriousness. “Herron not want to marry you! Why, you’re not in earnest about his not having spoken?”

At last I was making progress. “I assure you, he has not spoken. Nor has he indicated that he means to.”

She shook her head so vigorously that her new earrings blurred. “Now, listen to me, child,” she commanded. “I am not a young woman, and I’ve had a certain amount of experience in these matters. Do you think me blind? Whenever I see the two of you together, it is perfectly obvious what your feelings are.” Her expression turned roguish. “But I need not describe them to *you*—a young woman in love! Suffice it to say that it is clear even to an observer that there is a powerful attraction between the two of you.”

That I could not deny; but “Is that what a marriage should consist of?” I could not help asking.

A reminiscent smile touched her lips, and her eyes took on a faraway look. “In part, my dear, most assuredly.” She glanced back at me, and laughed at my expression. “How astonished you look! Well, no doubt mine is not the conventional view. But in the experience of someone who has been twice a bride, a marriage cannot be built solely on mutual respect and affection. To be sure, those qualities must be present; a marriage without them would be a crime and a travesty. Something more is essential, though: a truly passionate attachment. Without that, all the respect and admiration in the world are but hollow consolation.” Her voice had grown pensive, distant. “When you shudder every time your husband takes you in his arms, there is no true marriage.”

There was a long silence. She was once again regarding something only she could see; as she had done once before, she seemed to have forgotten my presence. Was she recalling her first husband? It had already become plain to me that she had found something in her new marriage that had been lacking in the previous one. I knew something of the late duke's austerity, his forbidding demeanor; now I knew, or guessed, how difficult it might be to be married to such a man. To be forced to acquiesce to his kisses, his embraces… I shivered, and the duchess seemed to come to herself.

"Forgive me," she apologized. "I had not meant to lecture. I only meant to say that I am glad—so glad—that there is no difficulty between you and Herron in that area." She tweaked my chin playfully. "I am certain the two of you will be vastly happy as man and wife—and as mother and father."

"Good heavens," I said faintly, confronted with yet another startling new idea, and the duchess laughed again.

"I've shocked you, have I? Perhaps I spoke too freely. But I want to see you happy, my dear, and if someone had only spoken as frankly to me… well, no matter."

"I appreciate your interest, ma'am," I said, not at all certain that I did. "I do hope, though, that you won't try to, er, hurry the matter along."

"I promise I'll not mention the subject again until you come to me and tell me that your engagement is to be announced." She plucked the lace from my hair—I had forgotten it—and dropped the snowy folds back into their box. "In the meantime, show this to Herron if you like; and see if that will make him come to the point!"

* * *

I did not, I need hardly say, show the lace to Herron. The last thing he would have on his mind now was marriage; there was no room for it among the specters that thronged his thoughts. If this caused me a twinge of regret, I pushed it aside. Now was not the time to think of myself; his welfare should be my first concern.

Later, though, when this whole unhappy business was over…

I did not even see Herron again until dinner that night. After a day crammed with jollity, Christmas dinner was the crowning event, culminating in a flaming plum pudding as big as a coal scuttle. Afterward the festive mood continued in the drawing room, where a crowd gathered around the piano to sing to Felicity's playing. Some of them, like Lord Claude, had been availing themselves freely of the wine, and their boisterous revelry finally drove me to seek refuge elsewhere. As much as I had enjoyed the day—and it had been the most delightful Christmas of my life—I was unused to so many people, and so hectic a level of celebration.

I began to ease my way through the revelers to the door, but I did not see Herron among them. Doubtless he had already made his escape; little wonder if he had found the celebration grating.

On the threshold of the drawing room I paused. Across the vast expanse of the entrance hall, a dim glow of firelight emanated from the morning room. As I came nearer I could hear low voices, and I found that a small group had wandered away from the main party to the seclusion of this room, where they had gathered around a table by the fire.

I saw Miss Yates, and stout dignified Lady Van Horne, and several younger women. There were very few men in the party, but Aminta's husband was one of them: he glanced up and gave a half-guilty start when he saw me.

"Ah, a newcomer! Will you join us? We were just indulging in a little harmless entertainment. But, of course, if you don't approve of these things..."

From his words and manner I expected to find a card game in progress when I approached the table. But if this party was gambling, it was in no fashion I recognized. The table was completely bare except for little India's alphabet blocks, which were laid out in a circle; two slips of paper bearing the words "yes" and "no," at opposite points in the circle; and an upside-down wine glass. I looked to Miss Yates for elucidation.

"We are trying to communicate with the spirit world," she explained, with the same slightly apologetic air I had discerned in Lord Montrose. "Those who have departed this life have been known to send messages to the living by these means. And, of course, since it *is* Christmas..."

"It seemed the perfect time," finished one of the young ladies, who did not seem to be burdened with the embarrassment evinced by her elders. "Everyone always tells ghost stories at Christmas, so why not talk to the ghosts themselves? It is just the season for spooks."

"Oh, I see." I knew of the growing popularity of séances, but I had never before seen an attempt to communicate with the dead. This would explain why no one had lit the gas; spirits would undoubtedly shy away from a brightly lit room. "Have you had any success?"

"Indeed, yes." Lady Van Horne nodded in majestic excitement, setting her necklaces chattering. "It has been quite gratifying. My first husband communicated a most affecting message. What was it he said, Wilkins?"

I saw now that her maid sat beside her, with paper and pencil—for the purpose of taking dictation from those spirits disposed for conversation, evidently, for she adjusted her spectacles and read out in a flat voice: "'Augusta I am here safe and happy do not grieve all is bliss no pain golden light we shall be reunited soon dearest love.'"

"How touching." Privately I thought I would find it grim to be informed of my approaching death, but Lady Van Horne was sighing in a rapture of sentiment. "Have you, er, received word from anyone else?"

"Oh, yes," Lady Van Horne hastened to inform me. "A number of friends and relations, and Miss Deveraux's favorite cat—"

"Struck by a carriage last summer, poor creature," Miss Deveraux explained.

"—and even a few figures from history. Although I *did* consider it to be in rather objectionable taste for Mr. Bonaparte to use such language."

"After all, ma'am, he was a soldier," Lord Montrose reminded her with a straight face. "Are you certain you won't join us?" he asked me. "It's quite a diverting way to pass an evening."

Miss Deveraux, with flushed cheeks and round grey eyes, confirmed this. "It's positively thrilling. Those who have passed Beyond the Veil can see with greater clarity, you know; even into the future. They can tell you whom you will marry, and when, and where you will live; even how many children you will have."

"Do take a turn," suggested Miss Yates. "I confess I am baffled as to how the thing works, but it has been answering all sorts of questions. Here, there's room for you beside Miss Wilkins."

I wavered only a moment before taking the offered place at the table. I knew it was silly to expect to speak with the dead by means of a wine glass and a child's building blocks, but the excitement was contagious; even the more skeptical members of the party, like Miss Yates and Lord Montrose, betrayed a guilty fascination in their manner. I drew my chair up so that I could place one finger on the glass, as the rest of them did.

Lady Van Horne sent one of the gentlemen to shut the door, and the noisy cheer from across the hall was abruptly silenced. The crackling of the fire was now the only sound in the room. Gathered at our table, we seemed to huddle in a shrinking pool of firelight, while around us shadows fingered the walls. I felt my pulse quickening with the same anticipation I saw in the faces across the table from me, an anticipation tinged with a delicious hint of fear.

"Now, you must concentrate," Lady Van Horne commanded. Her voice was hushed. "Ask a question, and it will spell out the answer. Do not try to force it or push the glass; it will move of its own, in its own time."

Wary, a little self-conscious, I fixed my eyes on the wine glass. "Is anyone there?" I asked tentatively.

For a few moments nothing happened. Then the glass, with all of us still touching the base, slid slowly across the table to rest beside the "yes" card.

"Who are you?"

Another pause, but the glass gradually picked up speed as it moved from letter to letter. A, F, R... "a friend," whispered Miss Yates, drawn into the moment in spite of herself.

I repressed a frown. The reply was too vague to inspire confidence. "Can you give me your name?"

The wine glass seemed to waver for a moment, as if pulled in different directions, and finally swung over to rest beside "no."

"Very careful of his privacy, this fellow," muttered Lord Montrose, grinning, and Lady Van Horne shot him a withering look.

"You must not annoy it," she said sternly. "If the spirit senses doubt, it will not answer at all. Skeptics interfere with its ability to communicate." I had time to wonder how she had acquired her expertise before she turned back to me. "Ask it something about the future," she instructed.

I was certain now that my companions were merely pushing the glass. Most likely they were more interested in inventing amusing messages than in creating credentials for their fictitious informant. "Very well," I said indifferently, and addressed myself again to the glass. "What lies ahead in the new year?" Surely that was a question the "spirits" would have no trouble answering.

Nor did they. The goblet flew from one letter to the next without hesitation.

"DANGER."

Startled, I asked, "What kind of danger?" This was not what I had expected.

Again the glass darted across the circle, spelling out the answer. "DEATH."

"Heavens, how gruesome," murmured one of the young ladies, to be promptly hissed into silence by the others.

My certainty of a hoax began to falter. This was hardly the kind of message the others would devise. "Is there any way to escape this danger?" I asked, and the goblet, in evident agitation, raced around the table so rapidly we could scarcely keep our fingers in contact with it. Miss Wilkins's pencil flew as she jotted down the letters.

"WARN DEATH ALL AROUND FLY."

"Goodness, how laconic he is," commented one woman, raising her lorgnette. "It could hardly cost him so great an effort to be a trifle more explicit."

"It seems clear enough to me," said Lord Montrose. We were still speaking in hushed tones. "He wishes to warn us that death is all around us, and urges us to fly. Clearly a spirit who does not believe in wasting words, or ectoplasm, whichever applies."

"Unless he (or she) wishes us to warn someone else," pointed out Miss Deveraux. "Is that what you want, spirit?"

Later none of us could agree how it happened. The glass began to shudder under our fingertips, and I remember glancing around the circle of faces, searching for signs that someone was moving the glass deliberately. Somehow, while my eyes were not on it, the goblet must have been lifted off the table, for suddenly it fell with a crash, shivered to pieces.

We dispersed rather hurriedly after that. It was growing late, and that made a convenient excuse for us to escape from the room, without having to admit to each other the cause of our haste. Even phlegmatic Lord Montrose cast a nervous glance over his shoulder as he swept India's blocks off the table and into their box.

In the hallway the party bade each other brief good nights without lingering. Evidently most of the house had already retired: the singing in the drawing room had dwindled to a duet between two young men, drunk as the lords they probably were, and the rest of my relatives had vanished. Lord Montrose caught up to me at the first floor landing.

"I hope we don't all dream of haunts after that message," he said, with a laugh that seemed the slightest bit strained. "Aminta will scold me for having taken part in such fancies. Shall I see you to your room?"

"Thank you, but that isn't necessary. Good night."

"Good night." As he strode away I thought I heard him muttering, "From ghoulies and ghosties and long-legged beasties..."

When I gained the top floor I was relieved to see that there were still signs of human, as opposed to supernatural, activity. Most of the guests had brought valets or maids with them, and the rooms near mine were, many of them, housing these domestics. After that eerie session in the morning room, it was reassuring to see maids whisking down the hall to their rooms and to hear windows being opened and doors shut. Tonight I would not have welcomed my usual solitude.

But it need not be solitude, I remembered, my footsteps quickening. Herron might have gone to my study to wait for me. Penitence seized me as I remembered how peevish I had been that morning, how I had selfishly resented him for casting a pall over my enjoyment of the day. I would not blame him if he was angry with me, but I hoped that, angry or not, he might still be waiting for me.

He was. As soon as I opened the door I saw him, sound asleep in an armchair.

Softly I shut the door behind me and stole up to him. His sleep was peaceful, with none of the restless twitches and mutterings that signaled one of his nightmares. His breathing was deep, and all the tension and anger had eased out of his face, leaving it as serene and vulnerable as a child's. The sight squeezed my heart, and I leaned over to kiss him very gently. I would not wake him. He had little enough sleep, I suspected, given his nightly walks on the leads.

Then a startling idea flashed into my mind, and I straightened. Since Herron would not be making his rounds tonight, why should I not take his place? Then he need not berate himself later for having missed a night, and, more importantly, I would have a chance to see for myself if his father's ghost really did walk. If the company in the morning room had felt this to be a promising night for haunts, I should not let the occasion go to waste.

Had it been any other night I honestly believe I would have recognized the folly of this plan. Even had I overcome my doubts about the existence of ghosts, I would have seen how foolish it was to expect one to appear more or less on demand—on the one night I took over Herron's vigil. But that night my head was still clouded with thoughts of messages from beyond the grave, and there seemed nothing strange about changing out of my dinner gown and donning my boots and black cloak to go seek a ghost.

Pausing only to drape a blanket over Herron, I hastened down the hall to the stairs that led to the roof. Cold air seeped down through the stairwell, and when I reached the landing I pulled the hood of my cloak up before opening the door.

All the same, the chill and the darkness came as a shock. I stood in the lee of the tower to wait for eyes and body to adjust, berating myself for not having brought a light. The roof was almost as exposed as a mountain top, and as completely desolate. The shrill whistle of the wind around the chimneys seemed to mock me, and I was increasingly aware that I did not want to be abroad tonight, at this season of haunts. With longing I thought of my warm room and down-filled coverlet. Perhaps I would only walk once around the roof and go to bed.

I was still nerving myself to step away from the comparative shelter of the tower when something disturbed me. I have never known what it was—a faint sound, or a wisp of motion in the corner of my vision—but for a moment I caught a sense of another presence. I took a step forward in search of the cause, and as I moved a stunning weight glanced my shoulder, sending me staggering.

Gasping, I looked around to find what had struck me. Almost invisible at the base of the tower lay a massive piece of pale stone, roughly square; not a rock, but something cut by a mason. The same stone from which the tower was built. I gazed up at its faint silhouette against the sky, but all was still: if something had dislodged the stone, there was no sign of it.

Ellsmere is an old house, I told myself; mortar disintegrates, and stones come loose from their moorings. But if I had not moved in the very instant it had fallen...

My shoulder was beginning to throb. I darted back to the door, wrenched it open, and plunged down the steps toward my room, and safety. “Fly,” the message had urged. Perhaps the very house itself was repeating the warning.

Chapter Eleven

By next morning my left shoulder had bloomed in a magnificently hideous bruise. My day dresses hid it completely, but when I changed for dinner I had to put on a shawl to cover what the lower neckline revealed.

In the light of day I had found it easy to dismiss my fear that the so-called spirit message had been a true warning. In fact, I had resolved not to mention the episode to anyone. My mishap on the roof was a result of no supernatural force but of simple ill luck, and I hoped it would go unnoticed.

The duchess's eyes were sharp, though.

"My dear, why are you all bundled up?" she demanded in the drawing room after dinner. "Have you caught a chill?"

"There seems to be a draft in the room," I lied.

"Well, come sit by the fire then, by all means. There's no need to wrap yourself up like a Christmas present." Before I could stop her she had twitched the shawl from my shoulders. She gasped. "Good heavens, child, what has happened to you?"

I started to shrug in dismissal, then winced. "It's nothing, ma'am. A loose stone from the tower—"

"The tower! Where on earth were you?"

"The roof," I said unhappily. The other ladies were listening raptly. "Truly, ma'am, it isn't worth troubling yourself over."

At this moment the door opened to admit the gentlemen from the smoking room. "Claude!" cried the duchess, sighting him. "Only see what has happened. We shall have to make some immediate repairs to the tower; this could have been a nasty accident."

"Why, what is it?" He, too, came to scrutinize my shoulder. I was beginning to feel like one of the exhibits at the Crystal Palace. "Good heavens, you must have that seen to. Jenkins, send for the doctor."

"Thank you, but there is no need," I said firmly, pulling my shawl up around me; "I am quite well." In truth, my shoulder was swollen and sore, but I wanted to put an end to the discussion.

"How did it happen?" asked Charles, joining the ever-growing crowd.

I restrained a sigh and repeated my story. The duchess turned to appeal to her husband.

"We must have the tower repaired immediately. When I think of what could have happened, how near we came to disaster—the child could have been struck on the head, Claude! Or it could have been Herron up there on the roof, having stones fall on him. When I think of all the times my son has been at risk of this—!"

Something hunted came into Lord Claude's face. He had looked haggard all day, probably from last night's overindulgence, and he recoiled under this barrage. "Now, Gwen, you're exaggerating. Let's not borrow trouble."

"But you *told* me!" she insisted, seizing his arm. "You told me that he walks on the leads every night, and why—"

Herron erupted through the group to face them, and she fell silent. His eyes were blazing, and he clenched and unclenched his hands spasmodically. I felt a hollow dread at what was to come.

"You knew?" he thundered at his mother. "How could you come to know such a thing?"

"Why, Claude told me, dear," she said, taken aback by his vehemence. "Surely you can't object to his telling me?"

With a wordless snarl Herron rounded on his uncle. “Yes, it would be you. Have you been creeping around in my footsteps, spying on me?”

Lord Claude licked his lips nervously. “Of course not, Herron. Be sensible. Why would I—”

“No, you’re right. You’d not follow me. You haven’t that much enterprise, have you? Who, then?”

The guests were utterly still, trying to pretend they were elsewhere. Most had averted their eyes, but a few, like Miss Deveraux, were staring in fascination.

“Herron, calm down,” said the duchess. “You’re making a spectacle of yourself. Why should anyone have followed you?”

“It’s obvious that someone did. Who did you pay, uncle? Who is the flunkey you’ve bribed to report everything I do to you?”

Lord Montrose made a shocked sound. “Come, Herron, this is beneath you.”

“This is none of your affair, Montrose,” said Herron through his teeth, not even glancing in his direction, “so I’ll thank you to keep out of it.”

It was not out of honor that I acted as I did, but from the simple fear that in another moment Herron would do violence to his uncle. He was breathing in quick spasms, poised on the balls of his feet as if about to launch himself at Lord Claude, and before I could change my mind I stood up. “It was I, Herron,” I said.

He whirled toward me. “What?”

“I am the one who told your uncle.”

“You...” he choked. “You *Judas*.”

For a long moment everything seemed to hang suspended as we stared at each other, Herron with damnation in his face, and everyone around us frozen. The shocked white faces of those around us were motionless as if drawn on paper. Charles’s hand had reached out almost imperceptibly as if to hold Herron back.

Then the illusion vanished. In one swift movement Herron flung himself out of the room, and in his wake everything burst into motion: the duchess calling out as she started after him, Lord Claude catching at her and shaking his head, the women putting their heads together and making shocked clucking noises, the younger gentlemen sprinting to the door to see where Herron had gone.

My knees buckled, and I sat down abruptly. Out of nowhere Aminta appeared and silently put an arm about my waist. She was holding a glass of sherry.

"Drink it," she said simply.

I drank, coughed, drank again. The duchess was flitting around the room in an effort to restore normalcy, and it was a credit to her that she achieved it so quickly. At her bidding Miss Deveraux took a seat at the pianoforte. Sprightly music filled the air, putting an end to the scandalized murmur of conversation; and the guests, choosing tact over gossip, composed themselves to give their attention to the music. No doubt they would all dissect the incident later, but they would not insult their hostess by scrutinizing it further in her presence.

"Are you all right?" asked Felicity, materializing at my elbow.

I nodded. "I am not the one who received the worst blow."

"If that's true, it is only in the metaphorical sense," commented Charles. "That looks like a thoroughly nasty blow your shoulder took. Will you let me examine it?"

"Really, Charles," Aminta reproved him. "You should know better than to propose that. It's hardly proper. Besides, can't you see she's upset? This is hardly the time to treat her as a laboratory specimen."

"I am doing no such thing. Has it not occurred to you that our cousin may be in some pain from her injury?"

I rose, interrupting the exchange. "Excuse me," I said. "I must speak to Herron."

They stared. "Don't you think you should give him some time...?" Charles began.

"I'm sorry, but I must go. I must find Herron."

"Oh, bother Herron," I thought I heard Felicity say, but I was halfway across the room by then and paid no heed.

He was not in the library or the morning room, where the seekers after supernatural knowledge were once again assembled. I ran upstairs and checked his rooms. Empty. Dismayed, I hovered on the landing, wondering where to look next.

Far down the hall, an open door caught my eye; no light came from the chamber beyond, but the door stood ajar as if I was expected. I hurried down the corridor and looked inside the room.

He had not even lit the gas, and the only light was the pale frosty moonlight that came through the uncurtained windows. He sat on the floor with his back against a window, so that the diffuse light formed a hazy aureole around his head; his face was in darkness, as it had been the first time I saw him. I stepped over the threshold. This must have been a music room at one time, for a shrouded harp hunched in the corner, but now it had been stripped bare in preparation for new furnishings. The light from the windows fell in gleaming bands across bare floorboards that echoed to my footsteps.

He was slumped against the window with his head bowed, and when I moved toward him he only looked up for a moment before letting his chin drop back to his chest. I had expected rage, shouting, accusation; this silent apathy filled me with dismay and tenderness.

"Herron," I said softly. "I want to talk to you."

His shoulders moved in a shrug. "It seems futile to try to stop you from talking," he said tonelessly, and I flinched at the jibe.

"I can understand why you would feel that way. But if you'll let me explain—"

"What explanation can there be? You had a choice before you, and you made it. You chose to side with him against me. And all the time you led me to believe you were on my side."

"It isn't a matter of taking sides, Herron. What I did, I did for you." He said nothing, and, encouraged, I came nearer, until I knelt beside him; he made no effort to stop me. "We spoke of proof, do you remember? Of the need for something that would resolve your suspicions? Well, that is why I told him what I did. I broke your confidence, yes—and hated doing it—but it was in order to test him."

A pause, while he digested this. "How?"

I explained the reasoning behind my ploy. "And he did not react as a guilty man would have, Herron. So you see, your fears were groundless. Your father's death was not his doing."

He was silent for even longer this time, and then he raised his head to look at me. "Did you tell him anything else?"

"Why—no."

"You hesitated. What else did you tell him? What other pieces of my soul did you sell?"

I sprang up from my place beside him and put the width of the room between us. "I sold nothing," I said, trying to keep my voice under control. "You have no right to suggest it."

He gave a guffaw. "I have no right! You are the turncoat here, not I. It was my trust that was betrayed."

"But I've told you why I—"

"Or perhaps you didn't set out to peddle my secrets after all," he said consideringly. "He might have charmed them out of you, as you did with me. He's as persuasive as Eden's serpent when it suits his purpose. Poor Ondine! Trapped by your own snare." His voice turned harsh. "I ask again, what else did you tell the murderer?"

"Nothing else! Only—only that I feared for his safety." I turned back toward him, holding out my hands in appeal. "That is all, I swear."

"That is quite a lot, for someone who professed to love me," he jeered.

"How can you doubt that? Oh, dearest..." In a moment I was beside him, reaching my arms around him, but he endured the embrace stiffly and without responding. "Herron, it is because I love you that I went to your uncle. I fear so much for you; I see how you brood over your grief and your suspicion, until they threaten to swallow up everything else in you. I am trying to save you from that, Herron. I can't bear to see you destroyed by your distrust."

"And my uncle?" From his voice I sensed that he was softening, but not yet persuaded.

I bit my lip. "I... Herron, I like him. I know what you believe of him, and I can even understand your resentment of him, but I had to warn him. My conscience would never let me rest if I had not." This brought no reply at all; nervous, I rushed on. "It was as much for your sake as his, Herron: if he is on his guard, you will not have the opportunity to—to do him harm. I'll not stand by and watch you become what you most revile. That much at least I can prevent."

"Do you really believe that I would kill him?" The question sounded almost wistful.

"No," I said, and in that moment I believed it. "But I didn't want you to have to face the temptation."

I held my breath, the sound of my heartbeats measuring the moments of silence. At last he sighed, and in that one long sigh he seemed to expel all his lingering suspicion and anger.

"I see," he said. "I should not have mistrusted you."

In a moment I felt his arms creep around me. A gasp of pain escaped me as he clasped my injured shoulder, but it was quickly forgotten in the relief and joy that washed over me.

"You can always trust in me, Herron. Always."

He did not reply, but secure in the circle of his arms I was comforted.

* * *

When, much later, I retired to my room, I found that someone had left me linen compresses and a basin of water that must have been hot in the recent past. On top of the neat stack of linen rested a jar of wicked-smelling ointment and a note: "For your shoulder. I hope you can find it in your heart to forgive a loose-tongued old man."

I smiled at the gift, but of course Lord Claude did no less than he should to apologize for repeating what I had told him, as I had imagined, in confidence. With some difficulty, I unfastened the basque of my gown. How could Herron persist in believing the worst of his uncle? I wondered, as I made gingerly dabs with the once-hot water. He seemed determined to make him a villain, in the face of all evidence. Why, Lord Claude had been so sympathetic when I approached him...

...So sympathetic that I had forgotten my mission halfway through our conversation in concern for his own welfare. The realization was like a slap in the face, and I stood gaping stupidly until I found out I was dripping cold water down my back. I wrung out the cloth and put it aside. My cheeks burned at the memory of how easily I had been distracted from my design to "test" him. How could I have become so muddled that I lost sight of my entire reason for seeking him out?

But I already knew the answer. Unhappily, I remembered that caressing voice, the hypnotic tenderness. Herron had said it himself: his uncle was gifted with an almost uncanny power of persuasion. And I had fallen victim to it. I had let him make me his tool.

I muffled a cry: "No!" It had not been like that. Lord Claude was not that sort of person. Why, look at the consideration he had shown in sending unguent for my wounded shoulder. It was one more proof of how compassionate he was.

And how wise, pointed out a cool side of my brain, not to give me anything more valuable. Had he sent a gift of his usual extravagance, it would have looked as if I were indeed being paid for sharing my knowledge. But there would seem to be no dishonest motive behind the innocent proffering of medical supplies.

"And there was none!" I snapped at the mirror. Why must I see a dark motive now behind his kindness? Why must a charming manner be the mask and symptom of a corrupt heart?

Herron's distrust was infecting me. That was what was the matter with me. He was so convinced of his uncle's vicious character that he saw its blazon in every facet of the man, and his conviction had planted the distrust in me as well.

Miserably, I pulled off my dress and threw myself into bed. All the contentment of my reconciliation with Herron was destroyed. It isn't fair, I thought childishly. At last I find a wonderful family who loves me, and I cannot even be allowed to trust that love—to trust them! Against my will, against all my efforts I was being forced to choose a side. I was heartsore for Herron's troubles, but why, why did they have to poison my life as well? Why must he drag me into his private vendetta?

My last waking thought was a disloyal echo of Felicity: bother Herron.

* * *

Guests were arriving now in droves. Every day carriages deposited a steady influx of people, and the vast front hall was constantly thronging with servants carrying trunks and valises. More and more, conversation after dinner turned to the coming ball, which was to be the crowning event of the house party, and frequently the drawing room was the site of merry galops and waltzes for those who did not wish to wait until the great night.

Charles was teaching me to waltz; he had regained his strength to such an extent that he scarcely ever carried his cane any more, and in the afternoons, when the drawing room was deserted—or in the morning room, where there was another pianoforte—we would seize Felicity or Aminta and make her play, while Charles practiced with me. Sometimes Felicity, who loved to dance but was not old enough to attend balls, would partner me while Charles played for us, and we would as often as not end up convulsed with laughter in the confusion of deciding which of us was leading. Zeus added to the chaos by romping around our feet and barking his enthusiasm.

Once Lord Claude came upon us during one such session, and he wheedled us into allowing him to join in: I found that Charles had spoken truth when he talked of his father's fondness for dancing. Lord Claude was a nimble partner and an enthusiastic one, and deftly swept me around the room. I enjoyed dancing with him, but I did not enjoy the doubts that seized me whenever I saw him now. Herron's suspicions had clouded my trust, however slightly, and I was never quite able to enjoy his uncle's company without being needled by misgivings.

Of Herron himself I saw little. At first I thought, with reason, that he was trying to avoid the onslaught of company, who would have accorded not at all with his desire for contemplation and solitude; later I realized that he was avoiding me as well. There were still evenings when he would seek me out in my study, but they grew more rare. He also ceased to confide in me. He spoke less and less of what was in his heart, although he brooded, if anything, even more. His silence frightened and depressed me. He was withdrawing from me, and I did not know how to fight it. He did not reject me, nothing so definite; but he was less giving of himself, more remote, and when he kissed me now it was without any emotion at all. In vain I urged him to tell me what I could do to make things right between us; when I spoke, now, he scarcely listened.

This much I did know: he still harbored a gnawing distrust for his uncle. My test had not convinced him—had even, I suspected, inspired him with distrust for me as well. I could not help but think that this was the cause of his new reticence, his drawing away from me. Even though he had seemed to accept my explanation, his behavior toward me changed from that time forth. If the truth were told, I clung to this explanation for his coolness. I could not face the possibility that he simply no longer loved me.

That he persisted in cherishing hatred toward his uncle was soon made amply plain—not only to me, but to the entire household.

"No music tonight," commanded the duchess, perhaps a week after that dramatic scene in the drawing room. "I won't have everyone wearying of dancing before the night of the ball. Tonight we shall have tableaus instead." An excited murmur rippled through the room; evidently this was a popular pastime. "I give you an hour in which to choose your confederates, decide upon a scene to enact, and make your preparations. Jenkins and Mrs. Appley" (this was the housekeeper) "will be happy to assist you in locating whatever properties and costumes you need. In one hour, then!"

The company surged into activity, as groups formed and began to pick over ideas for scenes to enact. Charles and Aminta immediately seized upon me. "You must be in our tableau," Aminta decreed. "I've had such a clever idea, although Charles thinks it silly. Where is Felicity? We'll need her as well."

"She seems to have been claimed already," said Charles, and there was a note in his voice that made us turn and look in the direction in which he was staring. It was Herron who had drawn Felicity apart, and as I watched he also extracted grave Lord Pettifer from the crowd.

"I had no idea Herron would be interested in joining in," said Aminta, with the same puzzled tone as Charles. "I wonder what he can be up to."

Neither Charles nor I challenged the assumption that he was "up to" something. Herron had made it plain that he wanted no part of the festivities up to this point, persisting in observing mourning for his father. Indeed, he had been conspicuous every evening for his gloomy demeanor and his habit of sitting apart to watch the merrymaking with a cynical eye. I wondered if the others shared my misgivings at this sudden participation in the revelry.

I had no time to ponder the matter further, however, since we had to prepare for our tableau. Aminta's idea was that we should portray the judgment of Paris; since we had lost Felicity, we whistled for Zeus and cast him as the third goddess. "Venus, of course," Charles proclaimed, and found some yellow crepe hair to provide the spaniel with alluring golden locks.

Because of Zeus, the company had some difficulty in identifying our tableau when at last our turn came; Lord Montrose, still wearing his costume of Henry II from the scene in which he had taken part, did at least guess that our scene was taken from classical mythology: he declared that we represented Orestes being pursued by the Furies. But he may only have meant to tease his wife.

After the duchess and Lord Claude had guessed the correct answer and we had resumed our places among the audience, Herron and his group took their turn. One end of the drawing room was serving as the improvised stage, with chairs for the non-participants ranked at the other end. Footmen had brought in folding screens to mask the preparations from our view, and I wondered with some trepidation what would be revealed when the screens were put aside. Aminta leaned over and whispered, “Do you know what Herron plans to do?” and I shook my head.

“I know no more than you.”

In the event, we did not have to wait long. In a very few minutes the footmen were beckoned to remove the screens, and the murmur of speculation died away in expectancy.

The lights had been dimmed for effect, but the tableau seemed to leap out at us: Herron, crouching grotesquely and wearing a padded hump on one shoulder, was instantly recognizable as that paragon of villainy, Richard III. He was eerily convincing with his face distorted in an evil leer, one arm drawn up like a broken wing, as if withered. His gold velvet costume suggested medieval garb, although I was puzzled by the false beard he wore; had not Richard been clean-shaven? He bent over the apparently dead body of Lord Pettifer, who lay covered in a black pall, his hands folded on his breast. Light glinted off a saber in Herron’s good hand, and he slowly and deliberately wiped the blade on the funeral drapings, as if cleaning it of blood.

I knotted my brow, wondering what episode from Richard’s checkered career this represented. This could not be the murder of the little princes in the tower; but who?

Then Felicity entered, clad in mourning and pantomiming tears, to fling herself upon Lord Pettifer. Evidently she was his grieving widow. At the sight of Herron she started back with an expression of loathing, but he silently urged her to stay, kneeling and offering her the sword. He held it out to her hilt first across the corpse, with an ingratiating smirk; she seemed to shrink away, yet hesitated, half fascinated by him in spite of the hatred she should be feeling.

For I knew now what this scene was, and from the way others were nodding, I saw that they had recognized it as well. Herron had chosen to portray Richard at the moment when he wooed his future wife over the body of her husband, whom he had killed.

Sure enough, Felicity seized the sword and made as if to stab the murderer with it; but as Herron continued to pantomime devotion, she weakened, and the sword slipped from her fingers. Her final submission was sealed when Herron placed a ring on her finger.

I saw Aminta and her husband exchange glances. Herron's lack of delicacy in choosing this subject was glaring—his own mother was so recently a widow, after all—and then the connection broke upon me like a cloudburst.

I saw now why he had donned a beard for clean-shaven Richard: to heighten the resemblance to his uncle. In just the same manner he had chosen Felicity for her likeness to his mother. She had even dressed in the violet mourning gown the duchess had passed on to me after wearing it so briefly. And Herron's velvet doublet, I realized dully, was actually Lord Claude's mustard smoking jacket. Even Lord Pettifer had been carefully selected—for his magnificent long beard, so reminiscent of the late duke's.

Herron had taken pains to make his implication clear, and a shocked murmur in the room showed that the similarities were not lost on the rest of the company.

"Good Lord," I heard Charles say. "What does he think he's doing?"

I was beginning to think I knew, but it was almost too awful to believe. My eyes sought the place where Lord Claude and the duchess sat, close to the "stage." From where I watched I could not see their faces, but I could see Lord Claude's hand, gripping the arm of his chair. The knuckles had gone white.

No one had spoken aloud; even for those who had not grasped Herron's implicit accusation, the scene was so tasteless a choice under the circumstances that the company was too embarrassed to recognize it. Awkwardly, the guests fidgeted, none wishing to speak, all wishing for an end to the predicament.

It was plain by now that no one was going to call out the name of the tableau. Slowly Herron broke his frozen stance, his head turning to sweep a long look around the room, as his teeth bared in a feral grin.

"What, are you all struck dumb?" he mocked. "Surely there is one here, at least, who sees something he recognizes?"

He was looking straight at his uncle. But it was not Lord Claude who rose to the bait; with a movement so sudden it toppled her chair, the duchess stood.

"How dare you." The words were so low I could scarcely hear them. Herron's eyes widened in a parody of innocence accused.

"Why, mother, has something upset you?"

Her lips tightened, but she would not dignify the query with a reply. The only sound in the room was the angry snapping of her fan as she opened and shut it spasmodically. I could only guess what a struggle it was for her to restrain herself from expostulating with him in front of the guests.

Felicity was looking from one to the other in consternation. Clearly she had had no idea of the import of the tableau. "Is something the matter—?" she began hesitantly, and Lord Pettifer sat up to blink owlishly around him. Without his spectacles he too was at a loss as to what had happened.

"Evidently our tableau lacked conviction," Herron said lightly. "I must say I thought we had presented quite an authentic depiction of the episode. But perhaps my mother means to offer a suggestion for improvement."

Felicity stared at him, uncomprehending. "Did I do something wrong, Aunt Gwendolyn? I did just as Herron told me to."

The duchess seemed to come to herself. "Nothing is the matter, Felicity; you were lovely." She turned her back on the three of them and faced the company with a bright artificial smile. "I'm certain everyone will agree that it would be impossible to find a successor to this last tableau," she said easily. "In fact, I believe it would be pointless to compete with it. Shall we have some whist? Charles, Aminta, you know where the cards are. Now, gentlemen, if you'll just help with these tables..."

I don't know how she finessed it, but within five minutes the impromptu stage was dismantled and tables and chairs had been set up for card games. The audience had broken into small groups and were already dealing cards. Lord Claude had still said nothing, and when I looked around he was overseeing the rearrangement of the furniture. His smoking jacket lay crumpled on the carpet, and as I watched, he picked it up and tossed it onto a chair.

Herron had vanished.

Chapter Twelve

Felicity came running up to me as I stood looking for him. The truth must have dawned on her; she was wringing her hands, and tears were starting down her cheeks.

"I had no idea," she cried, and I believed her. Felicity would not have imagined her cousin capable of such cruelty. "Oh, what must Aunt Gwendolyn think of me? I never would have imagined Herron would be so hateful. If I had known—but how could anyone play Old Crouchback as Papa! You must explain, cousin," she pleaded. "Tell them that I never intended to hurt them."

I took her hands to soothe her. "They know it," I assured her. "I am sure they do not blame you. Go, change your dress. You can make your apologies later, in private, but your stepmother needs you now."

She fled accordingly, and I was pleased to see her return in less than ten minutes wearing a social smile worthy of the duchess herself. As if nothing unusual had occurred, she set herself to play loo with Lady Van Horne. Had she dissolved into tears in the middle of the drawing room, the evening would have been wrecked past salvaging; as it was, she was able to help her aunt restore a sense of normality.

Lord Claude, too, was helping to reclaim the evening. Lines around his eyes showed strain, but he was perfectly composed; indeed, as he moved from group to group, making certain that glasses were filled, I could see the tension dissipate, and often his remarks, too low for me to hear, were met with laughter. I shook my head in admiration at this family. They were little short of magicians in the skillful way they could avert what promised to be social disaster. As I watched the card players, the duchess caught my eye and made a faint motion of her head that brought me to her side.

"I want to speak to Herron," she said in an undertone, raising her fanned playing cards to screen her words from the other players. "Will you find him?"

I nodded.

"Good. I shall plead a headache in half an hour. I'll expect him in my boudoir. Tell him so."

It took me nearly my allotted time merely to locate Herron. I finally found him on the back terrace outside the long gallery. Inside, servants were already beginning to prepare the room for the ball, and there was a comfortable bustle of dust cloths and floor polish; outside that warmly lit room was a wilderness of cold, darkness, and icy wind. Herron, seeming oblivious to the gale, leaned over the balustrade, staring out to sea.

My breath emerged in smoky puffs as I told him of his mother's command—for invitation it certainly was not. I could not prevent myself from voicing some of my own indignation as well.

"Whatever were you about, Herron?" I demanded, as we re-entered the house and started through the empty corridors. "That was tantamount to an accusation of your uncle, and before the entire county. Why would you perform such a foolish, hateful prank?"

He laughed shortly. I saw now that his face wore a hectic flush, more than the ruddy color whipped up by the wind; he looked as if he was taking a fever, and there was something in the too bright glitter of his eyes that made me wonder if he might be slightly delirious. "Did you see the expression on his face?" he demanded in turn. "Did you see him flinch? I could not have asked for more. Come, tell me you saw."

"I was not close enough to see," I said shortly. "What are you talking about? Do you mean to say you put on that entire display for the benefit of your uncle? I would not have thought you so vindictive."

"Vindictive?" His surprise seemed genuine. "But this was your idea."

It was my turn for surprise. "What can you mean?" I said blankly.

"You spoke of proof, remember? You told me of the way you tested him, of how you gauged his reaction for evidence of guilt. But I had to see for myself. So tonight I presented him with a performance of something like his own crime—and watched for his response."

The reason for his fever finally penetrated, and I felt my stomach lurch in dread. "You cannot mean you saw proof of his guilt."

The flash of his teeth in that wolfish grin answered me even before he spoke. "More convincing proof I can never hope for. His face, Ondine: you should have seen it. As if I had risen up out of the grave to accuse him." He actually rubbed his hands together, for all the world like the stage villain he had played tonight. "I have never seen a man more horrified."

"As well he might be! I am horrified myself. His own nephew—no, his own son now—has the breathtaking impudence to accuse him of fratricide. I would be appalled if someone I loved and trusted turned on me in such a manner. And before all his friends and relations, Herron! You have just maligned him in front of everyone whose respect he cherishes. How did you imagine that he would react to such an act on your part? I am amazed he did not horsewhip you."

During this harangue my disapproval actually filtered through his euphoria, and he pulled up short to fix his eyes on me. "You aren't convinced, then."

The irrelevance made me fling up my hands in sheer frustration. "What does it matter whether I am convinced or not?" I exclaimed. "You are making it impossible for anyone around you to live in peace; why, you may be wrecking your mother's happiness. More, you are placing yourself in a very tenuous position, Herron. Have you not thought of that?"

He waved dismissively and walked on. "Why should I care what they think of me? I had rather be anywhere else than here, watching the two of them fawn on each other, if it comes to that."

"It well may," I said grimly, and then we reached his mother's door. "I've little doubt that she will speak to you even more roundly than I have."

"Good." His eyes narrowed, and a tight unpleasant smile appeared on his face, as if he relished the prospect before him. "It is time we had words, my mother and I."

Even before we gained the duchess's door we had heard voices raised in agitation. Felicity had evidently closely followed her aunt; I wondered irrelevantly if Aminta had been left to bear the mantle of hostess alone. Felicity's voice sounded tearful in its protestations of regret; the duchess's voice was lower, more grave and composed, but did not seem to be rejecting the apologies of the niece.

Herron did not wait for the voices to die down, but flung the door open and entered.

Silence fell as abruptly as a guillotine blade. After a night of tableaus, another one greeted us: the duchess was seated on the divan, still toying with her fan, and Felicity was huddled on the floor before her. When they looked up and saw Herron at the door, for a moment neither moved: the duchess's carefully schooled expression did not change, but Felicity's brows lowered in anger and indignation. She scrambled to her feet and flew to the door to confront Herron.

"Have you not caused enough of a disturbance this evening, cousin, that you must follow us here?"

"Ah, but I had no choice; I received a summons."

At that, the duchess rose gracefully. "I asked him to come, Felicity; he is not trespassing here."

"I see." Felicity drew herself up and gathered her dignity about her like a protective cloak. Her eyes were red, but they did not waver when she fixed them on Herron. "I hope you have come to apologize, Herron. It seems to me that you have used us very ill."

His mouth quirked in a condescending smile, and he tousled her hair, unimpressed by her queenly manner. "Run along, little one," he told her. "There's no place for you here."

She jerked angrily away from his hand, and the duchess's voice, cool and distinct, cut off the hot remark rising to her lips.

"Put your mind at ease, Felicity; he will answer for what he has done. But that is not for you to enforce. I shall see you in the morning."

It was both absolution and dismissal. Felicity made a stiff curtsey, shot Herron an injured look, and withdrew from the room. I made to follow her, but again the duchess's voice came, stopping me before I had quite withdrawn.

"No; stay." She moved closer to Herron, three deliberate paces. "I would like a witness."

"As would I." Herron's gaze locked with hers. "If I am to be accused, I would like someone here to speak on my behalf."

The duchess's nostrils flared. "You showed no such tender concern for justice when you accused your stepfather in front of a jury of his peers. I could scarcely believe what I saw. That I have raised a son who would do such a thing! How could you insult your father in such a manner?"

He took a step toward her, closing the distance between them, so that she was forced to tip her head back to meet his eyes. "Mother, it is you who have insulted my father."

I gasped as his meaning struck home, and the duchess too knew at once which father he referred to. Her voice lost, for the first time since I had known her, its careful control, rising until Herron flinched at its force.

"You dare—you have the audacity to suggest that I have smirched your late father's memory?" He actually fell back a step as she advanced on him, her skirts rustling; even her garments seemed to be seething with anger. "I have nothing whatever to reproach myself with," she flared. "While your father lived, I was his true and loyal wife, and I did not so much as open a window without thought of his welfare. But he is dead, Herron." The words were clipped, relentless. "No amount of grieving can change that. My allegiance to him died with him, and I have only myself and my husband to answer to now."

"Your husband!" The hateful word brought him rallying. "How can you dignify that—that gargoyle, that satyr, with the name of husband?"

"You'll not use such language about your uncle again, Herron." Her voice had dropped: not wavering, but warning. The low steady words were hard as iron, cold as snow, and she was like a woman carved of ice; shivering at the implacable anger that emanated from her, I saw again the core of steel beneath the gentle surface. "As your stepfather, he deserves your respect; as your uncle, he deserves your love. Indeed, you gave it freely once."

"That was before he tried to take my father's place." Herron was not yet done fighting; the freezing tone had little effect against the heat of his indignation. "You talk of my audacity, and yet has he not proven himself to be the most brazen, most arrogant impostor imaginable? To believe that he could actually replace my father, that he could efface the memory of the best man who ever bore our name, when he was never worthy to wipe my father's boots—that, Mother, is audacity. It is complete, colossal insolence."

He was almost spitting the words at her, and for a moment amazement mastered her anger.

"I have never heard you be so hard," she said in wonder. "What has changed you, Herron?" And the icy surface cracked as she reached her hand out to him helplessly.

For the space of three heartbeats he said nothing. His mother's entreaty seemed to move him where her authority had not, and he hesitated, unsure of himself for the first time.

"A great deal has changed," he said, avoiding her eyes. "Not only I, but he has changed. Have you not seen it?"

Now it was her turn to drop her eyes. "I have seen nothing," she said, but her voice lacked certainty, and like a hound on the scent Herron seized upon that glimmer of doubt.

"Oh, but you suspect something, even if you cannot place your finger on the change. If you did trust him completely, he would be here now, so that the two of you could face me together. But you aren't entirely sure of him, are you? Not so sure that you could bear to watch the two of us have it out, for fear you would learn too much. Yes, that was wise. You might learn what he is truly made of, this charlatan you married."

The instant of her vulnerability had passed, and now she was in possession of herself again. "That is enough, Herron," she said in a low voice.

"It is nothing like enough. I won't stop speaking out against him, Mother. Not until you recognize just what it is that you have yoked yourself to."

"I say that is enough. Do not try me too high."

Her composure nettled him; he was the one losing command of himself now, his voice coming thin and shrill as the situation slipped out of his grasp, and as his own words inflamed his ire. "Does your conscience not torment you? How can you bear to think on what you have done? To have gone from the paragon of men to this bloated, smirking buffoon"—his hatred was choking him, getting in the way of his words—"a drunken, aging, tobacco-stained Lothario—"

I thought for a moment she had struck him. The echoes of the sharp crisp sound were still vibrating in the room when I realized they had another cause. The duchess had snapped her fan in half.

She was so angry that her earrings were trembling, and even Herron seemed to realize he had said too much. Half abashed, half defiant, he lifted his chin and met her glare.

"You have made your feelings quite clear," she said at last. Anger made her voice shake. "Now it is my turn to speak. What I have to say is only this. You are my son, Herron, and it is for that reason only that I have tolerated so much from you. I understand why you are behaving in this extraordinary way: you disapprove of my marriage, and you resent your uncle for seeming to take your father's place. I don't deny your right to be unhappy. What I cannot fathom is why you express your unhappiness in so ill-bred, intractable, and childish a manner. You seem determined to hurt me with these malicious displays; well, you have succeeded."

"I never meant to—"

"But if you intend to persist in these outbursts, you will not do so under this roof. I am not"—she held up her hand as Herron again tried to break in—"I am not, I think, unduly harsh when I say this. Herron, I love you, and I hope I always will. But my marriage is none of your affair. You are my son, true; but you are grown now, and my first duty is no longer to you. It is to myself, and my husband. So if you cannot bring yourself to look kindly on Claude, and to behave in a more filial fashion toward him, I must ask you to leave this house."

Outrage quivered in Herron's voice. "But I am the duke. How dare you treat me as—"

"I treat you like a child because you have behaved as one. You have no right, Herron, no right at all to pass judgment on me. Nor have you the right to persecute your stepfather and to embarrass our friends. Yes, Herron, you have the title; but have you the bearing of a duke? You think Claude so unworthy a successor to your late father, but how have you compared in that capacity? Your recent behavior has not been such as he would approve."

His silence seemed to acknowledge that her words had struck home. Defeat showed in his bowed head and slumped shoulders, and seeing this she softened slightly. She touched his face, and he flinched but did not move away from the contact. "I do not want to turn you out, Herron. Do not force me to do so."

"Ellsmere is mine," he protested, indignation conquering for the moment all other feeling. "You cannot turn me out of my own house."

A faint, sad smile touched her lips, and she dropped her hand. "You will not be twenty-one for another two months, Herron, so by the terms of the trust the estate is not yet yours. I hope you will not force me to make use of that technicality."

He stood breathing heavily for a moment, his eyes darting unseeing over the carpet as he assimilated all that she had said. The duchess moved over to the mantel and stood facing him, waiting. At last he raised his head.

"I see that I have little choice," he said in a growl. "You have the whip hand of me, Mother. But it may be of interest to you in your complacency to know that had you not made use of these noble tactics, I would have left Ellsmere of my own accord."

Her composure crumbled. "Herron, dearest, I don't wish you to go—" He raised a hand, as she had done before, and she faltered to a stop.

"Oh, you needn't try to retract it; it's clear that my presence offends. But I see now that I was wrong to think of going. Only a coward turns tail after battle has been joined. Very well, Mother: you'll not hear another word from me about your husband—whatever the cost."

She inclined her head at the concession. Questions hovered at her lips, but he gave her no time to voice them.

"One more word, and I'll leave you. You have expressed bewilderment at what you are pleased to call my malice. It might behoove you, mother, to ask yourself if there might be a method behind it."

"What method?" It was a whisper.

A mocking smile flitted across his face, and he turned to go. "Ah, but you have forbidden me to speak ill of my uncle," he said, with his hand on the doorknob. "You must seek elsewhere for an answer to the riddle. Perhaps it lies in your own heart."

After the door shut behind him there was a long heartbroken silence. The duchess lowered herself to the divan, moving slowly and carefully like an old woman. For the first time her age showed, and I could see the marks left by the passing years in her face. I sat down beside her, wondering if I should fetch Lord Claude. I had never seen her so dispirited; her defeated bearing was the more surprising since she had borne herself with such resolution and force in the confrontation that had just passed.

She held her head in her hands as if its weight was too much for her to sustain. "What did he mean?" she whispered. "Do you know, child?"

I had no time in which to consider my course. But it took no thought to know that not for the world would I have robbed her of her husband now that she seemed to have lost her son. "I have no idea what he could have meant, ma'am," I said.

She made no move. Anxious, I put my arm around her shoulders. "He is not lost to you forever, I am sure: in time he will come back to us, out of this prison he has made for himself."

She raised her head at that, and I was shocked anew at the weary hopelessness of her eyes, the tired lines that leapt into sudden relief. "It may be so," she said tonelessly. "But it may be that this prison is stronger than time—or love."

Her face dropped into her hands again. After a moment I crept silently from the room, and left her with her grief.

I, too, was more troubled than I could let her know. Herron's increasing isolation from those who loved him, the virulence of his suspicions, his growing refusal to trust—all filled me with a terrible sense that he was moving irrevocably into a purgatory of his own making, and from which none of us could reclaim him. Dully I wondered if it might not be better for him to leave Ellsmere. Of course, there was his continuing vigil to consider; he would not wish to give up the hope of seeing his father's spirit again. In spite of his defiant words about refusing to run from battle, I knew that part of his reason for staying here had to be the belief in a visitation from his father. Herron would scarcely brook his mother's conditions otherwise.

I thought then of the game with the blocks and wine glass, and wondered if it might be a way to expel his obsession. Herron might not share my skepticism: if his mother and I could persuade him to attempt to contact his father by those means, we could arrange for some benign message to come to him, to dispel his fears and suspicions...

And if after all there was a murderer at Ellsmere?

What harm would it do to let him be?

All ideas of justice went against such a thing. And yet—the duchess was happy now, or would be, if her son would let her. Lord Claude was the perfect husband for her, everyone agreed, and was proving to be an excellent landlord as well, beloved by his tenants and improving the quality of their lives. Why could he not be left in peace? If he had actually killed his brother (an idea I still could not believe) he had certainly committed a horrible crime; but it was a crime not without a beneficial effect for the survivors.

And Lord Claude was a good man. I was convinced of that: murder was not instinctive to his nature. He was a loving husband and father, a kind friend to me, and caring toward those on the estate; what kind of justice would it be to destroy his life and forestall all the good he might yet do? All that would be accomplished was the ruin of his family and the loss of another worthy man's life.

But there was no hope of convincing Herron of that.

I sighed, and looked around me. I had wandered onto the main landing of the stairs, overlooking the great hall, where footmen were hauling in trunks. Another guest must have arrived, although the hour was very late; delayed, perhaps, by a late train. The thought of returning to my room depressed me—I would only spend hours in the futile pursuit of sleep—and I decided to postpone retiring as long as I could. I could go to the library instead. The company of great quantities of books usually had a restorative effect on my morale, and the prospect quickened my steps as I made my way there.

As I had hoped, the air of tranquility in the library was soothing. After turning up the gas and stirring the banked fire into life, I climbed one of the ladders to the gallery. Above the fireplace the gallery was walled to frame a small tunnel or alcove, which was always pleasantly warmed by the chimney, which formed the inside wall. Partly for that reason, it was one of my favorite places to retreat with a book, and in a very few minutes I was comfortably ensconced there, idly sifting through a shelf of books I had not yet explored.

The books in the gallery seemed to have been selected more for their contents than for their bindings, which was not always the case in the lower part of the room. Many of the volumes I browsed through seemed to be castoffs from different members of the family. I found several volumes of Scott that bore Charles's name; here were a great many three-volume novels, possibly the duchess's; and the French grammars had to belong to Felicity.

A much-written-in copy of *Sartor Resartus* made me pause. The owner had plainly been much affected by Thomas Carlyle's account of his struggle with doubt and faith. As I glanced over the pages my eyes alighted on a passage that had been underscored with vigorous strokes:

"Is there no God, then; but at best an absentee God, sitting idle, ever since the first Sabbath, at the outside of his Universe, and seeing it go?"

In sudden dread I turned to the flyleaf to look for the name of the owner. It was as I had feared: the book was Herron's.

I put my head down on the page in despair.

The sound of approaching footsteps made me stiffen. I did not want to face company at that moment. Hunched over the open book, I sat perfectly still, willing whoever it was to go away and leave me unmolested. But the click of the latch, closely followed by voices, told me that I would not have my wish.

"The gas is lit," observed the first voice. "I thought you said we could speak privately here."

"One of the servants must have left it on." I recognized this voice as that of Lord Claude. "There's no one about but ourselves; you can see that for yourself."

I realized that where I sat, in the small alcove, I must be invisible to them. Embarrassed at intruding on their conversation, however unintentionally, I started to get to my feet to make my presence known. But then the first voice came again, and this time I recognized the speaker. My heart seemed to make one great leap, and I froze. After that I did not stir except to breathe; not for anything would I have alerted them to my presence.

"You should have sent for me sooner," the voice said. "You haven't done much with your time, from what I can see. I expected to find the matter concluded by now."

"You don't understand how difficult my position is," pleaded Lord Claude, with a diffidence that appalled me. "What you ask is very delicate, very—ah—involved."

There was the sound of a match being struck, and a pause while the first man evidently lit a cigar; the rank smoke came drifting up to me in my hiding place. "I cannot see the difficulty." The voice was dry. "With all your native ingenuity and strength of character, what could be easier?"

"You don't realize just what it is you are asking."

"Of course I do." There was the creak of someone sitting back in his chair. "What you seem to be forgetting is that this is not some caprice of my own; circumstances are forcing our hand. You know what the consequences will be should you persist in dithering about and shuffling your feet. We haven't much more time." I heard a clinking sound, probably that of a decanter against a glass, for the voice added wryly, "Does it always take liquor to summon up your courage, man?"

A crash as of a fist smashing down made me jump. "Damn it, you have no right to criticize me. You know I've tried. I'd like to see you do any better, if it comes to that. You're a fine man for talking, but when it comes to a crisis, you find it very convenient to let someone else take on the responsibility."

The other did not seem to be offended by this; if anything, he sounded amused.

"Now you have it, old boy. That's just the dash and mettle this enterprise wants. Approach the situation in that spirit, and the thing takes care of itself. Before you know it, the whole nasty mess is behind you."

There was a groan from Lord Claude, and when he spoke again his voice was muffled, as if he had buried his head in his hands. "Damn you!"

The other clicked his tongue. "Temper, Reginald." More smoke came drifting past my alcove. The tense nature of the conversation did not seem to be distracting this man from enjoyment of his cigar.

When Lord Claude's voice came again it was bleak, all defiance gone.

"The boy suspects something, you know."

"So you said," was the idle reply. "I confess I am at a loss to see how that affects our plans."

"You're a coldhearted bounder! When I think of how you lured me into all this—when I think of how I let you persuade me, against all my better judgment—! Mephistopheles was nothing compared to you."

"Come, come, you were fairly begging to be persuaded. Don't try to shrug the burden of your guilty conscience onto my shoulders." A low chuckle made me shiver. "And look at what you've gained. Why, you wouldn't be able to offer me these fine cigars otherwise. Don't work yourself into a fit of the vapors, Reginald. You may rely on me. Now that I'll be staying here—"

I started, and the book slipped from my lap and fell to the floor with a bang that resounded through the room. There was an instant's startled silence, and then "Who's there?" cried Lord Claude, on a thin rising note of panic.

My mouth had gone dry, so that I could not answer even had I wished to. I stepped out from the alcove and looked out over the two men below.

At the sight of me, Lord Claude gasped out a great sigh of relief and collapsed into a chair. His face was a dreadful pasty white, and he refilled his glass with a hand that trembled.

Of the three of us, he was the only one who seemed truly surprised. His companion appeared slightly startled, but rose from his chair without haste and moved closer. Without removing his eyes from me he flicked cigar ash into the fire. From where he stood before the fireplace, the flames cast diabolic lights and shadows over his face, and his eyes seemed to glow red. Mephistopheles was right, I thought.

"Good evening, daughter," he said.

CHAPTER THIRTEEN

"What are you doing here?" I said.

His grin widened, and the firelight gleamed redly on his teeth. "A cold greeting, my girl. Haven't you more of a welcome for your loving father?"

This was the mood in which I feared him most, when he was so satisfied with himself that he indulged in a mordant levity. It was in this temper that he most enjoyed baiting me. I clasped my hands behind my back to hide their shaking and took comfort from the fact that I stood out of his reach.

When I did not answer, his brows lowered and his voice lost some of its gaiety. "Come, girl, speak up. Or has this touching reunion robbed you of the power of speech?"

"Let her be, Pembroke." Lord Claude spoke without moving from his chair, looking as if he had aged twenty years.

"No," said my father sharply. "The girl heard every word we said, I'll wager, and we must find out what her feeble little brain has made of her eavesdropping—if anything. Come down here, daughter."

"I had rather not."

He flung his cigar into the fire. “Would you prefer that I dragged you down?”

He was quite capable of doing it. I moved hastily to the ladder and descended to the library floor, hoping to salvage some of my dignity by complying under my own power. My father gave a nod of satisfaction and turned back to the desk, where he extracted a new cigar from the humidor. Even though I had come to understand something of the nature of their relationship, it still shocked me that my father did not so much as glance at his host before making himself free with Lord Claude’s cigars. As he addressed me, he was rolling it between his fingers and inhaling its fragrance.

“I’m certain you found my conversation with your host most interesting, if a bit obscure. Tell us, what do you think we were discussing?”

“It isn’t any of my affair.”

“Ah, but it is now, you know. More’s the pity. Had we known you were skulking up there... but then, you always have been an inconvenient child. I vow I used to feel I could not take a step without tripping over you. You have a positive genius for being where you aren’t wanted.”

Lord Claude, unused to my father’s manner of addressing me, shifted uncomfortably. “Pembroke, the girl can’t do us any harm. She just wants to get away.”

“Yes, she is probably champing at the bit to run to auntie and tell her all about it. I’m afraid we can’t allow that.” Before I could move, he had sprung across to me and seized my wrist, wrenching my arm up behind my back. The breath hissed through my teeth as I tried not to scream.

Lord Claude had risen to his feet and taken a half step forward as if to come to my aid, but the look my father cast at him halted him as effectively as a bullet. Unhappy but compliant, he retreated.

“Now, my girl. Tell us what you think you heard.”

A vicious twist of my arm encouraged my cooperation. I gritted my teeth. “It seems perfectly clear,” I said tightly. “You are exerting pressure on Lord Claude to procure money for you, probably from his wife or nephew. I expect you are blackmailing him. Otherwise I cannot imagine why he would endure your presence here.”

My answer must have surprised him, for the painful pressure on my wrist relaxed. “What a bitter little minx it is,” came the amused comment. “But there’s sense behind your venom. I must commend you, Reginald: a few weeks in your care, and the mouse has learned to think—and to bite as well. Yes, daughter, you are correct. Reginald here is my unwilling banker, and I find myself in urgent need of funds."

He let me go, and I backed away, rubbing my wrist. His admission astonished me. But of course, he was too intelligent to expect that he could persuade me into thinking I had not heard what had been all too clear.

"If you have finished with the interrogation, I'd like to retire now," I said.

His narrow smile showed what he thought of my attempt to sound composed. "Yes, it's time all good little spies were in bed, isn't it?" he mocked. "But you aren't to go yet; not until you have heard the entire story. You are doubtless curious as to the nature of my hold over Reginald."

"I am not." I was already grieved and sickened to see Lord Claude in my father's toils, reduced to this obsequious posture; I wanted to know no more.

"Oh, there's no need to lie, my girl; curiosity, after all, is woman's downfall. It's an unsavory tale, to be sure, but not an unusual one, eh, Reginald? A nubile young dancer, fresh and tempting; a brief indiscretion, quickly regretted. Not a story that would shed any glory on the fine old name of Reginald."

"You'll not tell Gwendolyn?" This from Lord Claude, who gazed at me with haggard appeal.

"Of course not," I exclaimed, revolted. "I've no wish to cause pain to her—or to you, sir." In spite of my distaste I still felt pity for Lord Claude, and I had no wish to destroy his marriage to a woman he obviously loved. Too, the episode might have happened before his marriage. There could be little good in advertising the unsavory situation to the family.

"A touching display of loyalty," observed my father. "Why do you not show such devotion to me, my dear?" He pinched my cheek, harder than affection called for, and I jerked my head away.

"You've done nothing to earn it."

He threw back his head and laughed. Lord Claude winced at the sound. "What a brazen tongue you have, now that you've found other protectors! You must be very pleased with yourself. Indeed, I must admit I had not guessed you capable of such enterprise, or even such ambition. I almost like you better for it, daughter. You'll make me proud of you yet."

"Nothing I did was with the thought of pleasing you."

"Perhaps not, but the result is the same. You leave my house an orphan and within weeks are as good as engaged to a duke. Do you gaze into your mirror at night and congratulate yourself, and picture that drab little face crowned with diamonds?"

I knew it was safer not to rise to his mockery, but I could not let this pass. "After marrying for money and rank yourself, you are probably incapable of conceiving that someone could wish to marry for love. You are so entrenched in wickedness that you cannot understand anything else."

"Ah, so it's true love that binds the two of you together, then? A noble stance, my girl." His eyes narrowed on my face, then swept over my figure with contempt. "But young men are usually attracted to more, shall we say, tangible qualities. I am curious as to how you managed to ensnare your duke. It wasn't with your ideals, I'm sure. Might it be that you have been engaging in a spot of blackmail yourself...?"

I pushed past him to the door, unable to bear his presence any longer. "I've only one thing more to say to you," I told him. "Until you found that I had become attached to the Reginalds, you were content to deny me. Well, I say that once having done so you cannot undo it. I do not consider you to be my father, and I wish to see as little of you as possible while you are here. That is all."

I wrenched open the door, but was halted by the sound of applause behind me. "Brava, daughter!" his voice rang out. "You have already mastered the haughtiness of a duchess. As for your dislike of my company, you may please yourself; but you will find little protection from your loving relatives should I wish to make any claim on you. Your precious Lord Claude is but a broken reed."

Unwillingly I turned back. The brandy had finally done its work: Lord Claude had slumped over onto the desk in a stupor, the empty glass still clutched in his hand. My pity was tinged now with a kind of understanding. Little wonder that he sought solace in a bottle, if my father was holding the strings that made him dance.

Well, he would find that he no longer held my strings.

* * *

It was a shock to see my father at the breakfast table in the morning. The strange scene of the night before had seemed so unreal remembered in daylight that I half expected to find that I had imagined it. The sight of my father placidly spreading marmalade on a scone shattered any hope that his arrival had been a dream.

As soon as I set foot in the room he was on his feet, with a rather overdone courtesy.

"Ah, good morning, daughter," he greeted me, beaming with every evidence of delight. From his manner no one would have guessed just how little interest in me he had shown throughout my life. "So nice to start the day with one's nearest and dearest, is it not? Do have some of the marmalade; it's exceptional."

His geniality was even worse than his cruelty. I hesitated, on the point of leaving, but it would look strange to turn and walk out now; I contented myself with ignoring him and went to the sideboard to fill a plate. I would eat as quickly as possible, I decided, and escape. In future I must ask for breakfast in my room.

As I returned to my seat I noticed some of the ladies casting surreptitious looks at each other, marking my rudeness to my father. The gleam of amusement in his eye showed that he noticed them too. Leaning over to Lady Van Horne, he informed her in a stage whisper, "She's angry at me for something I said about her new bonnet. She's very sensitive; you know how girls are when they reach a certain age and haven't married."

"Indeed I do, Mr. Pembroke." Lady Van Horne nodded sagely, understanding the foibles of girls approaching spinsterhood. I felt my face grow hot, and kept my eyes on my plate.

"Are you feeling well this morning, my dear?" came the diffident voice of Lord Claude. When I looked up, he was smiling anxiously, as if trying to convey an apology. For my father's behavior? For his own failure to come to my aid? I could not tell how much he might remember of the previous evening, since he bore all the signs—unmistakable to someone who had seen Lionel after many a debauch—of too much liquor the night before.

I tried to smile in return. He may have lost a great part of my respect, but nevertheless I could not help liking and pitying him. And his query was kindly meant. "Perfectly well, thank you," I said. "Although a bit weary."

"You had difficulty sleeping?" he inquired quickly, perhaps to forestall anything my father might say.

"No more than usual," I said thoughtlessly, but then I caught myself up. "I suppose I am overexcited, like all the other ladies, because of the coming ball."

This was patently untrue, but I thought it a good enough excuse for my harrowing hours of wakefulness. My father was quick to seize on it.

"My dear girl, it isn't healthy to spend so many sleepless nights," he exclaimed, instantly assuming a solicitous manner. "I appeal to you, Lady Van Horne. She will put herself at risk of taking ill, will she not?"

Lady Van Horne agreed at once. "Nothing is more dangerous for the constitution, Mr. Pembroke, than sleeplessness," she declared.

Clearly my father had already wooed her over to him. I wondered if she would have agreed with him had he maintained that insomnia led to lycanthropy.

"And it has a devastating effect on the complexion, especially when one is past one's first youth." My father's voice was all tender concern. "My dear Miss Deveraux, is there nothing you can suggest for my daughter? I cannot bear to think of her spending every night in such discomfort."

Miss Deveraux blushed prettily at his appeal, but confessed herself stymied. I wished I could pull the tablecloth over my head. The entire table was involved in the exchange now. I knew now what people meant when they called a situation nightmarish.

In the end it was Lord Pettifer who thought of the solution. "Laudanum, Mr. Pembroke," he proclaimed. "That is the most effective thing for sleeplessness. A few drops every night will cure the most virulent case of insomnia."

My father's gratitude was touching; at least, I imagine it must have been to those who knew him less intimately. He had Lord Claude promise to send one of the servants to procure a bottle for me. By that time Father had probably convinced everyone at the table, excepting Lord Claude and myself, of his heartfelt concern for his daughter's welfare. I forced down my breakfast over a rising tide of nausea.

At last some respite from the charade came. Lord Claude rose, saying, "Good morning, my dear," sounding so nervous that I looked up. The duchess had entered and was regarding my father with astonishment, and not a trace of pleasure.

"Good morning, everyone," she said. "Mr. Pembroke, you must forgive me; I was not informed of your arrival. I would have made sure of being there to greet you had I known."

He bowed, with a courtesy finely shaded between sincere respect and mocking subservience. Clearly he was no more fond of her than she was of him. "You have nothing to apologize for, Your Grace," he said, but the silken undertone of the words implied just the opposite. "I arrived very late, and I could not expect you to disturb your rest for my sake. I was treated most hospitably by your husband."

As the words were calculated to do, they instantly shifted her attention to Lord Claude. Under her inquiring gaze he seemed to shrink, and hurried to defend himself.

"I did not have the chance to tell you, my dear, that Pembroke unexpectedly found himself able to join us. I had the servants put him in the Bavarian Room. I trust that will not upset your arrangements, Gwendolyn, but that was the only room that suggested itself to me at the time. There was no chance to consult with you, you see. I'm certain Pembroke won't mind shifting to another room if—"

Mercifully, she cut off the flow. "The Bavarian Room sounds like a perfectly acceptable arrangement, Claude. As long as our guest is satisfied with it, of course." She allowed a pause just long enough for my father's assurances, and then said sweetly, "I believe I would like a pastry, Claude, if you wouldn't mind."

At once her husband moved to the sideboard. She took a seat gratefully, and regarded my father as she poured tea. "We will have the pleasure of your company for the ball, I hope?"

"Indeed," said my father, "I would hate to miss it."

This was as close as she could come to ascertaining how long he would stay, I saw. Abandoning that line of inquiry, she deftly turned the conversation to the plans for the ball and kept it there while she broke her fast. She behaved as graciously as if she had been awaiting my father's arrival, but I was now certain that she had been as unprepared for his appearance as I was. As soon as she was through with her meal—a greatly abbreviated one, I suspected—she confirmed my thoughts.

"You will excuse me, friends, but I have some final arrangements for the ball that I must attend to. Will you be so good as to assist me, my dear?" she asked me, and I assented at once. Lord Claude rose to hold her chair as she stood, and my father, to my great discomfort, performed the same service for me.

Following her from the room, I was not surprised when she proceeded not to the long gallery but to the morning room.

"We may speak here without risk of interruption," she said briskly. Once the door was shut, she turned to me. "My dear child, what can I say? I had no idea of your father's arrival. I have never been so astonished in my life as when I saw him at the table. Please believe that I had nothing to do with his coming here. Knowing, as I do, your unfortunate history with him, I would never have subjected you to such a painful meeting."

"I never doubted that, ma'am." I was surprised that she did not take a seat, but hovered restlessly by the windows that overlooked the terrace, twisting her rings. She seemed more upset than I; but, then, I had had some warning of his presence this morning. "I could tell you were as surprised as I was at his arrival."

"Surprised? Appalled is more accurate. What on earth was Claude thinking, to ask him here without consulting me? The guest list has always been my domain, just so that such disastrous mistakes should not happen. It was inevitable that we should have to deal with the man, but not here, not now."

I felt a twinge of sympathy for Lord Claude, who would surely face her indignation later.

"Perhaps Lord Claude had a good reason for asking him here," I said, and then the realization struck. He had in fact sent for my father; I had heard that much last night. But why would a man send for his own blackmailer? Now too I recalled the sense that both were involved together, however unwillingly on one side, in whatever urgent business it was. My father had deliberately misled me. Was he too being blackmailed, and dependent on his hold over Lord Claude to protect himself? But what was the nature of that hold, if he had invented the story of Lord Claude's indiscretion for my benefit?

I was so startled by these reflections that it took me a moment to realize the duchess was speaking again.

"I beg your pardon?" I apologized, dragging myself with an effort back to the matter at hand.

She had stopped pacing, but she was still twisting her rings in agitation. Her face wore such a strange combination of pity and hesitancy that my heart gave an apprehensive thump. She must have something awful to impart.

"My dear girl, I think it is time you were told the truth," she said.

"The truth about what, ma'am?"

She took a deep breath and came to sit by my side on the divan. The sunlight streaming through the broad windows picked out her golden hair in a fiery halo, and she looked like an angelic messenger forced to impart tidings, not of great joy, but which she would rather have kept to herself. She took my hands, which had gone clammy with dread, and looked into my eyes with great tenderness.

"I have something to tell you that may be very terrible to hear," she said softly. "Believe me, I do not wish to cause you pain" (had I not said that, or something like it, long ago?) "but, circumstances being what they are, I feel it best that you should know this. It is about your father."

I let out my breath. "Oh," I said, without meaning to, and she smiled ever so slightly at the relief in my voice.

"I frightened you. I'm sorry, child. But what I have to tell you concerns you as well as him. Otherwise, it is something best never spoken of. It is, after all, in the past...

"You may have wondered why, in all the years since your infancy, the Reginalds have made no attempt to contact you or your father; why you grew up in isolation from your mother's relations; why, to be plain, your father was cut by the family." She permitted herself a tiny, un-duchesslike grimace. "Besides, of course, the innate undesirability of his company."

The conversation was taking a stranger turn than I had expected, but I was eager to hear more. "Yes," I said, marveling; "I suspected there must have been some breach between you, since Father never even admitted to the existence of this side of the family; and Father is not one to keep silent about connections to the peerage."

She gave a sad little nod. "Yes, he always was slavishly devoted to rank. It was something that worried my father; he was not wholly certain that Hugo wanted your mother for herself, and not just her family. She had no rank, of course; but by that time I was married to the duke, and I could give her *entrée* into the highest circles... along with her husband."

My mother was part of this. I realized with amazement that I had not thought to question the duchess before about her, when one of the reasons I had been so overjoyed to be taken under her wing was the hope that from her I might at last learn more of the mother I had not known. How could I have forgotten about my quest so completely in so short a time?

But the answer was not difficult to find. Herron had seized my heart and mind so strongly and suddenly that there was no room for anyone else; he had become all in all to me before I was aware of it, and had supplanted all other loves. How much I had changed in so short a time, and how poorly the change reflected upon me, to be so easily distracted from what had been so important to me. At once all my wistful eagerness for knowledge of my mother came thronging back to me, so swiftly that words rushed to my lips and threatened to stifle me.

"Is it something to do with my mother? Will you tell me more of her? Did your parents disapprove of her marriage, and was that why they denied the connection?"

"Nothing that simple, I am afraid." She still held my hands in hers, and I waited in bewilderment for what she was having such difficulty in bringing herself to say. "I know you have little love for your father, child, and less reason to love him, but what I am going to tell you cannot be easy for any daughter to hear. You know that your mother drowned, here at Ellsmere, less than a year after your birth."

"Yes," I whispered, a terrible vague dread creeping over me.

"You were just a tiny baby, of course; you could not remember what your mother was like. I am certain she married your father in the full confidence that he returned her love. For she did love him, foolish girl, for all his arrogant vanity and ambition." Her voice had died to a thread, and her eyes were squeezed shut, but she gave herself a little shake and seemed to collect herself. When she spoke again there was steel in her voice. "None of us knows for certain. That is the dreadful thing, and it is one of the reasons I did not turn him out of doors this morning. In the end we had no proof."

Again, no proof, I thought fleetingly.

"Nor were there any witnesses. But I knew my stepsister." She flung up her head now, and her jaw was set, her eyes hard as flint through her tears. "Before her marriage she was a happy girl. She would never have drowned herself. But something happened after the marriage to change her. I would never have thought she could abandon the baby girl she loved so much. I would have thought her capable of enduring anything for the sake of you and Lionel."

"What did my father do to her?"

"Oh, child, if only we knew. I know he was unkind to her. She would not tell me what passed between them; she was too loyal. Loyal to him! But she changed so after the marriage, became so melancholy and nervous. And he—it was plain he was not satisfied with her income. He was always so profligate, always in need of more money." I thought suddenly of the endless supply of fine cigars and brandy in my father's house, of his elegant suits and collection of fine cravat pins. He still had expensive tastes.

"How did it happen?" I asked, and was surprised that my voice was so steady.

"That afternoon we were having tea outside, on the terrace. Hugo and your mother had taken you for a walk; you were just beginning to be able to toddle around on your own, and she was so proud of you. She always regretted that Papa had not lived to see you and Lionel; but he died not long after your mother married. I always wondered if he might have known something was wrong, and if he was too grieved to find the heart to rally when he fell ill.... Your nurse went after the three of you, but in less than a quarter of an hour she came hurrying back in great distress: when she came in sight of you and your father at the edge of the cliffs, your mother had vanished. Pembroke told the girl that she had suddenly let go your hand and run to fling herself off the cliff before he could reach her. We sent for the fishermen from the village for assistance. All that night there were lights moving back and forth on the water, as the men in their boats searched for her body."

"But they did not find her." That much I knew.

"No. That is what led some to claim that Hugo had invented the story and that she had run away from him." Her voice had regained some of its strength and resolve. "But I knew your mother, and how well she loved you and Lionel. She would never have abandoned you. That is what convinces me that only some terrible torment could have driven her to take her life and leave the two of you in Hugo's care."

"You mean my father deliberately drove her to her death."

She rose abruptly from the divan as if she could sit still no longer. "We were never certain of it, but that is what I think all of us felt in our hearts. Ambrose—my husband—was sure enough to ban your father from the house. He told Hugo that we would not recognize him and did not wish to see him again. It sounds harsh"—she turned to gaze at me with a kind of defiance, even though her husband was well out of reach of my disapproval—"but Ambrose would never have acted so had he not excellent reason. In the family it was accepted as the most likely explanation that your father was responsible for her death."

My silence seemed to prick her conscience. "Should I not have told you?" she asked anxiously, drawing closer and reaching out to me. "It is a dreadful story, I know, and one that I do not relish having to tell—"

"You did right." I stood, gently putting her hands away from me, and made my way slowly to the door. I could feel her eyes following me, and I knew I should reassure her, but at that moment I could not spare any words for her; my mind was too wholly taken up with recovering from the series of shocks it had been dealt, and trying to rebuild what I knew to be true of my past.

For all of my remembered life he had cast her death up to me. And now to find that not only was I without blame, but that he himself, thinking perhaps of the legacy he expected, had probably provoked her suicide.

If it was true. It might not be. The duchess, for all her reliance on her late husband's judgment, still had no proof but her own instinct for her theory. But from what I knew of his character I could believe him quite capable of driving my mother to take her life, baiting her in so hateful and punishing a manner that it drove her at last from him, to run to the oblivion of the waves.

At least I knew now that she had loved me, I tried to tell myself. But the knowledge almost caused more pain than consolation: now I knew the true magnitude of my loss.

"Are you all right?" came a voice, and I found that I had wandered unseeing out to the front terrace. I realized that I was cold, and that Charles was standing before me. He had not been at breakfast, I recalled dimly. He was regarding me with concern. I must have looked peculiar, to say the least.

I shook my head, more to clear it than to reply. "I've just learned something disturbing." Then I realized, with a jolt, that he must know the whole story; the entire family must know. "The duchess has been telling me about the family's opinion of my mother's death," I said.

"I see." The deep voice was very quiet.

I was glad that he did not rush to fill the awkward moment with meaningless condolences or explanations. "Will you walk a bit?" I asked. "It's cold, and I don't want to go in." He offered me his arm, and we walked for a time in silence. "What I most regret is that I still have no knowledge of her," I said at last. "It may seem strange to you, but for me the real tragedy has not changed. My father had already robbed me of my mother, whether or not he killed her in fact."

There was another long silence, and I did not know whether Charles had even been paying attention. Then he said, "She was one of the loveliest women I've ever seen."

"What?"

He was gazing into the distance, his bright eyes pensive. "Your mother. I was madly in love with her. Even though I was only six years old at the time, I still remember how I worshipped her."

"You knew her!" Of course he would have; I chided myself for not having realized. But how could I have known that he would remember? When I found the breath to speak, I begged, "What was she like?"

His eyes dwelt consideringly on my face. "Very like you, in fact, although I think she was taller—but I was still so young everyone towered over me. I used to pretend she was a dryad," he admitted, half abashed. "She looked like the spirit of a willow tree, slender, with long white hands and big, sad eyes; I realize now she can't have been very strong. I remember her in shadow, mostly, lying on a sofa with the shades drawn because the light hurt her eyes."

I did not dare to speak, for fear he would stop.

"She used to sing to you and Lionel, and I envied you that; she had a beautiful voice, very low and sweet, and she would sing you to sleep with old ballads. I'd hide outside the door to listen. When she realized I was spying she didn't scold me, but let me sit on the hearth rug and listen."

We stopped walking. He gave me his handkerchief, and I held it to my eyes for a few minutes. "Thank you," I said at last. "You've given me something I never had before."

"You truly knew nothing of her?"

"Only that she had chosen my name." I managed a quavery laugh. "And that was such a strange legacy. Lionel used to hector me by saying I was named after the window."

His laugh was a comfortable sound, something reassuringly normal after all the strangeness of the morning. "Don't tell me you believed him? I thought you a better scholar." When I stared at him, he shook his head at me, gently teasing. "Remember your Latin, Oriel? Your mother had a pet name for you, although you wouldn't remember it. That is why she chose the name she did. She used to call you her golden one."

"Of course," I said softly, and found myself smiling back at him. "From *aureolus*." I felt like a simpleton for having failed to recognize it before, but that did not matter now. Now, after all these years of wondering, I knew something of her, something I could claim and hold to. And I knew that I had been loved.

Suddenly a shout broke upon us. From across the lawn, in the direction where the stables lay, Herron was approaching us. He moved haltingly, and he cradled one arm as if it was injured. His face was white with what seemed equal parts pain and anger. It was he who had hailed us.

Charles gave an exclamation. "Whatever have you done to yourself, Herron?" he said, and we hurried down the terrace steps toward him.

"The beast threw me," Herron said shortly. "That blasted Caesar. Tell your father he's a miserable judge of horseflesh, Charles; that animal should be destroyed."

Charles was too busy testing Herron's injury to heed him. "It looks like no more than a sprain. It should be fine once you have it bound up. Destroyed? Aren't you overreacting, Herron? We all take a toss now and then, but there's no reason to feel it so personally."

"I'll send a servant for the doctor," I volunteered, picking up my skirts to start for the house, but Herron stopped me.

"No, don't trouble; I'll have my man bandage it for me. And then I'll send him to shoot that horse."

Pushing past us, he strode up the steps into the house, and we stood looking after him in silence. We could hear him shouting for his valet.

"Will he be all right?" I asked.

"Oh, without a doubt," said Charles encouragingly. "His wrist should heal completely in a few days."

But that was not what I had meant.

CHAPTER FOURTEEN

"There you are at last, child! Come in, do; there's so much to be done. Jane, help her off with her things."

It was the evening of the ball, and at her request I had come to the duchess's room to dress. The scene that greeted me halted me on the threshold. Clad only in her underclothes, the duchess commanded a flurry of activity, issuing orders as briskly as a general in battle even as Mary laced her up. Jane immediately bustled over to urge me inside the room and unfasten my dress. One of the tweenies was touching up the ruffles on the duchess's ball gown with a hot iron, and another was sorting through a gossamer tangle of stockings.

All the women wore the same expression of concentration mixed with excitement. While Mary and Jane tried to affect a more worldly air, as befitted their station and experience, the tweenies giggled and whispered openly over their work, and the atmosphere was festive. The air was scented with perfume, fresh flowers, and the warm smell of the iron and curling tongs.

I surrendered myself to the ministrations of the handmaidens, for once not unwilling to let others fuss over me. After the strain of the last few days, the excitement was a welcome diversion. Herron's coolness, my disappointment in Lord Claude, the horrifying revelation of my father's probable involvement in my mother's death, even the misery of being under his scrutiny once again—all were swept away now on a rising tide of anticipation, and I gladly succumbed to it.

"It's a shame Felicity won't be able to join us this evening," I said, as Jane spirited my day dress away. "She's talked of nothing else for the past fortnight."

"And well I know it! Poor child, it is hard for her."

"Could she not come to the ball, even just for an hour? Surely it would not do any harm." As my own spirits revived, I wanted everyone else to be happy too.

The duchess sighed, but without disturbing her contented expression. "I could have indulged her, true, but she's so young to be out in society, and she'll be marrying all too soon, I fear. I can't bear the thought of it just yet; I'd like to keep my new daughter by me a little longer."

I had wondered before why the duchess had not, with her cavalier disregard for inconvenient proprieties, allowed Felicity to anticipate her debut into society. I could sympathize, though, with the duchess's wish to keep Felicity out of the marriage market as long as she could. It was all too likely that once out she would be quick to find a husband, and she did seem very young to marry. It was difficult to remember that the duchess had been no older than Felicity when she herself had first married.

"I told her she could come and see us in all our finery, though," she continued. "And if I know her, she will find a hiding place behind a curtain and observe the dancing as long as she can stay awake. But what of you? Are you not excited to be attending your first ball?"

I assured her truthfully that I was, and watched with fascinated eyes as she was helped into her ball gown. It took Jane and Mary both to lift the dress over the duchess's head and fluff the abundant skirts out over the supporting crinoline. Her gown was the delicate pink flush of the inside of a seashell, and the skirts were fashioned in layers like the petals of a flower, with frothy frilled edges at her bosom and arms, so that, with the fairness of her hair and complexion, she looked like nothing so much as a great pink rose. Indeed, her gown would have been more befitting to a girl at her first ball than for a matron of more than twenty years. But it suited her fair coloring and softly rounded figure, while I would have felt ridiculous in so girlish a dress.

I was to wear the sea-green gown I had coveted so when I had first seen it, and I sighed with pure pleasure as the maids produced it. It was, perhaps, too mature for one my age, with its spare, simple lines, unrelieved by flounces or lace, and its bold and unusual color, but the duchess dismissed these considerations with her usual unconcern. She kept interrupting her own toilette to look after my preparations.

"Is she laced properly, Jane? Remember that gown has only an eighteen-inch waist. Here, Becky"—to one of the tweenies—"these ferns are for her hair; can you pin them? Yes, that's perfect. Now, you need jewels. Mary, have you seen my emerald parure? And my diamond combs? Here, my dear, you'll need just the merest touch of powder..."

The preparations were a long and painstaking process, but even the process of being laced by Mary could not dampen my spirits. True, the deep décolletage of my gown showed a great deal of my shoulders and bosom, and I was alarmed at first when I observed this, trying to pull the gown higher on my shoulders. When the duchess noticed my unease she laughed.

"You have nothing to fret about," she said comfortably. "You look perfectly lovely, child; did I not tell you that the dress becomes you?"

"Are you sure—it is not too much—"

For answer she placed her hands on my shoulders and propelled me firmly to the mirror. "None of that, now. Have a look at yourself. I declare, Herron will not be able to resist you! I will not be at all surprised if he proposes tonight." The reflection framed us side by side like mother and daughter, as if her prediction had called up a vision of a future in which she had become my mother-in-law.

I did present a striking contrast to the dainty, pearly-hued duchess, as I'd feared. But it was not a displeasing contrast. The duchess was right: the gown was suited to me. The blue-green satin was luminous, its color shifting like the sea under a storm-laden sky, and the tint was reflected in my eyes, which shone in a way they never had before. The huge skirts billowed out gracefully, rendering my waist almost nonexistent, and I enjoyed the sensation of the hoops as my dress bobbed and swayed around me like a great bell; I felt as though I moved in the center of an orbit of shimmering color, like a soap bubble.

Even the low neckline was becoming. Aided by my stays, my bosom rounded out above the corsage in an undeniably feminine way; and fortunately the bruise on my shoulder had faded until it could be completely hidden by the judicious application of powder. Jane had worked her magic on my stubborn hair, coaxing it into an elaborate arrangement set about with ferns and long, springy curls that brushed my bare shoulders. From my ears dripped emeralds that quivered at the slightest motion of my head.

The duchess watched with amusement as I turned and preened. At last I said wonderingly, when I could discover no angle from which the reflection was flawed, "I think you are a djinn after all, ma'am."

"Oh, come. There is nothing magic about a pretty dress, with a pretty girl in it." She glanced at my face as I stood staring at my reflection and said more gently, "Someone has taught you that you are plain. Am I not right?"

I nodded. That was a mild way of describing the lesson I had learned, but I did not correct it.

"But you see now that they were wrong, don't you?"

"I... I suppose so."

She gave me a gentle shake at the doubt in my voice. "Look at yourself again—a real look! You are no plainer than you believe yourself to be. That is the real secret of beauty."

I turned to her, flushed with gratitude and happiness. I could almost even believe her words.

"Thank you." Shyly I embraced her, and she responded with an affectionate squeeze—carefully, so as not to crush our dresses.

"My dear child, such solemnity! One would think the girl had never had a new gown." We smiled at each other, and then she returned to her former briskness. "Now, let us see to gloves. Becky, have you found my ivory fan?"

She was off again to sort through more finery. I turned back to the mirror, still in wonder. The duchess could treat this lightly, but it was the first time anyone had spoken so to me, and the first time I had felt that I might not be the homely creature I had always been treated as. I beamed at my reflection with genuine good feeling. Tonight, for once, I did not feel that I would disgrace my patroness's efforts.

And the thought of what Herron would say when he saw me gave me a surge of secret exultation. Surely his icy, distant manner toward me could not help but melt under the influence of this mermaid gown. The breach that had grown between us would vanish, and he would come back to me; we would be as we had been, happy, as one. It might even be that the duchess's prediction would come true, and by the end of the evening Herron would be asking the company to toast our happiness. I could see the scene as if it were unfolding before me now: Herron, gazing down at me with love rekindled in his eyes; the duchess and Lord Claude, smiling their delight; my father, confounded for once, looking as if he had swallowed a bad oyster…

"Come, dear, we aren't finished with you yet." The duchess was rushing back to me to proffer gloves, fan, and bracelets, and I turned away from the mirror and my fantasies to be bedizened even further.

A knock on the door announced Aminta and Miss Yates. Aminta was dressed in her usual quiet elegance in an amber watered silk that complemented her burnished hair. At her ears and throat she wore topazes that glowed like sunlight through honey. Both she and the duchess had nosegays of camellias—white for Aminta, pink for her aunt—while I was to carry orchids from the hothouse.

Miss Yates, though, was the most striking of us all. Her ensemble was an eye-popping shade of cerise, with (I counted quickly) twelve flounces edged in black lace and a plunging décolletage more revealing than my own. Her figure was splendid for a woman of her age and she wore the gown with assurance, but it seemed strangely at odds with her matronly greying hair. I wondered if, at her age, the pleasure she took in wearing what she loved mattered more than obeying the dictates of decorum. I thought of the jewel-colored velvet dressing gowns I wore only in my room, and felt as if Miss Yates and I had something in common.

"Felicity won't rest until she can come in and see you both," she informed us with a smile. "I must say I will be glad when this night is over; the only French I have been able to force into her head this week is dance steps and fashion terms. She may never recognize the subjunctive mode, but she has no difficulty at all with *mousseline, peau de soie*, and *broderie anglaise.*"

"I imagine that such a vocabulary will be perfectly adequate for her needs," commented Aminta without rancor. "Should my sister ever travel to France, she will surely spend most of her time with modistes, discussing the cut of sleeves that season. Aunt, you are a vision. And our cousin! You should wear green more often. Not one woman in twenty can carry it off so well."

Of course I had to return the compliment, and in the midst of our chorus of mutual admiration Felicity came charging in. When she was excited, as now, she tended to forget Miss Yates's teachings in ladylike deportment, and bounced and bounded like a puppy.

"Oh, you all look so beautiful!" she cried, plumping onto the divan with a moan of commingled delight and despair. "Aunt Gwendolyn, that is the most utterly divine gown. You look just like an angel, like you're going to simply float away on a cloud. Oh, can't I come to the party? I'll not even dance if you don't want me to. I'll stand behind a palm and just watch. Please, Aunt?"

"Ah, this flattery has a purpose!" The duchess planted a kiss on her forehead. "No, my dear, not this time. But it will only be a few more months before you'll be going to parties every bit as grand as this one."

"But—" Felicity caught her stepmother's eye, which although affectionate was not to be argued with, and subsided. "Very well. But it seems terribly unfair that just because I'm not yet eighteen..."

"I know, dear," said Aminta consolingly. "But we have all had to wait our turn, our cousin longest of all."

Felicity's indignation waned at once at this reminder. She might even have been blushing when she turned to me. "I am sorry, cousin," she said, holding out her hands repentantly. "It was selfish of me to begrudge you your first ball. Aminta is right; surely I can wait another few months when you have waited so much longer."

She was so obviously contrite that I could ignore the sting of that blunt reference to my age. "Indeed, it's a kindness to me that you aren't also debuting tonight," I said. "With you in the room, I would never be asked to dance at all. Since you won't be there to eclipse me, I may actually draw a few partners."

"Oh, you're just trying to quiet me," Felicity scoffed, but her smile had reappeared. "Very well, you have shamed me sufficiently. I'll behave; you needn't perjure yourself further! But perhaps," she appealed to her aunt, "I can have a dance with Charles in the hallway if we are quiet?"

"I think Miss Yates and I can manage to look the other way for the space of one dance," said the duchess, generous in the face of this penitence. At the girl's insistence, we paraded our finery before her, as she sighed in bliss. Finally the duchess said we should go down to meet the guests and beckoned me over to the dressing table for a final dab of face powder. Promising to stop by Felicity's room later to tell her about the young men who attended, she glided out in a drift of pink tulle, and with hasty goodnights to Felicity the rest of us followed.

My memory of the long gallery as a place of dim drowned light and half shadow found nothing familiar in it tonight; like me, it had undergone a complete metamorphosis for the ball. The carpets had been removed, and most of the furniture as well, except for some chairs for chaperones and weary dancers (and wallflowers); the long expanse of floor gleamed in its new coat of beeswax under the dazzling light of the chandeliers. The walls were swathed in lengths of green and gold. The orchestra was tuning up at the far end, and Jenkins was directing the placement of punch bowls and champagne glasses in the smaller rooms opening off the gallery. The curtains had been drawn across the French doors that gave on the terrace, so that the early darkness did not intrude on the warmth and light of the festivities. Potted palms and huge floral arrangements created the illusion of summer in the midst of winter.

Aminta heard my gasp of pleasure and turned to me with a smile.

"It is a sight, is it not? On occasions such as this I think Ellsmere must be the loveliest place on earth."

"It is to me," I said simply. In truth, even had it been a poky little hut with a smoking fireplace, Ellsmere would have been beautiful to me because it was the place where I had discovered how to be happy.

The duchess had asked me to stand in the receiving line with her, and with some trepidation I joined her to greet the first guests. After the first two dozen I stopped trying to remember names, but the duchess always greeted people by name and asked after their children or interests. I contented myself with smiling and offering greetings. Soon the gallery was crowded with people, their voices an energetic hum, the ladies' gowns bright pools of color amidst the formal black garb of their escorts.

Although the duchess was doing me an honor by letting me receive with her, I was impatient to dance, and my heart lifted when the orchestra started to play in earnest. I craned my neck to search the room for Herron—he had not received with us as he should have—but I had not seen him by the time Charles came up to lead me into the opening dance. Herron had been more outwardly tractable since his confrontation with his mother, but still took every opportunity to disappear from company. As we took the floor I sent one last glance around the crowd, but I did not greatly mind standing up with Charles for the quadrille. He was a considerate partner, and coached me in an undertone through the difficult figures.

The dignified tempo of the music allowed me to observe the other dancers. I saw Lord Montrose partnering his wife, ungainly but doggedly perseverant, while she murmured encouragement. Lord Claude, benignly handsome, was leading the duchess in obvious pride; tonight he, too, had cast off his agitation and looked almost like his former self. I could almost believe that my father had never arrived to cast a shadow over us.

After the quadrille came waltzes, and to my surprise, which was quickly submerged in delight, I did not lack for partners. Lord Claude and Lord Montrose asked for dances, as I expected, but even had duty not impelled them to partner me I would not have been neglected. Indeed, so busy was I that for long stretches of time I forgot to look for Herron at all.

True, some of my partners were elderly gentlemen who wheezed and breathed punch into my face and stepped on my feet, but there were plenty of young men who came to claim dances as well, and in their eyes and voices I saw that it was not duty that impelled them. For the first time in my life I knew what it was to be noticed and admired. Instead of retreating into the shadows to become no more than a sort of extra coat rack, I stepped confidently into the light; I gathered eyes instead of shunning them or, worse, repelling them. It was a heady feeling, and I was aware of a giddiness that had nothing to do with the champagne I sipped between dances.

My strange new clothes and adornments—and perhaps, as well, the alien sensation of being observed with real interest and pleasure—seemed to heighten the acuity of my sense; my bared throat and bosom tingled in response to every current of breeze; the bob and sway of the jewels in my ears made me hold my head with a new self-awareness that was far from unpleasant. The grip of the corset, so uncomfortably tight at first, had become a snug embrace, making me conscious of the slenderness of my waist. Every inch of my skin was newly aware of itself, as my ringlets bounced silkily against my shoulders, as the warmth of my partner's hand met my body through satin and kid.

For that was most intoxicating of all. The admiration that lit up the eyes of the young men—eyes that looked into mine with a smile and an intimacy as tangible as their gloved hands lightly clasping my waist and hand. Their eyes moving over me left a warmth on my skin as if from a touch, and I guessed that this sensation agreed with me; when Charles came to ask for a waltz he told me he had been forced to rout a number of rivals.

"I practically had to horsewhip my way through," he said lightly. "You are quite the belle this evening, Oriel."

I laughed and shook my head, setting my earrings swaying. "Only this evening? Do you mean to say you've been oblivious to my charms all this while?"

"Not at all; I have always known you are beautiful. The only difference is that tonight you seem to have discovered it yourself."

"Flatterer. I can well see why you are so popular with the ladies, if you say such things to them."

He shrugged. "Please yourself, if you wish to think I do. In any case, I spoke only the truth."

Truth to tell, I had seen no evidence of the flirt in his behavior; he had danced frequently with his relatives and Miss Yates (making time for a surreptitious waltz with Felicity in the empty hallway) and no more than once with any of the female guests. But in my heedless happiness I could not resist baiting him, if only because I had never done so before.

"Just what a true gallant would say!" I teased. "Next you will tell me I dance as if I had winged heels."

His surprisingly deep laugh rang out. "That would be vaunting myself, since I take credit as your instructor."

"And a very fine instructor you were."

"Now who's the flatterer?" But he smiled at me with an affection I did not often see in his candid blue eyes. "This is a transformation indeed. I'm glad to see you so happy."

Even when my father came to claim a dance, my spirits did not quail. I had not been able to see him without a twinge of revulsion since that revealing conversation with the duchess, but at the same time I felt newly free of him. Now I knew him for what he was, and knew that I owed him no allegiance. I was finally released from the guilt he had forced on me for so long.

But even without this new perspective on my father I believe I would have faced him without dread. That night I could have waltzed with Cerberus and bantered with Hades—the latter situation, in fact, having many of the same qualities as conversation with my father.

"You're doing well for yourself this evening," he greeted me. "I see that you've discovered how to make men forget your lack of beauty."

"You are pleased to be chivalrous," I said lightly. "Perhaps you abandoned hope of me prematurely."

"Perhaps I did," he said. And that was the closest my father ever came to paying me a compliment.

My triumph, however, was not yet complete. Dancing with Charles had reminded me of the one I had not yet been partnered with, whose approbation meant more than all the praise a regiment of young blades could heap on me. I had caught only glimpses of him as the night progressed, and he was never among the dancers; always he stood apart, watching.

At last, during the last waltz before the supper break, I found Herron at my elbow. He cut a handsome figure in his evening dress, the stark white and black setting off his olive complexion, and my breath caught with love and awe.

"There you are at last!" I exclaimed, unintentionally parroting the duchess. "What a truant you've been. I've been waiting all evening for you to ask for a dance."

"Have you? You were quick enough to dance with everyone else." His voice was gruff, and now that I looked closer I could see that his face was flushed with what might have been temper. Or perhaps he had been indulging in too much champagne.

"I didn't want to be left sitting alone all night," I said, surprised. "And I could hardly refuse every gentleman who asked me, could I?"

"Perhaps not; refusing men does not seem to be something you are capable of doing."

This was a new and unpleasant mood. Could he be jealous? If this was jealousy, I could not understand why so many women exulted in being the cause of it. Had it been manifested in someone else, I might have called it petulance.

"Well, are you going to ask me to dance or not?"

He did not answer, but seized my arm and led me into the waltz. What was the matter with him? Why was he not exclaiming over my transformation, gazing at me with the delight and adoration I had expected? I could feel my euphoria ebbing away.

"Isn't this a lovely company?" I said brightly, hoping to wake him out of this mood. "I didn't expect to have such an agreeable time. I was afraid everyone would ignore me but you, and Charles. But all the guests seem so amiable. I've been enjoying myself tremendously."

"I noticed"—curtly.

"Not that I could really enjoy the evening until I danced with you," I hastened to add, but I don't think he even heard. He was steering me around the floor as if under sentence by law.

I gave up and fell silent, defeated by his ill humor. I had never seen him like this. Suddenly the room seemed hot and overcrowded. The babel of voices and the clamorous music battered my head, and I realized that my feet were sore from dancing. The weight of my skirts seemed to drag at me.

He said abruptly, "That dress is obscene."

"But I thought you would like it," I said, astonished. "I've had so many compliments on it, and even your mother said it suited me. Don't you think so?"

"It would be better suited to an actress, or a Paris courtesan."

"You must at least approve of the color," I persisted, trying not to be hurt by his coarse comment. "It's so like the sea—just the color for an ondine."

Again he made no reply. I searched his face, trying to discern the cause of his strange behavior. "Herron, won't you tell me what is troubling you?" I said finally. "You act like a different person tonight."

"A different person!" That, for some reason, halted him completely. "That is a fine thing to hear from you of all people."

Still in waltz position, we stood facing each other as the tide of dancers swept past us; they cast curious looks at the couple rooted to the spot. He darted a grim glance around the room, then propelled me through the crowd toward the doors to the terrace. "Come. I cannot tolerate this." When I hesitated, he seized my wrist in a surprisingly hard grip and pulled me through the doorway so violently that I stumbled.

He was moving with rapid strides, almost running, and my hoops jounced wildly as I tried to keep up. The cold night air was startling after the heat of the dance. He flung open another door from the terrace, pushed me roughly inside, and shut it behind him with a bang. Still he had said nothing.

I glanced around, struggling for breath in my tight stays, and saw that we were in his stepfather's study. There was a low fire burning, left perhaps from Lord Claude's sojourn here during preparations for the ball, and its dim red glow was the only light in the room. I could see Herron only indistinctly where he stood against the door, so I had no warning before he strode up to me and seized me by the shoulders.

"What in heaven's name were you thinking, getting tarted up like this?" he hissed, shaking me. "This is my mother's work, dressing you up like a cheap copy of herself, rouged and powdered and curled like the Jezebel you are."

"I don't know what you mean," I protested, shocked. "If the gown is too daring, I'll go and change; but I am still the same as ever."

"Don't try to lie to me. I see now what you are. To think that all this time I let myself believe you were as pure and true as you pretended to be, when underneath you're just like all of them. Cheap, deceitful, treacherous—" He shook me again. His fingers bit painfully into my upper arms, and I struggled in alarm that was fast becoming something like fear. "And all of this tinsel and gilt, these pretty artifices, are just another lure for us. Paint the harlot with enough rouge and she'll pass as a lily, is that what you believe?"

I searched his face, wondering in panic how to soothe him; this man was a stranger to me, and in the dim light I could only be sure of the fury in his face. "Herron, I swear I never deceived you. I only wanted to look nice for the ball."

He gave a bark of laughter, a sound I had never heard from him before.

"Only to display yourself to every man in the county, eh? Only to make a whore of yourself, make us want you, make us idiots with desire for you, for your body under ours, your skin, your mouth—" Without warning he ripped at my hair, pulling the careful ringlets into a tangle, and as I put up my hands to stop him, he seized the bodice of my gown and yanked it so fiercely that the hooks gave with a popping sound and it came away from my shoulders.

"Herron, stop—"

"So clever, aren't you, with your plots and wiles." Another vicious tug and my hoops fell with a muffled clank around my ankles. "Thinking you can cloud a man's judgment, turn him into a lapdog, so you can tear out his heart and sell it to the highest bidder." The gown followed, and Herron, cursing, flung it away, as I lost my balance and fell to the floor. He lunged after me, clawing at the hoops, flinging them after the dress. I squirmed backward, away from his hands, until my back was against one of the bookcases and I could go no further. He was crawling to me, two blazing spots of scarlet on his cheeks, his eyes bright with anger and purpose.

The silence frightened me most. He was no longer cursing at me, and the only sound was our breathing, as we both panted with the exertion of pursuit and retreat. He seized one of my high-heeled slippers and screwed it off my foot, then the other. He sent them after the rest of my garments.

Almost sobbing, I drew my knees up to my chest, trying to shield myself, but he held me by the ankle and fumbled up my leg, brushing aside my frantic efforts to push him away. The delicate silk of my stocking ripped, and he flicked it from his fingers like a cobweb before attacking the other.

I was wearing only chemise, drawers, and corset now. Any moment his true nature would emerge and the mauling would cease. But evidently he meant to strip me of all artifice, because he pushed me around to grab the back of my corset and struggled with it. The whalebones bit sharply into my skin and I could not keep from crying out.

But Mary's lacing held firm. I could feel Herron's rapid breath on the back of my neck and his hands tearing at the corset, his efforts shaking me about like a puppet, but I heard no rending of cloth. With an exclamation of wrath, he flung me away and staggered to his feet.

I crouched gratefully where I fell, hoping he had done with me, but in a moment he was back. There was a blade shining in his hand, and in a sort of detachment I saw that it was a letter opener. The grim pressure on my ribs began to relax as he sawed at the laces, and the corset dropped away. Seizing my shoulders again, he forced me to sit up, my back once more braced against the shelves, so that we faced each other. When he brought his arm up, I thought for a moment he was actually going to strike me, and I flinched; instead, gripping my chin with his other hand, he dragged the sleeve of his evening coat across my mouth and cheeks until he was satisfied that I wore no rouge. Then he released me.

I held my thin chemise against me with both hands, feeling the rapid thud of my heart. His face was inches away from mine. If he moved to strip me further I would kick out and claw. But surely he would not. “Herron,” I whispered; it was almost a prayer.

It was quiet, so quiet. His breathing was uneven, and his eyes flicked restlessly over my face. But he did not attack my pitiful remaining garments. When his hands moved, it was to slide from my shoulders down my arms, slowly, almost caressingly, and his mouth came down on mine.

I cannot call it a kiss. That animal embrace, hot and greedy, was nothing like the kisses we had shared before. He held me against the shelves, my head forced back while he sated himself on me. When he raised his head my lips were stinging, and I tasted blood. My skin burned where his hands had clenched me.

Abruptly, he stood. We stared at each other for a long moment, and I did not recognize what I saw. Then he turned and strode away. The door to the hallway shut behind him with a faint sound, and I was alone.

CHAPTER FIFTEEN

I do not know how long I remained there. In the dim study, hunched against the book case, I stared at the door through which he had disappeared. My brain was so dulled with shock that I could not even put a form to what I thought or felt. Only some time after, there was a knock on the door, and I blinked and stared at it in renewed fear.

It moved open a crack. "Oriel?" came a low voice. "Are you there?"

I could not speak, but the door opened cautiously to reveal Charles. When he saw me he stifled an oath, stepped into the room, and shut the door swiftly and silently behind him. His eyes took in the clothes flung across the carpet and came back to rest on me. They were mirrors of the shock I felt.

"Are you hurt?" he asked quietly. He did not move toward me.

I shook my head.

"Who did this to you?"

"Nobody. I..." There was no possible explanation I could offer. I fell silent.

His mouth tightened, and for a moment I saw an anger as implacable as that I had seen in Herron's face, but it was not toward me. Then it was gone, and his voice was gentler even than before when he said, "Would you like me to ring for one of the maids to help you, or fetch Aunt Gwendolyn? She would certainly—"

"No!" I pulled myself to my feet, one hand pressed to my chemise like some miserable Botticelli Venus. My voice was not quite steady, and I took a deep breath before trying to speak again. "I don't want anyone to see me like this."

He nodded, politely moving his eyes to a space six inches to the right of my face. "In that case, may I help you to your room? I think we can repair your, er, disarray so that you can reach it without unwelcome attention."

I felt tears start at his kindness. The conventional phrases deferred to me and were a delicate indication that no matter what he felt at seeing me this way, he would still treat me with respect. His consideration was stronger even than pity—or disgust. My face burned with humiliation and I turned it away from him.

"If you please," I said, avoiding his gaze.

And so we began a bizarre re-creation of my preparation for the ball. Now, instead of giggling, bright-eyed maids who dressed me and coiffed me, it was Charles who helped me step into my hoops, who lifted the gown over my head and hooked it up, who smoothed the crumpled skirts into something like their former glory. The stockings were ruined, and he hid them in a pocket, also concealing the useless corset under his evening coat. He rescued the discarded slippers and steadied me while I stepped into them. Finally he offered me his handkerchief, without commenting on the state of my face.

"You would make a very good lady's maid," I said, with an unsteady attempt at levity.

He smiled, but it was a stiff imitation of his normal smile. "I'll keep that in mind, should my medical ambitions come to nothing," he said, matching my tone.

When I was dressed again, the sash disguising the gap in my bodice left by the absence of corset, there remained the wreck of my hair to mend. I tried to gather it up into a coil, but my hands were shaking and I was forced to let it fall back around my shoulders.

"If you'll allow me?" said Charles. "I can't hope to create something worthy of the *Journal des Demoiselles*, but I think

I can provide a temporary solution." Again he waited and did not move to touch me until I nodded and turned my back so that he could dress my hair. He seemed to realize how nervous I felt of being touched, and had been careful not to do so without my permission during this strange toilette.

His hands on my hair were gentle as they smoothed and pinned, and so lulling was the touch that I felt almost calm when he had finished. He did not trouble me with questions or exclamations over my plight, nor did he voice any indignation or horror, and when I realized this later I was grateful for his silence. I was not in any fit state to contend with such a conversation.

When Charles seemed satisfied with his repairs, he opened the hall door a cautious crack and took a long look. Then he returned to me and offered his arm. "Lean on me if you need to."

I did not lean on him, but I was grateful of his arm all the same during that long strange walk to my room. Sounds of clinking china and voices raised gaily in the dining room told me that supper was still in progress, but to my great relief we encountered no one: I knew that in spite of his valiant efforts to repair my appearance, I must still look alarmingly disheveled. The ball seemed like something that had happened years ago, or something I had read in a novel, and I felt numb surprise at the realization that so little time had passed since Herron had dragged me from the dance floor.

"You'd do well to ring for some tea and a hot-water bottle," Charles said when we reached my door. "You've had a bad shock." He stood with his back to the hall, shielding me from view should anyone happen by.

"I don't feel like seeing anyone. I'll be fine."

The grimness was back in the set of his jaw.

"I should like to know who has done this to you," he said. "At the very least, he should be barred from the house."

If he hoped for my answer to give Herron away, he was disappointed. "He did nothing but frighten me," I said steadily. "I was not harmed. There is no need for you to do anything; this is a matter that concerns only me and one other, and you have already done more than chivalry could require." Even this brief speech had exhausted me, and I was conscious of a fierce headache drumming in my temples. My shoulders and arms throbbed where bruises were sure to emerge tomorrow. "I know that when I can think clearly I shall wish to thank you properly for your help."

"Don't," he said. "I am only sorry that help was necessary."

"Then if you would do one more thing for me?" I was beginning to shake in reaction, and I knew I could not hold together much longer.

"Of course, Oriel."

"I would be glad if you would not speak of this."

He did not answer for so long that I thought he would refuse. Then he said, "I won't promise to keep silent if I see the opportunity to exact some retribution for what you've suffered. But I will respect your wishes as much as I can."

It was more than I had hoped for. In some gesture toward normalcy I gave him my hand, which he held for a long moment. His eyes on my face, he seemed about to speak; then, releasing my hand, he turned silently and left.

In my room, I locked the door and leaned against it to steady my trembling legs. When at last I straightened and turned away, I caught sight of myself in the mirror. I looked as wretched as I had feared. My face was bloodless, except for my swollen mouth, which in cruel contrast was voluptuously red, as if I indeed wore rouge. My eyes were enormous, sunken in their sockets, and angry pink streaks burnt on my cheeks. My bared shoulders and throat no longer looked alluring but thin and pathetic. Slowly, numbly, I began unhooking my dress.

A quarter of an hour later, as I lay sleepless in bed, I heard a quiet knock at my door. My heart gave a thump of mingled apprehension and gladness: Herron, come to explain, apologize, comfort? When the knock was not repeated I crept to the door and put my eye to the keyhole.

A tea tray lay on the floor. Behind it Charles stood, still in his evening dress, talking to one of the parlormaids. He must have been giving her orders, because she nodded, bobbed a curtsey, and took up a post in the chair he placed opposite my door. With this sentry in position, Charles left once again.

I left the tray where it was and went back to bed. I lay waking far into the night, but Herron did not come.

* * *

The next thing I knew was a mercilessly cheerful voice saying, "Good morning, miss. I have your breakfast here."

Groggily I blinked and found that Jane had entered. Pearly grey light, the light of an overcast day, was shining through the windows. So I had slept after all.

"Breakfast?" I said, drawing myself to a sitting position. Jane had placed the tray on the bedside table and was bustling about retrieving the discarded bits of finery from the night before. I winced at the memory they stirred.

"Yes, Her Grace sent it up. She thought you might rather breakfast in your room today; many of the ladies are, after the late night." She picked up the ball gown—would I ever be able to see it again without feeling sickened?—and clucked over the broken hooks. Absently, her mind taken up with the dress, she added, "There's a note for you."

"What?" With one leap I was out of bed, snatching at the envelope that nestled inconspicuously against the toast rack. My hands were clumsy and it took me several tries to tear it open.

"My dear girl—"

My eyes dropped to the signature, and all my eagerness deserted me in a rush, leaving me hollow. I sat down on the edge of the bed and read it through, even though it had lost all interest for me.

> *My dear girl, I hope you are improved this morning. Charles told us of the headache that forced you to retire early. It may speed your recovery to know that your presence at supper was sorely missed! Take today to rest, as many of the other girls will be doing the same, and send word if there is anything I can do for you.*

It was from the duchess, of course. So she did not know. Charles must have been very plausible; it seemed I owed him another debt of gratitude.

"Is that all, Jane?" I could not stop myself from asking. "No one else sent a message?"

"No, miss; no one." My expression must have aroused her pity, because she inquired, "Would you like me to take a letter to anyone?"

"No, thank you," I said. A sense of injury told me it was not my duty to send the first word. It was for Herron to seek me out, to apologize, to explain why he had abused me in such a shocking fashion. "That will be all, Jane, except that I will take my lunch in my room today."

"Yes, miss." Her arms full of sea-green satin, she curtseyed and let herself out.

With a brief prayer of thanks for her unquestioning obedience, I retreated to my bed and dealt listlessly with toast and tea. I knew that I would not be able to face the rest of the company until I was forced to; dinner I could not miss without making some excuse, but at least I would not be subjected to the gantlet at luncheon. The bright chatter about the ball, the precise review of every detail, the debate over how many times Mr. X had danced with Miss Y—I could not endure that. And my father, with his uncanny talent for sniffing out my weak points, would guess that something had gone badly wrong between me and Herron; he had been making sly insinuations for days about the discord between us, and I knew that once he saw me he would not rest until he had ferreted out the whole unhappy story. And then would come the taunting... I could not face it. Not until Herron had mended things.

As the morning passed with no word from him, I began to wonder just how long Herron would be. In my self-imposed solitude I would pick up books, only to put them down after reading half a page, and drift back and forth through my two rooms. He was too ashamed to come to me, I consoled myself; remorse for his own behavior made him hesitant to approach me. Less consoling was the possibility that he had not exhausted his anger with me. I had seen how implacable his rage could be when it was directed toward others; was he going to continue to brood over his grievance against me?

And what, if it came to that, was his grievance? After lunch I found my thoughts turning increasingly in this direction, as my desolation turned to indignation. What had I done to offend him except dress and act like the other girls? If wearing a lovely gown and dressing my hair with curling tongs were grounds for such an explosion, I would have liked to have been warned. To accuse me of wantonness, of artifice, of—what else had he hurled at me?—of participation in some feminine conspiracy! I wondered if Herron's grief had festered in his mind to such an extent that he could no longer trust anyone, even me.

But as the afternoon passed my anger shaded into sadness. Herron and I had shared so beautiful an accord, had loved each other so deeply. How could it have vanished? For my part, I still felt that painful, sweet pull on my heart at even the thought of him. I was forced to wonder now if he still felt that for me.

By the time the daylight had started to fade I was growing restive. It was obvious that Herron was not going to seek me out; very well, I would seek him. I could not support any more doubts and uncertainties. We had to talk.

Finding him, however, was a test of my endurance. Whenever I put my head into a room to look for him among those gathered, someone would hail me and try to draw me into a conversation about the ball. I detached myself as quickly as possible from these well-meaning inquisitors, and without questioning too blatantly I at last gathered that Herron had been seen at one of his favorite haunts, the cliffs.

Indoors the atmosphere was listless, with everyone lethargic and spent after last night's revels, but outdoors the air held an electric quality. There was no rain, no lightning, but the sky still lowered; and the wind whipped relentlessly around me, tugging at my skirts and hair. I gulped it into my lungs, grateful for the refreshing cold vitality of it. It helped me convince myself that I felt brave as I approached the lone figure standing at the head of the cliff path.

He turned as I neared him. Then, after one brief look, he faced the sea again. Not a word; not a sign to show that he had marked my presence. His eyes simply took in my existence, then dismissed it as irrelevant.

"Herron?" I said in bewilderment, but he did not move.

"I've been expecting you," I tried next.

He spoke without moving. "Why?"

More than merely discouraging, it was humiliating, addressing his back. "After what happened last night, I thought you would wish to talk to me."

"I have nothing more to say to you."

His voice was not even bitter; it was distant, flat, as if he had spent all his emotion last night. I fought the urge to give up and turn back. He so clearly wanted nothing to do with me. I could have dealt with anger better than this complete absence of feeling; anger at least would have shown that I still had some effect on him.

"It's precisely because of what you said that I am here." Again, nothing. "At the very least you owe me an apology."

"I owe you nothing. All obligations between us are broken."

The meaning was starkly clear. I felt faint, as if all the breath had been squeezed out of my body. "What has happened to you, Herron?"

At this he turned to face me. His face might have been that of a marble saint, so unmoving, so beautiful it was in its cool remoteness. "You are a remarkable creature," he observed, the lack of any feeling in his voice belying the words. "So persistent in your pretended naïveté, even when I've shown you up for the false creature you are."

"I was never false to you."

He ignored this. "How completely you fooled me. You seemed so sincere and devoted, and all the time you were manipulating me, conspiring with the rest of my loving family."

"Conspiring! How, pray? Must you see everything that goes on in this house as a threat to you?" I retorted, aware that an edge was creeping into my voice.

This at last won some spark of response from him. "If you find me so absurd, you needn't force yourself to endure me any longer," he said coldly. "You may report to my uncle that your mission has failed, and that he will have to find another toady."

I reached out to him, hoping that my touch might bring him to his former self, but he shook my hand off almost absently. "Herron, what are you saying? I love you. I thought you loved me." But in his face I could find no remnant of love.

"I haven't loved you for weeks," he said.

Weeks.

He had not said it to hurt me. It was the plain truth.

Weeks.

When I had breath to speak I demanded, "Why did you say nothing? You should have ended it, Herron. It would have been kinder than letting me cling to a futile hope."

"I'm certain you won't be lonely for long," he said, uninterested. "You've made it plain that one man is as good as another. Why not Charles? He's good-looking enough, although perhaps too dim and bloodless to make the conquest a triumph for you."

"Don't say such things of him," I snapped. "Charles is a fine man, Herron; perhaps finer than you."

"And how quick you are to defend him," came the dry rejoinder.

"I must, if you are to persist in seeing only evil in everyone around you. First your uncle, then your mother, then Charles—why do you believe we are all conspiring against you? None of us would ever dream of doing you ill."

He shrugged, losing interest. "You know best, of course."

I might indeed have been appealing to a statue. Frustration rose in a red tide. "Very well, so you have lost faith in me. But I refuse to believe that you know your family as little as you pretend to. They have always loved you, and you persist in believing them capable of the worst kind of deception and vice. I don't know what you were like before your father's death, but it seems to have done something to you—made you suspicious and evil-minded—and I don't like what you have become."

To my horror, I saw his mouth curl into a sneer at my vehemence. "You really should be consistent, my darling," he purred, so nastily that I shrank back. "Only a moment ago you were prepared to swear on your soul that you love me. Which story am I to believe?"

He had never spoken to me in so caustic a tone, and his face was distorted into something that sickened me. I had spoken the truth when I said he had changed.

"Believe what you will," I said, shaken. "I know that I loved you: guilelessly, and sincerely, whatever you may claim. And I hope that some day you will come to realize that, and will recognize that you yourself were the ruin of it. I am blameless."

I turned to go, unable to bear the sight of him any longer. That in outward appearance he should remain as beautiful and desirable as he always had, when our circumstances were so changed, was the cruelest mockery. It was nearly impossible to conceive that I no longer had the right to kiss those lips, which I had kissed so many times; that I could no longer expect those velvet eyes to rest on me with delight. My mind could not hold the idea while my eyes still held him in their sight. I had to get far away from this man who was suddenly no part of me.

Before I had taken three steps his voice came from behind me.

"I let you make a fool of me for too long."

I turned back for an instant. "You made yourself a fool, Herron; I had nothing to do with it."

He shut his eyes as if succumbing to the weight of intolerable tedium, and turned away.

For only a moment I struggled with the desire to go to him, to shake him until this evil spirit that spoke through him had relinquished his hold and the Herron I loved looked out again through his eyes. I wanted to weep, to beg, to scream at him. But it would do no good. He was lost to me now; there was no changing that.

But I could not continue to stand there wrestling with my soul; blindly, swiftly I moved away, wanting only to put distance between us. The path to the shore beckoned, and I plunged down it, the recklessness of my descent dislodging pebbles and earth under my feet. I wanted the sea. I wanted to plunge into the icy water until the remembered touch of his hands and lips on my skin was blunted into numbness, until the roar of the tide obliterated his murmured endearments in my ears.

And the other voices as well, the ones that sounded like my father, saying how senseless I had been to believe he could love me. I clapped my hands to my ears, but it did not blot out the jeers ringing in my head. I could not stop seeing Herron's face, once full of trust and tenderness, transfigured into revulsion and scorn.

I was almost running when my feet touched the strand, and I kept running through the churning surf, as cold eddies sucked at my footsteps and the wind lashed at me until my skin was stinging and raw. When my strength failed I slowed to a walk, but I kept moving along the beach, following the foamy line of the tide, away from Ellsmere. Away from Herron.

* * *

When, hours later, I returned to the house, I had reached a point of more than physical numbness. I could not say I had begun to accept the end of Herron's love for me, but it had taken on an unreal quality; if I exercised the fiercest control over my thoughts and memories, and quashed him every time he tried, specter-like, to appear, I could endure.

This fragile self-possession carried me through the days that followed. Dinner every night posed the greatest challenge, since Herron was always there: after his mother's ultimatum he had been careful to join the family nightly for dinner, although he said little enough in his uncle's company. The sight of him at the dinner table on the evening after the ball was excruciating, and I avoided looking at him as much as possible.

The ordeal was made even worse by the certain knowledge that both of us were being closely observed by everyone else present. It was borne in upon me that our estranged behavior was prompting much speculative raising of eyebrows, meaning glances, and whispered comments, and whenever I raised my eyes from my plate I was sure to encounter a host of peering eyes. A shattered heart might be borne—I was not yet ready to make a definite assertion on that point—but it certainly should not be served up before an avid audience every night.

Fortunately, since the ball had marked the climax of the house party, the number of guests was diminishing. Every day the great hall was filled with luggage, and a carriage was always waiting in the drive for those who were departing. The number of places at dinner dwindled every night, and as the third floor gradually emptied my room regained its previous atmosphere of calm and privacy.

That was the pleasant part of the guests' departure; unfortunately, the end of the house party was not an unmitigated advantage. For one thing, my father showed no sign of departing. Every morning I felt the sinking of my heart as he presented his gloating smile to me over the breakfast table and asked with saccharine concern whether Herron and I had "made up that lovers' tiff yet." The duchess chafed, I thought, but did not ask him outright to leave, and I began to wonder if he would become a permanent member of the household.

The other disadvantage of the emptying house was that once more I found myself left to my own devices for the greater part of the time. No longer were the days and nights filled with a busy commotion of social activity; it was not possible to avoid Herron's company, and my own thoughts, by joining a group of guests and immersing myself in the company of others. My own rooms, once a refuge, were haunted by memories of Herron's presence; yet I was afraid that if I left them I would encounter him.

Somewhat to my surprise, Felicity emerged as a great help and comfort to me at that time. This came about from a simple question: she asked me one day at luncheon if it was true that I did not ride.

"Living in the city as I always have, there was little opportunity to learn," I explained.

"Well, you no longer live in the city, cousin," she reminded me, with a trace of smugness. "I shall teach you."

I tried to demur. "I would be a terrible pupil; I cannot make such claims on your patience or your time."

"Oh, you needn't worry that I can't teach you." Her amusement made me wonder, abashed, if my doubt had been that evident. "Charles and Aminta will tell you that I am a fine horsewoman. Come, it will be fun; now that the house is empty, we shall need something to keep us from being dull."

Aminta added her endorsement. "Felicity may look about as capable as a butterfly, but she is an excellent rider."

"There, you see? Do say you'll let me teach you. I promise that if after a fortnight you aren't pleased with your progress I'll not bother you any more." She put her head on one side and shook her curls in her most cajoling manner, and I smiled and gave in.

In spite of Aminta's commendation, I was surprised to find that Felicity was, in fact, a good teacher. She was unexpectedly patient with me, and quick to offer praise and encouragement when they were needed. In less time than I would have thought possible, I had become comfortable in the saddle. The day I was first able to ride to the village and back was a cause for celebration. I would probably never sit a horse with Felicity's apparently instinctive grace, but for me it was a triumph.

Perhaps just as therapeutic was having something with which to occupy my time and my thoughts. Even on days when I spent more time falling out of the saddle than riding, I was less desolate now that I had something to distract me from the ever-present pain of losing Herron.

Felicity was not the only one who helped me through those first terrible weeks. Aminta and her husband frequently had me to tea in the nursery with their children, in whose presence it was impossible to be self-absorbed. Charles and I took to spending an hour or two every afternoon playing chess; while we spent most of this time in silence, again I found that focusing my thoughts on strategy was an effective antidote to grief. The duchess took me calling with her, brought Mrs. Prescott in to fit me for spring gowns, and engaged my aid in selecting hangings and furniture for the redecoration of the third floor. With a tact that I welcomed gratefully, she refrained from expressing any disappointment in her hopes of a marriage between me and her son. In fact, she only mentioned him once, to note offhandedly that he had taken to spending all his time in his rooms, and I knew that she had told me this so that my mind might be eased, knowing I need not fear a chance encounter with him.

As for Lord Claude, he produced what was perhaps the most unexpected and dramatic means of taking my mind off Herron.

One night after dinner I was startled by a knock on my study door. I had been reading—or, at least, had been moving my eyes over the pages of a book—and jumped at the unexpected sound. It was a strange time for a visitor; the family and few remaining guests would still be gathered in the drawing room. "Come in," I said, trying to quell the faint surge of hope that rose in my heart.

It died of its own accord when the door opened to reveal Lord Claude. "Oh, good evening, sir," I said, hoping my disappointment did not show.

"Good evening, my dear. I hope I'm not disturbing you."

"Not at all." This, at least, was the truth, and I shut the book and put it aside as he took a seat. For the first time in weeks, he seemed at his ease; I guessed that this was because my father was not present. Lord Claude invariably looked tense and strained around him, as if my father wore a black shroud and carried a scythe. I imagined that I probably looked the same way myself when near him. Indeed, it was partly to escape my father's company that I had retreated directly to my room after dinner instead of lingering with the others in the drawing room.

"I know it is late for a visit, so I'll not detain you long," Lord Claude said now, with a smile that held something of its old charm. "In fact, I come as a messenger."

"Oh?" I said, that idiotic hope bobbing up again, and he must have observed it, for he was quick to put me out of doubt.

"From Charles."

"Oh," I said again; then, belatedly, "whatever for?" Charles had never resorted to such oblique means of communicating with me before. Indeed, he had no need to; I had seen him just an hour ago at dinner.

"The fact is," said my visitor, settling back into his chair and lacing his fingers comfortably across the front of his waistcoat, "Charles wishes to know if you would consider becoming his wife."

CHAPTER SIXTEEN

I blinked at him. He continued to regard me with perfect composure; I, on the other hand, had never felt so confused. "Charles?" I repeated, my voice an incredulous squeak.

He permitted himself a half smile. "He knew his suggestion would come as a surprise. In fact, if I had less confidence in your self-command, my dear, I would have come armed with spirits of ammonia before broaching such a topic. But, however sudden, the offer is serious. My son wishes to marry you."

"Why?" At this he did smile, and I put my hands to my head, trying to sort out my thoughts. "No, I don't mean why, exactly, but—yes, I do. Why should Charles propose to me? He has never given the least indication that he is at all interested in me, that way."

"Hasn't he?" Under Lord Claude's steady gaze I felt more discomfited than ever; all of a sudden I was forced to re-evaluate every meeting I had ever had with Charles in a new light. Could I have misread his behavior, been blind to the import of his seemingly platonic interest?

"Well, perhaps he was not very marked in his attentions," Lord Claude conceded, as I did not speak. "But you must admit that he had every reason not to be."

Of course. Until recently everyone had believed that Herron and I had an understanding—as I myself had believed. But I still had difficulty reconciling my amiable chess partner with this new vision of him as hopeful wooer. The idea seemed so farfetched, so different from the Charles I knew. This might be some ploy of my father's to better his own ends, or at best a cruel joke on his spinsterish daughter. It might even be the duchess, with her penchant for matchmaking, who had conceived the proposal.

"Are you certain it was Charles's wish for you to speak to me?" I asked warily.

His eyebrows rose as if he was injured, but then he sighed. "You have every right to ask me that, of course," he said, his voice a subdued rumble. "You have not been able to trust me as you used to since your father arrived."

"No," I admitted. His shoulders bowed under the weight of the word, and I added softly, "but the blame is my father's, not yours. The only thing I fear in you is my father's hold over you, and that is not your fault."

"You're a kind girl," he said slowly. "And an understanding one."

"I know my father; that is all. Lord Claude... what is the real reason for his presence here? Can you tell me?"

I was horrified to see his face contract in pain, his eyes shutting as if he was unable to face his own knowledge. "I cannot tell you that, my girl. In any case, you would not believe me. And better for you that you did not."

"I see." I saw nothing, except that I should not force him further; whatever my father's purpose here, it was one that seemed to tear at Lord Claude's soul. "I... I suppose, then, that you cannot say when he will be going."

He rubbed at the crease in his forehead, while his eyes slid away from mine. "It will not be much longer," he said, and the words seemed weighted with a meaning I could not discern.

"Then we shall be free," I exclaimed. "Surely we can endure him a little longer, if we know the time is short."

Impulsively, I reached my hand out to him across the desk, and he took it. I smiled at him, trying to extend encouragement to him, and for a moment we shared that intangible kinship I had felt once before. Then he released my hand, and the moment passed.

"In any case, I can assure you that your father has had no hand in this proposal," he said more briskly, straightening his shoulders; it seemed a relief to him to return to the topic of his astonishing errand. "Indeed, he knows nothing of it. Charles said he had spoken only to me."

"Why did he speak to you?" I could not help asking. "Why did he not approach me himself? It is unlike him to be so—so squeamish."

"Squeamish?" His father chuckled. "I can't wait to see his face when I tell him you said so. It was his thought that, since he had not spoken to you of his feelings, you might appreciate some time in which to accustom yourself to the idea before being confronted by him. His intention was only to spare you embarrassment." I felt ashamed of myself, even more so when he went on, "I thought it very considerate of him. If you had rather not face him at all, I shall be glad to convey your answer to him."

"Oh, no, I would not ask you to do that," I said hastily. "It would be unfair to Charles; he should be the first to know my answer." Lord Claude's frankly inquisitive raised eyebrows made me laugh self-consciously. "And no, sir, I do not yet have an answer. I need time to consider."

I rose, and he was on his feet at once, never questioning my wish to end the interview. "Of course," he said warmly. "Charles will understand perfectly. Only do not keep him on tenterhooks too long, my dear."

I could not help but smile at the incongruity of the image his words conjured up: genial, unflappable Charles, wasting away in a pale languishing fever of love denied. "I'll not draw out his agonies, I give you my word." Then, as we reached the door, I thought of one more thing to ask.

"What do you think of his wish to marry me, sir?"

He took my chin in his hand. "I think," he said, "that I raised a very bright son." And, with a little shake of my chin, as if to chide me for a foolish question, he bade me goodnight.

I could think of nothing the next day except that baffling proposal. I had wondered if Charles's manner toward me would be changed, if he would even (heaven forbid) ask me directly what my answer was. But he treated me with the same friendly courtesy he had ever shown me, as we conversed about the weather, my ride with Felicity, the new books to be ordered for the library. It was I whose manner had changed; I felt unnatural, awkward around him, suddenly conscious of hitherto unguessed possibilities between us. It was bewildering trying to divine what his thoughts might be, and making the pretence of normality; by the time dinner was over I was exhausted and glad to take refuge in the solitude of my room.

Once alone, however, I found my mind was still teeming with questions. I was too restless to retire, but nonetheless I changed my dinner dress for the comfort of one of my velvet dressing gowns. As always, it was a relief to shed my corset and take my hair out of its net and remove the pins. All the weeks of my new life had not accustomed me to wearing my hair up; often my head ached from the pins, or from the sheer weight of my hair, and it was always with a sense of release that I unbound it in the evening and brushed it out. This evening I brushed it for a long time, as I thought.

I could not help feeling slightly annoyed with Charles for not having made his offer in person. This was unfair to him; he was only being tactful and considerate of my feelings. Nevertheless, I felt somehow cheated. It was so difficult to take his proposal seriously, offered as it was through an intermediary; had he spoken to me himself, perhaps I would have been more convinced of his sincerity. Unless he had doubts himself about his choice, and had sent his father in order that he might have another's opinion as to the wisdom of proposing to me? Perhaps he was being cautious.

As well he should be. The hairbrush stilled in my hand. He was, in fact, taking quite a risk in asking me to marry him, knowing so little about me. Having discovered me half naked in compromising circumstances, he had every right to entertain doubts about my suitability for marriage. And he knew of my attachment to Herron. Most gentlemen would never even consider proposing marriage to a young woman who had been so intimately connected with another man. No wonder if he had chosen to court me with such caution; it would not be like him to take so important a step impulsively.

But it occurred to me that I might not know Charles as well as I assumed. I knew he was kind, tactful, considerate; he had proved that beyond a doubt on the disastrous night of the ball. He was amusing, sometimes even silly, but undeniably intelligent and perceptive. He had never seemed prey to self-pity, even when he had been half crippled by illness. But of his feelings I knew little. Certainly I could not imagine what would lead him to pursue marriage with an obscure, undowried girl whose father was suspected of uxoricide. True, we did seem to get along well. But could there ever be between us what I saw in the duchess's face when she looked at Lord Claude, or what I had felt for Herron?

Impulsively, I put the brush down on the dressing table and slid my feet into chamois-soled slippers. It was late, but not so late that he would have retired. Most likely he would just be returning from the drawing room. I peered around the edge of my door; a solitary maid vanished around the corner with a stack of linens, and then the hall was empty. I made my way to his room silently and, in my sapphire blue dressing gown, almost invisibly.

"Come in," he called at my knock, and when I entered he swung around with a friendly smile, evidently in expectation of a valet, for it faltered when he saw me. To my dismay I saw that he was already undressing; his coat and waistcoat were discarded, and his hands had frozen in the act of unknotting his tie. I felt blood mantle in my cheeks, and realized too late how my own attire might be construed at such an hour. But his first words reassured me.

"You must have come to discuss my offer," he said. "Won't you have a seat? Please excuse my informal dress; I was not expecting to entertain."

"Thank you." I took the chair he indicated, and he seated himself opposite me. I was suddenly at a loss as to how to conduct this conversation; we were meeting on such different terms than usual. I was still having a difficult time reconciling the Charles I knew—or thought I knew—with my impulsive wooer.

For his part, Charles seemed determined to conduct himself as if this unconventional visit were a normal occurrence. He was regarding me with a pleasant, amiable expression as he attempted to reknot his tie. Had he not mentioned his proposal, I would have thought it the furthest thing from his mind. Certainly I saw no evidence that he was anxious to be put out of his suspense, and his next words did nothing to change that impression.

"Would you care for some refreshment?" he offered. "I'll be happy to ring for some tea."

"No, thank you."

"You're right, that wouldn't be wise. Sherry, perhaps? But I don't keep any in my rooms. I could brew you a nice cordial of hydrogen peroxide and formaldehyde in my laboratory, but I'm afraid that is all I have to offer."

I had to put an end to this; evidently the only way was to be direct. "I won't keep you long," I said. "I'm sorry to disturb you at this hour, but I had to speak with you alone." He nodded as if this were perfectly natural, but again I paused, watching his continued efforts to put his tie in order. By now it was in a hopeless state, but when he ceased struggling with it, he seemed not to know what to do with his hands.

At this rate I would never accomplish what I had set out to do. Mentally giving myself a shake, I plunged in before I could stop to think about what I was saying. "Your offer of marriage is very generous, and I'm certain it was kindly meant. But we have known each other so short a time that I wondered how you could have any idea of whether we would be compatible."

"Compatible?" he repeated, his eyebrows climbing. "I think we have been acquainted long enough to have an idea of that. We both enjoy dancing, narcissus, strawberry preserves, the works of Sir Walter Scott..."

A sense of depression began to steal over me. "Yes, of course; you are perfectly right."

"That is not what concerns you, is it?" His deep voice became serious for the first time during this interview. I shook my head, grateful for his perception.

"Tell me what you are thinking, then," he requested.

Now that he was regarding me so steadily and expectantly, I found it difficult to be as frank as I would have liked to be. I kept my eyes on my hands, which were pleating and unpleating the fabric of my dressing gown. "Your aunt has a theory about marriage—perhaps she has shared it with you?—that it should consist of a, shall we say, more than temperamental compatibility. I daresay you find the idea unorthodox."

"On the contrary, I think it a very sound theory."

I darted a look at him, but failed to catch even a glimmer of laughter in his eyes. He seemed perfectly grave. This was heartening, and I was able to continue with more confidence.

It should be possible, after all, to conduct this experiment in a matter-of-fact, intelligent fashion; we were both sensible people, and he seemed receptive to reason. "Had you considered whether that, er, compatibility is present between us?" I asked bravely.

He nodded, again with perfect composure. "For myself, I can assure you that I anticipate no disappointment in that quarter."

"Oh?" I hoped I was not blushing. I had not expected to hear that he had even thought about the matter.

"But I would hate for you to feel any uneasiness," he said cheerfully. "If you are uncertain of my charms, you have only to say so."

"I have wondered," I admitted. "That is not to say that I dislike you, or anything of the sort. But I had never thought of you as—as a—in that capacity, and..."

"Perfectly understandable. What can I do to assist you? I am at your disposal."

A hysterical urge to laugh bubbled up in me; he might have been offering to carry parcels for me. "I think it might be a good idea if I were to kiss you," I said.

"Of course," he said readily. "An admirable suggestion." This time I knew there was an undercurrent of laughter in his voice, but it had the strange effect of easing my nervousness; it reminded me that this was Charles, after all, not some stranger.

"You are too kind," I said, and at my tone he smiled outright. This would not be so difficult after all; I thanked heaven he had a sense of humor. I rose, and he followed suit. "If you will just stand there..."

"Your wish is my command." He stood straight, his eyes fixed on the distance, as if awaiting a firing squad—not a comparison very flattering to me, but one that removed any threat of unwelcome familiarity. "I think I had better keep my hands behind my back," he added, clasping them together. "I wouldn't want them to... well, I think it would be best," he ended lamely.

I surveyed him. He was certainly a good deal taller than I had realized. "I shall have to ask you to stoop down a bit," I said. "And if you don't mind I'll put my hands on your shoulders."

"That seems reasonable. Would you like me to close my eyes?" I gave him a look, and he said humbly, "Never mind; I'll do what I think best when the time comes."

With my hands braced on his shoulders I was able to raise myself comfortably to tiptoe. In my preoccupation I forgot to close my eyes at once, and had time to notice that Felicity had been right about his long eyelashes before being distracted by other observations.

The kiss was delicate at first, almost tentative, as if each of us was afraid to startle the other. I was fleetingly aware of the not unpleasant tickle of his moustache. His lips were gentle, but at their touch tendrils of warmth began to uncurl through my veins. My lips parted under his. Hardly aware I was doing so, I moved in closer to him; I could feel his shiver at the instant our bodies touched, and he murmured my name before his arms slipped around me to hold me closer still.

Minutes passed, or hours, or seconds. Finally he sighed against my lips, and raised his head to look at me. The intense blue of his eyes filled my sight. I could feel the rapid beat of his heart, or perhaps it was my own.

After a long moment we released each other. Without speaking, he turned and went to the washstand. As I watched, he soaked a towel in the basin, wrung it out, and applied it to his face. "I owe you an apology," he said, his voice muffled through the linen. "The last thing I wanted was to offend you."

I found my way to a chair; my legs were quite incapable of supporting me any longer. "Did I appear to be offended?" I demanded. My response could have left little room for such misinterpretation.

His smile kindled his eyes to such a blaze of azure that it made me breathless again, and I had to look away. "Perhaps that was a poor choice of words. Let's say I was afraid that I might have seized privileges you aren't ready to bestow on me."

"To bestow on anyone but Herron, you mean," I interpreted, and after a moment's pause, he nodded. "I did not think of him until this moment," I admitted, surprised, pleased, and slightly ashamed to discover that this was true. While Charles held me in his arms no comparisons or memories had thronged to me; I had not thought of Herron for an instant—indeed, I had scarcely been capable of thought at all. I dragged myself back to the present.

"You needn't worry that you were too forward. Believe me, you have nothing whatever to reproach yourself with."

At this emphatic speech, a smile tugged at his lips again, and I found myself smiling as well. Well, there was little purpose now in trying to disguise my reaction. "And I," he said, his voice rumbling with suppressed mirth, "must return the compliment."

At that, we both burst into laughter, and the shyness that had threatened to come between us was vanquished. He dropped into a chair opposite me, and we regarded each other with something like our former camaraderie, although tinged now with a new awareness. I noticed for the first time that his hair was tousled, and realized that it must have been from my fingers. "So," he said, "where does this leave us?"

The laughter died in me; I was still for a long time. "I wish I knew," I said at last. "I had not bargained for this. I thought it would be so simple." Even to me my voice sounded plaintive. "I was going to accept you."

"Was?" I think he said, but I was not paying attention.

"It would have been so easy simply to accept all that you offered: a home, security, companionship, with no need for any depth of feeling on my part. I was willing to use you in that way, I admit it, to marry you without any emotion other than affection and gratitude." Ashamed of the sound of it, the callousness of it, I dropped my eyes. "I suppose you will wish to withdraw your offer now. You must think me completely without scruples."

"I think I know you better than that," was all he said to this; then, "What feelings did you suppose prompted my offer, if those were the feelings that would have motivated your acceptance?"

I had not come to any satisfactory conclusion about what he felt. I had to cast about me now for a likely answer. "You are of an age to be looking for a wife," I ventured. "And I think you are fond of me."

His mouth twisted in a wry smile very like Herron's. "Is that all? I am not certain which of us you are undervaluing."

"I'm sorry; I don't seem to be thinking very clearly. I should have waited until a more appropriate time to speak to you." I rose to go, and although he seemed on the point of protesting, in the end he accompanied me to the door without any attempt to detain me. I gave him my hand in farewell.

"I'm very grateful to you, Charles, but I can't give you an answer just yet."

"Wait, Oriel, please; I'd like to say something before you go." His eyes dropped to my hand, which he still held. His fingertips moved lightly over it, tracing my veins, my bones. "I know you love Herron; I also know it will probably take you a long time to stop loving him, even after what he did to you the night of the ball—yes, I knew it was he," as I started to speak. "I understand that you can't be ready to think about loving me. But I couldn't help but see how things have changed between the two of you, especially since that night, and I thought I might have a chance." He was still concentrating on my hand, as if memorizing it, and his words seemed to come from far away. "Perhaps it was conceited of me, but I even wondered if you might find me a pleasant change after my cousin's cruelty."

The tender pressure of his fingers had lulled me into a half daze; the last words wrenched me out of it. "Cruelty!"

"I don't mean that he's cruel by nature," he said quickly, his eyes holding mine, willing me to listen. "I still believe that Herron's a good fellow at heart. But he is very young yet, and sometimes acts without considering others—and, unfortunately for you, you were one of the people closest to him, and so most at risk from his thoughtlessness. I call him cruel because that is what his treatment of you was. But it was not consciously so."

I had never before thought of Herron in this way. But was it not true? I myself had seen his growing detachment from us change his treatment of his family, of me.

"It is true that he hurt me," I said slowly, groping my way through this new perspective. "Not deliberately. But without meaning to, without even realizing that he did. He is so consumed by his own distrust, by suspicion, that I don't believe he really understands how his behavior can injure those around him." I had been gazing into space as I thought this through; now I realized that Charles was watching me attentively. "I think he did love me, though; as much as he could love anyone, when he was so absorbed in his own anguish."

He nodded, his brows drawn, as if he had come to the same conclusions and had found them as troubling as I did. "I know he loved you. But I believe you're right in thinking that there was little of his heart left for you, when the greater part of it is occupied with thoughts of his father and himself. I hoped that you would come to see that before…"

He was too kind to finish, but I could say it. "Before he discarded me." I smiled faintly. "It would have been more merciful had it happened as you wished, but I doubt I would have seen what was bound to happen." No, I had been too much in love to have believed.

"But it need not happen the same way again," he said gently. "Not if you choose someone who loves you too dearly to do anything that might hurt you."

I found it strangely difficult to speak; never had I expected this.

"Do you mean you love me?" But as soon as the words left my lips I felt I had been too abrupt; I shook my head and exclaimed, before he could speak, "Please do not answer; I don't know what I'm saying. I should not have asked you that."

"Of course you should ask it, if you truly do not know the answer." He was very close, close enough to kiss me again; but instead he raised my hand to his face and held it there, my palm against the warm skin. "Don't you?"

I could not think under the intensity of that blue gaze. I don't know what I might have said if he had not suddenly cocked his head, frowning. He did not seem to notice when I eased my hand out of his grasp.

"Do you smell something?" he asked, in a different voice.

"No, not a thing," I said truthfully, but his alert, attentive stance did not change.

"It's smoke. Something is burning." He opened the door, first making certain that I was shielded behind it, and leaned out. In a moment he drew his head back into the room.

"It's coming from the direction of Herron's room," he said briefly. "I'm going to have a look. You should probably stay here; I'll let you know when it's safe to leave. It will be best for you if you aren't seen here." He was right; the repercussions would be dire if I were found to have visited his room at night. He gave me a quick smile, meant to reassure, but clearly his mind was already on the other matter. "If there's any danger, I'll be back for you," he said, and then he had gone.

Startled by the suddenness of his departure, I remained where I stood by the door. I was almost grateful to this emergency for having given me a chance to regain my composure. So much had happened that I welcomed the time alone.

For a few minutes I thought that Charles might have been called away by a false alarm, for no smell of smoke had yet reached me; had he been misled, or were his senses so much better than mine? But then, gradually, the smell of smoke began to permeate the room. Running footsteps came—probably servants, alerted by Charles; voices raised in questions indicated that the hallway was beginning to fill with curious bystanders.

I eased the door open a cautious sliver. Smoke was curling from an open doorway down the hall, and sounds of men stamping on flames emanated from the room. As I watched, Charles and Herron emerged in the same instant. Charles was half supporting his cousin, who shook with coughing. He was in night clothes, and must have been sound asleep—would have been asleep still, I thought in shock, if Charles had not noticed something awry and gone in after him.

"They need more help in there," Charles commanded, and several men obligingly rushed into the chamber. There were more calls for water, and some of the ladies emerged with jugs and basins slopping over in the anxiety of their errand.

"What is this disturbance about?" came a peremptory voice that I recognized as my father's. Immaculate in a ruby-colored dressing gown, he gazed with distaste at the two disheveled men, rescuer and rescued.

"A fire started in Herron's room. Don't worry, he's unharmed, and the fire is only a small one." Charles eased Herron into a sitting position on the floor, with his back propped against the wall. My father curled his lip at the spectacle.

"No doubt you were smoking in bed and fell asleep," he said. "A dangerous habit, as you nearly discovered to your cost."

Herron glanced at him with what was, under the circumstances, forgivable resentment. I knew he did not smoke. He tried to speak, but his voice was choked from the smoke he had breathed; he went into spasms of coughing again.

Charles handed him a glass of water and stood over him so that he would drink it. "It would be more constructive to help solve the immediate problem, Mr. Pembroke, rather than indulging in futile speculation as to its cause. Will you lend Herron your dressing gown? He needs to be kept warm after the shock he has suffered."

"I've never heard of anything so absurd," my father huffed. "You suggest that I give up my dressing gown and subject myself to all the perils of a draughty hall in the middle of the night for the sake of this young idiot who could have burnt us all to death in our beds?"

Charles stared at him for a moment, then shrugged.

"I'm sure Herron would rather contract pneumonia than put you at risk of a head cold," he said drily. "If you won't make yourself useful, will you kindly get out of the way so others can? Here, Montrose, hand me that blanket."

After Charles had wrapped Herron in the blanket and gone back into the chamber to see what more he could do, my father hovered over Herron, looking down his nose at the hunched, smoke-stained figure. "It seems you've been smoked out of your hole, my boy," he said, and I wondered if I imagined the dislike in his voice. "You won't be able to go to earth as you have been."

Herron, after one glowering look, turned his head away. He did not answer.

The fire was out, but the house could not settle down immediately. Herron had to be provided with a place to sleep, and he steadfastly refused to share a room with any of the other gentlemen; in the end a divan was moved into the music room for him. Fortunately, the duchess and Lord Claude had not been roused by the commotion, but everyone else wanted to linger in the hall and discuss the cause of the blaze and their own narrow escape from a fiery death. My father seemed to enjoy simply loitering about and making a nuisance of himself. In the end, though, Charles and Lord Montrose managed to restore order. Not until everyone had cleared out of the hall did Charles return to his room, and to me.

"I'm sorry to have left you for so long," he said when he had shut the door. "It couldn't be helped."

"I know." The smell of smoke clung about him overpoweringly, and soot had left smudges on his face and shirt. His eyes were startlingly bright in his dirtied face. "Will everything be all right now?" I asked.

"Yes, there's nothing to worry about. Herron will be fine."

I would not have blamed him if he had spoken ironically, but he did not. I felt a strange strangled feeling in my heart. But "How did the fire start?" was all I could think to say.

"It seems to have started in the bed curtains, but I don't know how." He raked his hair back from his forehead with a grimy hand, and I knew he must be almost too weary to stand, but he was too much of a gentleman to ask me to leave, no matter how tired. I should go, I knew; it wasn't kind of me to stay and keep him from his rest.

"Is it safe for me to leave now?"

"It should be. I think everyone has gone back to their rooms."

"Good night, then." Still I felt that I wanted to say something more; but this was probably not the time, even had I been able to think of it.

He did not move as I stepped past him. "Good night, golden one," he said quietly, and I closed the door on the sight of him standing there.

By now it was late, but all the excitement of that evening had made me more wakeful than ever. And I wanted to sleep. My meeting with Charles had aroused too many ideas, most of them disturbing; I did not want to confront all the implications of that unexpectedly sweet encounter. There was also the mystery of the fire. So sudden a blaze, with no discernible cause, and after all the other strange occurrences—it was a puzzle that nagged at me tiresomely.

For once I wanted not to have to think. I was beginning to feel as Herron must, trapped in the maelstrom of his own mind, slipping farther away from anything outside of it, and so that I might have a few hours' respite I took out the bottle of laudanum my father had procured for me. I measured out the proper number of drops into a glass of water and drank it down. At least I might be able to ease my too-active brain for tonight and find some peace in sleep.

But even if my waking mind was lulled by the drug, I found I could not escape so easily. Perhaps because of the laudanum I found myself trapped in endless, frenzied dreams.

I did not often dream. I had never been subject to the kinds of nightmares that made Herron thrash and mutter in his sleep; nor had the increasingly dramatic events of my new life played themselves out in scenes before my sleeping self. But tonight I dreamed.

I was watching Herron and the duchess confront each other again on the night of the tableaus, only this time it was I wearing the duchess's evening dress and diamonds, and it was I Herron was berating.

"Not enough that you should be a harlot, running to the arms of any man who beckons," he was snarling at me. "Not enough that you can change your attachments as some women change their gown. No, you must add to your wantonness folly as well. Can you not see what he is about? Why should he care for you? No man would willingly open his arms to a woman who has passed through those of another man, without good reason of his own."

Then, horribly, Herron's figure shifted and wavered, melting into another familiar form, and now it was my father who loomed over me and castigated me for my behavior.

"I was right to think you a dunce," he boomed. "You haven't even the wits to see that he is wooing you to save his own skin. You're so besotted with him now that you will never cry murder against him or his father. They are safe from you now, and all it took was a few honeyed lies, a quick cuddle in a dark room—you sell your silence cheaply, my girl. How does it feel to be kissed by a killer?"

With a huge effort I jerked myself awake. The silence of the room greeted me like a friend, but I dared not sleep again. I rose and walked the floor of my room until daybreak; but it was not so easy to outpace the accusations that still rang in my ears.

Chapter Seventeen

The next forty-eight hours were to be among the strangest of my life.

When I went downstairs next morning the first thing I saw was a clutter of trunks in the great hall. The last remaining guests had been routed by last night's fire, and were departing. I was disappointed to see that my father's luggage was not among that in the hall. So we were not yet rid of him.

The house was very quiet that day, from the absence not only of guests but of some of the family as well: Aminta and her family, taking Felicity and Miss Yates with them, had gone to spend a few days with friends. Even Charles, while not accompanying them, had made himself scarce, perhaps so that I would not feel compelled by his presence to give him an answer to his proposal—an answer I could not yet give.

Herron was more in evidence than usual, now that he could not retreat to his rooms for refuge as he had been doing, but of course his company was not something I courted. The duchess and Lord Claude had been shocked when told of the events of the night before, and the duchess fluttered around her son with pillows, rugs, and cups of broth, as if he had been suffering from a chill. Herron did not brush her attentions off, as I had expected; he suffered them quietly, if not gladly, although I noticed that when his mother's back was turned he poured the broth into a potted palm. I would have smiled at this childish gesture if he had not looked so grim; his air of constant wariness had not diminished, even though he looked so tired and hollow-eyed that my heart twisted when I saw him.

By dinner that night it was plain that something was in the air. While the duchess was even more vivacious than usual out of her relief at her son's narrow escape, a strange moodiness seemed to afflict the rest of the company: Charles was unusually silent, as was my father, who seemed to be brooding. His glowering presence at the table, however, had the effect of making Lord Claude nervous. For the hundredth time I wished I knew the nature of the strange link between them.

Herron himself seemed to have been sobered by his experience. He ate little, and when I bent down to retrieve my dropped napkin I saw that he was passing his food down to Zeus, who sat waiting by his chair. He watched his stepfather with a fixed concentration that seemed even more marked than usual. Lord Claude was not unaware of this scrutiny, and by the time the last course was served he seemed to have made up his mind to try to lighten the atmosphere.

"I have something special for you tonight, Herron," he announced, with a geniality that did not seem wholly genuine, when the dessert plates were being set out. "I know how fond you are of that particular type of Chartreuse, so I ordered a bottle for your birthday. Of course, it's almost a fortnight yet until the great day, but I thought you might like to open it tonight—to celebrate your lucky escape."

"Thank you," said Herron, but his voice gave no indication as to his feelings. "That's very kind of you."

"Yes, darling, what a generous thought." The duchess smiled at her husband. I was certain she was encouraged by the fact that Lord Claude and Herron could find some common ground, even if it was only a bottle of liqueur. "And we must toast Charles as well, as Herron's rescuer."

"There's no need, Aunt Gwendolyn. I'm just glad that I smelled the fire in time."

"Indeed, it was fortunate for him that you did," my father observed, but there was a dry undertone in the words that the duchess seized upon.

"Well, of course it was fortunate!" she exclaimed. "A few minutes more, and Herron might have been—oh, I cannot even think of it. Charles, how glad I am you were there!"

As Jenkins opened the bottle, one of the footmen placed a liqueur glass before Herron. No one else received a glass. "You'll join me, I hope, Uncle?" said Herron. It sounded more like a challenge than an invitation, but his uncle smiled comfortably.

"I'll not be so selfish as to ask you to share your favorite, my boy; I bought it for you. I'll have the port, Jenkins."

The other two men chose port as well. I was content not to be offered the drink; the strange color of the liqueur did not appeal to me, but "I shall have some" proclaimed the duchess, and beckoned for a glass. "If we are observing Herron's birthday early, then I certainly want to join my son in a toast."

"But, Gwendolyn," objected Lord Claude, and I was surprised at the urgency in his voice. "You detest Chartreuse."

She laughed. "I am not yet so old, I hope, that I cannot acquire a new taste. If my son wishes to have Chartreuse, I shall learn to like it." She watched approvingly as the glasses were filled; her husband, in contrast, seemed distressed. I saw him pass a finger around the inside of his collar.

"Gwendolyn, I really do think you have had enough spirits this evening," he said. "Thomas, take Her Grace's glass."

But she waved the footman away. "Really, Claude, don't be stuffy. Why shouldn't I have a glass of liqueur?"

"Why not, indeed?" Herron agreed, and his eyes were narrowly watching his uncle. "Is there some reason no one will share my birthday drink? I must say it's a bit hard that my own stepfather won't drink to my health, even if—I admit it—I have not been a model son of late." This dignified admission won an approving smile from his mother, and he continued with a humility I had never seen in him. "I would be glad if you would have a glass with me, uncle, to show that you forgive my recent behavior."

There was utter silence. The duchess was beaming at this unexpected gesture, but Lord Claude's face had gone a pasty grey. He did not look as gratified as he should have at hearing his rebellious new son capitulate. His hesitation was so marked that his wife felt the need to prod him.

"Come, Claude, you must have a glass with him now. A toast to mark a new beginning for our family!"

"Yes, Claude," said my father, smiling as if amused. "You can scarcely refuse now."

With a sudden, decisive movement Lord Claude pushed his chair back from the table. "No, Herron, I will not drink with you. I cannot so easily overlook your misconduct. You have caused great embarrassment to your mother and me, to the Reginald family name itself, and I will not simply sweep the matter under the rug when it pleases you."

He might have said more, but his wife was watching him with her lips thinned in an expression that boded him no good. "I am sorry you are so unforgiving, Claude," she said shortly. "Herron, I hope you will forgive your stepfather his stubbornness. I am certain he will come to see there is no good in such obstinacy." The look she sent her husband promised that she would personally enforce this change of heart if necessary. "Until then, my dear, I raise my glass to you."

Herron hesitated, then held his glass aloft as she did. His eyes were on his uncle, as if waiting for some word or sign, but none came. The candlelight gleamed palely through the drink, a strangely mesmerizing sight. Then the duchess moved to bring her glass to her lips, and Herron slowly followed suit. But the instant she moved, Lord Claude gave a great shout and knocked the goblet out of her hand.

Bright drops of liquor showered the air like jewels in the moment before the glass shattered against the floor. Then Herron's voice came, ringing out in triumph.

"I knew it!" he shouted. "It was poisoned!"

There was a slice of time in which no one made a sound, and I saw Lord Claude breathing quickly, as if he had lifted some enormous weight. I was aware of the intent expression on my father's face, the shock on Charles's, the wide astonished eyes of the duchess. Suddenly everyone seemed to be standing.

"I don't know what you mean," said Lord Claude, but his voice was unsteady. "There was a wasp on your mother's glass—"

Herron was laughing, his face mottled with red. "Your soft heart spoiled your plan, didn't it? You hadn't allowed for the possibility that Mother would wish to share the wine. Too bad, Uncle. A bit more resolution, and you'd have been rid of me—and you'd have inherited your wealthy bride's fortune as well."

"Herron, you aren't well," whispered his mother. "You don't know what you are saying—"

"That is what I have been trying to tell you, Gwendolyn." Lord Claude's voice was harsh with strain. "The boy's mind isn't whole. He needs to be sent away. I know a place where they can treat cases like this, where he'll be safe from these delusions—"

Herron laughed again, and advanced on his uncle with a deliberation that was frightening to see. "Oh, it would suit you very well if I were mad, Uncle, I can see; I would be as good as dead, but without the inconvenience of another murder. You'd not even have the poisoned wine to explain away."

"As if I needed an explanation." Lord Claude fell back a pace as his nephew continued to advance. "How could there be anything in the drink? Where would I possibly get poison?"

"It's easily found, if you look. But then, you wouldn't even have to look very far, would you? Not with your loyal son and his laboratory." He was closing the space between himself and his uncle, bearing the glass before him purposefully. "He could have obliged you easily by stirring up something lethal."

"Herron, that is enough," Charles commanded, moving to intercept him. "Put down that glass."

"Not until my uncle drinks." Herron's eyes never wavered from his uncle's face. "That is the only way he can clear himself now."

With an attempt at dignity, Lord Claude straightened. "You are speaking wildly, Herron. I will not dignify these insane accusations by listening to them further." He turned to the duchess, whose face had gone white, and held out his hand to her. "Come, my dear; we need listen to no more of this."

Her eyes flicked back and forth between him and her son, and she made no move toward his outstretched hand. Suddenly Herron lunged at Lord Claude, but Charles was there first, seizing the arm that held the goblet, forcing it out of Herron's hand. In the scuffle the liquid slopped out of the glass and onto the table, staining the white cloth pale yellow. The duchess gave a thin shriek, and Lord Claude staggered backward, knocking over his chair.

"Get out of the way, Charles," Herron hissed. "My uncle and I have a score to settle."

"This is not the way to settle it." Charles had grasped Herron by both arms and held him firmly.

"He is right, of course," came my father's voice, lazy and offhand; when I looked, I saw that he was the only one not on his feet. He reclined in his chair, one hand idly toying with the stem of his port glass. "The proper way to settle such accusations is with a duel."

"This is a family affair, sir, and we'll thank you not to interfere." I had never heard Charles so angry. "No one has mentioned duels."

"It was only a matter of time," my father returned, with no change in his languid posture. "The boy has made a grave allegation against your father. When one man insults another in such a fashion, the accused must defend his honor. You insolent puppy, you were begging to be called out."

"No." The low whisper came from the duchess, but it went unnoticed.

"I shall certainly not call out my own stepson," returned Lord Claude, with new spirit, seeming to revive; there was authority in his voice now. "The boy is raving, in any case, and should be locked up. I see that we have been too lenient with you, Herron; we should have had you sent to an asylum long before now."

"Herron isn't mad." It was Charles's voice, strangely distant and very, very quiet. "The Chartreuse was poisoned."

All eyes turned toward him as he pointed to something that lay on the floor beyond the foot of the table. It was Zeus the spaniel, who had been lapping up the spilled liqueur. He lay too quietly for any living thing.

"Oh, no," I cried. I had not believed until now that the drink had been poisoned, that someone could have died, but here was brutal proof. All the security I had felt came crashing down around me. Death had found its way into the house.

Until then, I think the men had forgotten that there were women present. My cry had startled them into remembrance.

"Gwendolyn, you and the girl should not be here," Lord Claude declared, his voice charged with shock and something like outrage that we should have been witness to all this. "This is not a scene for ladies."

"I will not leave." The duchess's chin was set at its most formidable angle. "You cannot ask me to go at such a time."

"It is precisely because it is such a time that you must go!" Her husband paused to regain control of his voice, and Charles put in quietly, "I would be grateful if you took Oriel away, Aunt. She, at least, need not be subjected to this."

"No, I won't leave," I said, but after a considering pause the duchess raised her head in acquiescence.

"Come, child," she said to me. "We had better go." The men were motionless, all discord suspended until they could resume their contention out of range of feminine ears. The duchess gave me a look that brooked no argument; miserably, I followed her from the room.

"How can you bear to leave?" I burst out, when the door had been shut—and locked—behind us. "It may be Herron's life at stake, or Lord Claude's—"

"Hush," she ordered. She was moving swiftly toward a small door down the corridor, and I hesitated only a moment before following; there was a purpose in her gait that suggested she was not accepting her banishment so easily as I had thought. "Keep very quiet and follow me. We must know how this ends." She wrenched open the door and without even glancing behind to see if I was there she caught up her skirts and began ascending, quickly, nimbly, two steps at a time.

The narrow stair smelled of must and disuse, and I had no idea where we were going. I had shut the hall door behind us, in case any of the gentlemen thought to look for us, so that we ascended in almost complete darkness. Busy as I was, clutching at my too-abundant skirts as I felt my way upward, I had no time to wonder what our destination was.

We emerged suddenly into a long slice of room, one side of which was constructed of a pierced, decorative wooden screen. Voices were audible through this, and the duchess, with a warning glance at me to remind me of the need for silence, moved slowly over so that she could look through. I followed, holding my hands against my skirts to still their rustling, and looked through the screen. The long expanse of the dining hall spread beneath us, and I realized we must be in the old minstrels' gallery. We would be invisible to those below, even if they were not so absorbed in their brutal conversation.

Evidently while we had removed to our hiding place, as short a time as we had been, Herron had again launched himself at his uncle in an attempt to do violence to him;

Charles was struggling to regain his grip on him. My father's voice was the first we heard.

"This is shabby behavior from a duke," he commented, and his voice still held that undercurrent of detached amusement, as if the scene concerned him as little as a pantomime. "You would rather throttle your stepfather than fight him honorably in a duel."

"I would not trust him in a duel," shouted Herron. "A man who resorts to something as underhand as poison would stoop to any treachery."

"If you were anyone else, Your Grace, I would call that cowardice."

Herron's struggles to free himself ceased—out of resignation, I sensed, rather than any shame called up by my father's accusation. He was breathing heavily, and his evening jacket was torn. Charles, too, was disheveled, but his grip on his cousin did not weaken. Lord Claude had armed himself with a poker from the fireplace; now, evidently judging that the immediate danger had passed, he reached cautiously behind himself to replace it, never moving his eyes from Herron.

My father continued, untroubled by the lack of interest his words inspired. "But, of course, I should expect such dishonorable behavior from you: the cad who discarded my daughter after leading her to believe that you had an understanding."

Now he had their attention. "There was no understanding," Herron said, his voice tinged with bewilderment at this change in topic.

At last my father rose, and when he spoke his voice had hardened. No longer was he the disinterested observer. "I say that there was," he snapped, "and only a blackguard would deny it. Now, what should a father do under such circumstances? Horsewhip the young scoundrel? Quite possibly. Call him out? Most certainly. Your Grace, you have trifled with my daughter's honor, and I demand satisfaction."

Herron's body had gone slack in consternation, and I felt equally baffled. What did my father have to gain by calling out Herron? Why was he using me as a pretext? I could tell from her face that the same questions were passing through the duchess's mind. She looked at me for answers, but I shook my head helplessly; all we could do was listen.

“This is preposterous,” Herron was saying, impatient now, trying to dismiss this nuisance. “You have no occasion to challenge me.”

My father started to speak—to goad Herron further, I had no doubt—but he was forestalled.

“I, on the other hand, do,” said Charles, and I gasped before I remembered the need for silence. A block of ice seemed to form in my stomach. I had a terrible feeling I knew what he was going to say, but I could not guess why he was going to say it.

Charles’s grip at last relaxed, and Herron turned to stare at this new, unexpected accuser. “Whatever have you to do with it, Charles?” he demanded, wonder overcoming even his anger.

I wished I could read Charles’s face. From above, all I could see was the top of his head. “I found Oriel,” he said quietly, “the night you attacked her.”

There was silence at this; Lord Claude and my father looked equally confused, and the duchess slanted a look at me.

“You did indeed behave like a cad to her.” Charles folded his arms across his chest and stood unmoving, facing his cousin. “You stripped her almost down to the skin and then abandoned her there. I do have cause to challenge you, Herron, and the cause is a lady’s honor.”

The duchess whispered, “Did Herron do this to you?” and I nodded. At the sight of the shock that flooded her eyes, I averted my gaze. She was learning things tonight she should not have had to know.

“If this is true,” said my father, and his voice resounded not with indignation but with satisfaction, “then it is my place to defend my daughter’s honor.”

“No, it is not,” Charles returned strongly. “I hope to become Oriel’s husband, so it is my place, and mine only, to challenge her attacker. And Herron has questioned my honor as well, by accusing me of brewing poison to kill him. I have two reputations to defend.”

“Charles, you will not defend anyone.” Lord Claude had rallied from his surprise. “No one will fight. It is preposterous to debate questions of honor with a lunatic.”

“This madman has enough honor to avenge those you and your son have wronged,” snarled Herron. “I’ll meet you both, if you wish, one after the other.”

There was argument over this. Lord Claude did not want Herron to duel anyone; my father and Charles both claimed the right as theirs. They haggled like cooks at a butcher's shop, and had it not concerned the men dearest to me, I could have found the situation to be not without humor. I wondered desperately why Charles was so insistent, why he was so eager to duel Herron.

Under cover of the men's raised voices, the duchess leaned over to me and murmured, "Charles must love you very much to be so quick to defend your honor against his own cousin."

I shook my head, baffled. "There must be another reason," I insisted. "Herron did me no harm; Charles knows that."

"Enough," thundered Charles at last. The squabbling died away. "Herron, I am calling you out. Even if you care nothing for the lady you dishonored, you will surely not let pass the chance to spill the blood of your poisoner."

Herron's eyes shifted; now that it came to the crisis, his certainty seemed to waver. "My uncle was the poisoner."

"You can't be sure of that. After all, as you pointed out, I am the one who has the readiest access to deadly chemicals. Besides, you know your stepfather will never fight you. I am his champion, if you will." Charles half smiled at his father, who stepped forward in horror. "Whatever quarrel you have with my father, you have with me. We are the same person, as far as this matter is concerned."

"Very well, then." Herron spun away from them, strode toward the door. "If you are to be my uncle's scapegoat, then I will meet you."

"Herron—" Lord Claude started to speak, but trailed off when Charles gave a warning shake of the head.

"At dawn, then, at the potter's field," he said calmly. "We'll expect you and your second."

After that, the duchess and I crept away. There seemed little reason to stay. In silence we walked to her room, and I bade her a bleak goodnight.

Her hand shot out to grip my arm before I could move away. "Go change your dress," she commanded. "We cannot possibly go in these gowns; we would be far too conspicuous. Your green riding habit should do." I stared at her blankly. My riding habit, at this hour? "I shall meet you in your room as soon as I have changed," she went on, her voice sure and decisive. "We shall have to saddle the horses ourselves—we can't let the servants know what is happening—but I believe that if we are careful we won't be seen."

"What are you talking about?" I whispered.

I had never seen such determination in those soft blue eyes. "You cannot imagine I will let my son and nephew duel each other and not be present? We must be there when they meet."

"Do you think we can stop them?" The idea sent hope blazing through me.

"No, my dear. There is nothing we can do to change the course they have set for themselves, not now that honor is involved. In affairs such as these, men will never hear reason." I must have looked as stricken as I felt, for her voice softened momentarily. "But we may at least be there to see what happens. You would not forgive yourself if the man you love were killed, and you not there in his last moments."

My mind reeled at the word. I had not allowed myself to think that Charles or Herron—or both—might die. Please, I prayed fervently, please let it not come to that pass. "If we cannot prevent it, can we not at least send for the doctor, so that he will be present?" I said faintly.

"One of the gentlemen will do that, dear. It is usual at these meetings."

With a brief consoling pat on my shoulder she vanished into her room, and I made my way to mine. I fumbled my way into my riding habit by myself; I could not ring for Jane, I knew, and risk her spreading word of my strange activities. In a few minutes a low tap on my door announced the duchess. She, too, was in her riding habit, a dark blue one, and had draped her bright hair with a black silk shawl. "If the gentlemen see us, they will postpone the meeting," she explained. "We must keep completely out of sight; fortunately there are woods where we can conceal ourselves. Now, try to get some sleep. We have hours to wait."

"How can we be sure they will not start early?" I asked. "Their tempers are so inflamed—what if they are at each other's throats even now?"

"Hush, child. They are men of honor; they will follow the procedure." She took a seat on the divan, from which she could see the clock, and arranged her skirts to make herself comfortable.

How comforting, I thought numbly, to know that there is an etiquette to killing. How could it be that honor had so many contradictory meanings?

That night was the longest I have ever spent. The duchess and I kept our vigil separately, wrapped in our own thoughts, yet united in fear of what the dawn would bring. We spoke little. Shortly after we had settled in for our long watch, she had lifted her head with a perplexed frown to ask, "What is that noise?"

"Herron, on the roof," I answered, and saw pained comprehension cross her face. We listened in silence to the footsteps that marked the passage of the night. "How have you borne it?" she asked softly, after a time.

I knew she meant to ask how I had endured that nightly reminder of Herron after he had broken with me. I had suffered keenly at first, until I had thought of a solution, mundane but effective. "Cotton wool in my ears," I said briefly.

"He'll wear himself out," she murmured. "By dawn he will be exhausted." Then her thoughts seemed to return to the scene we had observed from the gallery; when she spoke again, it was on a new topic. "Herron taxed Claude with intending *another* murder. What did he think was the first?"

I decided it was useless trying to shield her now. "The duke," I said, as gently as I could.

All she said was "I see," but I could tell that in the light of that new piece of knowledge she was reliving the last months with belated understanding, revising all her ideas of what she had thought she knew, finally aware of what had been passing through her son's head.

After that we were silent, and the lonely pacing continued overhead, regular and inexorable.

I could only guess what thoughts kept her company during that long dark night. Mine were far from cheering. Once again I was forced to confront the likelihood that someone I thought I knew possessed a hidden side, one I could not trust. Charles had seemed always to be so reverent of human life, the last person to voluntarily take one. I remembered now what Herron had said about Charles killing in battle, and shivered. He might kill Herron tomorrow.

He might have tried before.

The thought I had been trying to force out of my mind ever since the night before had to be faced. Perhaps the reason I had not smelled smoke last night until after Charles left me was that he set the fire himself. But then why pull Herron from the blaze, after having set it? Perhaps others responded too quickly, and their presence had forced him to rescue the man he had tried to kill. And, having been thus thwarted, he had poisoned the wine tonight, only to have been discovered by his father.

Why, though? How could Herron's death possibly benefit him? I was certainly not worth killing for, and in any case there was no need of it: I had not even refused Charles. Had I been too quick to dismiss Herron's thought that he could have been in league with Lord Claude? But I could still not believe that even loyalty to his father would cause Charles to involve himself in murder.

Then the ugly idea came to me that Charles might inherit his cousin's estate, if Herron did not marry. That would be reason enough to kill Herron and to court me—to keep me from marrying Herron and inheriting Ellsmere. And, hateful as it was, this theory even explained two earlier incidents. The block that had fallen upon me from the tower might have been meant to kill me, to remove the threat I posed as Herron's potential bride. And Herron's fall from Caesar could have been easily engineered. Felicity's careful checks of our mounts' saddles had shown me how small a thing could cause an accident: a burr under the saddle, a loosening of the girth... someone may have meant for Herron to receive a far more serious injury than a sprained wrist.

I flung out of my chair and walked to the window. I could see nothing, but I could sit still no longer under the needling agony of my own thoughts. This was all the wildest conjecture, I told myself firmly. I had no way of knowing who Herron's heir was. And in any case, his mother had said that the estate was still in trust; that was why she still had the power to bar him from the house if she chose. So Herron's murderer would gain nothing unless he waited for his birthday, when he came into his inheritance. Relieved at this recollection, I returned to my chair. Charles could not be after the estate; the idea was laughable even without the logical flaws in such a theory.

But why, came the thought circling back, inevitable and persistent, why challenge Herron?

Hours later, the duchess stirred and stretched. "It's time we were going," she said. "We still have to saddle the horses, and we must be on our way before the others reach the stables."

"How will we find our way?" I asked as I pulled on my cloak.

"I know the place; I can take us there. Come, it's nearly dawn."

CHAPTER EIGHTEEN

We reached the stables without encountering anyone. The duchess instructed me in saddling my mount—something I had never had to do for myself—as she performed the same office for her own. After a brief check to satisfy herself that I had done an adequate job, she led the way out into the night.

The landscape lightened as we rode through the woods; nothing as definite as sunlight met us, but the shapes of the trees gradually grew more distinct, and all at once I realized that color had come into the world. We rode in silence, listening for the men so that we might not blunder across their path. The duchess's unquestioning acceptance of the duel forced me to realize that it was something that we could not forestall. If we tried to interfere, the men would only change the time and venue of their meeting; no matter what we said or did, they would carry it out regardless.

And still I did not know which man I more feared for.

"We must leave the horses here," said the duchess presently. "We are coming close now, and the horses will be seen. We must walk, and carefully." Tethering our mounts to branches, we made our way on foot through the thinning woods. When we reached the fringes of the forest, she gestured for me to stoop down; the scattered trees provided less concealment now, and we might be seen. At the edge of the woods we crouched down behind some straggling bushes that provided a screen, and waited.

In the growing light I was able to discern the scene before us. We had an excellent view of the field, which was not a large one: longer than it was wide, its uncropped grass grew knee-high. Across from us, another band of trees marked the boundary. I could no longer hear the sea, and I imagined that this place must be well removed from any dwellings; even I knew that dueling was illegal, and must be carried out in privacy.

My mouth went dry as the sound of horses' hooves came to my ears. The men had arrived.

Charles and his father rode abreast; was Lord Claude acting as second to his son, I wondered, or was he there as a concerned bystander, like the two of us crouched in the shrubbery? Behind him came a man I did not know; he was elderly, dressed in sober unfashionable garments, and held a black bag before him on the saddle. "The doctor," the duchess mouthed at me.

Herron came last. He was the only one who had not changed his clothes; he still wore his evening dress, and the elegance of the stiff shirt and white tie was startlingly incongruous in this deserted field at dawn. His jaw was set, and he stared straight before him. The breeze tossed a lock of dark hair into his eyes, and he brushed it away absently with the back of one hand. He looked spent, and very young.

I glanced at the duchess; how could she bear this without speaking, without moving to stop them? Her face wore a frozen calm, and was perfectly still. Only her hands moved; they plucked absently at the dead grass we sat on, pulling up blade after stiff blanched blade. I looked into her eyes once and did not look again. Her whole soul was poised there.

The doctor seemed to be in charge of the proceedings, perhaps because he was the only truly disinterested party. He was inspecting the pistols with an efficiency that suggested he had performed this duty before, and as we watched he gave one to each of the duelists. Herron had brought no second to check his gun, and glanced at it only perfunctorily before loading it, but Charles took a few minutes to perform a more thorough inspection of his weapon. His expression was serious and intent as he handled the gun, and his hands were steady; he was not going to collapse from sheer exhaustion, as his opponent might. I wondered how he could be so calm when preparing to fire a pistol at a blood relative.

"I'm ready," I heard him say. The sun was rising. There was no brilliant glow in the sky, simply a lightening from grey to white; it promised to be an overcast day. The doctor looked inquiringly at Herron, who gave a curt nod.

"Very well, then, gentlemen. As we have discussed." The doctor's voice was deep and faintly resigned, as if he had attended at many of these affairs of honor and had grown almost accustomed to watching young men blow holes in each other. Perhaps he had. "Take ten paces by my count and turn. When I drop my handkerchief, fire one shot each. If neither strikes home, Reginald as the offended party decides whether to continue. One—"

"Charles, wait." Lord Claude burst out suddenly as they stepped out from each other. "I cannot let you do this. It isn't your quarrel—"

"I have made it mine. Please let me pass, Father."

Charles moved inexorably on, taking the proper number of paces. His father trailed after him, his hand still reaching out in appeal, before drifting to a stop several yards away from where the doctor stood.

Charles and Herron stopped and turned to face each other. It was very quiet; not even the birds were singing. I could hear the duchess's breathing, quick and shallow. Very distantly, I thought I could hear sheep bells.

The lack of ceremony was jarring; how could everyone be so matter-of-fact, so perfunctory? This was no way to die, without time to prepare, without even glory, just a bullet fired across an abandoned strip of weeds.

Someone must stop this, I thought. I could not believe this stupidity had progressed so far. I made a panicked movement, and the duchess's hand closed around my wrist in a grip like stone.

Charles and Herron raised their pistols to point squarely at each other. For a few moments they stood like that, unmoving, awaiting the doctor's signal. Men of honor, observing the courtesies as each stood poised to send a deadly ball of lead tearing into the other. What is the doctor waiting for? I thought feverishly.

Then several things happened almost too quickly to see. The handkerchief dropped from the doctor's hand. Herron suddenly jerked his pistol to the side, away from Charles, and a gun's report came with deafening force into the silence. There was smoke, and shouting, and then I saw that someone was down. Not Charles, but Herron. It was not his gun that had fired.

A thin shriek burst from me, but it was the duchess who was on her feet and running, fast as a hare, for the place where her son had fallen. The gathered men drew aside for her as she flung herself down next to him.

"He can't be dead," I gasped, as I caught up to her. The duchess was stroking her son's forehead, and his face was so white, so still, that the breath choked in my throat. I knelt down beside them, groping for his hand. His eyes were closed.

"He isn't," said the doctor shortly; "not yet. Make room, child. We need to stop the bleeding."

"Here," said Charles: he had taken off his coat and folded it into a bundle, and the doctor took it without question and placed it under Herron's head. I noticed the blood now, what seemed a terribly great amount of it, so much that I could not tell where Herron had been hit.

"How bad is he?" asked Lord Claude, from behind me.

The doctor did not reply at once; he was cutting away Herron's blood-soaked shirt to reach the wound. "The bullet went straight through the shoulder, very clean," he said presently. "But he's losing blood, and there's always a chance of complications. I presume honor is satisfied?" he asked dryly of Charles, who nodded briefly.

"We must get him home at once, then, where the wound can be cleaned and where he can rest." The duchess was in command again. "Claude, our horses are three hundred yards into the woods. Fetch them, and get the blankets from my saddlebags. Doctor, can he ride?"

"Pillion, I think. Best let him go with Mr. Reginald; he is the strongest."

I watched in disbelief as the duchess assented. As a compress was hastily bound against Herron's wound for the journey, I plucked at her sleeve. "How can you let him ride with Charles?" I hissed at her. "For the love of heaven, he just tried to kill Herron."

She barely glanced at me. "Charles will take good care of him. The important thing is to get him home."

I stared at her open-mouthed. I could not believe she would entrust her own son to the care of the man who had shot him. Lord Claude had returned with the horses now, and after Charles mounted, Herron was lifted up to sit crosswise on the saddle before him, held securely in Charles's arm. No one else seemed concerned about the wisdom of this arrangement.

"Have you got his gun?" Charles called to his father, who held it up in answer. All the others were readying themselves for the ride back to Ellsmere. I tightened my lips and mounted, wondering what everyone else seemed to understand that I did not.

It was a silent, tense ride. The others rode at a jog-trot that seemed maddeningly slow, but the doctor warned against a faster pace that might jar Herron's wound and set it bleeding more freely. Once I managed to maneuver my horse next to Charles. The duchess had ridden ahead to Ellsmere to make things ready, and the other two men had fallen back out of earshot.

"Is he conscious yet?" I asked shortly.

"No. Better for him; he'd be in considerable pain." The ghost of a smile flickered over his face. "And distinctly unhappy at his escort."

"You've given him good reason to be so," I retorted. "How could you do such a thing?"

He looked at me over the top of Herron's head. The brilliant eyes were dimmed with what might have been sadness or simple physical weariness. "I had to," he said quietly. "He was aiming at Father, he was going to kill him. It was the only way to stop him."

"You didn't have to shoot him."

"There was no time for anything else, Oriel, even had he not been past listening to argument. It wasn't exactly easy, either, shooting to incapacitate him but no more. Do you think I wasn't frightened that I would kill him?"

I gnawed at my lip as I struggled with disbelief. I could not dismiss the horror of the sight that had faced me as I ran across the field: Charles holding a smoking pistol, standing over the man he had shot down. "You did not have to duel with him at all."

"Perhaps not. At the time it seemed the only solution." He sighed, and the movement of his chest brought a faint groan from Herron. "We'll talk later, Oriel. After Herron is safe. Just tell me one thing. Why does your father want Herron dead?

* * *

It was many hours later before we spoke again. Herron was put to bed in the room next to his mother's, which teemed with bustling, frantic activity: an army of servants hurried to provide everything the doctor and the duchess thought he needed, and my father shoved his way into the room to pelt us with questions as to his condition. We all crowded around as the doctor worked over him. At length the doctor professed himself satisfied enough with his patient's condition to leave him.

"He's very lucky the wound was not worse," he said, and I thought of Charles's words. Had it really been design, rather than luck? "Dueling is a dangerous business, Your Grace, and it could easily have cost him his life."

The duchess was almost as pale as her son, but she was the most composed of all of us. "Thank you for your care of him, Doctor. I assure you that this will not happen again."

The doctor looked skeptical. "I should hope not," he said sternly. "I trust I do not need to remind Your Grace of the laws against dueling. Next time perhaps the young men can find a less dangerous way to settle their quarrel." But he let himself be shown out of the room.

No one said a word until the door shut behind him. Then the duchess whirled, not on Charles, but on my father.

"This is your doing, Hugo," she accused.

My father's hand flew to his heart in a show of shock and injured feelings. "My doing! My dear Gwendolyn, it cannot have escaped you that it was your nephew who put the bullet in your son. How can you possibly blame me for that hotheaded young man's doings?"

"You were the one to introduce the idea of a duel; if not for you, there might have been some fisticuffs, but nothing more serious. It was you who goaded the others on and did everything in your power to ensure that someone would be killed. Don't trouble to deny it; I heard everything. I don't know why you would be so malicious, Hugo, but you will not subject my family to your vicious sense of humor any longer. You will leave this house today, and you will not return."

Lord Claude's face had gone ashen. "Gwendolyn, do you not think you are being harsh?" he began, but my father smiled gently and bowed his head.

"Very well, madam. I am sorry to have caused you inconvenience. I will not darken your door again. I wonder, though, if I might have a few more hours' grace in which to prepare for my departure? You will not deny me that scant favor, I hope, since it will be the last."

His graceful capitulation was unexpected and, I think to all of us, a distinct relief. I was not surprised when the duchess said grudgingly, "Until tomorrow noon then."

"Thank you." He bowed himself out of the room with his usual touch of insolent exaggeration. The rest of us gazed at each other with surprise, but a lightening of the heart. Perhaps now we would have a chance to mend what had passed.

Finally there came a moment when the room had emptied of people and I was alone at Herron's bedside. The duchess had ordered the room cleared so that he could rest, and had herself gone to oversee the preparation of a hot drink for him. He was asleep or unconscious, pale and small in the vast expanse of white linens, the bedclothes turned back to reveal the taut fragile lines of his throat. His eyelashes lay on his cheeks in two startlingly black crescents. I touched his forehead, smoothed his hair back; there was no fever, at least. Not yet. I let my hand linger, feeling the sweet familiarity of the shape of his brow under my palm. He looked younger and more defenseless than I had ever seen him. I could not help but recall the night he had first come to me for comfort, how his vulnerability had wrung at my heart, making me want to protect and soothe him.

"Here now, don't cry," came a voice, and I half turned to find Charles behind me, watching Herron too. "He should be all right; you heard the doctor."

"But he also said he's very weak." I fumbled for my handkerchief and wiped my eyes. "He hasn't been eating or sleeping enough. What if he doesn't recover?"

His hands closed around my arms and lifted me from my place by the bed. "Come and get some air," he said. "There's nothing you can do for him just now, and you aren't doing yourself any good, hovering over him."

Still sniffling faintly, I let him shepherd me into the morning room and ring for tea. "I don't want any," I told him, but when the tray came, the fragrance of hot buttered toast and muffins reminded me that I had not eaten since the night before, and I fell to without shame.

"Aren't you eating?" I asked. Charles had taken a cup of tea, but nothing else; he sat back in his chair regarding me as he drank.

"I had something earlier. I don't believe in dueling on an empty stomach."

I felt better after I had eaten: stronger, more calm. At last I sat back with a sigh, my fingers curled around the comforting warmth of a full teacup, and looked at him. In the bustle over Herron, no one had thought of Charles; he looked as if he would have been the better for a hot posset and a long rest himself. He had not even taken time to find another coat to replace the one he had given up to Herron; he was still in his shirt sleeves. I was glad the fire had been lit in the morning room.

"Well," he said finally, "you haven't fled my presence yet. Does that mean you have decided to trust me?"

I looked into my teacup and considered this. "I think so," I said. "I suppose you had to challenge Herron to prevent my father from calling him out. But I still believe Herron would have refused to meet him."

"Possibly. But he was certainly ready to kill someone, and it seemed very likely that it would be Father. If I hadn't goaded Herron into a duel, he wouldn't have rested until he had the chance to point a gun at my father's head. As indeed he proved this morning."

"Did you know he would do that?"

"I thought he might. That was why I had to be the one facing him; Father would never have shot Herron, even to save his own life."

"But once Herron recovers he will try again to kill Lord Claude." I put aside my tea and propped my chin on my fist, gazing out the windows at the bleak grey day that was so exactly a mirror of my mood.

"Possibly," said Charles again. "But the situation may have changed by then; I hope so. Why do you think your father was trying so hard to stir him up?"

"I've no idea," I said wearily. "He delights in causing trouble, and for some reason he seems to dislike Herron. And there is something peculiar between him and your father. He seems to have some hold over Lord Claude, but I don't know what it is."

"I've noticed that too." After a moment he said, slowly, "Then there's the poisoned wine."

"Do you think–who do you think did it?" I asked, hesitant to delve into what seemed the most dire of recent events. Poison had a deliberate, an irrefutable quality to it: this was not a spontaneous crime of temper, but something coldly planned and plotted. And it looked as if the plotter had to be Lord Claude. My heart constricted again as I thought of poor little Zeus–Felicity would be inconsolable–and realized that Herron had been using him as a taster at dinner. Even then he had been suspicious... and with good cause.

Charles had not answered. When I looked at him, he had shut his eyes and was rubbing his temples. There was so much defeat in the gesture, and it was so unlike him to give in to such an emotion, that I almost rose to go to him. "It was Father," he said without opening his eyes. "It must have been. But I can't understand why he would do it. Even if Herron believes him to have killed the duke, there's no proof, nothing that would make him a threat to Father. I can't understand it."

It was painful to see him struggle with the idea that his own father was capable of such an act. It seemed that all of us were being forced to realize that, after all, we could never truly know the people dearest to us. "Perhaps he did it under duress, at my father's behest. He had something to do with it, I'm certain."

But he seemed to find nothing in my words to ameliorate the conclusions that were forcing themselves on us. "There's too much death around here," he said, opening his eyes to stare into the fire. "This house is becoming steeped in it. I thought it would be a haven after war, but it isn't after all."

This time I did go to him, and sat on the arm of his chair. I took his hand and held it, and we sat without moving or speaking for a long time.

* * *

By bedtime it had started to rain. The sky that had threatened all day was finally fulfilling that threat, and that night I brushed my hair to the rushing, pattering accompaniment of the storm.

Herron had slept the greater part of the day, and by evening had shown signs of improvement. He had eaten a hearty dinner and grew restless as night fell; I knew he was eager to keep his futile nightly tryst, but he was still too weak to do so. Perhaps getting shot will be good for him, I thought; at least it will keep him in bed for a few days so that he can get the rest he so badly needs.

We did not take the evening meal in the dining room. Although two of the gardeners had removed poor Zeus's body and buried him that afternoon, the awful scene of the night before was still so vivid in all our minds that the duchess decided we should dine in the breakfast room. There were so few of us that the smaller room would have been more appropriate in any case: Herron was confined to his bed, and my father had pointedly informed us that he would be too busy overseeing the packing of his belongings to join us. I doubt his absence caused any of us grief.

None of us spoke aloud about the strange events that had passed since last we had dined together, but I know all of us were thinking of them. It was a strained, silent meal, and afterwards we all dispersed to our rooms without even the pretense of lingering in the drawing room. Now, alone, I tried again to make sense of what I knew.

I could not construct a theory that accounted for everything. My father's involvement still troubled me. He had been ready, even eager, to fight Herron. But poison was not consistent with his character. Like Herron, he would have been more direct: fingers around his throat, or a knife in the ribs...

It must after all have been Lord Claude who had tried to poison his stepson. Yet he would not duel him. Was he a coward, or so unwilling to commit this murder that he could only make use of the most indirect means? This made sense; by all accounts he was genuinely fond of Herron. But why, if he was so reluctant to kill Herron, would he do so at all? Again I thought of my father. If Lord Claude had murdered the duke, I thought recklessly, perhaps Father had proof, and used that power over Lord Claude... to force him to murder Herron? It still made no sense. What possible good could come to my father from Herron's death?

I frowned in concentration, trying to recall more of that dialogue I had overheard. It had not been the conversation of a blackmailer and a victim, I had decided; there was a sense that both were entangled in something equally, but my father was the only one willing to use that situation against the other. There had been such a sense of urgency, too; my father had berated Lord Claude for delaying in executing his mission. What could they both be involved in that required such immediate attention?

And then I knew. The solution came to me whole and complete. It was so logical, with what I knew of Lord Claude and my father; it was so perfect that I wondered why Charles had not thought of it. I would have pieced the truth together sooner had I known as much as he surely did about the settlement of the estate; but then, he had not been privy to the conversation I had overheard, which rendered everything so clear.

At least Herron is safe from my father tonight, I thought with a rush of relief. And after tonight all would be well: my father was leaving tomorrow, and once he had gone, Lord Claude would not be able to bring himself to try to harm Herron again. Then, if I spoke to the duchess, if we could use that trick with the blocks and the wine glass to convince Herron of his uncle's innocence, the family would be whole again.

For the first time in weeks, my heart felt light. I knew that the family would never quite be the same; no one would be able to forget the glimpse of something treacherous and hateful that we had seen last night. But we could leave it behind us; we could heal. I climbed into my bed with a sigh that was almost contented.

With my mind at ease, I thought I would sleep the night through. But hours later something woke me. I lay there, groggily wondering what it had been, when it came again. It was a noise.

From out in the hall I heard footsteps, moving slowly and ponderously, and a long sibilant sound that I could not identify. Moving as noiselessly as I could, I slipped out of bed and across the room to put my ear to the door. The sounds were receding in the direction of the stairs to the roof. At once I dismissed the idea that it was Herron; he was not strong enough to come so far under his own power. And no one else had any business on the roof.

I waited until I heard the door to the stairs shut. Then I stepped out of my room and followed.

The footsteps were moving so slowly that I had to stop and wait more than once, at the bottom of the stairs and then at the door to the roof, to avoid catching up with them. I did not know who I followed, but I knew I should not be seen. Finally they grew fainter and stopped altogether, and I opened the door to the roof.

It was still raining, and in the bright moonlight the wet roof gleamed like a sheet of silver. I hovered behind one of the chimneys to conceal myself, but I need not have bothered. My father was not looking in my direction.

He stood over the crumpled figure of Herron, which he had deposited a few yards away. My father was breathing heavily, and I knew now that the mysterious sound I had heard was Herron's body being dragged across the carpeted floor. I could not tell if he was alive: he lay so still, his limbs sprawling, like a doll whose sawdust had leaked out. But then I saw him move his head, and heard him groan.

My father nudged him roughly with his foot. "None of that, boy; we can't have you raising the house." Having caught his breath, he made as if to pick up Herron again, and I stepped out from behind my hiding place.

"Let him be!" I commanded. My father's head jerked up, and at the sight of me he gave a sort of choking gasp and fell back a pace, his face draining of color. I realized then what an eerie appearance I must present: in my white nightgown, under moonlight, I could have been a ghost.

I smiled to myself. At last, Herron would have his phantom, and she might just save his life.

Raising my arms in what I hoped was a ghostly fashion, I moved closer, trying to drive him away from Herron. But as I neared, the illusion was destroyed. My father laughed shortly, and his hunched shoulders relaxed.

"You gave me a start, daughter," he said almost gaily. "I never expected you to be here. I thought you would be deep asleep, sunk in a laudanum-induced stupor. What a nuisance you are. Can't you do anything I want of you?"

"What are you doing?"

"Killing young Herron. He takes a great deal of killing, this lad. I'm losing count of the times his uncle and I have tried."

"His uncle!" My heart sank, and he chuckled at the dismay in my voice.

"Ah, you had hoped your father was the only villain, had you not? But I could not always be here. It was Claude who dropped that block of masonry on you, for example."

"But why should he try to kill me?"

"Oh, but he didn't, you see; the mistake was so typical of Reginald. He insists that from above, in your cloak, you could have been Herron, and after all it was Herron he expected to be there. He hesitated too long, though, and botched the job." Clicking his tongue, my father shook his head in annoyance. "Claude is entirely too soft-hearted for this sort of venture. He hasn't sufficient ruthlessness."

I felt a wave of genuine hatred toward this man, who had worked on a good man's weakness to turn him to murder. "And Caesar—that was another attempt to kill Herron, wasn't it? He insisted that the horse was dangerous, but we didn't listen."

"Isn't that always the way?" His voice oozed mock sympathy, and I thought what a bizarre picture he made, conversing with me so calmly while rainwater streamed over him, running in rivulets over his face, dripping down the lapels of his dinner jacket.

"The fire was his doing as well, I suppose?"

"No, that was mine. It was so exasperating when that Charles came blundering in. And, of course, you know about the poison. I had to put a great deal of pressure on Claude before he agreed to that. He has the most irritating soft spot for his nephew; it's been our greatest obstacle." He eyed me curiously. "You haven't demanded an explanation, daughter. I find it impossible to believe you this incurious."

"Oh, I know what the explanation is," I said, and I could not entirely suppress the selfish flicker of satisfaction I felt at the surprise this called into his face. "You and Lord Claude are the trustees of the late duke's estate, aren't you? And you have been spending Herron's inheritance as if it were your own. Lord Claude's generous gifts to his family, his improvements to the tenants' houses, your self-indulgent extravagance—all came out of the money that was to become Herron's on his twenty-first birthday." His expression told me that my surmise was correct and, boldly, I continued. "But you could not let him live that long, to discover what you had done. If he died before coming into his inheritance, he could not bear witness to your crime—and what happens to the estate then? Does it revert to the trustees who have already bled it dry?"

He swept me a theatrical bow. "Reginald and I continue to administer it, yes. You have impressed me, daughter: I never thought your feeble brain capable of such feats. Or"—his eyes narrowed—"did someone help you with your thinking?"

My mind worked rapidly. It would be unsafe for me to admit that I had told no one of these conclusions. "It was Charles's idea, in fact," I improvised. "He is the one who recognized your intentions. Soon everyone will know."

But to my dismay his face split in a grin. "Ah, so the stalwart Charles is your confidant. Excellent! He will never open his lips. It would destroy his father's reputation or put him in danger of prison. I could not have chosen a better way to keep the matter secret."

Horrified, I watched as he turned back to Herron. "Well, enough of this badinage, daughter; I have a task to complete before I take my leave. Young Herron's suicidal yearnings are well known now, thanks to you, and it should surprise no one when he is discovered to have thrown himself off the roof. Particularly in the wake of a disastrous love affair."

Desperately my eyes darted over the roof. There was nothing I could use as a weapon, nothing with which I could alert the sleeping household. All I could do was delay him and pray that someone would notice Herron's empty bed and come in search of him.

If only Herron were not so helpless; if only he could overpower my father while I distracted his attention. But he lay shivering in the rain, his eyes unfocused, spent and broken. I could not rely on him for help. My father had flung one of the flaccid arms around his neck and in a moment he would pick him up and carry him to the parapet.

"What about my mother?" I blurted, and he paused.

"Your mother, child, had nothing to do with this," he said with exaggerated patience. "Not directly, in any case. I suppose you could say that it was due to her that the duke made me a trustee; he felt guilty about completely cutting me off from the family after her death, and he gave me this appointment as a kind of sop. Not a bad arrangement, as it turned out."

Again he turned to pick up Herron. "How did she die?" I demanded. "Tell me the truth."

He gave a mighty sigh. "This is scarcely the time to go into the whole painful story, daughter. Suffice it to say that Ambrose was right to blame me—although he had no proof."

The idea I had scarcely dared to consider rose up before me. "You murdered her for the inheritance you expected, didn't you?"

"Precisely. And I would have sent you with her, you miserable little brat, if that fool nurse hadn't arrived so quickly." He straightened, forgetting Herron in his remembered anger at me, and I felt true fear born in me at the loathing that gleamed in his eyes. "It would have worked so beautifully: push her over the cliff, and drop you after. Two broken bodies on the rocks, and a tragic story. The doting mother finds that her child has wandered to the edge of the cliff, and in a fit of maternal tenderness she rushes to the rescue, only to lose her footing and fall after you." Now he was biting out the words. "But you, you damned little eel, you were so slippery and quick that I couldn't catch you to throw over before the girl arrived. So your mother became a suicide, and her family blamed me for it. You cost me more than you can ever imagine."

A sort of dizziness was creeping over me, a strange feeling that there was no longer ground under my feet. So my mother had been denied even that last solace I had imagined for her: she had not run willingly into the welcoming sea, and had felt nothing but fear in her last moments of life.

"You are a monster," I whispered.

He smiled. With his hair sleeked down by the rain his face had the sudden appearance of a death's-head. "What an extraordinary coincidence," he purred. "Those were your mother's last words. How fitting that they should be yours as well." He advanced on me, and I backed up hastily in sudden fear—but at least I was leading him away from Herron now. "Perhaps you will go over the roof with your beloved. That would be very touching: having discovered the young duke's suicide, you were too distraught to live, and flung yourself over the parapet after him. Yes, that should do nicely." Then, to my horror, he turned and moved back to Herron. Again he reached for the limp form and gripped him under the arms. "But you'll have to wait your turn."

His hold slipped, and he dropped Herron with a thud, cursing the rain. I knew that once he started dragging him to the parapet I would be able to do nothing. Now, before I could think, before I could hesitate, I ran at him. I put my head down and my arms out, and plowed into him with all the force I could muster.

He slipped, skidded, struggled for balance, and for a moment he could have fought me back; but as I pushed against him I felt a great surge of power from some unknown source, and I knew that something I could not see was adding its strength to mine.

Together we forced him over, until without a sound he vanished over the parapet.

CHAPTER NINETEEN

After a moment I moved toward the edge of the roof to look down.

"Careful," came a voice, and strong hands on my shoulders restrained me. The suddenness made me start, but he held me securely. "Best step away from the edge," Charles advised me, his voice steady and calm. "You've seen how dangerous it is up here. We can't afford to have you slip and fall like your father."

"Like my father?" I repeated stupidly.

"You needn't reproach yourself, Oriel; I saw you try to save him. Not that he deserved it." He was wrapping something around me, something warm and dry, and I realized abruptly how cold I was. Rainwater plastered my nightdress to my body, and the chill seemed to bite into my bare feet. All of a sudden I was shivering.

"Is he—?"

He went to the parapet and looked down. Then he nodded.

It seemed impossible; my father could not be defeated so quickly, with so little outcry. But Charles was already turning his back on the parapet and the sight that lay below.

"Can you help me with Herron?" he asked. "We need to get him inside, and warm, or he'll be in danger of pneumonia on top of everything else."

I had almost forgotten Herron. He was in a pitiful state, his whole body shaking from the cold; his eyes were glazed and blank, but they were fixed on me.

Cold as I was, I felt a wave of something colder flood through me. What if he had seen? Would he tell Charles I had deliberately pushed my father?

For the moment I did not have to worry; he was in no condition to talk. Charles flung another blanket around him—he had come well prepared—and raised him to a sitting position. I hurried around to take Herron's other arm and draped it across my shoulders. As we lifted him to his feet, his head fell forward, his eyes closing; he had lost consciousness again. The two of us half supported, half dragged him across the roof toward the door. It was a slow, precarious progress, the rain-washed roof slick under our feet.

"How did you know to come?" I asked presently.

"I couldn't sleep and went to check on Herron's condition. When he wasn't in his room, and when I found that your father was gone as well, I guessed they would be either here or on the cliffs. I tossed a coin." His smile was a trifle wan. "Lucky for Herron it came up heads."

Once we had made our way across the roof and inside the stairwell, Charles simply picked Herron up and carried him in his arms like a child. I caught up the lamp Charles had brought and lit the way down the stairs. He had not yet asked me what had happened, and I was devoutly glad of it: I had to decide how much of the truth I could tell him.

Outside my door Charles paused, his arms full of his dripping, shivering burden.

"You should change into dry things right away. I'll see that Herron is taken care of."

"No," I said, pulling the blanket more securely around me to quell my shivering. "I'll go with you."

"Oriel, don't be so stubborn. I can't look after the both of you." When I still did not move, his lips tightened briefly. "Very well, I won't drive you from his side when you've risked your own life to save him. Come, then."

The scene that unfolded shortly thereafter in Herron's room was like a repetition of the morning. I roused the duchess and Lord Claude, while Charles rang for the servants and sent for the doctor again. I shall never forget the expression on Lord Claude's face when he entered the room and saw Herron, feeble but alive: panic and relief chased each other over his face in a quick succession, but I think relief won out. In spite of the danger to himself posed by Herron, I believe he was glad his nephew was still alive. I felt a rush of hope that I had not been wrong in believing Lord Claude to be a good man at heart.

The duchess's reaction was more straightforward. "Good God," she exclaimed, and flew to wrap her arms protectively around her son. "What has happened now?" she demanded, on her knees beside him, hugging him to her breast. She looked from me to Charles expectantly.

"Oriel knows more than I," said Charles, when I did not speak. "But this may not be the best time to—"

"Of course; you are both soaked to the skin. Go and put on dry things, while we see to Herron. Then I want to hear everything."

It was almost a relief to be ordered about by the duchess; her air of efficient command held the assurance that Herron would be all right—she would not allow him to be otherwise. The respite also gave me time to decide on my story. I thanked heaven Charles had not seen more, and had misinterpreted what he had seen. Otherwise I imagined that even now the duchess would be sending for the police.

I shuddered at the thought of prison, the trial, and then—what? Hanging? Or, if she shrank from the scandal of an arrest in the family, at the very least she would have me thrown out of the house. This time I would be completely without connections, without fortune or position. The world did not deal kindly with such creatures.

If only Herron did not talk, or if I could convince his family that it was his delirium speaking. I hurried to dress, hoping to be there when—if—he spoke against me.

We were a solemn little group gathered once more around Herron's bed. He seemed to be slipping in and out of consciousness, and his mother's brow was knit with concern as she bent over him. Finally she sighed and looked around at the rest of us: Lord Claude, Charles, and myself. "Tell me," she said.

I explained that I had been awakened by a noise and followed it to the roof to find Herron and my father. “I must have frightened my father,” I said. “I suppose he had heard about Herron’s watch for the duke’s spirit, because when he saw me he seemed truly frightened. He lost his footing, and I reached out for him.” I waited for Charles or Herron to interrupt me, to correct, but neither spoke; more confidently, I concluded, “But it was too late; I couldn’t keep him from falling.”

The duchess sat back in her chair, and I took a furtive peek at her face. Her expression was bleak, but not skeptical. “He is dead?”

“Yes,” said Charles. “I came in search of Herron, when I found he was not in his bed, and I saw Pembroke slip and fall over the edge. There was nothing either of us could have done to save him.”

Lord Claude released a long breath of relief, as if he had been afraid to breathe until now. The duchess only gave a single slow nod. “It is a fitting end for him,” she said. “But a mysterious one. What was he doing with Herron? I won’t believe he was trying to help him back indoors. Indeed, I wonder that Herron was able to make his way to the roof at all.”

I looked appealingly to Charles; I did not know how much to say, how much they would believe about my father. But the decision was taken out of my hands.

“Herron did not go of his own volition,” said Lord Claude. “Pembroke dragged him to the roof to push him off.” His voice was low but steady, and he met our eyes without hesitation. “Since he had been ordered to leave Ellsmere tomorrow, he was forced to act tonight. If the girl did frighten him, she probably saved Herron’s life.”

“Claude.” The duchess’s voice held fear for the first time. “What do you know of this?”

“More than I wished for you to learn, Gwendolyn.” He looked at me. “You know the whole story, don’t you?”

“Most of it, I think,” I answered, and since he seemed to expect me to tell it, I tried to comply. “When the late duke died, as you all know, he left his son’s inheritance in a trust to be administered by my father and Lord Claude. I’m not certain who succumbed first, but access to so much money was too tempting. I expect it was my father who first thought of what was to be gained by exploiting that access. Lord

Claude is a generous man; naturally he found it difficult to resist all the possibilities offered by this wealth." I realized I was pleading Lord Claude's case for him, trying to make the others see his actions as I did. "He was tempted by the chance to make improvements on the estate, to buy his new bride expensive gifts—"

A tiny sound from the duchess made me break off. Her eyes were wide and pleading as they sought her husband's, but he did not give any word or sign to deny what I had said. I felt a terrible aching pity for her. As harrowing as the last two days had been for all of us, for the duchess they were tantamount to crucifixion.

After a moment, I continued.

"But as Herron's twenty-first birthday neared, they know they faced exposure. Therefore..."

"Therefore Herron could not live," said Charles, almost gently. He seemed regretful but not surprised, and I wondered if he had come after Herron with a better understanding of his peril than he had revealed. "The fire and the duel were engineered by Pembroke to ensure that Herron died before turning twenty-one. I should have recognized earlier what was in the wind, but I did not realize until tonight when I found Herron missing." He paused, and his father waited with doomed eyes for his next words. "I'm sorry, Father," he said quietly. "It's time this came out, for all our sakes."

There was a long silence, while we waited for the duchess to speak. She had risen from her chair, and stared at her husband as at a stranger. That look came nearer to breaking Lord Claude than anything that had yet come to pass.

"Gwen, I didn't want to hurt him," he cried. "But don't you see, if he went to the law, I would have been arrested, jailed—I would have lost you." His whole heart was in the last words.

Still she did not move. "Then it was not Hugo who poisoned the wine. It was you."

"I had no choice! Pembroke threatened to expose me if I did not dispose of the boy. He knew it meant condemning himself, but he would have done it to spite me. He had less to lose, and could assure himself a lighter sentence by informing against me. You cannot imagine what it has been like, knowing that the only way I could keep you was to kill my own nephew."

"Claude, you would not have lost me." At last she went to him, and he seized her hands desperately, as if afraid she would slip away. Tears stood in her eyes, but she faced him serenely, standing calm and strong like a queen. "Did you think you needed jewels and gifts to hold me? If you had only told me of this, we would have found a way. Men like Hugo cannot command us. There might have been disgrace, but I would not have abandoned you to face it alone."

His face shone as if he were seeing a vision from heaven, but he could not yet allow himself to believe in his redemption. "But there may yet be scandal. On Herron's birthday—"

"I have money of my own, Claude; I had a careful father too, and he made sure I had money my husbands could not touch. We will restore Herron's inheritance with that. We may need to find a sympathetic lawyer, but we shall find a way to right this." The gentle, measured tone did not change as she added, "But if you dare to think again of harming my son, I will see you hanged."

With a great gasp of relief he snatched her into his arms. I felt myself relax. With her strong guidance, and without my father playing on his weakness, he could be recovered. I only hoped it was not too late, and that his wife could still love him as she once had in spite of what he had tried to do. As for Herron...

"He's awake," announced Charles suddenly, and the duchess tore herself out of her husband's arms to return to Herron's side. The unfocussed look had left his eyes, and he regarded his stepfather with something like his old glare.

"Darling, how do you feel?" the duchess pressed him. "It's all over now, dearest. There has been a terrible misunderstanding, and Claude owes you a great apology, but you're safe now."

He licked his lips, and spoke in a voice that seemed to come from far away. "I heard," he said, and Lord Claude moved to the bedside.

"My boy, I can't expect that you will forgive me," he said, with a dignity I could not help admiring. "But maybe, in time, if I can earn your trust again—"

"Did you kill my father?"

The words were weak, but unmistakable. Caught off balance, his uncle gaped. "What?"

"He isn't himself yet, Claude; don't listen to him." The duchess stroked her son's hair, trying to soothe him.

But Herron, weak as he was, was attempting to push himself up in bed, the better to stare down the man he still thought of as his enemy. Without a word, Charles helped raise him and propped him up with pillows.

"Did you kill my father?" he repeated. "You might have done it for the money, or to marry my mother, or simply because you resented him for being all that you never were and never could be." The outburst seemed to exhaust him, and he struggled for breath, but did not relent. "I have to know, or this cannot end."

In the silence his labored breathing was loud, and I saw Charles glance with concern at his bandaged shoulder, where fresh blood was showing. But he did not intervene. Lord Claude straightened, and met Herron's eyes without rancor. "I—"

"Stop," ordered the duchess. "Don't say a word, Claude. You shall not answer that question." She glanced at him to ensure that he would obey her; then, satisfied, she turned again to Herron. Her chin was set at the determined angle I had come to know and respect, and she spoke to Herron gently but firmly.

"You are never to ask that of your uncle again," she informed him. "And I must insist that all speculation on the subject end here, Herron. We have had enough of death in the past, and it is time to leave it in the past. Claude is a good man, and I have faith in that goodness. I will not have you tormenting yourself, or the rest of us, with these groundless accusations."

I am not certain which of us was the most astonished. "Gwendolyn, are you sure—" began Lord Claude.

"I am sure. I know you, and I know you are not a murderer. You could never bring yourself to kill, Claude; remember how you warned me against the wine, when doing so could only alert Herron of the danger? No, you are not a murderer." She turned a formidable gaze on her son, who lay in stricken silence. "Anyone who says otherwise forfeits forever his place in my heart—and in my family. Do you understand?"

If he had not been so weakened by his ordeal he might have defied her. But his eyes wavered for an uncertain moment, and then he nodded.

A tiny smile of triumph flitted across the duchess's face. She leaned forward to kiss him on the brow. "Good," she said softly. "Sleep now, dearest."

* * *

Herron was ill with a fever for four days. It was a harrowing time; his mother and I scarcely left his side, and the doctor left only to visit other patients. More doctors were called in from London, so that at any time a crowd of them could be found, shaking their heads and muttering, around his bed. We hung on every minute change in his color, his breathing, his pulse, hungry to see improvement.

As for me, I felt as if my own soul hung in the balance with his life. No just universe would allow him to die after I had killed to save him; I could not have become a murderess for nothing. Sometimes I felt that if he died, or continued for long in this half-existence, my mind would give way from the strain.

On the fifth day the fever broke, and we knew he would not die.

After the crisis had passed, his convalescence progressed slowly but steadily. When he had grown strong enough, on fair days he liked to be carried out to the terrace off the gallery, from which he could see the ocean reaching out to the horizon. His illness had changed him. He seemed older, and it was not just because of the spare new contours of his face that had emerged as he had grown thinner; his defiance and anger had grown into something more reflective. Somewhere in the ordeal he had undergone, his childhood had been left behind.

As the weeks went by and he grew more alert, he seemed not to mind my presence, so I would busy myself with a book or embroidery while he lay absorbed in his thoughts. Sometimes we would talk: mild, placid exchanges about his progress, the gradual approach of spring, the acquaintances who had asked after his health. Sometimes we would just sit in companionable silence. The threat that he would expose me never ceased to haunt me, but it began to recede.

One afternoon, while I was sitting by Herron's bedside as he napped, Charles called me out into the hall.

"I'm leaving for Edinburgh tomorrow," he said without preamble. "Now that Herron's out of danger, I should be going."

The unexpectedness of it stunned me; I had to put my hand to the stair rail to steady myself. “But why?” I exclaimed. “You hadn’t planned to go until summer. Why must you leave now?”

He looked into my eyes with such a pointed meaning that his answer was redundant. “I stayed to make sure Herron would be safe, and to learn what you had decided to do. You don’t need me here, Oriel. Knowing that, I’d rather go.”

“But I do need you. I don’t want you to go.”

His face brightened a fraction. “If you truly don’t want me to go, I won’t,” he said. “You have only to ask me to stay.”

I opened my lips to tell him to stay. But the word froze on my tongue; my eyes darted back to Herron’s door, and I knew Charles had to leave. I could not risk having him learn that I had killed my own father. Better to send him away now than see him shrink from me later. And even if Herron did not talk, Charles did not deserve a murderess for a wife. I could not live with myself if I let him marry me, knowing as I did what I was capable of.

Stricken, I stared at him wordlessly, and he gave a short, resigned nod.

“I see,” he said, his deep voice very quiet. “You have made your decision.”

“Charles, it isn’t what you think. I don’t love Herron any more. Or if I do, it is as a sister, or a cousin; not as I used to.” I faltered to a stop. There was no reason he should believe me.

“You don’t have to explain, Oriel; all I want is your happiness.” My eyes blurred at this; I could not have been less happy at that moment. “But remember that if you ever need me, all you need do is send for me. I’ll come whenever you ask.” His smile didn’t reach his eyes. “And you needn’t fear that I’ll see your writing to me as an indication that you have changed your mind about marrying me. There are no conditions, no obligations.”

“Thank you,” I said inadequately. “You’re very kind.”

He said nothing.

“When are you leaving Ellsmere?”

“Tonight. My train is early in the morning; I’ll stay the night in the village.”

So this was probably our final parting. “I hope you have a pleasant journey,” I said, and chafed at the inanity of the words. I seemed to be trapped in the conventional phrases that revealed nothing of what I really wanted to say. We could not part this way.

"Will you kiss me goodbye?" I asked.

There was a pause, long enough for me to begin to regret the words; then he said, "Of course, if you wish," and bent toward me. I tipped my face up readily, and felt his lips brush my cheek, chaste as any brother's. "Goodbye, golden one," he said. "Be happy."

Then he turned and walked away.

I did not see him again before he left. Ellsmere, in fact, was emptying rapidly. The duchess had decided that she and Claude should have a belated wedding tour, and they were departing for Italy as soon as Herron was well enough to join them. I knew that the voyage was in part an opportunity to let their marriage, as well as their relationship with Herron, recover from all the strain of recent events. Inevitably, there had also been a certain amount of scandal about my father's dramatic death, even though we had decided to describe it as a tragic accident. I felt optimistic that the couple would find a way to put things right between them; the duchess had enough strength of will, and her husband enough devotion, to guarantee that they would regain some, if not all, of their former happiness. I was less certain that Herron and his uncle would ever be reconciled. But, in any case, I knew my presence would not make their way easier.

Felicity and Miss Yates had already left Ellsmere; it had been decided that Aminta, in their stepmother's absence, would sponsor Felicity at her debut, so she and her governess—soon to become governess to Freddy and India—were to live with Aminta's family at least until the duchess and Claude returned. Soon I would be the only member of the family remaining there. Aminta and her husband had assured me I was welcome at their house, but I had put them off. In truth, I had not expected Charles to leave, and I was unprepared for the desolation his departure left in me.

At breakfast next morning the duchess cast a long look at my bowed head and said brightly, "Dear, I wonder if you would do me a favor? I would so appreciate your advice before I begin my packing for Italy. Perhaps this morning you wouldn't mind going through my things with me and helping me decide what to take."

This was nothing more nor less than an attempt to keep me from being lonely; her maid would be far more help than I ever could.

"If you can manage without me, I had hoped to take a walk."

To my relief, she did not press me. "Very well, my dear," she said. "I'm sure the fresh air will do you good. I shall see you at luncheon, then."

I did not answer, and as soon as I decently could, I excused myself and left the house.

Almost without conscious thought my feet found the path to the shore. I had come out without a bonnet, and a warm breeze ruffled my hair as I made my way down the incline. The sea glittered and twinkled at me, playful in the sunshine, but I paid it little heed as I walked down the beach.

Herron and I had once talked of the uses to which men put their lives, of the capacities that lay within all of us. Now Charles was going to explore his, by setting out to become a healer. He had found the role that would allow him to realize his potential, and his would be a life of fulfillment, of usefulness, of purpose.

I, too, had discovered what capacities lay in me. The ability to kill.

I had known the horror of seeing those around me revealed to possess unguessed qualities, but it was nothing to what I felt upon discovering this hidden darkness in my own soul. Never mind the mitigating circumstances; forget that I may have saved Herron's own life. When the choice lay before me, my instincts had led me to commit a crime I abhorred. Without thought, without mercy, without hesitation I had with my own hands ended a human life. I had become like my father.

I could not live with that knowledge.

I came to the border of rocks around the little bay, and climbed over them. The water was calm, the bay like a cup of light as it reflected the sunlit sky overhead. The water was warm where I waded in, but grew colder the deeper I ventured. When the water was up to my waist, my feet were so cold I could scarcely feel them, but I did not care. My skirts and petticoats floated around me in a profusion of white ruffles, and if there had been anyone to see, he might have fancied that I stood among water lilies. But soon enough the water would weigh them down.

The sea pulled at me as I walked further out, until each step was a dragging, slogging effort. My progress grew slower and slower. Then, in the space between one step and the next, there was no ground; my feet strained for the feel of sand under them, and trod nothing but water.

This was as far as I needed to go. I lay back against the surface of the ocean and let myself float now, the water cradling me. I shut my eyes. My face, turned up to the sunlight, was warm; my back, clasped by the sea, was cool. The gulls screamed faintly, but everything else was peaceful. The water lapped at my fingertips, drawing out my thoughts. It was like being rocked to sleep, just as I had imagined.

My breathing became slower. Every exhalation allowed another piece of me to slip under the surface of the water. My fingers were drifting down into the shadows. I lay quietly, feeling the water creep coolly up my arms. My shoulders. My temples. I breathed as gently as if I feared waking myself.

The water slid over my face. I was under water, all sound abruptly blotted out. All was quiet, muffled, distant. I breathed in...

...and burst choking and gasping from the water, my feet churning for ground, hands flailing for a hold. Thrashing against the sea, I stared wildly around, and found rocks looming their comforting solid presences over me. I gripped one and hauled myself up, feeling the welcome roughness rasp against my palms, painfully dragging myself onto the rock until I could lie there, my legs still drifting in the water, and breathe the air, panting.

At last I rolled over on to my back, my lungs still struggling for air. How had I come to be this close to shore, I wondered dimly, when I had walked so far out? I opened my eyes, stinging from salt, and looked around me. The tide was coming in, and I had not even noticed.

I began to laugh, lying there half in and half out of the water, drenched and half drowned. I had thrown myself into the arms of the sea, and it had thrown me back.

Suddenly the entire scene was ridiculous. How earnest, how sentimental I had been, running to meet a romantic death. And how many times had I remonstrated with Herron for seeking such an end to his fears and griefs?

"Fool girl," I muttered to myself, but I was smiling. "Do you even listen to what you tell others?"

Spent from coughing and from laughter, I lay on the sun-warm rock and let the breeze dry me. I reflected that my father, wherever he was, would have been pleased had I drowned myself. It would have proven that I was unable to contend alone with the world and to throw off his yoke. There was no good in punishing myself for what I had done; it would undo nothing, and the only way I could live down my fears about myself was to set about proving that I was something more than a girl who had killed, and that having done so did not destine me to kill again. My life could be more than that.

Presently, when I had lain there long enough, I stood up and wrung the salt water out of my skirts. Then, only slightly unsteady on my feet, I started back to the house. The sea still twinkled and glittered at me as it had before, unconcerned with any epiphany experienced by one mortal girl. I waved goodbye and turned my back on it, to face what lay ahead.

CHAPTER TWENTY

Herron, too, had come to new understanding about himself. I came to recognize this later that day, when I had changed out of my sodden clothes and joined him on the terrace. For a time we sat in the pale sunshine, saying little, as I worked at some embroidery.

"Oriel," he said presently, "do you feel like talking for a bit?"

Until now we had not talked about the past, but something in his manner suggested that he was finally about to confront it. "Of course."

"I have been thinking about what I should do with my future," he said seriously. "I would like your opinion."

"Well, heavens," I said, startled, "you are the duke, you know. You have your role set out for you."

"Yes, if I choose to accept it. But Claude is much better at being duke than I am, even if the title isn't his. He truly enjoys administering the estate, keeping up with the tenants' concerns and the rents and the crops, and he has a rapport with the tenants that I've never tried to forge."

I tried not to betray my surprise at hearing him speak so generously about his uncle. "And you think your path lies elsewhere?" I queried.

He nodded, his eyes gazing past me out to the sea. "I have been thinking about this a great deal recently—I have had plenty of time in which to think, you know." For a moment his familiar wry smile flashed out at me, but then he sobered. "I have decided to go into the church."

It took me a moment to absorb this. "You sound very definite," was all I could think to say.

"I believe it would be the right life for me. I used to think I understood the way life and death worked, and what love and justice and forgiveness were. Now I realize I am only just beginning to learn what they mean. I want to keep on learning about them, about why we are here. Do you remember that conversation we had, a long time ago, about the purpose to which we put our lives?"

"Yes," I said. "I do."

"I think I know where to look now for the answer." He smiled at me again, only this time it was an uncertain, wistful smile. "Do you think I'm right?"

I reached over to put my hand over his. "I think you are very wise to find a life that will give you the answers you seek, Herron."

"Thank you." He hesitated, then added in a low voice, "I haven't told you everything, though. There is another reason I've chosen this direction. Something that made me realize how many forces there are in the world that are still unknown to us."

I waited, and he rested his head against the pillows and told me.

He told me of the night my father had dragged him to the roof. Herron had been too weak to follow all our conversation, but he knew my father planned to kill him. Too feeble to do anything in his own defense, he had waited almost with detachment to see what happened.

"He bent over me," he said, "and I knew I was about to die. Then you came flying at him, with your hair streaming out and the most splendid look of wild determination on your face, like a warrior queen out of the history books." I smiled at that. "And you went smashing into him like a tidal wave. I thought for a moment you'd saved me, until he started to regain his balance. But then the strangest thing happened.

"I saw a bright golden glow appear next to you. It was taller even than your father, and it had a shape—a slightly hazy shape, or it may have been my vision that was hazy. But it was pushing against him just as you were doing." He turned his eyes to me. "It wasn't very distinct. But it looked like my father."

When I did not reply, he hurried on, embarrassed. "I don't expect you to believe me, after all my fruitless waiting for his ghost. And this was nothing like what I thought I'd seen before, on the day of the funeral. I had hoped that you might have seen it yourself, so that you would understand—"

"But Herron, I felt it." It was awe that had silenced me, not disbelief. "I could not see it as you did, but I knew I felt something beside me, helping me save you." I shook my head, marveling. "All the time you were searching for him, he was simply waiting until a moment when you truly needed him."

We gazed at each other in wonder that was too joyful to contain fear.

"Have you told anyone else what you have told me?" I asked after a moment.

"No, I'm certain they would just tell me it was my delirium, the loss of blood, a trick of the moonlight. I don't want to hear it reduced to that. I'm glad you believe me, Oriel."

For a time we sat in companionable silence. Then Herron shifted restlessly against his pillows.

"Are you uncomfortable?"

"No, I'm fine. Only that it's unpleasant sometimes, the way things one did in the past come thronging back to one's mind." Awkwardly he said, "I—I was a brute to you, Oriel."

I picked up my embroidery again. "Not all the time," I said lightly.

But he did not take the chance to make light of it. "I owe you an apology. You were right about so many things, and I couldn't or wouldn't admit they were true." He fell silent, perhaps sifting through them, and added quietly, "I was thinking always of myself; I never spared a thought for you or your feelings. And you weren't the only one; I must have caused everyone a lot of pain."

I did not deny this; let him take responsibility, finally, for his actions. But I was delighted to see this evidence of the change in him. He possessed a maturity now he had lacked before.

"And the night of the ball—how I must have terrified you." He shook his head, remembering. "It was unforgivable of me; no wonder Charles flung it up at me later. You seemed so different that night, and it frightened me, that feeling that I hadn't known you after all."

"I know what that is like," I said.

"But I should never have attacked you," he said miserably. "The truth is that I found you very alluring that night, very—well—tempting. And I was angry at myself for being so drawn to that side of you."

I looked at him in surprise. "That was why you were so furious? I thought you believed I was working against you, conspiring with your uncle."

"I could hardly tell you the truth. I'm not even certain I recognized it myself at the time." Then, "At least I know that you have found a better man," he said more cheerfully. "Charles will make you happy, I'm sure."

I frowned in concentration over my embroidery, and said nothing.

"Where is he, by the way? I haven't seen him today." His voice trailed off as he sensed something amiss.

"He is gone," I said, snipping off a thread.

"Gone! When?"

"Yesterday evening. He apologized for not saying good-bye to you in person."

I found that I had dropped my blue silk, and bent to retrieve it. I sensed Herron beside me struggling to understand this new development, but he hesitated to ask a direct question that might wound me. Presently he inquired, with such elaborate casualness that I almost smiled, "There hasn't, I hope, been some trouble between him and—er—Claude?" Poor boy, he was trying to be tactful.

"Not at all," I said. "It is just that I don't think it is best for us to be together." I sounded so sensible, so poised. Perhaps I had learned something from the duchess: how to give the appearance of being in command of a situation—or at least of my feelings.

"What will you do?" Herron demanded, almost indignantly.

I tried to shrug offhandedly. "I have a few ideas; you needn't worry about me."

"You could go abroad with my mother and Claude, you know; I'm certain they'd enjoy your company, especially when

I tell them I'll be returning to university instead of accompanying them."

"No, I would only be a hindrance. They need some time by themselves."

"But you haven't had any opportunity to travel before," Herron persisted. "And if you and Charles aren't... well, you would meet many young men abroad." A mischievous light came into his eyes. "Italian noblemen. You could become the first *marchesa* in the family."

"Oh, I don't think so," I said, unable to keep from smiling. "I don't seem to be very good at keeping suitors."

He laughed self-consciously. "You shouldn't count me, you know; this suitor was too foolish to realize at the time how lucky he was in you. Your only mistake was settling for so dense a lover." Then he grinned, and went on in a more cheerful tone. "No, next time we must find you a fellow intelligent enough to appreciate you properly. Perhaps a scholar, like yourself, and you can conduct your courtship in Greek verses."

I laughed, and we went on to talk of other things. I had come to realize that in some ways I had loved Herron as I had loved Lionel: Herron had aroused the same protective impulse within me. But that was not what married love should be. Nor was it the comfort Herron had sought in me, when he had needed someone to give him the devotion he felt his mother had transferred to Lord Claude. What we had felt for each other had been sweet, but it could not last, and I could look back on it now without regret.

I might even be ready to start looking forward.

* * *

By the time Herron left for university to embark on his new course of study, spring was coming to Ellsmere. The sere garden plots, so drab during the past months, were tinted in delicate pale green hues, and trees seemed suddenly fat with leaves. The air grew so balmy that the duchess took to ordering tea laid on the terrace every afternoon. I supposed she was already imagining herself in Italy, where she and her husband could take all their meals on the veranda of a palazzo under the Mediterranean sun.

Herron refused to let us accompany him to the train station; we had to make our adieus at Ellsmere while the coach waited. I could not help but be reminded of the day my father and I bade Lionel farewell—for that was what we had believed it to be: farewell, not goodbye. A pinprick of fear touched me. But Herron was not going to war, I reminded myself. If he continued on the course he was starting now, he would become someone I could be proud to have known. I blinked firmly to discourage a few foolish tears, realizing I would miss him.

He kissed my cheek and smiled at me. "I'll write to you, Oriel."

"I'll hold you to that," I said, smiling back.

His mother took him in her arms, but she did not weep or plead with him to stay. It was the embrace of a duchess, warm but dignified, and soon she held Herron away from her so that she could look into his face. There was sorrow in her eyes at the parting, but pride as well. "Don't forget us, dear," she said only, before she pressed a kiss on his forehead and released him.

One more remained to take his leave of Herron. Lord Claude and his nephew faced each other, and the duchess and I waited in apprehension. The two men had not overcome their estrangement, but had avoided each other throughout Herron's convalescence. Although I knew Lord Claude was anxious to convince Herron of his contrition, he was always on edge in his nephew's presence, and Herron, while never reverting to his former hostility, still regarded his uncle with forgivable wariness. He had confided in me the day before that he hoped his theological studies would teach him how to forgive his uncle, since he had not yet succeeded in doing so in spite of his efforts.

The past few weeks had aged Lord Claude as well as Herron: his hair bore wide streaks of grey, and his face was more careworn than of old. I felt a pang of compassion for him, and saw the duchess's hand sketch a motion toward him, quickly stilled, as if she had been about to reach out and steady him.

It was Herron who spoke first. "You have it in your power to do me a favor, sir," he said, his voice polite but betraying no emotion. "While I am gone, Ellsmere will need an overseer. You have filled that role so well since my father's death that I wonder if I may depend upon you to do so again when you return from your travels."

Surprise and pleasure had dawned in his uncle's face as Herron spoke. "I would be honored to have Ellsmere in my care."

"Excellent. I thank you." There was a silence, and then Herron gave an abrupt nod. "Goodbye, then."

"My boy," said Lord Claude, and held out his hand.

Herron said nothing. Strain as I might, I could not read his face. But then he put out his hand and clasped his uncle's.

Beside me, the duchess smiled. Our eyes met, and we shared a moment of silent relief. It was a start.

* * *

The night before the duchess and Lord Claude left for Italy, the three of us dined at Lord Montrose and Aminta's house, five miles away. It was pleasant to see them again and to recapture for the evening the atmosphere of former times. The absence of Herron and Charles left a sad gap in our company, but we were able to be merry in spite of this. The candlelight glowed as cheerfully as at any Ellsmere dinner, and we drank many toasts: to the absent ones and their success in their respective endeavors; to the end of the war in the Crimea; to the safe voyage of the duchess and Lord Claude.

"And to my success in catching a fine husband this season," added Felicity impishly, raising her glass. Finally eighteen years old, she wore her first true dinner gown, with long skirts and a décolletage, and her hair was dressed no longer in the girlish ringlets but in an elegant chignon like her aunt's. Her cheeks were pink with excitement, but she already possessed a poise that showed she was ready to venture into the world. Aminta caught my eye and smiled.

"Very well; why not? A toast to Felicity as she goes forth to seek her destiny. May she show as much discrimination as I did."

"Hear, hear," seconded Lord Montrose, with a broad grin for his wife, and we all laughed and raised our glasses to Felicity's future.

At the end of the evening, when we were taking our leave, Felicity drew me aside.

"I did not want to be tactless and ask after you in front of all the others," she whispered. "Aminta felt it would be best if we did not mention your father tonight, and of course I agreed. But I thought—I wondered—well, even though Aunt says he was never a true father to you, and we know so many dreadful things of him now, I was afraid you might be missing him."

Her eyes were filled with such sincere concern that I could not resist hugging her.

"It's kind of you to ask, Felicity. I can't claim to have loved him—certainly not as you do your father—but it is strange all the same to know he is dead." I tried to ease the anxious expression on her face. "I have had some time to accustom myself to the idea, though, and I am perfectly fine."

Her dimples broke out at once. "Oh, I'm so glad to hear it. Now, are you certain you won't come to London for the season with us? I should so love for you to be presented with me. Think of all the parties and balls we would attend! Between the two of us, we would break every heart in the city."

"Perhaps I will," I laughed, as the duchess beckoned for me to join her in the carriage. "If I weary of Ellsmere, I may appear on your doorstep one day."

"Do," she urged. "I shall tell Aminta to air the second guest bedroom for you." There was no time to say anything further, so she and Aminta waved goodbye, and until we passed the curve of the drive we could see them waving, standing against the warm lighted windows of the house.

We had left Ellsmere a threesome, but now we were four: Miss Yates was accompanying us back to the house so that she could be my chaperon and companion while the duchess and Lord Claude were in Italy. The arrangement had been my idea, so that I could stay on at Ellsmere instead of joining one of the two sets of travelers. I knew the duchess would never let me stay there alone, and I had no wish to leave, at least until my future was more certain. Miss Yates had agreed readily.

"Lady Montrose's children don't yet need me; their bonne will be sufficient for the season. And the prospect of seeing Felicity launched, I must confess, makes me nervous. I'm certain I'll be fighting the urge to intrude every moment. She will be better off without me there to keep her under my watchful eye."

She was to be installed in rooms across from mine, so when there was a tap at my door later that night, after we had returned to Ellsmere and retired for the night, I assumed it would be Miss Yates. Instead I found it was the duchess.

"I'm not disturbing you, I hope?" she inquired. "I can never sleep the night before starting a journey, and I thought you might feel like talking."

"Of course," I said, and we made ourselves comfortable before the fire. She curled up gracefully on the divan, tucking her feet beneath her as if she were a schoolgirl instead of a duchess. Indeed, in her frilly dressing gown, with her hair in a braid down her back, she looked no more than sixteen. Somehow all the recent shocks had not seemed to age her; unlike her husband, she bore no signs of strain in her face. Her next words showed that even now she continued to think of others before herself.

"Will you not be lonely here while Claude and I are away?" she asked. "I hate to think of you alone in this great house. I would feel much easier in my mind if you would come to Italy with us."

"I am perfectly content with my own company, and I shall have Miss Yates when I tire of solitude."

"But you will find it very dull," she insisted. "With no guests, and no parties, the days will be very empty."

I went to my dressing table and retrieved a letter, which I handed to her. "I will have something with which to occupy myself. A few weeks ago I contacted a publisher in London and sent him some of my translations. He believes they will find a receptive audience."

"But how wonderful!" she exclaimed, scanning the letter. "So you will be doing more such work, I gather."

I nodded. "He has told me of several texts I've read that lack adequate translations. I plan to start work on them right away."

"Oh, my dear, I am so glad for you." She leaned over to kiss my cheek, then sat back, beaming. "I see I need not have worried; you seem to have found your path, as Herron has. I am very proud of you both."

"You'll miss him, won't you?"

She forced a smile. "Terribly. The more, since I am not certain how much I shall see him in the future. His life will take him elsewhere, I'm sure, and Claude and I may not ever return to Ellsmere."

"What?" I cried. "You mean, you will stay in Italy?"

"I don't know." She hesitated, then continued. "There are so many unhappy memories linked to Ellsmere now that I'm not certain we could ever live here in contentment. We would be constantly reminded of so many things that we would rather forget—indeed, that we must forget, if we are to find peace."

"But you must have many happy memories here as well," I protested. "This has been your home, and your family's home, for so many years."

"I know, child," she sighed. "I am not saying the decision is made. It is far from an easy one."

"And what of the estate?" I pressed her. "Without Herron to see to it, Lord Claude's presence is vital. Herron depends upon him to oversee everything for him."

That brought pleased reminiscence to her face. "Yes, there is that. He has entrusted Ellsmere to Claude, and Claude will not lightly reject such an overture. It was splendid of Herron to make such a gesture, and Claude knows it well." She spread her hands. "We shall see; I cannot say now what will happen.

"But before we part," she added in a different tone, "I have something for you. I was not entirely honest when I claimed that I came here because I could not sleep; I had another reason as well." From the voluminous folds of her peignoir she produced a small box, which she handed to me. "I wanted to give this to you before I left. Somehow the right moment never presented itself today."

I gasped when I opened the box: nestled inside was an antique brooch of the Reginald coat of arms, enameled and set with jewels. Enclosing the coat of arms was a round border on which tiny diamonds spelled out the family motto. I gazed at it in wonder for a long while before I could tear my eyes away to look back at the duchess.

"It belonged to the first Duchess of Ellsworth," she said. "She gave it to her daughter-in-law on her wedding day. When I was married it became mine, and now it is yours."

"But, ma'am, it is not for me to have. I am not the next duchess, nor ever will be—"

"It belongs to whomever I give it to, and I want you to have it." Softly, distinctly she added, "It is small enough thanks for saving my son's life."

The room went very quiet. All I could hear was the gentle crackling of the fire. Not daring to look at her, I found myself staring at the motto that encircled the brooch. To be, rather than to seem. I thought how ill suited any of us was to wear it: all of us at some time had seemed one thing and been another.

"You are too generous, ma'am," I managed. "Perhaps my presence that night was lucky, but you do me too much credit."

"Oh, I think not," she said evenly, and in uncertainty my eyes sought her face. She was watching me with a faint, sweet smile. "Herron came to me before he left and told me what you did. It was you who saved him, child, and I'll not forget it. I can never thank you enough." Leaning forward, she clasped her hands over mine, folding my fingers around the brooch. "I only wish you had trusted me enough to tell me the truth," she said reproachfully. "What did you think I would do? Cast you out, or throw you on the mercy of the courts?" When I did not answer, her voice gentled. "Surely you know me well enough to realize I would understand that you only did what you had to do."

"I was afraid of what you would think of me," I admitted. "You have always been so kind to me, but this was something you never bargained for when you took me in. I was certain you'd believe you had been deceived in me, that I was an evil woman you would not want to associate with." Not even the knowledge that Herron and I had felt some other force helping me fight my father had entirely absolved me of this fear.

"Evil! You!" She burst out in mirth. "Oh, my dear child, I should not laugh at you; you must have been in torment, fearing your secret would come out. But there is nothing in what happened to make me see evil in you. In fact, given the right circumstances, I think everyone is capable of killing. I know that I am."

"You could never murder anyone!"

"Oh, I could; but, in any case, acting as you did—to save another life—that is not murder. You are no more capable of cold-blooded, deliberate murder than... than Claude. There is some situation in which everyone will kill, whether it is to save her own life or that of someone she loves. That does not make her a killer by nature, or mean that, having destroyed once, she will ever do so again." Seeing that she had made her point, she went on blithely. "Now, I am made differently. I am entirely capable of committing murder, just as Hugo was."

"I do not believe it," I said warmly. "You could never be so malicious."

"It is not a matter of malice, my dear; had I known what Hugo was about, I could most certainly have killed him. I would have, to protect Herron and Claude. I could have calmly and deliberately planned to end his life, and I would have taken the proper steps to do so."

Incredulous, I looked at her curled there on the divan, speaking so serenely of murder. With her spun-gold hair and frothy gown, she resembled a murderess about as much as a kitten. Curiosity got the better of me, and I asked, "How?"

She put her head on one side with a thoughtful moue. "Poison would have been effective, although it has a number of drawbacks," she mused. "Perhaps I would have sent for him to meet me in my boudoir and then, when he arrived, stabbed him with my letter opener; I would then have spread the story that he had made an indecent advance, and I had been forced to defend my honor. Or I could have suggested an archery competition and accidentally shot him. (I am an excellent archer.) I could have crept into his room at night and used a pistol on him, then hidden the silver and claimed a tramp had broken into the house." She shrugged carelessly. "There are all sorts of ways."

"I see," I said, dazed, and her trilling laugh rang out again.

"Now I have shocked you. Don't worry, my dear; unless Herron or Claude is ever in danger again, I don't expect I shall have to act upon my deadly impulses. I may be capable of murder, but I would not engage in it without good cause. Now," she commanded, leaning toward me, "tell me your fears about all of this have been set at rest."

"They have," I said gratefully. "I am sorry I did not trust you, ma'am."

"And you will never hesitate to trust in me in the future, will you? There is nothing in your character that could ever cause me to turn against you."

"How can you be so sure?" I could not help asking it, even though I did not want to find fault with her kindness. "How can any of us really be certain we know what those around us are capable of?"

She rose to her feet and shook out her gown. "Sometimes we cannot, dear, but often our hearts tell us enough. In any case, we cannot depend on absolute certainty; sometimes we must take people on faith, and trust them even if we risk being hurt."

She moved to the door, but I sat motionless and continued to ponder this. "It is a risk," I said slowly. "But I suppose that if we refused to take that risk—protected ourselves by regarding everyone with suspicion and caution—we would never have a chance at happiness." I remembered Herron as he had been, cut off from all human connections because of his fear and distrust, and knew that I had been doing the same thing since my father's death.

Shaking myself out of my reverie, I rose to see the duchess out. "Thank you for everything you have given me," I said. "My home, my brooch, my peace of mind."

Beaming, she held out her arms to me, and we embraced. "You are most kindly welcome," she said. "Now, don't you think you should write to Charles and tell him to come to you?"

"I already have," I said, and she laughed and departed.

* * *

Charles returned on a golden evening in spring. I had been daydreaming over a book on the back terrace, but when I heard the sound of carriage wheels on the gravel drive I leapt to my feet and ran around to the front of the house. Charles was just alighting, and when he saw me he smiled broadly and opened his arms. I ran to them.

"Something is different about you," I said after a time, when he had released me long enough for me to speak. "I can't tell just what, though. Kiss me again."

"Gladly," he replied, and did so with an enthusiasm that left me breathless. When I emerged again I cried, "Your moustache is gone!"

He grinned down at me, his eyes so brilliantly blue they seemed the color of heaven. "I thought it a fitting gesture. Leaving behind the last vestige of my life as a soldier to become a husband."

"Well, perhaps we should talk before you make any definite plans." Firmly I fought down my elation, reminding myself that I must get the thing I dreaded over with before I could be secure in my happiness. The coachman and Jenkins were both watching us with interest and barely concealed amusement, as was Miss Yates from the morning room; we needed privacy. I slipped my hand into Charles's to lead him away.

"I wondered what had made you change your mind," he commented, as we walked across the terrace away from our audience. "When I got your letter, I thought—I hoped—that your doubts were resolved. Is something still troubling you?"

"No," I said, seating myself on the wide stone balustrade and drawing him down beside me, "but it may trouble you when you learn of it." I took a deep breath and faced him. "You may not wish to marry me once you know the truth of what happened to my father. He did not slip and fall from the roof accidentally, as you thought. I pushed him. I did it deliberately, knowing it would kill him, because it was the only way I could think to keep him from murdering Herron."

Then I waited.

His eyebrows drew together in bewilderment. "That is why you sent me away? Because you feared I would discover this?" When I nodded, he said gently, "But Oriel, I knew it already."

"You knew?" I gasped.

"Of course I did. I saw you. My God, when I remember racing up to the roof and arriving just as you flung yourself at him, too late to do anything but watch as the two of you grappled at the edge of the roof... that was the worst moment of my life." He pulled me into his arms again, and I was too amazed to resist, even had I wished to. "You seemed so horrified at yourself that I let you think I had misconstrued what I saw."

"Then you don't despise me?" My voice was muffled against his chest, but he caught the words.

"Despise you!" he retorted. "Oriel, you saved Herron's life that night, and almost certainly your own as well. If I had gotten there first I would most likely have acted just as you did." His voice took on a teasing note. "Even had he not been an embezzler and a would-be murderer, I could never have endured Pembroke as a father-in-law. Now, does that make you feel better?"

"Yes," I said joyfully, turning my face up to his, "much better," and whatever else I might have said was lost as his lips met mine.

Much, much later, when we were again disposed for conversation, we strolled to the cliffs to watch the sun set. He told me of the progress of his medical studies in Edinburgh, and I told him of all that had passed at Ellsmere since his departure—omitting a certain foolish soaking of mine.

"By the way," said Charles, as we looked out over the sea, stained rose and gold in the setting sun, "would you rather have a big, showy, pretentious wedding in society, with a reception for three hundred, that takes months to arrange; or would you prefer a charming, intimate, expeditious ceremony on the way to Edinburgh?"

"Since you won't state a preference," I said demurely, "I'll choose the second. You realize, though, that it will mean risking Felicity's wrath by robbing her of the opportunity to be bridesmaid."

"I'm willing to chance it," he said comfortably, his arm snug around my waist. "My life has been so placid these last few weeks that a bit of danger will add some welcome savor."

I could not repress a shudder as I recalled some of the "savor" we had lived through at Ellsmere. "It's sad, but I won't be entirely sorry to leave," I reflected. "The duchess was right; there are a great many unhappy memories here."

"And some very pleasant ones."

"Granted. But I still wonder..."

"What?" he asked, when my voice trailed off.

I glanced up at him apologetically. "It's probably unkind of me to mention the possibility to you. But since he's to be my father-in-law... do you think your father killed the duke?"

Leaning against him, I felt him sigh, and when I looked up again he was staring unseeing at the horizon. "I've wondered that too," he said. "It seems significant that he was killed just months before Herron's birthday. That would suggest that the trust was a motive, and it would mean that my father would have had excellent reason, apart from his wish to marry Aunt Gwendolyn. But all the same, I find it hard to see him deciding to kill his own brother. I might believe it if his own life had been at stake, or Aunt Gwendolyn's."

"I keep coming to the same conclusion. Oh, I shouldn't have mentioned it at all; I suppose Herron's suspicions just planted themselves in my mind..."

"It is a mystery, though." We fell silent, and presently Charles said, slowly, "One explanation did occur to me. It's probably farfetched, but it would explain things."

"Go on," I urged him, when he seemed to hesitate. "I'm sure any theory of yours is quite sound."

He threw me a quick glance of affection, and continued. "The two of them were hunting alone, which did not often happen; usually they went out with a party of guests and neighbors, or at least with the grooms. Perhaps one of them took the opportunity to bring up something that had become an obvious source of discord: my father's love for Gwendolyn.

"Father might have asked Ambrose if there was any possibility of divorce; or perhaps my uncle had lost patience with Father's all too evident affection for his wife. But however the subject arose, I think both of them realized that they could not continue as they had. The matter had to be resolved." He turned to gaze behind us at the woods. "My uncle was a fierce defender of what he considered fairness. I can imagine the sort of solution that would have presented itself to him in that situation."

"What?" I demanded.

He turned back to me with a grim smile. "A duel," he said.

"But in the middle of the woods? In full daylight, with no seconds?"

"There are open stretches in the forest where they would have had unobstructed aim at each other. They had guns with them already, for the most natural of purposes, and precisely because they were known to be hunting the sound of gunshots would arouse no suspicion. It is just the kind of practical, cool-headed, cold-blooded plan that my uncle would have thought of, and my father would not have been able to refuse. My father fired first, as the challenged party, and my uncle went down."

"But why claim it was an accident?" I wondered.

"Perhaps precisely because he had such good reason to want his brother dead, and knew what rumor would say. Or perhaps because he was afraid that Aunt Gwendolyn would hold her husband's death against him." Sheepishly, he inquired, "What do you think? Is it a ridiculous theory?"

"From what I have learned of your father and the duke, it sounds very likely," I said, when I had considered it. It explained a great many things. "Are you going to ask your father?"

He did not even have to pause to think. "No," he said. "I don't know what good it would do. If I'm wrong, I'd prefer not to know; I don't want to have to wonder about my father's integrity for the rest of my life. And I would rather not distress Aunt Gwendolyn. It's in the past now; there's nothing to be gained by dwelling on it." He looked down at me with a real smile now, the sort that made my heart turn over. "I would rather concentrate on the future."

"So would I," I said, and hand in hand we walked back to the house.

AFTERWORD

Sea of Secrets had its earliest origin in my crush on Hamlet. Not on the play, but on the character. When I first read Shakespeare's tragedy as a teenager, I felt like I'd found my soulmate in the troubled prince. His tragic romance with Ophelia fascinated me, and I felt that their story was even more heartrending than those of other famous Shakespearean couples. Romeo and Juliet at least died secure in the knowledge of the other's love. Ophelia died without such comforting knowledge; not until after her death did Hamlet admit how much he loved her.

I wanted to see more of their time together, and especially to see what their love affair might have been like before murder, political intrigue, and madness tore them apart. So I wrote a novel exploring the events of speare's play from Ophelia's perspective, showing I felt her relationship with Hamlet might have played in the moments not shown onstage.

When I started submitting that manuscript to publishers, a generous editor fished it out of the slush pile and took the time to phone me with feedback and suggestions. "Get further away from Shakespeare" was what his advice boiled down to. "Make the story your own." But it wasn't until years later that I discovered how to do that.

By then I was working on my doctoral dissertation under the guidance of Dr. Anne Williams, whose fields of expertise include gothic literature. I can't remember when the epiphany hit me, but I realized that *Hamlet* was very gothic indeed—it had murder, ghosts, madness, dark secrets from the past, and a deeply messed-up family dynamic at the core. I had been steeping myself in nineteenth-century fiction and poetry, and I could easily see the story transplanted to that era. Hamlet himself seemed like a natural companion to such Byronic characters as Edward Rochester and Heathcliff.

The only wrinkle was that my feelings about Hamlet himself had changed: I had realized that in real life the brooding loner preoccupied with his own pain generally makes a crummy boyfriend. I had also read enough gothic romances to become weary of the tradition that the moody dark man who treats the heroine badly is always destined to be the hero, while the nice fair-haired chap with decent manners inevitably turns out to be stringing the heroine along for some nefarious purpose. This time, I decided, the nice guy was going to be just that. The trouble was, nice guys were scarce on the ground in my source material. So Charles was invented out of the whole cloth to serve as Herron's opposite and a contrast to the general angst.

The coda to my story is an amusing one: when I submitted *Sea of Secrets* to the editor whose advice had made such an impression on me, he responded that the story had now strayed too far away from its Shakespearean source material. But by that point, Oriel and the other characters had taken on a life of their own, independent of their Shakespearean counterparts, and I was happy with the story that had grown up around them.

Because the story has evolved so far from its origins, however, I've saved disclosure of the *Hamlet* connection for this afterword. My hope is that readers who recognize the echoes of *Hamlet* as they read will enjoy the Shakespearean elements in Oriel's story, and that those who don't notice the parallels will nonetheless enjoy *Sea of Secrets* on its own merits.

Book Club Discussion Questions for

Sea of Secrets

Warning: contains spoilers!

If you have not finished reading *Sea of Secrets* and don't want to know what happens, stop reading now!

1. *Sea of Secrets* is clearly inspired by Shakespeare's *Hamlet*. What are some of the parallels? What are the biggest differences? Does *Sea of Secrets* give you a different perspective on *Hamlet?* Do the parallels between the two works enhance *Sea of Secrets?* If so, how?

2. Very rarely is the heroine, Oriel, addressed by name. Instead, those around her use endearments, nicknames, or other ways of referring to her (e.g., "daughter," "Ondine," "my dear"). What do these different forms of address reveal about each character's relationship with Oriel? Who actually calls her by her name, and is this significant?

3. The sea is a recurring presence in the book, and Oriel feels she has a special relationship with it. Why is this? In what ways does this connection manifest itself? Is the ocean a symbol? If so, what does it symbolize, and does this meaning change over the course of the story?

4. Different characters offer a variety of perspectives on the late duke, Herron's father. What kind of picture emerges from their descriptions and implications?

5. A turning point in Herron and Oriel's relationship occurs when he strips her on the night of the ball. Why does he do this? What does it reveal about his feelings toward women in general and Oriel in particular?

6. Over the course of the novel Oriel gains two suitors. What traits in each man attract her? How are they different? What qualities in Charles may make him a better match for Oriel than Herron?

7. How does Oriel change over the course of the story? In what ways does she gain wisdom or maturity? Do you feel that she is a stronger person at the end of the novel than she is at the beginning? What do you envision that her future will be like?

8. In the 1850s, when the story takes place, the position of Victorian women was still greatly limited. Based on the female characters in the story, what impression do you get of the expected role of the Victorian woman? In what ways do different characters adhere to that role or defy it?

9. Oriel is haunted by the fear that she may take after her father. Do you see any resemblances between them? What are her father's chief personality traits?

10. *Sea of Secrets* follows in the tradition of classic gothic romance novels like *Jane Eyre* and *Rebecca.* What traditional gothic elements do you see in the story? Are any of the gothic conventions altered or overturned in this novel?

More Victorian Romantic Suspense From Amanda DeWees

WITH THIS CURSE

Winner of the 2015 Daphne du Maurier Award for historical mystery/suspense

Can a curse strike twice in a woman's life?

In 1854, seventeen-year-old chambermaid Clara Crofton wa dismissed from Gravesend Hall for having fallen in lov with Richard Blackwood, the younger son of the house Alone in the world, Clara found a tenuous position as seamstress, but she always blamed the Gravesend curse fo the disaster that had befallen her—and for Richard's deat soon after in the Crimean War.

Now, more than eighteen years later, Richard's twin Atticus, seeks out Clara with a strange proposal: if she wil marry him and live with him as his wife in name only t ease the mind of his dying father, Atticus will then endow he with a comfortable income for the rest of her life. Clar knows that he is not disclosing his true motives, but whe she runs out of options for an independent life, she has n choice but to become Atticus's wife.

For Clara, returning to Gravesend as a bride bring some triumph . . . but also great unease. Not only must sh pretend to be a wellborn lady and devoted wife to a ma whose face is a constant reminder of the love she lost, bu ominous portents whisper that her masquerade brings grav danger. "This house will take from you what you mos treasure," her mother once warned her. But the curse ha already taken the man Clara loved. Will it now demand he life?

Interior file SOS 10-26-17 Maurice edit AD 2 10-29-17

Cover file
Sea of Secrets paperback cover 10-27-17 1+3
11-13-17 1+2

Made in the USA
Columbia, SC
14 November 2017